ROBERTS

P9-CRP-970

Like Father, Like Son

Leon's eyes narrowed as he riffled through the pages. He paused at the glossy photo insert in the center of the book and stared at one of the black-and-white pictures. It took him a second to realize what he was looking at. When the recognition hit him, his whole body gave a little jerk, as if the book were an electrical device that had just short-circuited in his hands.

Looming over him, his mama grunted. "Hard to believe, ain't it?"

Leon gawked at the photo. It was a mug shot of a meek-looking middle-aged man whose mouth was twisted into a silly little grin. He was wearing a denim work shirt and had a plaid deer-hunter's cap cocked on his head.

The caption below the picture read: "Official police photograph of Edward Gein, grave-robber, ghoul, and collector of female body parts."

"Damn," gasped Leon.

He was staring into the face of his father.

Praise for the Incredible True-Crime Books of
Harold Schechter

Voted Best Nonfiction Book of 1996 by *Rocky Mountain News*

THE A TO Z ENCYCLOPEDIA
OF SERIAL KILLERS
by Harold Schechter and David Everitt

"This grisly tome will tell you all you ever wanted to know (and more) about everything from 'Axe Murderers' to 'Zombies' . . . Schechter knows his subject matter. . . ."

—Mark Graham, *Rocky Mountain News*

"The ultimate reference on this fascinating phenomenon."

—*PI Magazine*

DEPRAVED
The Shocking True Story of America's
First Serial Killer

"A meticulously researched, brilliantly detailed and above all riveting account of Dr. H. H. Holmes, a nineteenth-century serial killer who embodied the ferociously dark side of America's seemingly timeless preoccupation with ambition, money and power."

—Caleb Carr, bestselling author of *The Alienist*

"An astonishing piece of popular history. I unhesitatingly recommend [it] . . . to round out your understanding of the true depth, meaning and perversity of the uniquely American brand of mayhem."

—*The Boston Book Review*

"[Schechter's] writing keeps you turning the pages. . . ."
—*Syracuse Herald-American*

"As good as the best work of Jack Olsen or Ann Rule. As chilling as *The Silence of the Lambs* and as blood-curdling as the best Stephen King novel. It's destined to be a true-crime classic."

—*Flint Journal* (MI)

DERANGED
The Shocking True Story of America's Most Fiendish Killer

"This biography of the ultimate dirty old man, Albert Fish . . . pedophile, sadist, coprophiliac, murderer, cannibal, and self-torturer . . . [is] as horrifying as any novel could be."

—*American Libraries*

"Compelling . . . grippingly fascinating-repulsive."

—*Booklist*

DEVIANT
The Shocking True Story of Ed Gein, the Original "Psycho"

"A solidly researched, well-written account of the Gein story."

—*Milwaukee Journal*

"[A] grisly, wonderful book . . . a scrupulously researched and complexly sympathetic biography of the craziest killer in American history."

—*Film Quarterly*

"Schechter's account of Gein's unspeakable acts and their cultural fallout is top-drawer true-crime writing."

—*Booklist*

Books by Harold Schechter

Outcry
The A to Z Encyclopedia of Serial Killers
  (with David Everitt)
Depraved
Deranged
Deviant
Dying Breath (with Jonna Semeiks)

Published by POCKET BOOKS

For orders other than by individual consumers, Pocket Books grants a discount on the purchase of **10 or more** copies of single titles for special markets or premium use. For further details, please write to the Vice-President of Special Markets, Pocket Books, 1633 Broadway, New York, NY 10019-6785, 8th Floor.

For information on how individual consumers can place orders, please write to Mail Order Department, Simon & Schuster Inc., 200 Old Tappan Road, Old Tappan, NJ 07675.

OUT-CRY

Harold Schechter

POCKET BOOKS

New York   London   Toronto   Sydney   Tokyo   Singapore

The sale of this book without its cover is unauthorized. If you purchased this book without a cover, you should be aware that it was reported to the publisher as "unsold and destroyed." Neither the author nor the publisher has received payment for the sale of this "stripped book."

This book is a work of fiction. Names, characters, places and incidents are products of the author's imagination or are used fictiously. Any resemblance to actual events or locales or persons, living or dead, is entirely coincidental.

Lines from "Nobody" from *Complete Poems of Robert Graves* by Robert Graves © 1988 by Robert Graves, used with permission from Oxford University Press.

An *Original* Publication of POCKET BOOKS

POCKET BOOKS, a division of Simon & Schuster Inc.
1230 Avenue of the Americas, New York, NY 10020

Copyright © 1997 by Harold Schechter

All rights reserved, including the right to reproduce this book or portions thereof in any form whatsoever. For information address Pocket Books, 1230 Avenue of the Americas, New York, NY 10020

ISBN: 0-671-73217-X

First Pocket Books printing August 1997

10 9 8 7 6 5 4 3 2 1

POCKET and colophon are registered trademarks of Simon & Schuster Inc.

Cover art by Victor Stabin

Printed in the U.S.A.

For
Joe Coleman

The eyes were lifeless, and lustreless, and seemingly pupil-less, and I shrank involuntarily from their glassy stare to the contemplation of the thin and shrunken lips. They parted; and in a smile of peculiar meaning, *the teeth* of the changed Berenice disclosed themselves slowly to my view. Would to God that I had never beheld them, or that, having done so, I had died!

—Edgar Allan Poe, "Berenice"

OUT-CRY

Prologue

◆

Thirty miles north of Madison, the snow began falling—flakes so big that they seemed to strike the windshield with a splat. Stimpson flipped on the wipers and cursed. He'd meant to replace the blades a month ago. Now, the worn rubber edges did nothing but smear the wet across the glass.

Stimpson squinted through the windshield. Even with the beams popped to high, nothing shone in the headlights but a few yards of onrushing asphalt. Otherwise, the darkness was complete, the night as cold and black and empty as outer space.

Now I know how that damn mutt must have felt, Stimpson thought.

Two weeks earlier, the Russkies had launched another surprise, a second satellite, this one carrying a pooch named—what the hell was it again?—Latka or Laika or some such shit. The first satellite, Sputnik, had sent all of America into a panic. Like most of his countrymen, Stimpson still had trouble believing that the Commies had beaten them to the punch.

Now the experts were saying that there'd be a man up there pretty soon—and if the U.S. didn't get its ass into gear, that fellow's spacesuit would be sporting a hammer-and-sickle armpatch.

Sitting behind the wheel of his '54 Chevy, Stimpson had no trouble at all imagining what it would feel like up there, sealed inside a metal capsule, peering out a porthole as you were propelled through an endless expanse of black icy nothingness.

He let out a little snort. It would probably feel just like speeding through south-central Wisconsin in the dead of a wintry night, heading toward some godforsaken place where something bad had just happened.

Something that couldn't wait until morning for the services of the state Crime Lab's chief photographer.

The call had jolted him awake just after midnight—his gravel-voiced boss apologizing for the lateness of the hour before hitting Stimpson with the news. A woman's body had been found in a little farmhouse northaways. He didn't know all the details, but from what he'd heard, it sounded like a real mess up there.

Perched on the edge of his mattress, Stimpson copied down directions by the glow of his bed lamp, while his wife let out a little grunt of complaint, heaved her bulk away from the light, and went back to snoring serenely.

"Got it," Stimpson said when his boss was finished.

"And Lewis—"

"Yeah?"

"Bring plenty of film," said his boss. Stimpson had never heard him sound grimmer.

The snowfall slowed to a flurry, then eased until only a few scattered flakes sifted down from the sky. Moonlight leaked through the thinning clouds. In the spectral glow, Stimpson could make out a little clump of houses straight ahead: a tiny village flanking the highway. He kept his foot to the pedal—no need to slow down at that time of night;

the place was as dead as a ghost town. Before he had a chance to wonder what the village was called, it had already vanished behind him, swallowed up by the dark.

Though he'd lived in Wisconsin for nearly a dozen years since moving from his native Chicago, Stimpson wasn't especially familiar with that part of the state. His work didn't take him there very often. Not that people were less prone to violence in south-central Wisconsin. Far from it: murders happened all the time. But most of the killing was run-of-the-mill stuff, the bloody upshot of domestic quarrels or tavern brawls—nothing that called for a crime lab investigation.

As for the other homicides, the ones that made the headlines and baffled the local police, Stimpson was rarely needed to photograph the remains—for a very good reason.

No one ever found the remains. The victims simply disappeared.

Stimpson was still surprised at how often people vanished in that neck of the woods—farmwives from their kitchens, sportsmen from their campsites, children on their way home from school. Before he had moved there back in '45, he had always thought of Wisconsin as God's country—a rich, rolling pastureland, parceled into thriving farms. And that was true of certain parts of the state.

But not the part he was heading into now.

It wasn't a wasteland, exactly. But it was a hardscrabble region, dirt poor and sparsely populated. An air of desolation hung over the land, and the tiny communities scattered here and there were ingrown, cut off from the world, and leery of strangers. For the most part, Stimpson had found the citizens of his adopted state to be a friendly and hospitable breed. But the folks up around here acted different, as though they had something to hide.

It was hard country up here, and the locals existed in grim isolation, separated by miles and miles of dense, wooden terrain, where few men ventured—and where a missing body could molder to dust without ever being discovered.

He was hungry for a smoke. He reached into his shirt pocket for his pack of Camels, thinking back to the last time he had been there on a case, three years earlier, in '54.

A middle-aged woman named Mary Hogan, proprietress of a little roadside tavern, had disappeared from her establishment under highly sinister circumstances. A customer stopping by for some noontime refreshment had found the place completely deserted. A spent .32-caliber cartridge lay on the floor beside a drying pool of blood that was streaked down the middle as though a body had been dragged through it.

Hogan—a massive, hard-bitten woman whose language could make a teamster blush—was an immigrant from Chicago like Stimpson, and rumor had it that she'd been rubbed out by the mob. The case was still officially open, though no one entertained much hope of solving it.

Hogan's tavern was shut down for good shortly after her disappearance. It had been located in a little town called Pine Grove, just a few miles away from the place Stimpson was driving to now.

Forty minutes later, he spotted a sign and brought his car to a stop without bothering to pull onto the shoulder. There wasn't much risk of obstructing traffic. On the whole trip, he had passed exactly one other vehicle—a wood-sided station wagon with a spike-horned buck strapped to the roof, the fruit of the first day of deer-hunting season, which had officially opened the morning before.

Stimpson peered through the windshield at the sign:

WELCOME TO WAUSHARA COUNTY,
CHRISTMAS TREE CAPITAL OF THE WORLD!

He gave a derisive little grunt as the car picked up speed again. Seemed like every damn place in the country was the capital of this, or the birthplace of that, or had a museum dedicated to such and such. He remembered visiting New England years ago and passing through a village that proudly declared itself "The Cranberry Capital of the United States." Another time, while driving across Colorado, he found himself in a one-horse town featuring a little museum devoted entirely to the life and career of Joseph F. Glidden, the inventor of barbed wire.

People just can't accept being nobodies, he mused. *Everyone has to feel special about something.*

He squinted into the darkness, searching for the landmarks his boss had described.

Well, one thing was for damn sure, he thought. The town he was nearing wasn't famous for *anything.* Hell, he'd never even heard of it until his boss told him the name:

Plainfield.

He had been groping around the back roads for a full twenty minutes before he spotted the old farmhouse looming in a frozen clearing a few hundred yards away. As he turned his Chevy onto the property, he could make out a bunch of police cars parked by the side of the house. Stimpson pulled his car up beside them, surprised at the number of vehicles assembled there—at least a dozen.

Something else surprised him. Given all those cars, the house should have been a hive of activity. But from where Stimpson sat, the place looked completely deserted—the windows dark, not another human soul to be seen. Stepping out of his car and into the frigid air, he pulled his coat collar tight around his neck and took a moment to look around.

The sky had cleared by then and a nearly full moon floated overhead. Its light made the lonely old farmhouse seem especially desolate. Standing there in the raw November night, Stimpson shuddered—but whether from the cold or the forbidding look of the house, he couldn't say.

Suddenly, a small light winked in the blackness of a window. Frowning, Stimpson stepped over to investigate. Putting his face close to the glass, he saw to his surprise that the inside of the window was coated with something opaque—black paint or possibly tar paper. The place wasn't deserted after all. Through a little crack in the black coating, he could see a wavering glow, as though someone were moving about by flashlight.

As he turned away from the window, Stimpson heard voices rising faintly from the rear of the house. Fetching his camera and equipment bag from the trunk of his car, he followed the sound around back, where a shedlike summer kitchen abutted the house. Light gleamed dully from the half-open door and people were speaking inside. The words were too muffled for Stimpson to understand. But even from that distance, he could hear a peculiar tension in the voices.

As he approached the doorway, Stimpson saw several men in police uniform conferring in the junk-filled shed. He shouldered open the door and stepped through. The men swiveled their heads in his direction, and one of the officers took a quick step forward—Stimpson had the sense that the man was trying to shield him from something.

A floodlamp hooked to a large battery had been set up on an old wooden crate. Its beam was trained on the ceiling. Out of the corner of his eye, Stimpson was aware of something suspended from a rafter—a pale, beefy slab. He turned to look just as the policeman reached his side and clamped a hand around his upper arm, as though to steady him.

It took a moment for Stimpson to understand what he was looking at. The dangling thing seemed to be a large, butchered animal, though of a variety he had never seen before, and for an instant his mind cast about wildly, trying to place it in a comprehensible category: heifer, hog, ewe. When he could no longer fend off the truth, the shock was so jarring that he literally jumped back a step and would have gone tumbling over a rusted-out wheelbarrow had the police officer not been gripping him by the arm. Stimpson managed to choke out a few words—"Holy Mother of God"—before his throat clamped tight with fear.

It was a woman—or rather, the naked carcass of a woman—hanging upside down in the icy shed like a side of beef in a butcher's meat locker. The torso was split and gutted, so that the trunk was little more than a dark, scooped-out hole. Someone had decapitated the carcass, the way a deerhunter will remove a trophy head from a prize kill.

Stimpson was so staggered by the sight that he simply stood there gaping, unaware that the man beside him was saying something. Only gradually did the officer's voice seep into his stunned consciousness. Forcing his eyes away from the

7

butchered corpse—transfixing in its ghastliness—Stimpson turned toward the grim-faced policeman.

"Hard to believe, ain't it?" said the man softly.

Stimpson tried to speak, but no sound emerged from his fear-strangled throat. He swallowed hard, then managed to rasp out a single word: "Who . . . ?"

Still holding him by the arm, the officer led Stimpson over to the little knot of lawmen, one of whom—a local sheriff who introduced himself by a name that sounded like "Schieley"—filled him in on the basic facts.

The victim was a fifty-eight-year-old widow and grandmother, owner of the Plainfield hardware store. The previous morning, Saturday, the sixteenth, she had opened the place as usual, even though the town was largely deserted. Most of its male population—including her adult son Frank, who helped her run the store—had gone off to the woods for the first day of the fall hunting season.

When Frank returned around dusk, he'd found the store empty. The cash register was gone and the floor was stained with a dark trail of blood that led out to the rear parking area.

Suspicion immediately fell on the town oddball, a forty-one-year-old bachelor who'd been living alone in this remote, run-down farmhouse for a dozen years since the death of his beloved mother. Frank had told the police that the little man had been hanging around the hardware store lately, pestering his mother. The suspect had been arrested at the home of a neighbor, where he'd gone off to enjoy a nice pork-chop dinner after finishing up his butchery.

In response to Stimpson's next question, Schieley told him the suspect's name. It sounded like "Geen"—with a long *e*. Stimpson immediately thought of those freak-show performers known as geeks who entertained carny-goers by devouring rats and chewing off the heads of live chickens. He was surprised when he read the newspaper headlines the next morning and saw the actual spelling of the name:

Gein. Edward Gein.

"Quite a job ol' Eddie done on her, too," Schieley said bitterly. "Found her innards over there packed away in a suitcase. Still nice and warm."

Stimpson shivered and rubbed at his neck with a shaky hand. "How about the head?" he asked.

"Ain't come across it yet," said Schieley. "But we will."

Struggling to assume the professional detachment that made his work possible, Stimpson glanced around for a place to set up his tripod on the junk-littered floor. "Guess I might as well get started," he said dully.

"Maybe you'd better see the rest of it first," said Schieley.

Stimpson stared at him. "Rest of it? You mean there's more?"

"Hell yes," said the sheriff. He jerked a thumb toward the door that led to the main part of the house. "In there. Must be more'n a dozen deputies sifting through the place right now." Then he added something that Stimpson would never forget:

"Mr. Stimpson," he said, pointing his chin at the headless, hollowed-out carcass dangling by its heels from a rafter, "this here is just the beginning."

—From *Slaughterhouse,* by Paul Novak, Chapter 8, pages 112–119

Part One

~

Slaughterhouse

1

"**O**kay, so the cops find the poor woman strung up like a dressed-out deer carcass in this sicko's summer kitchen." Beneath his neatly trimmed moustache, Lemmick's mouth was pursed in distaste, as though it pained him to discuss such repellent topics. "What then?"

Paul Novak took a small sip of ice water and sloshed it over his tongue, hoping that the sound couldn't be picked up by the minimike clipped to his jacket lapel. Above him, the studio lights felt strong enough to give him a tan, but it wasn't the heat that was parching his mouth—it was nerves.

Though he'd just come off a nationwide tour, his TV appearances had been limited to local cable talk shows—the kind hosted by chirpy middle-aged women whose major qualification seemed to be that they were married to the station managers. But this program was different. This was *The Lionel Lemmick Show*, nationally syndicated during afternoon prime time, head to head against Oprah and Montel. A hundred pairs of eyes appraised him from the audience, and he could feel a million more behind the cold stare of the cameras.

Setting his water glass down on the side table, Paul looked straight at Lemmick, who was standing halfway between the stage and the tiered rows of spectator seats. "Then the sheriffs and deputies entered the main part of the farmhouse," Paul said. He paused a beat for dramatic effect. "And what they found inside that house of horrors defied belief."

Lemmick lifted his eyebrows. "Such as?"

"Chairs and other furniture upholstered in human skin. Soup bowls fashioned from the sawed-off tops of skulls. A shade-pull made from a pair of lips. A collection of noses." Paul could feel his jitters easing as he spoke. For all its ghastliness, this was comfortable territory—ground he had covered dozens of times during his publicity tour. "Inside the bedroom, the investigators found the preserved faces of nine women. The faces had been flayed from the skulls, stuffed with newspaper, and hung on the walls like hunting trophies. There was also a shoebox full of"—he hesitated for an instant, debating which term to use before deciding on the most neutral— "female genitalia."

Lemmick, however, clearly preferred something more vivid. "You mean vaginas?"

"Right," said Paul.

A murmur of mingled shock and incredulity ran through the gallery. But Paul could detect something else in the sound, too—an undercurrent of excited fascination. It was as though the audience were simultaneously revolted by the horror and hungry for more.

Lemmick let the noise subside before he spoke again. "So I guess it's fair to say, Paul, that this Edward Gein was one sick puppy."

Paul gave a thin smile. "I'm sure Sigmund Freud would have used those exact words, Lionel."

This time, the only response was a scattering of uneasy laughter, as though the audience suspected that Paul might be making fun of his host. *Schmuck,* Paul cursed at himself. *What the hell are you doing? You knew you weren't going to be swapping* bon mots *with Bill Moyers.* He silently vowed to avoid making anything that sounded even vaguely like a smart-ass remark. He was there to promote his book, not condescend to Lionel Lemmick.

Leave that to Wylie, Paul thought.

Out of the corner of his eye, he could see a man with

a headset standing beside one of the big rolling cameras, signaling for a station break.

Forming his right hand into a pistol—thumb cocked, forefinger rigid—Lemmick took aim at the camera. "Listen, my friends," he said solemnly, "if you have little ones at home, then please, I urge you, do not let them watch today's show. The same goes for any of you seniors with weak hearts. Believe me. The things this psycho did would give Jack the Ripper nightmares. Robbing graves, butchering women, making clothing out of their skin." He gave an exaggerated shudder, as though a chill were running down his spine. "We'll be back to hear all about it right after these messages."

As the audience clapped and the theme music burbled, Lemmick passed his mike to an assistant, stepped over to the stage, and seated himself beside Paul. "You're doing great," he said, leaning close and cocking his head toward the audience. "They're eating it up."

Sitting that near to Lemmick, Paul could see a web of ruptured capillaries leaching through the makeup on his nose—evidence of the hard-drinking nightlife that had made him the subject of endless tabloid gossip. But Lemmick's mostly female audience seemed infinitely accepting of his sins. All he had to do was flash his trademark lopsided grin and they were ready to fold him in their arms and squeeze, like a mother who can't help forgiving the adored, wayward son who is constantly breaking her heart.

"Just one little thing, Paul," Lemmick said. "You might want to keep your language a little less . . . ah . . . technical."

It took Paul a moment to realize that Lemmick was referring to his use of the word *genitalia*.

"All right," Paul said, nodding slowly. "I wasn't sure. I just didn't want to make the book sound too tacky. I mean, it's a shocking subject, but I want people to know it's a serious piece of work."

"Absolutely," Lemmick said. "It's a hell of a book."

He leaned even closer and lowered his voice a notch. "You just have to keep in mind that fancy words give most people a headache."

"Sure," said Paul, imagining what Wylie would say if she could hear this conversation.

"Terrific," Lemmick said with a wink. "You're my kind of writer, Paul. You and I have a lot in common."

I certainly hope not, Paul thought as he watched Lemmick hop down from the stage and head over toward the audience.

It was hard to know what to make of Lemmick. He genuinely seemed to regard himself as a serious TV journalist who took on the stories no one else had the courage to go after—the only man in America with the guts to tackle subjects like satanic baby sacrifice and the truth about the government's UFO cover-up. It was also true that, for all his unmistakable sleaziness, he had a gift for projecting an air of passionate concern—like a sideshow operator who really *cares* about the welfare of his freaks.

On the other hand, for all the viewers in America who were crazy about Lemmick, there were at least as many who saw him as a slimeball, pure and simple—Paul's wife Wylie among them.

An assistant trotted over to Lemmick and handed him the wireless mike and a copy of Paul's book. The theme music picked up, then faded again while the cameras focused in on Lemmick, who had climbed into the audience section and was standing halfway up the aisle.

"Welcome back, friends," Lemmick said, holding up the book. "We're talking to Paul Novak, author of the true-crime bestseller, *Slaughterhouse,* the shocking—and I *mean* shocking—real-life horror story of Edward Gein, America's most fiendish psycho." Lemmick kept the book at shoulder level while the camera zoomed in for a close-up of its red-splattered cover art.

"Before we dive back into the gory details," Lemmick said, looking deeply pensive, "let me ask you something, Paul. These crimes took place when? In 1956?"

Paul corrected him. " 'Fifty-seven."

"Okay. So we're talking about stuff that happened forty years ago. My question is this: why in the world are we still so interested in this creep? Lord knows there've been other homicidal monsters since then, some of them even worse—Bundy, Gacey, Dahmer."

Paul uncrossed his legs and stretched them a bit. "Maybe one reason is exactly *because* it happened so long ago." He was happy to find that his stage fright was almost gone. "You know, people remember the fifties as this innocent, golden age. I think they're fascinated to discover that it wasn't all Doris Day and Ozzie and Harriet—that there was a dark side."

"Happy Days weren't all they were cracked up to be," Lemmick said.

"Exactly. I also think our interest has to do with *where* it happened—the fact that such incredibly sick things were going on in this apple-pie little town, Wisconsin's answer to Mayberry."

Lemmick gave a snuffing laugh through his nose. "Kind of like finding out that Barney Fife was leading a secret life as a serial killer."

The audience guffawed, and even Paul broke into a big grin. He had to admit that Lemmick had a way with a punchy comparison.

"Another thing," Paul continued when the laughter subsided. "People are always fascinated when they find out that Gein was the inspiration for *Psycho.*"

"The original Norman Bates," Lemmick interjected.

"Right," said Paul. "I do want to correct one comment you made, Lionel. You said Gein was a serial killer. That's not exactly true. He did murder two women. But the rest of his victims—maybe a dozen in all, nobody knows for sure—were taken from local cemeteries. He was"—Paul was about to say *a necrophile* when he remembered Lemmick's injunction against polysyllabic words—"a ghoul."

"Someone who robs graves," Lemmick clarified.

"That's right."

Lemmick made a little *phew* of wonder into his microphone. "What in the world would drive a human being to do something like that?"

Paul smiled grimly. "You said it yourself, Lionel. He was a sick puppy. But the important word isn't just *sick*. It's *puppy*. Gein never grew up. He was a violently disturbed mama's boy."

"Like good old Norman," Lemmick said.

Paul nodded. "Gein's mother died in 1945. He desperately wanted to get her back, couldn't live without her. Her coffin was buried inside a concrete vault, so he wasn't able to reach her. Digging up those other women was the best substitute he could come up with."

"But then why did he do all these terrible things to their bodies—cut them up, turn their heads into soup bowls, make lampshades out of their skin?"

"Because his mother was a monster," Paul said simply. "She had done terrible things to *him* and this was his way not only of getting her back but of getting back *at* her. He hated her as much as he worshiped her."

"A split personality?" Lemmick asked.

"In that sense, yes."

Lemmick took a deep breath and blew it out again. "One more question, Paul, before I let the folks in the audience have their say. Did Gein ever have any normal relationships with women?"

"You mean sexual relationships?"

"Sure. Sex, friendship, intimacy—the whole schmear."

Paul frowned. "Not to my knowledge. At the time his crimes were discovered, there *was* one local woman who claimed that she had been Ed's girlfriend for a while—in fact, that he had asked her to marry him. But there's no evidence to support that story."

"What happened to this woman?"

"She disappeared. I tried to find her when I was researching the book, but—" he broke off with a shrug.

"Couldn't dig her up, huh?" Lemmick said.

"So to speak," Paul said dryly.

Lemmick chortled, then said, "Paul, I'm going to turn this over to the audience for a while. We've got some pretty impatient-looking folks sitting here."

It was true. Throughout the spectator section, people were waving their hands urgently, like famished diners frantic to get the attention of an oblivious waiter.

Paul folded his own hands in his lap and smiled, pleased with how well things were going. Fifteen minutes before, sitting under the harsh, overhanging kliegs, he had felt like a police suspect getting the third degree. Gradually, the merciless glare had softened. By now he was feeling completely relaxed, soaking up the limelight's glow.

Lemmick had worked his way along an upper row and was motioning to a plump, middle-aged woman. She wiggled out of her seat, tugging her checkered skirt down to a more decorous position just above her dimpled knees.

"What's your name, dear?" asked Lemmick.

"Sophie," said the woman in a Betty Boop voice. She wore the kind of cat's-eye glasses Paul associated with the maiden aunts of his childhood, though her white-blond hair was styled in a surprisingly flashy cut.

She glanced questioningly at Lemmick, who gave her a go-ahead look.

"I want to say to Mr. Novak, first, that I've read his other books, his short stories and novels, and I think he's a wonderful writer."

"Thank you," said Paul. "I appreciate that."

"What's your question, Sophie?" Lemmick prodded.

"My question to Mr. Novak is how could such a sensitive author write this kind of awful, trashy book?"

There were audible gasps from the audience but also some emphatic handclaps and even a few cheers.

Paul felt sucker-punched. His smile went rigid and he could feel his whole body clench.

"I mean," the woman continued, "here is an entire

book dedicated to this horrible little pervert who did the most disgusting things imaginable. Digging up the corpses of elderly women. Removing their faces and breasts and wearing them like some sort of awful Halloween costume. Why do we need this kind of garbage when there are so many worthwhile things to write about? Weren't you just trying to earn some dirty money by pandering to psychos?"

More applause. Paul was almost grateful for it, since it gave him a few seconds to collect his thoughts.

Lemmick had to hush the clappers with a few "quiet-down" hand motions before Paul could speak. "If I were doing it only for the money," he said, "I wouldn't try 'pandering to psychos,' as you put it." He was glad to hear that his voice remained steady. "I feel pretty sure that psychotics represent a relatively small segment of the book-buying public." He was struggling to sound un-ruffled, though it was hard to keep the sharpness from his tone.

"But you *have* made a bundle." This time it was Lemmick speaking. "We all saw those pictures in last week's *People*—those shots of you and your family in that big new house in Connecticut."

"Absolutely," said Paul. He was damned if he'd apologize for his success. "The royalties are rolling in. But in a way, that's the point. It isn't crazies who are buying all those copies. It's the average, everyday American public—the same people who were lining up at the multiplex to see Hannibal Lecter chew up some faces."

Paul paused, drawing in a breath. He was letting himself get too agitated. He continued. "Look, lots of people don't like to read or see anything scary or upsetting, and that's great—nobody's forcing them to. But there are millions of people who do. Even kids. Check out 'Hansel and Gretel' in case you've forgotten how horrifying it is."

Crossing one leg over the other, Paul assumed a professional air. "I think the issue isn't how disturbing the material is but how it's dealt with. I have to say that I think my book treats the Gein case very responsibly. It's not at all exploitative."

"Lionel! Oh, Lionel!" Someone was shouting from a far corner of the audience. Lemmick swiveled his head to look, then made his way hurriedly in that direction.

Even before he reached her, the shouter—a slender woman in her midtwenties, dressed in black jeans and an army-green tank top—was already on her feet, waving a copy of Paul's book in the air. Her long black hair framed a striking face: sharp bones, full mouth, flashing black eyes. Staring up at her from the stage, Paul couldn't help registering how attractive she was.

Lemmick had made it to her side in record time. "Sounds like there's something you want to get off your chest, uh . . . ?"

"Chris," the woman snapped.

"You're on, Chris," said Lemmick, tilting the mike in her direction.

"Here's my question for Mr. Novak." She spoke the name the way Paul's parents said *Hitler,* as though spitting out a curse. "How can that man sit there and claim his book isn't exploitative when it contains passages like this?" Flipping open the book to a place she had marked with a finger, she began reading aloud in a voice full of loathing.

" 'Standing by the foot of the bed, Ed moved the dead woman's legs apart and bent closer for a look. Abruptly, he pulled back, repulsed by the smell. On a table nearby lay his instruments. Picking up the sharpest of the tools, he turned back to the body and applied himself to his work. It was only a matter of minutes before the freshly excised vulva was nestled in his trembling hand. He carried it out to the kitchen, where—' "

Lemmick interrupted her. "I think we get the picture."

"Do you?" Chris shot him a look. "Then why are you letting that man use your show as a forum for promoting pornography? Because that's all it is. Snuff literature. A how-to book for psychos. A step-by-step, do-it-yourself guide to torture and dismemberment."

"That's completely ridiculous," Paul said heatedly. "You think sociopathic personalities are created by books? Believe me, these people have been warped out of shape before they're old enough to read."

"You don't think," Chris shouted at him, "that shit like this puts ideas in people's heads?"

"Excuse me," Lemmick broke in over the shocked cries of the audience. "We're on live TV."

"Good," said Chris. "Maybe your viewers will have a chance to hear the truth." She turned on Paul again, stabbing a finger in his direction. "I'm accusing you of being an accomplice to crimes against women."

"You mean *women* spelled w-o-m-y-n?" Paul sneered, embarrassed even as he said it. It was a cheap shot, delivered with a childish *nyah-nyah* tone of voice.

"No," Chris said, her own voice more subdued now but no less fraught with rage. "I mean 'women' as in your wife and your daughter. How would you like it if someone came after *them* with a meat cleaver and butcher knife?"

"I think that's completely uncalled for!" Paul shouted at her.

"And you know what I think?" she answered with a thin, contemptuous smile. "Of you and your lousy book?"

In a motion so fluid that she might have been practicing it for weeks, she ripped out the page she'd been reading from, crumpled it into a ball, and fired it at the stage.

It was a good throw—as strong and straight as if she spent her weekends playing centerfield in a women's softball league. Even so, the balled-up paper didn't have enough heft to carry as far as she'd intended. It sailed over the audience and bounced off the balding dome of an elderly gentleman sitting in the second row beside his white-haired wife. He touched his scalp tentatively and swiveled to gaze over his shoulder, like a man who didn't know what had hit him.

Paul knew exactly how he felt.

Up on the top row, Chris had already removed, crushed, and hurled another page. This one made it all the way to the front of the stage.

"Stop that now!" cried Lemmick, reaching out to grab the book from her hands.

Chris used an elbow to keep him at bay and tore out another page. Most of the audience hooted and booed, though a few women shouted encouragement. Chris seemed oblivious to both the catcalls and cheers.

She stood at her seat lobbing away while Lemmick beckoned for a security guard and Paul sat there shaking his head.

An hour later, he was shaking it again as he headed up Route 95 in his new silver Audi—like his house, another fruit of his recent good fortune. Reaching down to the dashboard CD, he lowered the volume of Neil Young's "Harvest Moon." Normally, Neil's strangled crooning had a soothing effect on Paul. Now, it just grated on his nerves. He was still brooding about the business with that woman, Chris.

Not that the show had been a debacle. Lemmick himself seemed tickled by the turn of events. The nastiness with Chris had been "confrontational TV at its finest," he told Paul as soon as the show was over. Indeed, Lemmick seemed prepared to rank it as one of the all-time high points of his program, right up there with the time the animal-rights activist dumped a bucket of Benjamin Moore house paint on the sable mink coat worn by a representative of the furrier's union and the memorable occasion when Lemmick himself—upholding the red-blooded standards of heterosexual malehood—got into a slugging match with a member of the North American Man-Boy Love Association.

Even Paul's publicist—who had accompanied him to the studio and watched the show on the monitor in the green room—had been pleased. "Controversy sells books," she assured him. She wouldn't be surprised if *Slaughterhouse* did another 25,000 copies by the end of the week.

No. It wasn't Chris's outburst itself that bothered Paul. He knew her kind—a member in good standing of the PC police, the type who insisted on calling fat people "differently sized" and condemned the word *masterpiece* as "phallocentric." ("What are we supposed to start calling the *Mona Lisa?*" Paul once asked a colleague of Wylie's during a heated dinner argument. "An artistic mistress-piece?")

No. Paul didn't take Chris's attack very seriously. He knew his book wasn't evil, even if the crimes it recounted surely were. But there was something else eating at him as he passed the road sign welcoming him to Connecticut.

He could picture that lovely face contorted with hatred as she said it. "I mean 'women' as in your wife and your daughter. How would you like it if someone came after them with a meat cleaver and butcher knife?"

Paul cursed aloud at the memory.

She gets up there and says that on national TV. And she accuses me *of planting vicious ideas in people's heads!*

The thought of it filled him with dread.

2

The town of Stoddard Bridge—pop. 2,617—sits on the banks of the Housatonic River in the Connecticut county of Litchfield. Its first English settlers erected their houses a century before the American Revolution, and the spirit of a bygone age still lingers in the community.

You can feel it on those soft summer twilights when its citizens settle down on the grass of The Commons for a band concert by the Original Stoddard Ragtimers—tootling away from the old-fashioned gazebo that stands in the center of the little park—and on those frigid Yuletide evenings when several hundred hardy souls gather at the same spot to carol Christmas songs under the stars. It is there in the weekly all-you-can-eat pancake breakfasts at the First Congregational Church on Main Street and in the monthly country auctions at Jameson's Treasure Barn at the southernmost end of River Road.

There are families who have lived in Stoddard Bridge for generations. Emanuel C. Stanhope, M.D.—the crusty pediatrician who has been practicing out of the same office on Maple Lane for the past fifty years—now treats the grandchildren of some of his original patients. Dr. Stanhope's ancestral plot in the local cemetery just off Route 44 contains several tombstones so antique that they were once featured in an article, "Graveyard Carvings from Our Colonial Past" in the *Bulletin of the Connecticut Historical Society*.

Of the big porticoed houses that flank The Commons,

the newest was built just before the Civil War. The town's tiny commercial district includes both a barbershop (complete with spiraling pole out front) and a beauty parlor, a hardware store, liquor shop (Stoddard Wine and Spirits), bakery (specializing in six varieties of all-natural muffins), corner pharmacy, real-estate agency, handicrafts gallery, and luncheonette. There is also an almost cloyingly quaint country store, which offers everything from penny candies to kitchen gadgets to a variety of decorative knickknacks (many of them featuring cats), and a rambling inn that draws weekend guests from as far away as Maryland. The largest building in town is the bank, an imposing structure with Doric columns and marble floors and polished brass grills at the tellers' windows. Stoddard Bridge is the kind of place where the bank manager, C. Howland Pearson, knows most of his customers by name.

Tucked away in the northwestern corner of the state, Stoddard Bridge lies too far from Manhattan for easy commuting. As a result, it has escaped the fate of several equally picturesque villages to the south, which have been transformed in recent years into havens for middle-aged Yuppies fed up with urban living. At the same time, the town is close enough to the city—just under two hours by car—that the transition from the jangling streets to the tranquil country lanes can feel slightly disorienting.

Paul Novak, for one, never made the trip without feeling a bit like H. G. Wells's time traveler—as though his sleek new vehicle were really a sci-fi contraption, propelling him back to a world where the evils of modern life had not yet intruded.

His dark mood had dissipated by the time he reached his exit. It was a golden July evening, just after seven. The Audi was equipped with a climate-control system that would keep the interior at any temperature he chose, but he switched it off and lowered his window as he turned onto Old Schoolhouse Road. In the city, summer meant rotten smells and smothering heat. Up here, the air felt so sweet that Paul wanted to bathe in it.

Knowing that the liquor store would still be open, he decided to treat himself and Wylie to a celebratory bottle of Puligny-Montrachet, their favorite wine. Detouring into town, he parked in the train station lot, nearly vacant at that hour.

There was one other customer in the liquor store—an elderly woman, white-haired but still trim, wearing beige cotton slacks and a blue-checkered top. Paul felt he had met her before at some local gathering but couldn't put a name to her face. He and Wylie had moved to Stoddard Bridge less than six months earlier, and they knew only a few of their neighbors.

The woman, however, recognized Paul immediately. Gripping him by the arm, she exclaimed that she had seen him on *The Lionel Lemmick Show*.

"Not that I spend my afternoons watching television, mind you," she hastened to explain. She had switched on the set only because a friend had called to tell her about a marvelous production of Mozart's *Don Giovanni* that PBS was rebroadcasting at four o'clock. She was searching for the channel when she spotted Paul's face.

She praised his performance, especially his "refusal to be browbeaten by that dreadful young woman." As soon as the program was over, she had called the B. Dalton bookstore at the Watertown Mall and asked them to put aside a copy of Paul's book.

"I'll have to smuggle it past my husband, of course. He abhors that sort of thing. 'What do you need horror stories for when you have the nightly news?' he says. But I enjoy a well-done shocker every now and again." She spoke this in a conspiratorial whisper, as though confessing a secret vice to a fellow sinner.

Heading back to his car a few minutes later, wine bottle in hand, Paul realized that he had become something of a celebrity. National bestseller. *People* magazine. *The Lionel Lemmick Show.* Immediately, he recalled the words of Andy Warhol: "In the future, everyone will be famous for fifteen minutes."

He made a wry face as he settled behind the wheel. *Okay. So maybe it doesn't amount to very much.* He placed the costly bottle beside him on the passenger seat and started the engine. *Still, might as well enjoy it while it lasts.*

He steered the Audi out of the parking lot, feeling like a lucky man.

The wooden structure that gives Stoddard Bridge its name spans the Housatonic River at the southern end of town. There is nothing especially picturesque about it. Roofed and unpainted, it resembles a long, narrow barn incongruously stuck over the water. It does, however, possess some historical significance. Dating back to 1826, it is the only extant covered bridge in Connecticut. As a result, it was declared a state landmark in 1953 and permanently closed to traffic.

To reach his house, situated on the west side of the river, Paul had to drive a half-mile north of town and cross a little steel-girdered bridge that rumbled hollowly under his tires. From there, he followed a hard-packed dirt road to a turnoff in the woods, marked by a flaking, red-painted mailbox nailed to a plain wooden post.

He swung the car onto the rutted track that ascended to his driveway, jouncing through a shadowy tunnel of maples and pines. A hundred yards up and the path became gravel. The trees thinned out on either side. Suddenly he emerged into a clearing, where his house stood on the crest of the hill.

Parking his car behind Wylie's blue Volvo, he sat for a moment and gazed at his home. It wasn't imposing by local standards—a nine-room stone farmhouse built in 1826—but its rough-hewn grace spoke of a vanished world of proud rural craftsmen, and the sight of it never failed to fill him with pleasure.

Paul had read somewhere—he couldn't remember the source—that all a girl had to do to become a woman was get older, but manhood was something you had to *earn*. In most cultures, that meant proving your skill at some physical challenge—hunting, fighting, sports. But whatever else it involved, manhood meant taking care of your family—making sure that your wife and children had food on the table and a roof over their heads.

He realized that this was a hopelessly old-fashioned, even retrograde, notion. He could just imagine what warrior-woman Chris would have to say about it. But in his heart, it felt like the truth. The sturdy old house—purchased through his own labor—validated him in some deep, fundamental way, as though investing him with its own solidity and substance. For the first time in his thirty-six years, he felt like a full-grown adult.

He stepped out of the car and stood there for a moment, savoring the air. The Novaks owned the entire hill, all six acres of it. Their nearest neighbors, the Keegans, lived a quarter-mile to the west, their roof barely visible amidst the treetops. Paul closed his eyes and listened to the stillness, which was broken only by the chirping of birds and a mellow rustle in the leaves. And then something else—a high-pitched shout, followed by a squealing laugh: the sounds of his children at play.

Reaching back into the car for the wine bottle, he shut the door and followed the sounds to the back of the house. His children, Matt and Diana—ten and seven—were busily engaged in Whiffleball, while Wylie worked at the cedar picnic table they used for al fresco dining when the weather permitted. Books and papers were scattered all over its surface. She wrote with her back to the landscape; behind her, the vista was distractingly lovely. A dense stand of birch trees, their dark leaves gilded by the evening sunlight, cast long shadows across the meadow that ran down to the river's edge.

Paul paused at the corner of the house and watched while Diana pitched to her brother—a wild, underhand throw that sent the ball sailing at least six feet over his head.

As Melville, the family's five-year-old black Labrador, loped off in pursuit of the ball, Diana spotted her father.

"Daddy!" she cried and came bounding at him. Matt dropped the plastic bat and followed behind.

Paul boosted Diana up as she hurled herself at him. She hung on his neck, her thin legs wrapped so tightly around his middle that he hardly needed to support her. With his free hand, he reached down and tousled the soft blond hair of his son, who hugged him around the hips.

Wylie glanced up and flashed him a bright grin. Raising a forefinger—a gesture that said "just give me a minute"—she returned to her writing.

"Daddy!" Diana cried again. "You were on TV!"

He kissed her on the forehead and said, "You didn't watch, did you?"

"Nah," Matt grumbled. "Mommy wouldn't let us."

"Yeah," Diana piped up. "She said it was too scary." She paused, frowning. "Did that man in your book really eat people?"

"No," Paul said with a soothing little laugh. "But your mom was right not to let you watch. We were talking about some pretty creepy stuff."

Matt snickered evilly. "Yeah, like chopping up little girls and making them into beef stew."

"No!" Diana cried.

"Hey, guy," Paul said, shooting his son a mildly reproving look. "Cool it." He set Diana on the ground and stroked her cheek. "There's nothing to worry about, sweetheart. That man I wrote about died a long time ago—before you were even born."

Turning to her brother, Diana stuck out her tongue at him.

Strolling across the grass to the picnic table, Paul set the wine bottle on the surface where Wylie would see it when she looked up. Then he stepped behind her and glanced over her shoulder. She continued to write for another half-minute, then set down her pen with a loud sigh of relief. He bent over and kissed the warm crook of her neck. She was wearing a yellow rayon tank top with spaghetti straps, and her strong swimmer's shoulders were sun-freckled and smelled of buttermilk soap.

"Hey, sweetie," she said, glancing up at him. "Good to see ya."

"Bought us a present," Paul said, nodding toward the bottle.

She picked it up and looked at the label. "Yum."

"How's it going?" he asked, gazing down at the title page of the paper she'd been working on. "The Transgressive Self: Gender, Art, and Ideology in the Poetry of Emily Dickinson," it said.

"Tough," Wylie sighed. "But I think it's good. I'm hoping the *Dickinson Quarterly* will take it." Wylie, an assistant professor of English at Connecticut State, was coming up for tenure in the fall and needed one or two more publications to nail it down.

She patted the bench beside her. "Come. Sit down and tell me all about the show. Not that I haven't gotten a complete rundown already."

He gave her a questioning look as he slid beside her.

"Let's see." She raised her right hand and ran through the names, counting them off on her fingers. "So far I've gotten calls from the Wilsons, the Eisenbergs, the Statlers, the Keegans. Your mother. *My* mother." By then, she had all five fingers in the air, plus the thumb of her left hand. She broke off with a little laugh. "There were a few others, too. And all of them said to tell you that they taped the show in case you forgot to set up the VCR."

"Oh, good," said Paul. "I always wanted my own video library. Of course, I was hoping for a little more variety."

"That doesn't include the copy *I* made. I was planning to watch it tonight when the kids are asleep."

He bent and kissed her bare shoulder. "I had slightly different plans for what we might do when the kids are asleep."

"Mmmm." She smiled, closing her eyes and leaning toward him for a kiss. It lasted a long moment. Then, straightening up again, she said, "So . . . I heard it turned out to be pretty wild."

"Wild *and* woolly."

She gave him a look. To his eyes, it seemed slightly sardonic.

"What's that supposed to mean?" he asked.

"What?"

"That expression. Like, 'Well, you were asking for it.'"

"That's not what I was thinking. You're imagining it. Still . . ."

"Yes?"

"Well, it's what you wanted, right? Notoriety. Or else you wouldn't have done it."

"Done what? Gone on Lemmick's show?"

"That, and written the book in the first place."

"Oh Christ," said Paul, his temper flaring.

"Don't get mad," she said. "It's just that—"

He cut her off. "Look, I know damn well you think *Slaughterhouse* is crap."

"I don't think it's crap," she answered sharply. "It's just that . . ."—she paused for an instant, as though debating the wisdom of giving voice to her thoughts—"It's just not the kind of writing I think you should be doing."

"Right," Paul said bitterly, reaching for the title page of Wylie's essay. "You'd prefer me to write the kind of artsy bullshit academics go for."

"That's very unfair, Paul." She bristled, snatching the paper out of his hand. "All I'm saying is that I think your earlier books are more worthy of your talents."

Paul sat tight-lipped for a moment, clamping down on his fury. Finally he said, "You don't seem to object to all this." He made a sweeping gesture that encompassed their home and its surroundings, "To what we've been able to afford—thanks to my book."

"No," she said softly. "But we were doing all right before."

"Right," he snorted. "On your assistant professor's salary. And the pittance my other books were bringing in."

"And my father's trust fund."

Paul shook his head. "We weren't starving, that's true. But you're no heiress, Wylie. Things were getting pretty tight."

She shrugged.

"And anyway. I didn't write *Slaughterhouse* for money. I wrote it because I *wanted* to. And I'm fucking proud of the way it turned out, too."

She sniffed. "Don't curse at me, Paul."

For a moment, they sat and glared at each other, not speaking a word. In the poisoned silence, they suddenly became aware of their children, who were standing across the yard, playing catch with the Whiffleball while Melville dashed back and forth between them, barking excitedly.

"Kids," Wylie called out in a taut voice. "Go inside and wash up for dinner."

Normally, Matt and Diana would have made at least a few perfunctory protests. But they could hear the tension in their mother's voice and see the grim look on Paul's face. Tossing the ball into the grass, Matt turned and trudged toward the front door, Diana at his side.

As soon as they were gone, Wylie turned back to her husband. "Look, Paul," she said, her voice flat and unappeasing. "I'm sorry this happened. All I wanted was to hear about the show, have a nice family dinner, then spend a few pleasant hours with you."

"Same here," Paul said in the same tone. "I'm just sorry you started in on this shit again."

With that, Wylie shoved herself off the bench and stalked toward the house.

Watching her go, Paul found that he was focusing on the curve of her hips and the swivel of her ass. Even through his anger, he could feel his hunger stir. Twelve years of marriage hadn't diminished his desire for her at all. Nor did it seem much affected by their fights.

He had long ago stopped wondering about the source of her power. She was a great-looking woman, no doubt about it—blond and leggy, with a lithe, athletic body and high, shapely breasts. But it was more than a matter of looks. She seemed to give off an essence that seeped into his skin.

Whatever it was, he felt helpless before it.

Their quarrel didn't outlive dinner. The wine made a difference. So did their long-held determination not to fight in front of the children. And then there was simply their mutual goodwill. They loved each other, and it pained them both to see the other upset.

Ten minutes into the meal, Paul reached across the table and covered Wylie's right hand, giving it a squeeze. She looked up at him and smiled. The relief they both experienced was palpable enough to suffuse the dining room—even the children could feel it. Warmth flooded back into the household.

Later, after tucking in the kids and kissing them good night, they retreated to their second-floor bedroom. By the time Paul came out of the bathroom, Wylie had changed into a clinging black nightgown, cut very low in back. She was seated at her dressing table, brushing her fine blond hair. Her hair and skin glowed softly in the lamplight, and her cheeks were slightly flushed from the wine.

Paul perched on the edge of the bed, watching her in the mirror as she raised the brush to her hair. Her breasts rose with the movement, pushing against the silky fabric. Her eyes met his in the mirror.

She smiled. "Soon." After a while, she lay down the brush and picked up a jar of pearly cream. Dabbing a bit in her right palm, she tipped back her head and massaged it gently into her long throat. The left strap of her nightgown slipped down over her shoulder, exposing her breast almost to the nipple.

"You're so lovely," Paul said, the hoarseness of his voice surprising him. She laughed—a rich, throaty sound. She knew what she did to him.

Rising, she came to the bedside, the nightgown shimmering in the lamplight. Pausing beside the bed, she bent to kiss him, tenderly placing a hand on the bulge of his crotch. She raised her eyebrows and smiled.

He reached up and slid a hand over her breasts, feeling the stiffness of her nipples beneath the silky gown. She took a step backward. Reaching down, she drew her nightgown over her head and dropped it to the floor in one motion. Standing there, she slowly pulled her panties down while he watched. She laughed at the look on his face.

"Come on," he said, grabbing her wrist and pulling her down. She collapsed on him with a little cry and then, smiling, rolled off.

Lying side by side, they kissed hungrily, mouths open wide, sliding their hands over each other's flesh, brushing fingertips over nipples. He almost hummed with pleasure when she began stroking him softly, insistently. His fingers inside her felt startlingly wet.

He pushed himself onto one elbow, bending low over one breast, his lips circling the hardened nipple. His head moved downward over the contours of her stomach, then between her widespread legs. Her smell was thick and deeply arousing.

When he slid his tongue inside her, he was struck by a coppery taste. He made her come that way, licking hard over her clitoris while his forefinger massaged the spot deep inside that tightened to a little knot as her convulsions began. By the time her spasms subsided, he was nearly trembling with his own urgency.

He slipped himself inside her and began to fuck. His orgasm was upon him in a minute. He groaned with both pleasure and disappointment—he had wanted to hold back but couldn't. "Yes, baby," she whispered into his ear, reaching down to cup his contracted balls. He came with a choking gasp.

Eyes closed, they lay on their backs, legs intertwined. Paul must have dozed. Suddenly, his eyes fluttered open as he felt her stir beside him, then leap from the bed.

"What's up?" he said groggily.

"I think my period's started," she said, hurrying for the bathroom.

Later, after she had returned to their bed, he got up to take a leak. Holding himself as he stood over the bowl, he could feel her drying blood thick on his cock. Moving to the basin, he adjusted the water to warm and rinsed himself clean.

In the basin, the bloody water spiraled down the black hole of the drain.

3

He slouched on the plastic-covered sofa in the airless room, the yellow shade drawn against the throbbing July sun—and the prying eyes of his neighbors. His sleeveless cotton undershirt, nearly as yellow as the window shade, clung to his sweat-soaked upper body.

He wore the shirt at home just about every day in the summer, putting it on as soon as *she* left for work. He would never let her catch him wearing it. She'd tear it right off his body and sling it straight into the trash. *Get that stinking thing off your back!* she'd screech. *Lord God, you're no better than a hog in its mire!*

So he always made sure to strip it off before she returned and bundle it away in his secret place, way back in his bedroom closet, where he kept all his treasures. Then he'd slip into one of his freshly laundered T-shirts to greet her at the door. She liked them best with the funny sayings on them, like the one with the picture of a cow's rear end and above it the words, "Welcome to Wisconsin. Smell Our Sweet Dairy-Air."

But for now, he could just relax and enjoy the sensation of the ratty old shirt against his body.

It was like putting on a second skin.

He glanced at the digital clock perched on the portable Sony—4:40 P.M. *Just a few minutes to go!*

He had already made his preparations. On the glass-topped coffee table in front of him sat his favorite midafternoon snack: a sandwich of Peter Pan chunky peanut

37

butter and Smucker's grape jelly on white bread. He had scraped out the last of the jelly in making the sandwich and used the empty jar as a drinking glass, filling it with Hershey's chocolate milk without bothering to rinse it clean. Lying beside his right hand on the plastic-covered sofa cushion was the remote control unit for the TV.

The big orange numbers blinked to 4:41. He could feel a tightening of excitement in his chest.

A dribble of sweat tickled his rib cage. He glanced down at himself. A tuft of mousy brown hair, beaded with moisture, poked out of his armpit. *Just like a woman's bush,* he thought, grinning lewdly. *All juicy and dripping and ready to go.*

He frowned suddenly, spotting a fierce red pimple on the white flesh of his upper arm. He scratched it off with the nail of his right index finger. He winced at the pain but was pleased by the solid feel of his bicep. For the past six months, he'd been working a part-time job delivering copies of *Modern Milwaukee* around the city, and all the loading and unloading of the bundled magazines had built up the muscles of his arms.

Christ! Look at the time!

The room was a sweatbox. He pushed his fingers through his plastered-down hair and his hand came away sopping wet. He flicked away the moisture. Then, fumbling for the zapper, he aimed it at the TV and thumbed the on button. The picture materialized in an instant, and he found himself staring at *The Lionel Lemmick Show.*

His brow furrowed. Why was the set tuned to Channel 11? Then he realized *she* must have been watching TV last night after he'd gone off to work. Probably that inspirational show she enjoyed so much: *For Goodness' Sake with the Reverend Victor Hobart.* It was just about the only thing she ever watched. All the rest, she liked to say, was "just so much manure for the mind."

He was about to switch channels when something caught his eye onscreen—a dark-haired young woman high up in the audience tearing pages out of a book. *What the hell?* She was a real slut, you could see that in a second, wearing nothing on top but one of those itty-bitty T-shirt things, and—*shitfire!*—you could see her nipples all right, poking right through the fabric like a big old pair of thumbs. He leaned forward on the couch for a better look.

He couldn't figure it out. She was balling up the paper and firing it straight at the guy onstage—some skinny, curly-headed Jewboy, by the look of him.

He watched for another minute, but the camera pulled back so you couldn't see her titties anymore, and anyway, it was almost 4:45!

Quickly, he hit the number 3 button twice on the remote control. The picture winked and *there it was!* His all-time favorite program, just coming on. AEROBICIZE WITH DEBBIE, it said in big, rainbow-colored letters, while the familiar bouncy music played in the background.

He leaned back on the couch, reaching down to undo the tie of his sweatpants. His hands were shaking slightly as he loosened the knot, then raised his buttocks and squirmed out of the pants and his Fruit of the Loom undershorts, yanking them down to his ankles. The plastic felt stiff and sticky under his bare ass as he settled himself back on the cushion.

Then, reaching forward, he picked up his sandwich and jelly-jar glass as the program began.

The set looked very phony. It was supposed to be a fancy health club, but you could tell it was just a big, empty room with a few pieces of gym equipment sitting in the corners—some dumbbells and mats and a bench for lifting weights. A dozen young women were gathered in the center of the room, loosening up for the workout—jumping in place and shaking their hands at their sides.

A few of the women were short and chunky. The rest were pretty good-looking. There were a couple of muscular young men there, too, wearing little white shorts and T-shirts.

He snickered. *Homos.* Raising one end of the sandwich to his lips, he inserted the tip of his tongue into the crack between the slices and licked out a dollop of purple-brown ooze.

Debbie, the instructor, was positioned in front of the little group, facing the camera. The way she stood—hands on her hips, feet spread apart—reminded him of Wonder Woman. She was slender but strong-looking. Her face was pleasant, though not really pretty. But there was something about her broad mouth that fascinated him. When she smiled—which was almost always, even when she was doing jumping jacks or shouting commands—you could see her big shiny teeth, like a horse's.

He was fascinated by her body, too. Her breasts were perfectly round and high up on her chest, like balloons. He closed his eyes for a moment and pictured them, floating up into the air, separated from her body. He wondered what it would feel like to have those big balloons attached to your chest.

He jerked his head and stared at the screen. Debbie's skin-tight leotard made her dirty part bulge. If he squinted hard enough, he could almost make out her crack.

He felt a stirring between his legs and glanced down hopefully. But his thing lay shriveled in the matted nest of his pubic hair, its pale head peeping up like a blind hatchling waiting for its mother to fly home with a bug.

He was beginning to get anxious, and the anxiety was making it hard for him to feel excited. It was growing later by the second: the clock read 4:52. He knew that she would be on her way home from work by now. Usually, she didn't arrive until the program was over. But sometimes she left the cannery a few minutes early, or the buses made better time, and she got back sooner.

Come on! he pleaded with Debbie. He couldn't tell if

he really yelled out the words or just shouted them inside his head.

He knew the exercise routine by heart. He watched the program almost every day. The part he liked best was when the girls lay down on their backs and opened and closed their legs like scissors to *firm those thighs!* That was what Debbie always shouted: *"Firm those thighs!"*

Oh please, he whined. What if this was one of those days when she made it back home before he had a chance to finish?

The thought made him so nervous that his hand shook as he raised the jelly jar glass to his lips, and some chocolate milk sloshed over the rim and splattered onto his undershirt, adding a brown stain to the yellow.

He glanced down at the stain uncertainly. Both of his hands were full—the right one with his sandwich, the left with his jelly jar. For a moment, he couldn't decide what to do. Then he set the jar down on the coffee table and tried rubbing the stain off his shirt with his fingers. It didn't work very well. He shrugged, licked his fingers clean, then bent forward to reach for the jar.

When he picked it up, he saw to his horror that it had left a circle of brown liquid on the coffee table.

Oh Jesus! he cried. He glanced up at the TV set just as Debbie called, "All right, people. Time to work on those thighs."

Panic surged inside him. What if she walked in right now and saw the wet mark on the coffee table? He had to clean it up quickly, just the way she had taught him— first with a damp square of paper towel, then with a dry square of paper towel. But the paper towels were in the kitchen, and he couldn't leave the room—not now!

A little whimper escaped his throat as he sat here, desperately trying to think. On the screen, the women were arranging themselves on their backs.

Suddenly, his frantic gaze fell on the *National Geographic* magazines stacked on a corner of the table.

Carefully placing his sandwich down on his crotch, he leaned forward, snatched the topmost issue, and laid it over the wet brown circle. The spot wasn't clean, but at least it was covered up.

He heaved a sigh of relief, then picked up his sandwich and polished it off quickly. His drink, too.

On screen, the whores were spreading their legs for him. He began to breathe faster and felt his thing stir to life. (That was what she called it whenever he took a bath: "Don't forget to wash that thing good," she would shout through the door.)

Eyes riveted on Debbie's crack, he began massaging himself with the fingers of his right hand. He could feel himself throbbing, swelling. He let out a groan.

Where should he finish? Fleetingly, he thought of doing it inside the *National Geographic*. But suppose she decided to read it tonight and found the pages stuck together? Or suppose he used it and then threw it away and she discovered it was missing from the stack? He knew she saved all the issues, keeping them—like everything else—in apple-pie order.

He was still pondering the problem when Debbie called an end to the exercises and announced that it was time to cool down.

He leaned back his head and howled with frustration. This time, he knew it wasn't just in his mind, because his upstairs neighbor pounded on the ceiling.

He had waited too long, wasted all that time because of his stupid carelessness with the jelly jar! (She was right—he was just a useless good-for-nothing!)

But he didn't want to stop now. He could feel it inside him—a big, steaming load almost ready to shoot. On screen, Debbie and her bitches were waving good-bye.

Fortunately, there was another way.

Reaching down, he yanked his sweatpants and undershorts up to his hips, heaved himself off the sofa, and scurried into his bedroom.

4

$\sim$

He locked the door behind him, flipping the metal hook into the eyelet. Not that he needed to. His mother hadn't entered his bedroom since she'd come across that *Reader's Digest* article, "Your Children Deserve Their Privacy, Too!" That had been nearly a dozen years ago, shortly after his thirtieth birthday.

Still, it made him feel extra snug and secure to have the door latched.

He hadn't known a single moment of privacy earlier in his life, especially during those long years when the two of them inhabited that hellhole on the western edge of Milwaukee where she'd moved after leaving her hometown right before he was born. They had stayed there for the first eighteen years of his life: a shabby one-bedroom apartment in a tenement where the roaches came out so thick after dark that you were afraid to get up and pee in the middle of the night, knowing what you'd see when you turned on the bathroom light.

It was all they could afford in those years on the pittance her parents sent her every month. But she refused to go to work back then. *Call me old-fashioned,* she'd say, *but I believe that a mother's place is at home. Not like these hussies today. Leaving their offspring behind while they tart themselves up and sashay off to some job. Spend all day sucking up to some big tub of guts who thinks that being a boss gives him the right to talk smut and lay his filthy paws all over 'em.*

So they'd stayed shut up in that apartment, day after day, year after year. Just the two of them, hardly ever going out at all. Sharing the same bedroom, so cramped there was space for only one double-sized bed.

It was funny. He couldn't really remember that period of his life very clearly, long as it was. But sometimes at night, just before falling asleep, a vision would rise up and overwhelm him—a crazy memory, indistinguishable from a terrible dream, that would leave him sweat-soaked and shaking:

The two of them together in bed. The weight of her head as it rested on his belly. Her trembling fingers unbuttoning his p.j. bottoms. Her voice, cracked and whimpering, "Oh, you don't know what it's like to be so lonely."

Then the moist suckling sensation down there, both sickening and unbearably exciting. The torturous release. Then her shrieks and curses and the frenzied blows on his face and arms until she collapsed onto the bed beside him; the mattress shaking with her wailing sobs.

But that was so long ago. Maybe it hadn't happened at all. Maybe it really was all a dream.

It was hard for him to tell anymore what was real and what was not.

One thing he knew for sure: in here, he was safe—here in his own little world.

He drew in a deep breath of pure contentment. The room was so much a part of him that he couldn't even smell it, though a stranger who had somehow found himself inside would surely have backpedaled out as quickly as possible, fumbling for a pocket handkerchief to shield his assaulted nostrils from the stench.

He kept the window shut tight and the shade completely drawn. The shade wasn't translucent like the one in the living room but a heavier kind that permitted no light to seep through. It was made of a dull greenish black material, roughly the color of bread mold.

The room was sparsely furnished: a rumpled bed, night table, and three-drawer maple-veneer bureau. The headboard, table, and bureau—along with a wood-framed wall mirror—made up a matching "four-piece colonial bedroom suite" his mother had purchased from the Sears catalog.

The floor was covered with a drab synthetic material with the texture of Astroturf. Only a few small patches of it were visible, however. The rest was hidden under a wall-to-wall carpet of fetid underwear and sweatsocks, dog-eared comic books and men's magazines, wadded tissues, crumpled cola cans, empty candy wrappers, and greasy take-out sacks from assorted fast-food restaurants.

In one corner lay a discarded inflatable object, like a punctured beach ball. This one, however, was flesh-colored and shaped like a flattened human being. It had a Kewpie-doll face and a puckered hole for a mouth. Its name, according to the box it came packed in, was Kandi. Kandi's mouth was lined with a six-inch rubber tube that was supposed to provide (according to the same box) "an amazingly lifelike sensation."

He had tried it a few times but found it far less satisfying than his own right hand.

The only other item of decor in the room was a corkboard mounted on the wall directly across from his bed. When he switched on the Tensor lamp on his night table, its beam hit the corkboard like a spotlight, illuminating his collage.

The collage was a perpetual work in progress, constantly changing shape. It consisted entirely of female bodies, scissored from his favorite magazines—*Hustler, Beaver, Gash*. Though the corkboard wasn't especially large, he was able to fit dozens of pictures onto it because he always eliminated the unnecessary parts of the girls—their heads mostly, but often their feet and hands. Or maybe just a few fingers or their toes. Sometimes, he removed a whole leg or arm if it didn't add anything to the girl's looks. It depended.

In other cases, he had done amusing things. On one

torso, for example, he had pasted a pair of big staring eyes where the tits should have been. On another, he had glued a picture of a gaping shark's mouth between the girl's widespread legs. He prided himself on his creativity.

Often before he went to sleep, he would lie on his bed and stroke himself while staring at the collage. But right now, he required something stronger.

He concentrated hard, listening for her, but the only sounds he could hear were the faint sounds and laughter of some neighborhood children playing in the weed-choked vacant lot that abutted the side of the building.

There was a closet in his room, as deep as a walk-in but very narrow. It, too, was heaped with rancid clothes and rubbish, as though he used it to store his surplus debris when his bedroom floor became so chaotic that even he had trouble moving across it. A forty-watt bulb dangled from a plastic socket in the closet ceiling. Yanking the cord, he dropped to all fours and crawled inside, making his way to the rear.

It was hard to breathe in the stifling space, and his sweat flowed so freely that he had to grope around for something to wipe his eyes with before he could proceed. A balled-up paper napkin from Domino's pizza, crusted with month-old tomato sauce, was the first thing that came to hand.

There was a small clear space, perhaps two feet square, all the way in back. Kneeling before it, he lowered his face until he could make out the outline of the little trapdoor he had fashioned in the floorboards. He hooked his untrimmed fingernails into the cracks and lifted out the wooden square, exposing a pair of boxes from Van's shoe store in the Grand Avenue Mall. The boxes were nestled side by side on the subflooring.

Reaching down, he removed the box on the right. The second box, the one he left in place, contained his most precious possessions. He had smuggled them back home years before, during his only visit to his mother's hometown. Even now, after all this time, they still held a powerful fascination for him.

They were his legacy.

But for the moment, he was more interested in the contents of the other box, the one he now held cradled in his arm as he scrabbled out of the closet.

He clicked on the Tensor, then perched on the edge of his mattress, placing the shoebox on his lap. Carefully he removed the lid. A single item lay inside. He lifted it out and raised it to his eyes.

It was a small Ziploc bag. Gazing at the object it contained, he could feel himself stiffening.

The object was a swollen cotton lump, roughly cylindrical and stained a rusty brown. It reminded him of those cotton rolls the dentist shoves up inside your cheeks when he's filling your teeth. Only this one was much bigger. And it had a little cotton string hanging from one end.

He had spotted it lying in the gutter the week before after making a delivery to a magazine shop on Center Street. He knew what it was right away, though he'd never seen one before. He had seen the packages, of course, on drugstore shelves and in the "feminine hygiene" sections of supermarket aisles. But never the thing itself. And never one that had been used!

Instantly, he had picked it up by its string and carried it back to his delivery truck, holding it as delicately as a butterfly collector who has just plucked a rare species of swallowtail from a tree blossom. Driving back to the garage, he had trouble keeping his eyes on the road, so excited was he by the magical object lying on the passenger seat only a few inches away.

By then, he'd already known what he would do with it. He would place it with the other treasures in his closet—add his own contribution to the collection he had inherited!

Since that day, his prize had provided him with hours of pleasure. Everything about it was wildly thrilling to him—its shape, texture, aroma. But most of all, the thought of where it had been! And of where those red-brown stains had come from!

He moved the box off his lap and yanked down his sweatpants and undershorts. Then, peeling open the lips of the bag, he held it over his nose and mouth, inhaling deeply. His eyes fluttered closed and he gave a shuddering groan. Reaching down with his free hand, he began to pull at himself violently.

His pleasure built quickly. His curled hand moved to a furious beat. He grunted in time to its rhythm.

His climax was almost upon him. His sopping face—twisted into a tortured grimace—flushed bloodred. His grunting grew louder.

Through it, he suddenly heard the faint sounds of a sliding deadbolt, then the opening and closing of the front door. Then the heavy shuffle of footsteps and a strident female voice, fraught with suspicion, calling, "Leon?"

His mother was home from work.

But there was no stopping it now. He squeezed his lips tight to muffle his cries as he exploded onto the bedsheets. Collapsing back onto the mattress, he lay there for a moment, drenched and panting.

By then, his mother had reached the living room. "What in *hell?*"

Frantically, he shoved the little bag under a pillow, pulled up his pants, and bolted for the door. He was just about to unlatch the hook when he realized that he was still wearing his undershirt. Tearing it off, he rummaged desperately in his dresser for a clean T-shirt. He found one printed with a funny saying: "My Mom Visited the Dells and All I Got Was This Lousy T-Shirt."

He struggled into it, flipped open the hook, turned the knob—and nearly fell backward at the sight of his mother standing just outside the door, her black eyes bulging with fury, her lipless mouth drawn back into a snarl.

"Get outta there!" she thundered.

As he stepped over the threshold, pulling the door shut behind him, she raised her heavy right hand and walloped him across the face, staggering him.

"You been messing up my living room, boy!" She raised her hand again. When he put up his own hand to protect himself, she grabbed it hard by the wrist and hauled him toward the living room.

"Lookit that mess!" she shrieked, pointing at the sofa and coffee table. "What in hell you been doing here?"

"Just eating something, Mama."

"How many times I got to tell you—?" Her voice was quaking with fury. "You get your fat butt in there and clean up your leavings. I ain't your housemaid, boy!"

He hurried to the kitchen and returned a few moments later with the necessary supplies—a roll of paper towels, a pail of soapy water, and a mini-Dustbuster. She loomed over him while he cleaned, her crossed arms as meaty as a pair of baked hams, her bosom ballooning beneath her shapeless polyester dress.

When he had completed the job to her satisfaction, he put away the supplies, then came back and stood before her. He smiled at her uncertainly.

Her eyes narrowed in their pouches. "You remember to brush after eating, boy?"

He blinked nervously.

She repeated the question, louder this time.

"No, ma'am," he mumbled.

Instantly her right hand shot out, a surprisingly deft motion, given the bulk of her arms. Grabbing him by the shirtfront, she half led, half dragged him into the bathroom. "The mouth is a breeding place of germs, Leon. If I told you that once, it must've been a million times. But you just never listen to nothing, do you, boy?"

Squeezing herself behind him in the cramped bathroom she stood there and made sure he brushed according to the method she had taught him: up and down for the front teeth, back and forth for the molars. When he bent to rinse his mouth, he could feel her enormous stomach pressed against his buttocks.

He spat out the last mouthful of foam, then gazed up and looked at her reflection in the mirror.

"Ain't you forgetting something?" she asked.

"Aw, Mama," he whined. "You know how much I hate that."

"Want me to do it for you?"

He sure as hell did not. The last time she had flossed him, his gums had bled for days.

Heaving a defeated sigh, he opened the medicine chest, removed the little white container, and performed the operation.

"Now you turn around, so's I can get a good look in there," she said. "C'mon, Leon. Open up and let Mama in."

He squeezed his eyes shut tight while she pried open his lips and examined his mouth, like a horse dealer checking out a potential purchase. He could smell the fish-stink on her fingers from her job in the catfood cannery.

Finally, she let him go. "Guess that'll do," she said.

When he opened his eyes, her face was only inches away from his. "You're a filthy thing, boy. But I reckon you come by it honestly." In her eyes, as in her voice, there was the strangest mixture of sadness and loathing.

She shook her head slowly, and as she turned around and made her way out of the bathroom, she continued to mumble in the same half-melancholy, half-disgusted voice: "No better'n that miserable father of yours. No sir, not one whit better'n that dead skunk that sired you."

5

Their morning had passed without so much as a nibble. Under the high midday sun, the big lake glared like a sheet of tinfoil. The two boys had been in a foul mood to begin with; the heat and their boredom only made matters worse.

"What a shitty vacation," muttered Tad Kahler. The fourteen-year-old boy was seated in the stern of the row-boat, his fishing rod clasped listlessly in his left hand, his chin propped morosely on his right.

Roger, his eleven-year-old brother, sat in the bow. "Yeah," he said. Then added wistfully, "Remember the Dungeon of Horrors? And that cool miniature golf place, Pirates' Cave?"

"Cove," Tad said. Pirates' *Cove."*

The previous summer, their parents had treated them to a vacation at the Wisconsin Dells—a solid week of water slides and wave pools, bumper cars and mini-Grand Prix racers, haunted houses, wax museums, wagon rides, and eat-out meals at neat places like Paul Bunyan's Lumberjack Inn and Ollie's Swedish Kitchen.

This year, however, their folks had decided on something different: ten days at a secluded cabin on Castle Rock Lake, thirty miles north of the Dells. When the boys had put up a fuss, their dad had explained the reasons. It would be a lot cheaper, for one thing. The week at the Dells had cost "an arm and a leg," whereas the cabin—owned by one of Bill Kahler's colleagues in the biology department at Beloit—was available for next to nothing.

"And it'll be a lot healthier, too," he enthused. "Ten days of fresh air and exercise. Hiking and biking and swimming and boating. Grilling our own fish caught right from the lake. And the scenery! It's God's country up there, boys."

Their father wasn't exaggerating. The big lake and the surrounding woods were spectacular, all right. The family had been there for nearly five days now, doing all the things Bill Kahler had described and more—sunbathing, bird-watching, berrying, picnicking.

So far, the boys had hated every minute of it.

"Jesus, it's hot," Tad said. Gripping his fishing rod between his knees, he pulled off his Milwaukee Brewers baseball cap, dunked it in the lake, wrung it out like a washcloth, and replaced it on his head.

The day was so still that the boat floated motionlessly on the water. Every now and then, Tad gave his rod a halfhearted tug, trying to stir up some interest in the waterlogged nightcrawler impaled on the end of the line. But there were no takers.

It was 12:23 P.M., Wednesday, August 12.

Roger shifted uncomfortably on his seat. "I gotta pee," he said, turning to his brother.

"So pee."

"You mean here? In the middle of the lake?"

"That's right, Roger," said Tad, as though addressing a mental defective. "Right here in the middle of the lake."

"I can't."

"Sure you can, Roger," Tad said in the same tone. "All you gotta do is stand up, whip it out, and aim over the side."

"But people'll see me," Roger whined.

Tad widened his eyes and glanced around him, as though checking the shoreline for spies. "You see lots of people, Roger?"

"No, but—"

Tad made an exasperated sound. "Awright, awright," he said, reeling in his line so fast that the hooked worm came shooting up out of the water in a prismatic spray. "Might as well get off this stupid lake anyway. This is a complete waste."

The rowboat was rigged with a small outboard motor. Yanking the starter cord, Tad ruddered the boat toward the little strip of beach at the eastern edge of the heavily wooded island. The boys had spent several lazy hours there a few afternoons before, reading from their trove of superhero comics. They had insisted on taking the comic books with them on vacation after learning that the cabin wasn't equipped with a TV.

The engine puttered along gently, the water lapping at the aluminum sides of the boat. The vast sky was dotted with puffy white clouds. They reminded Roger of whipped cream. His mom had promised to bake a wild-blueberry pie with homemade whipped cream topping as soon as she had gathered enough berries. Roger's stomach growled as he closed his eyes and pictured the pie.

He opened them again just as Tad cut the engine and the rowboat glided into the shoreline, hitting it with a little bump. Hopping out, Roger grabbed the prow and, grunting, managed to work the boat an inch or so onto the sand.

"Be back in a sec," he said, then turned and hurried toward the trees.

Tad stuck his elbows onto his knees and planted his chin on his hands. He stared at nothing while the voice inside his head grumbled a litany of complaints: against his parents for refusing to take them back to the Dells, against his pain-in-the-ass-y brother who was such a dork he needed a tree to pee behind, against this stupid, boring place where there was nothing to do all day except hang around and get sunburned, against—

Suddenly, something big splashed in the water close by.

Tad peered in the direction of the noise. The sunlight glinting off the water made it difficult for him to see. He squinted harder until he spotted it—a fat, golden-eyed bullfrog hunkered among some weeds in the shallow water maybe a yard and a half from the boat.

It was too far away for Tad to reach by hand—his preferred method of frog-catching. But if he leaned carefully over the side, he might be able to snag it with his short-handled fishing net.

He decided to give it a try. Then he'd wait until good ol' Roger came back and maybe slip the big slimy thing down the little dweeb's swimming trunks and watch him flip out. *That* would brighten up the day a bit.

Grabbing the net, he extended his arm and leaned way over the side of the boat. Then, very cautiously, he dipped the net so that its edge was just touching the surface of the water behind the frog's haunches. He knew not to bring the net straight down over the frog. Fat as it was, it would simply flatten itself down into the mucky lake bottom and shimmy away. The trick was to get the net *under* the frog and—

He had maneuvered the net into precisely the right position and would have caught the frog for sure if his brother's screams hadn't startled him so badly that he let go of the handle and fell back in the boat with a cry.

Even in the shadows of the forest, the temperature must have been close to ninety degrees. But Roger was shaking uncontrollably when Tad came crashing through the underbrush to his side.

"Rog! What—?"

The little boy's eyes were bulging and his skin had turned a sickly shade, as though beneath his suntan all the blood had drained from his face. A quaking whimper was the only sound he seemed able to make. When Tad grabbed him by the shoulders, Roger raised a finger and pointed. His hand shook so violently that for a moment, Tad wasn't sure where to look.

Then he saw it, partly covered with pine needles on the forest floor.

His first thought was that it was a department-store dummy—it looked so stiff and unnatural. But staring harder, he thought, *Department-store dummies don't have real boobs! Or hair between their legs!*

He could feel his own limbs begin to tremble.

Suddenly, he let out a shout. The eyeballs had moved! *She's alive!* he thought wildly. Until he realized that the movement was coming from the dark bugs crawling in and out of the eye sockets.

Still, it wasn't until he really looked at her mouth—a great gaping hole, boiling over with black ants and beetles—that Tad Kahler clutched at his stomach, turned away from his little brother with a moan, and puked out his guts.

6

Detective Sergeant R. B. Streator had taken Wednesday off, spending his free time the way he generally did when the weather permitted—boating with Ellen and the boys on Lake Michigan, doing a little fishing, a little reading, and a lot of basking on the cabin top with a Bud Lite in hand. By the time they'd redocked the *Ellie Belle* at the marina and driven back home, it was already after nine. Pleasantly enervated by his long day in the sun, Streator sacked out early, without bothering to check out the ten-o'clock news on TV.

So it wasn't until seven the next morning—when he fetched the Milwaukee *Journal Sentinel* from his front lawn and unfolded it as he entered the kitchen—that he learned about the latest horror.

"My Lord," he said, staring down at the story.

Ellen, wrapped in her pink terrycloth bathrobe, turned away from the refrigerator, Tropicana carton in hand. "What's the matter, Arby?"

He held out the newspaper so that she could see the front page. Her brown eyes widened and she raised her hand to her mouth, drawing in a startled gasp at the headlines.

WOMAN'S BODY FOUND IN WOODS
Second Torture Victim in Two Months

MOUTH, OTHER PARTS MUTILATED
Possible Serial Killer, Say Police

"Better get right over to headquarters," Streator said grimly, tossing the paper onto the kitchen table.

"What about your breakfast?" Ellen protested.

"I'll grab something downtown," he said, moving past her toward the hallway.

A few minutes later, he reappeared in the kitchen, car keys dangling from his right hand. Ellen was seated at the table, looking down at the paper and shaking her head.

Streator came up behind her and put an arm around her shoulder. They had known each other since their sophomore year in college. Since then, Ellen had put on a few pounds. But Streator, a lanky six-footer who could still fit into the suit he had worn on their wedding day twenty-two years before, liked the feel of her extra flesh. Her body had always been a comfort to him and (as he never failed to tell her when she began fretting about her weight) there was that much more of her to enjoy.

"We'll catch him, sweetheart," he said softly. When she gazed up at him, he saw that she was crying. She gave him a stricken, tight-lipped smile and nodded.

Kissing her on the top of her head, he strode to the back door. He was reaching for the handle when Ellen cleared her throat and spoke.

"You know," she said in a voice hoarse with sadness, "I used to feel bad sometimes that we never had a girl. But when you read about what's going on in this . . ."— she paused for an instant, then spat out a word that had never crossed her lips before, at least not in Streator's hearing—"this *shitty* world . . ." Her voice quavered and broke, and she had to stop speaking.

Streator regarded her for a long moment, wishing he could find the words to make her feel better and knowing there were none.

He pulled open the door and made for his Chevy.

The drive to headquarters from their split-level home in municipal Meadows, a tidy suburb in southwestern

Milwaukee much favored by cops and firefighters, took twenty-five minutes. Along the way, Streator mulled over Ellen's parting words. After all their years together, he had no trouble completing her thoughts.

I'm glad we didn't have a daughter. That's what she was about to say when her emotions got the better of her.

Streator understood exactly how she felt. *Hell,* he thought, *if I had a teenage girl for a kid, I'd be nervous every time she went out after dark—probably right up to the day she left for college. And then I'd probably worry about her being off on her own!*

Sometimes, it seemed as if the whole damned country was crawling with sickos who got their jollies from hurting women. Not that there hadn't always been wife-beaters and rapists, but in the past ten, twelve years, the situation had gotten much worse. Crimes against women were increasing all the time. And the violence itself had gotten a lot uglier. Drunken husbands going after their wives with the jagged ends of broken whiskey bottles. Jilted boyfriends blinding their ex-lovers with acid. Divorced men blowing away their ex-spouses with assault rifles.

Streator had seen it all. And worse.

Still, he thought, raising sons wasn't the easiest job in the world, either. It was tough to bring up teenage boys with the right values these days. To teach them that women were meant to be loved and respected. That being a man wasn't a matter of putting notches on your dick.

Streator was perfectly aware, of course, that sexual scorekeeping was not a recent phenomenon. He clearly remembered the way his high-school buddies competed with each other to see how far they could get with a girl on a date—first, second, or third base (hardly anyone made it all the way in those days). But as the baseball comparison suggested, there was something playful about it all.

These days, the game had taken a vicious turn. Girls weren't seen anymore as an exhilarating challenge, a prize to be won. They had become prey to be hunted, bagged and tagged like prize kill during deer season. Pieces of meat.

Streator's brow furrowed. Something had drifted into his thoughts, faint but distinctly unpleasant, as though a grim, long-buried memory had given off a foul stench. He spent a few moments trying to identify it, then abandoned the effort.

No need to dredge up something dead and buried from the past, he thought. *Things are rotten enough right here in the present.*

They were about to get a lot nastier, too, if that story in the newspaper meant what he thought it did.

The phone was trilling as he stepped into his office. He snatched up the handset. "Yeah?"

"Is this Detective Sergeant Streetor?"

"It's pronounced 'Straighter.' As in 'less crooked.' "

The voice on the other end chortled. "Good name for a cop."

"So I've been told. What can I do for you, Mr.—?"

"Heckley. Stan Heckley. I'm a freelance journalist, Sergeant Streator. Maybe you've heard of me. I blew the lid on that preschool teacher up in Madison, the one running the kiddie-porn racket?"

"Sorry," said Streator. "Doesn't ring a bell."

"Ah. Well, anyway, the reason I'm calling—I'm doing a book on this serial killer running loose here in Wis—"

Streator broke in, raising his right hand in a "slow down" gesture, as though Heckley were there in the room. "Hold it, hold it. What in the world are you talking about, 'serial killer'?"

"Come on, Sergeant. First Carolyn Dearborn. Now this new one up in Adams. I'm sure you've noticed a connection." There was an edge of sarcasm in Heckley's voice that caused Streator's stiffening hackles to rise even higher.

"Look, Mr. Heckley. I just got in about thirty seconds ago, and all I know so far about this latest killing is what I read in the paper. Yeah, there seem to be some similarities between the cases, but—"

Heckley barked an unpleasant laugh. "I'll say. Two teenage girls with all their teeth yanked out and their cun—excuse me, *vaginas*—stitched up with surgical thread."

"What I was going to say," Streator continued darkly, "is that I haven't seen any official details yet on this recent incident, so I have no reason to assume it's the work of the same perpetrator. Could be a copycat for all I know."

There was a pause at the other end of the line, as though Heckley was reconsidering his strategy. "Look, Sergeant Streator," he said after a moment in a crudely ingratiating tone. "All I'm asking for is access to your investigation. If this *does* turn into something big, there's a lot of potential here. Book-club sales. Movie rights."

"Golly," Streator said. "Maybe Burt Reynolds could play me in the TV miniseries."

His acid tone seemed lost on Heckley. "Stranger things have happened, Sergeant."

"Well, Mr. Heckley," Streator said. "As they say in Hollywood, don't call us, we'll call you." Then he slammed down the receiver.

He sat there for a few minutes, silently cursing Heckley and his ilk—the media vultures always scavenging for a fresh tragedy to feed on. Battening on death, the grislier the better.

When he finally got his indignation under control, he picked up the phone again, placed a call to the Adams County Sheriff's Office, and spoke to a deputy named Dick Southerfield, who gave him a brief rundown on the investigation so far. Next, he put in a call to the office of the state medical examiner. It took him a few minutes to get hold of the ME, who promised to fax him the autopsy report within the hour.

Hanging up the phone, he gazed briefly at the plastic photo cube standing on the desk. It held six pictures altogether, though he could make out only three of them from where he sat. One was an old faded Polaroid of Ellen in a beehive hairdo and one-piece bathing suit. She was standing at the edge of a swimming pool, striking a mock-provocative pose, one hand on her cocked hip, the other on the back of her neck. The other two photographs were of his sons, Bobby and Junior, when they were small boys. Bobby was dressed in his Little League uniform, Junior in his Cub Scout blues.

Just your typical American family, he thought. At least that's what he used to believe. Nowadays, families like his—a hard-working dad, a stay-at-home mom, and two well-brought-up kids who still addressed their elders by "ma'am" and "sir"—seemed as rare as peregrine falcons. Another endangered American species.

An audible growl from the pit of Streator's stomach roused him from these thoughts. Swiveling in his seat, he looked out at the window and saw Chuckie's Snack Wagon parked across the street at the corner of West State Street and Seventh. A few people were milling beside it, enjoying their breakfasts al fresco. When Streator's stomach gave another loud complaint, he decided to join them.

Heading for the elevators, he ran into a member of his squad, Detective Franklin Turner, just arriving for his shift. Turner was a mountainous bull-necked black man who looked as though his idea of a good time was bench-pressing four-hundred-pound free weights. His suits invariably seemed a size and a half too small for his iron-pumped muscles, as though the slightest flex of his biceps or pecs would cause the clothes to explode off his body, an impression that inevitably invited comparisons to the comic-book figure the Incredible Hulk. For a while, in fact, he had been known around headquarters as "the Black Hulk," a nickname that some stationhouse joker had abbreviated to "the Bulk."

Turner was not fond of his nickname, though a few of his colleagues persisted in using it.

Not, however, to his face.

Turner's mouth, framed by a lush Fu Manchu moustache, formed itself into a deep frown as Streator filled him in on his conversation with Chief Deputy Southerfield.

"Fuckin' mess," Turner grumbled.

"Look," Streator said. "We won't know anything for sure 'til we have a chance to look over the autopsy report." He stuck out his wrist and consulted his watch. "Why don't you drop by my office around ten and we'll see what we're dealing with?"

Outside the air-conditioned building, the day already felt oven-hot. It was going to be a scorcher. Streator loosened his tie as he crossed West State Street and got in line behind half a dozen young office workers alongside Chuckie Frewer's white-painted food truck, which was decorated with brightly colored decals of ice-cream bars, cola cans, hot dogs, and fries.

Chuckie Frewer wasn't exactly a walking advertisement for the nutritional benefits of his offerings. He was thin and pale—a little sickly looking, in fact—with his hair shaved so close to his skull that its color was hard to determine. Still, he always seemed energetic enough, and he greeted Streator with a bright, horse-toothed grin.

"How goes it, Sarge?"

Streator waved off the question with a dismissive "don't ask" gesture. "What's good today, Chuckie?" he asked, peering through the clear-plastic cover of the pastry tray resting on the grimy countertop built into the passenger side of the truck.

"Try a jelly-filled cruller. Fresh as they come."

"You sold me. And a coffee. Large."

In less than thirty seconds, Streator's order was sitting before him on the metal countertop. He dumped the contents of three Domino sugar packets into his coffee before lifting the Styrofoam cup to his lips.

"Sure got a sweet tooth, Sarge," Chuckie said.

"Always have," said Streator through a mouthful of cruller.

"Lucky you still got all your teeth. Which is more than you can say for that gal they found up in Adams."

Streator shot him a black look.

"Sorry," Chuckie said, looking abashed. "Sick humor."

"I'll say."

Chuckie watched Streator take another chomp of pastry, then said, "What do you make of the coincidence? Her body being found in Adams County and all?"

Streator frowned. "How's that?"

"You know. Adams being right next door to Waushara. Where Eddie Gein came from."

Something clicked inside Streator's head. "Funny. I was just thinking about him this morning without even knowing it." He blew on his coffee and took another sip. "That's going back a ways, Chuckie. Way before *your* time."

"Well, sure. Hell, I wasn't even born 'til 'sixty-three. But you don't grow up in Wisconsin without knowing all about ol' Eddie Gein, the Mad Butcher of Plainfield. Hear there's a new book about him, too."

"Big surprise," Streator said dryly. "Not enough new perverts to keep the public satisfied; gotta dig up the ones from the past." He made a face so sour that he might have been munching on a kosher dill instead of a sugar-glazed pastry full of strawberry jam. "I'm still trying to figure out that big coincidence you were talking about."

Chuckie gave a little shrug. "Maybe that wasn't the right word. Just seems like that part of the state breeds some major-league psychos."

"Chuckie," Streator said, "you'll travel far and wide

before you find a place in this country that doesn't." He wiped his lips with a napkin, tossed his garbage into the wire-mesh basket hanging from the passenger window, placed a buck on the counter, and said, "Gotta get back to work."

Crossing the street, Streator recalled the disquieting sensation he had experienced that morning while driving to work. *So that's what it was.* When he'd thought about the way young men went after women these days—*like hunters after prey*—his mind had made a subconscious connection to Eddie Gein, whose final victim had been strung up, gutted, and beheaded exactly like a dressed-out deer.

Funny how the mind works, he thought.

Funny, too, the way a mental case like Gein had become a legendary figure around these parts.

Like most people his age in Wisconsin, Chuckie Frewer had undoubtedly grown up hearing all kinds of stories about the Plainfield horrors. He was probably one of those kids whose parents kept them in line by telling them that ol' Boogeyman Ed would come and get them in the night unless they did what they were told.

7

When Frank Turner showed up a few minutes after ten, Streator was seated behind his desk, tapping his steepled fingers against his tightly drawn lips as he stared out the window. In the center of his desk lay a few curling sheets of fax paper, held down by a souvenir beer stein emblazoned with a Brewers logo and containing an assortment of ballpoint pens and pencils.

As Turner approached the desk, Streator stirred from his reverie and glanced up at him.

"That it?" asked Turner, pointing with his chin.

Nodding, Streator reached out a hand and removed the makeshift paperweight from the autopsy report.

Turner lowered himself into the molded plastic chair next to the desk, scooped up the report, and began to read, though he had already inferred the worst of it from the look on Streator's face.

Streator watched as the big man studied the report. Standard office furniture never seemed large enough for Turner. Perched on the plastic chair, he looked like the father of a second-grader trying out his child's seat during parents' visiting night at the elementary school.

A sound like steam hissing from a radiator whistled through Turner's clenched teeth as he finished the report. When he looked up, his eyes met Streator's.

"Same one," said Turner grimly.

"Yup."

"We got ourselves a problem."

"Yup," Streator said again. "Real big problem."

The victim, Darlene Redding, was a pretty sixteen-year-old brunette from Elm Grove who had been missing since the afternoon of Thursday, August 6, when she'd bicycled off to meet a friend at a local shopping center and never arrived. As in the case of Carolyn Dearborn—the nineteen-year-old waitress whose mutilated corpse had been found two months earlier in the undergrowth of Milwaukee's Shorewood Nature Preserve—all of Darlene Redding's teeth had been extracted and the outer lips of her vulva had been stitched together. Both victims had died of stab wounds to the heart.

During homicide investigations, it is standard practice for the police to withhold several essential details from the press in order to filter out phony confessions. Since sensational, highly publicized crimes often provoke a rash of imitations, the suppression of these facts is also a way of distinguishing copycat killers from the original.

When Carolyn Dearborn's body was found, the Milwaukee police had attempted to keep wraps on the precise nature of the victim's sexual mutilation, but a tabloid reporter had somehow gotten wind of this grisly detail. Within forty-eight hours, it was headline news throughout the state. Still, the detectives had managed to hold back three crucial details. Since all three were noted in the autopsy findings on Darlene Redding, it seemed certain beyond a reasonable doubt that both slayings were the work of the same individual.

First, both women had deep fingernail marks in their palms, evidently produced by the agonized clenching of their hands during torture. "Certainly the removal of the teeth and very possibly the suturing of the genitalia took place prior to death," the ME had concluded.

Then there was the matter of the disposal of the teeth. The newspapers had reported that none of the teeth had been recovered. But this was erroneous. In each case, two teeth—the canines—had been located during the postmortem examination.

The teeth had been inserted deep inside the victims' vaginal canals.

The final detail involved the suturing material used on the young women. Here, the police had deliberately planted a piece of phony information, announcing—after the tabloid story first appeared—that the victims' genitals had been sewn together with professional surgical thread. But in fact, the killer had used nothing so specialized.

He had used dental floss.

8

"Have some more clams, Doug." Wylie smiled at the thickset, balding man seated next to her. In the candlelight, her face was suffused with a honeyed glow.

Doug Heller wiggled his eyebrows up and down a few times, Groucho-style, and cast a covetous look at the few remaining steamers in the orange-glazed serving bowl.

"Tempting," he said to his hostess. "Mighty tempting." His own bowl held a dozen empty shells, glistening with the tomato-flecked broth Wylie had spooned over each serving, a recipe from *The Silver Palate,* her favorite cookbook. "Of course," he added, "I want to leave room for that *fine*-looking meat your hubby is grilling."

"Assuming it ever gets cooked," Wylie said. "It seems to be taking forever."

"Figure I oughtta go out there and lend him a hand? I mean, hell—what's a northern boy know about barbecuin' anyways?"

This was Doug doing what his wife Valerie called his "down-home routine." Though Heller was as sophisticated as they came—a senior partner in a prominent midtown law firm who had lived in Manhattan since his student days at Columbia—he liked to play the good ol' boy with friends. The pose was only partly a joke: Heller hailed from Galveston, Texas, and had a strong sense of pride in his native state.

"Just sit where you are, Doug," Wylie said, reaching out to ladle the last of the steamers into his bowl. "I'm sure he's doing fine."

"Don't overfeed him, Wy," said Valerie, refilling her wineglass with Riesling. She was a small-boned woman, half her husband's size, with fine brown hair worn in a smart summer cut and eyes so dark they looked black. An editor of college sociology textbooks at a major New York City publishing house, she was as sharp and tough-minded as her mate. Physically, however, they were opposite types—as incongruously paired as a blacksmith and a ballerina.

"Val's a little worried about the old waistline," Doug said, giving his midriff a few pats.

"And your cholesterol count was what?" Valerie said. "Two-fifteen when we got back from the Vineyard?"

"Damn," said Doug, detaching another clam from its shell and popping it into his mouth. "You're just fixed on spoilin' my pleasure in this seafood, aren't you?"

"Really, Wy," said Valerie. "I don't know how this man can even *look* at another steamer after our vacation."

Doug flashed Wylie a grin. "I guess I did put a pretty good dent in the local quahog population."

"*Decimate* is more like it," said Valerie. "Not to mention the lobsters."

"Couldn't get enough of them," Doug said. "Come dinnertime, I'd just zip into Edgartown, pick up a couple of two-pound beauties, take 'em back to the cottage, boil up a big ol' pot of water, and—" He brought the fingertips of his right hand to his puckered mouth and made an exaggerated lip-smacking gesture, like a French chef pronouncing on the perfection of his Béarnaise sauce.

Valerie gave a half-hearted shrug. "They were good, all right, but—"

"Come on, darlin'," said Doug. "You loved 'em."

"They tasted fine," said Valerie, then turned to look at Wylie. "I just can't stand to see them being boiled alive. Never seems to bother Doug, though."

"That's a fact," Doug said, gulping down the final clam. "Must be a man's thing."

"Actually," said Wylie, "I'm the one who always cooks the lobsters in our family. Paul's like Val—he hates the whole idea of it. Won't even come into the kitchen while they're boiling."

Valerie's eyebrows rose. "Really? I'm surprised."

"Why's that?"

Valerie shrugged. "You know. Given his interests and all."

This time, it was Wylie who lifted her eyebrows. "Val," she exclaimed with a startled little laugh. "You know how gentle Paul is."

"Like his book?" Val shot back.

Wylie stared at her friend for a moment before replying. "The book is one thing. Paul's another. You make it sound as though—I don't know—he's some kind of closet sadist or something."

Valerie opened her mouth to say something, then closed it again. She reached for her wineglass and took a long sip.

"Here, lemme clear away these dishes," Doug said suddenly, half rising from his chair and reaching for Wylie's bowl. "Hell, I ate most of this stuff anyway."

"Don't be silly, Doug," said Wylie, putting her hand on his forearm and pushing him back into his seat. "You two relax. I'll be back in a minute."

A little silence fell as Wylie scraped the empty shells into the serving bowl, stacked the dishes, and carried them into the kitchen.

Through the window over the sink, she could see Paul, barbecue utensils in hand, tending the butterflied lamb on the big grill out back. He stood in the warm glow of the smoldering charcoal, surrounded by the solid blackness of the country night.

Though Valerie's comment had discomfited Wylie, she decided to put it out of her mind. She had been looking forward to this evening for weeks. The Novaks and Hellers had been neighbors on the Upper West Side and good friends for fifteen years.

It was their annual custom to mark the end of each summer with a special dinner at Paul and Wylie's place on the weekend before Labor Day. So tonight—Saturday, August 29—was a very special occasion: the first of their farewell-to-summer dinners at the Novaks' new home. Wylie was determined to make everything go perfectly.

The children had been fed early and sent off to the family room to watch their favorite video, *City Slickers*. She had taken care of the food preparations in advance. The salad—endive, red bell peppers, watercress, and romaine lettuce—was crisp and ready to be dressed with a walnut vinaigrette. The baby asparagus were steamed to perfection. The herb bread she had baked that afternoon sat golden and fragrant on its wooden cutting board. Paul had uncorked the Merlot an hour before the Hellers' arrival. The two bottles stood breathing on the dining room sideboard.

Even the weather was ideal. Though the day had been unseasonably hot, the temperature had dropped to just below seventy after sundown. A westerly breeze, rising off the river, stirred the gauzy summer curtains that framed the kitchen window.

As Wylie picked up the big glass salad bowl and turned toward the doorway, she could hear a hushed exchange between Doug and Val. It ceased abruptly the minute she entered the dining room. Her two friends looked up at her with slightly strained smiles.

"So," Wylie said, setting the bowl on the table. "Tell me what's new in the city."

"Oh, please," Val said with an impatient little flip of her hand. "Don't get me started on *that*."

"Goin' to hell in a handbasket," Doug said. "Hear about that murder over at one twenty-three?" This was the number of the apartment building on the corner of the Novaks' old block.

"No!" Wylie said. "Who?"

"Some old widow lady. Hadn't been seen for a week.

Neighbors began noticin' this real *ripe* smell comin' from her apartment and called the police. Someone had broken in through her bedroom window. Tied her up. Raped her. Smothered her with her feather pillow." Doug shook his head. "Seventy-eight years old."

"Jesus," Wylie said softly.

"Lemme tell you," said Doug, "you and Paul did a real smart thing, gettin' out while the gettin' was good."

"Hey, Doug," said Val. "Why don't *you* write a gory bestseller so we can retire to the country, too?"

Wylie felt her cheeks flush. What the hell was going on with Val? She opened her mouth to give voice to the question.

Suddenly, a chill breath of wind whispered into the room, rustling the curtains and making the candle flames waver. The back door banged and footsteps approached. A moment later, Paul appeared in the doorway.

"Ta-da!" he trumpeted. Stepping to the table, he set down the platter of grilled lamb with the grand formality of a headwaiter presenting the pièce de résistance. Then he straightened up and looked closely at the faces of his wife and two friends. His smile evaporated.

"Have I come at a bad time?" he asked.

There was a tense moment of silence, broken by Doug's booming voice. "Hell, no. I haven't eaten a bite in almost five minutes. I'm *hungry*."

The others smiled. Paul sliced the lamb, Wylie served the side dish, Doug filled everyone's glass with red wine. Then the four of them settled down to enjoy themselves.

Val didn't say much for a while but grew more gregarious after two glasses of the Merlot. They chatted about their favorite topics: movies and novels, the latest doings on and off Broadway, the pleasures and pitfalls of parenthood, the sorry state of the world. It felt like old times.

Until Paul invoked the name of Edward Gein.

It happened about thirty minutes into the meal, when he turned to Val and said, "You'll get a kick out of this. I've been invited to give a lecture at the University of Wisconsin."

"On what?"

Paul grinned. "The sociological significance of Ed Gein."

"Oh?" said Val, her voice curiously flat. "Who invited you?"

"The chairman of the sociology department."

"Are you going?"

"Maybe. It might be fun. And I can do some book signings in Madison."

"They must love you out there," Val said dryly.

"In Wisconsin?" Paul shrugged. "The book's selling like hotcakes. I don't think the citizens of Plainfield are too thrilled with me, though."

"Plainfield?" asked Doug.

"You know. Where Gein came from."

"Right. Forgot the name. What've they got against you in Plainfield?"

"Publicity. They'd just as soon forget that Gein ever existed. Too many painful memories. Plus, it's not exactly the kind of thing you want to be known for."

Doug chortled. "I bet. Imagine living in a place where your only claim to fame is that your neighbor used to be this guy who liked to dig up female bodies and make 'em into furniture."

"Exactly. And my book's stirred up a lot of new interest in the case. I hear there are all these people, college kids mostly, making pilgrimages up there every weekend to visit Gein's grave."

Val shook her head. "So sick."

"Think so?" Paul said lightly.

"You don't?" Val snapped back.

"Not really," Paul said, slightly taken aback by her tone. "People are fascinated by monsters. Even little kids."

"Come on," Val said. Her expression remained neutral, but there was a sneer in her voice.

"You come on, Val," Paul said. "Take a look at fairy tales—like 'Hansel and Gretel.' It's a horror story. Plain and simple. And kids gobble it up. So to speak."

"He's got a point, darlin'," said Doug. "Remember how Lauren used to make us tell it to her every damn night when she was real little? And how she always wanted me to pretend I was a werewolf comin' to eat her up when I tucked her in bed?"

"The stuff in your book," Val said to Paul, "is no fairy tale."

"But it's exactly the same kind of story," Paul said vehemently. "Think about it—here's this lonely little house way off the beaten track inhabited by an oddball character who turns out to be an ogre. It's exactly the kind of story kids are always making up to scare the shit out of each other. Only this time, it turned out to be true."

"But that's a big difference, Paul." This time it was Wylie who spoke up. "I think Val's point is precisely that there were real people involved. A real psychopathic killer. And real victims."

"They're gangin' up on you, big guy," Doug said with a mischievous grin.

"Look, I'm not defending serial killers. I'm just saying that reading books about them is totally harmless."

"You think the stuff going on in Wisconsin right now is harmless?" Val asked, her voice hardening. "With these teenage girls being slaughtered? While your book is 'selling like hotcakes,' as you put it?"

Everyone stared at her for a moment. Finally Doug said, "You're not blamin' Paul for *that?*"

"That's not what I said," Val answered. "But it's a pretty striking coincidence. Some psycho running loose out there, mutilating young women. Removing body parts and keeping them as souvenirs."

"Most serial killers take trophies," Paul said quietly. "And Gein wasn't into teeth."

"And what about this insane business of sewing them up?" Val's face was a mask of disgust.

Paul nodded. "Gein did some sewing, all right. But not on living victims."

"I see," Val sneered, as if to say, "Big difference."

Paul leaned closer to Val. "Listen. People don't commit psychotic crimes because of what they read in books. Or see in movies. You notice a big upsurge in chainsaw massacres down in Texas?"

"All I know, Paul, is that books put ideas into people's heads. That's what they're *for*. And sometimes, they can put very bad ideas in there."

"I'm telling you, Val: I've studied a lot of case histories; it isn't reading that makes these people evil."

"Really? What about Gein? He loved reading stories about sex crimes and Nazi torture and South Seas headhunters. You said so in your own book."

"Sure. He was a desperately sick individual. What'd you expect him to read—*Curious George?*" His mouth felt dry. He reached for his wineglass and drained it. "Hey, when I was a kid, I was into all kinds of crime comics and monster movies and horror magazines. And *I* didn't turn out weird."

"Oops," said Doug. "I think you might've just blown your own argument, good buddy."

The others smiled—even Val.

"Say, can we change the subject?" Doug asked. "This conversation is startin' to give me a powerful case of heartburn. How about something a little more *upbeat?*"

"Here's an idea," Wylie said with a little laugh. "Why don't we discuss gender, art, and ideology in the poetry of Emily Dickinson?"

"I surely would," said Doug, "If I knew what the hell you were talkin' about."

"I like a look of agony," muttered Paul.

"What'd he say?" Doug asked Wylie.

Wylie cast a sideways glance at her husband. "He's being a smart-ass. It's the first line of a Dickinson poem:

'I like a look of agony.' All about death and pain and suffering."

Val looked at Paul. "So what's your point? That there are disturbing things even in Emily Dickinson?"

"There are disturbing things everywhere," Paul said. "And you don't have to look very hard to find them. Just turn over any rock in the garden."

Val pursed her lips for a moment before replying. "I couldn't agree with you more, Paul. The difference is, I don't feel the need to go looking under rocks."

"Afraid of what you'll find, huh?"

"No. Afraid of what might come crawling out from underneath," she answered. "And find *me.*"

9

Though her nightmare had ended hours before, Sheila Atkins was still out of sorts as she moved hurriedly around her kitchen at 7:42 A.M.

It had been another bad dream about Richard. In it, she had been relaxing in the living room, listening to the hammering overhead as her husband repaired their leaky roof. Suddenly, the sound was coming from the front door. Rising from the sofa, she had gone to open it. There stood Richard, looking hollow-eyed and shockingly pale. He was wearing a state trooper's uniform and having trouble breathing, as though the collar was constricting his throat. Sheila had reached up to loosen the button.

As she did, he ripped open his shirtfront and stared down at himself.

Under his shirt, below the neck, he was a skeleton, all white ribs and vertebrae. Seeing this, he began to moan in horror and sorrow.

Sheila had awakened with a jolt, her heart jackhammering against her breastbone. It was her own moaning, not her dead husband's, that had jarred her from sleep.

Turning toward the clock on the night table, she squinted at the glowing figures: 3:06 A.M. She lay wide-eyed in the darkness for more than an hour before falling into a fitful doze. When the alarm began beeping at 6:30, she had reached out blearily, hit the off button instead of the snooze button, and ended up oversleeping by twenty minutes.

Now—Wednesday morning, September 16—both she and her fifteen-year-old daughter, Patti, were running late, and Sheila was dashing about frantically, trying to make up for lost time. A secretary in the billing department of Milwaukee General, she was cursed with a sour-tempered supervisor who would hit the roof if Sheila wasn't at her desk by 8:30.

"Better hurry up, Patti," she shouted down the hall. Her daughter had less than twenty minutes to catch the school bus.

Pulling a plastic-wrapped loaf from the bread box, Sheila removed four slices of whole-grain and dropped them into the slots of the GE toaster. While they browned, she hurried back to her bedroom and clipped a pair of pearl earrings onto her lobes, frowning at the image that stared back at her.

The lack of sleep hadn't done much for her appearance. In the harsh morning sunlight, she looked older than her forty-two years. Her hair was good—thick and shiny, without a hint of gray. But her skin looked deeply lined. A pair of furrows formed dark parentheses around her mouth, crow's feet ran from the corners of her eyes, and her brow was creased with wrinkles.

She gave a philosophical shrug. Life was full of hardships, and if you were human, they left a few scars on your face. Nothing to be done about it, short of plastic surgery, an indulgence Sheila Atkins regarded with passionate scorn. *Rather have my face show a little character than let some knife-happy bozo turn it into a phony beauty mask.*

She *could* do something about her weight, though. She tugged irritably at her flower-print skirt, which felt even tighter than it had the last time she'd worn it, just a week before. Not that she was fat—more like what her father used to call "pleasingly plump." Except that it didn't please her or anyone else.

With a good night's sleep, a little help from Revlon, and a lot more self-control in the kitchen, she could still be attractive. She was relatively young. Not quite ready for a rocking chair, anyway. Suppose she met a man she liked?

Instantly her conscience jabbed her. Four years since the accident and she still felt disloyal for even thinking about other men! But why shouldn't she entertain such notions? *I have a right to a life, don't I?*

The bell on the toaster pinged. Still frowning, she returned to the kitchen and began buttering the slices. *How hard would it be,* she wondered, *to take off twenty-five pounds?*

Footsteps came hurrying up behind her. "Those for me?" piped a breathless young voice.

Turning, Sheila smiled at her dark-haired daughter, who was dressed for school in black Levi's and a short-sleeve, V-neck, button-front blouse. Plucking two slices of toast from the counter, Patti stuck them together like a sandwich and crunched off a corner while she stood beside her mom.

"Sit down and eat right," Sheila said. "You'll choke if you wolf down your food like that."

"No time," Patti mumbled through a mouthful of crumbs.

Patti stood only five feet four and had the chubby-cheeked looks of a preadolescent. But over the past nine months or so, her figure had ripened to maturity. There was, in fact, such a jarring discrepancy between her face and physique that Sheila was constantly reminded of the ads for a risqué movie Richard had dragged her to years ago: "A child's mind! A woman's body!"

"Sorry things are so crazed this morning," Sheila said. "I had a crummy night."

"Thinking about Dad?"

Sheila pressed her lips tight and nodded.

Patti leaned over and kissed her mother on the cheek. "Poor Mom."

She meant it, too. Patti's warmth and sympathy were genuine and quick; they had won her a large circle of friends. But her pity was all for her mother, none for herself.

Her father had perished four years earlier on a rain-slicked highway in the western part of his territory. Killed, ironically enough, while out selling insurance against accident and death. His loss was a hard blow for Patti, who adored him. But (to all appearances at least) she had come through the trauma largely unscathed, embracing the world with a sweet, youthful ardor her mother could only envy.

"Here," Sheila said, pulling open the refrigerator and removing a carton of Minute Maid. "Drink some juice before you go."

Patti gulped down a glassful, then headed for the door.

"Wait," called Sheila. "You coming straight home from school?"

"I thought I'd stop off at the mall first. Just for a little while."

A mild alarm sounded inside Sheila. The school bus ran right by the Mayfair Mall. Once dropped off there, most kids could walk the rest of the way home. Last year, Patti had spent so much time hanging out at Uno's Pizzeria with her friends that on several occasions, she had done poorly on important tests.

"Patti, I thought we had an understanding."

"Mom," Patti said with mild exasperation. "I'm not going to waste any time there. I just want to pick up a couple of things. Then I'll come right home, I swear."

"What things?"

"A leather skirt. Oh, Mom, Nancy got one and it's so beautiful! French Leather Works is having a back-to-school sale. And this skirt is really cheap and soooo cool!"

"How cheap?"

"Twenty-five dollars."

Sheila looked skeptical. "Can't be very good."

Patti's eyes rounded. "It's *beautiful*. It's really reduced; that's the only reason it's so cheap."

Sheila looked at her daughter for a moment, then gave an acquiescent shrug. In fact, she felt secretly pleased. Patti's wardrobe consisted largely of jeans and T-shirts, and Sheila was glad to see her daughter interested in something a little more grown-up.

"Is that it?" Sheila asked.

"Basically. Also a book."

"That's a switch," Sheila said, genuinely surprised. She'd expected Patti to say the latest CD by Heavy Perspiration or whatever weirdo group the kids were listening to nowadays. "What book?"

Patti hesitated a beat and then said, *"Slaughterhouse."*

"Uh-uh. Absolutely not."

"Mom—"

"N-O," Sheila said again. "It's garbage, plain and simple. I can't believe decent people who ought to know better are reading it."

"Mom, it's supposed to be *good*. It's about stuff that really happened right here in Wisconsin."

"I know exactly what it's about. And you may *not* buy it. You want to read something disgusting, there's plenty in the newspapers—that sex maniac who's going around butchering young girls. Let me tell you, I wouldn't be at all surprised if that monster got his ideas straight from that awful book."

"Oh, Mom."

"Now you listen to me, Patti. That book is as bad as pornography. Maybe even worse. It's full of hateful, harmful things. Now, I can't stop that man from writing it or blabbering about it all over TV. But I *can* make sure I don't give him my money. Or you, either. And that's my final word. All right?"

"If you say so," Patti sighed, then bid her mother good-bye and hurried from the kitchen.

No point in arguing, Patti thought as she walked briskly to the corner, her book bag slung over a shoulder. She could tell that her mom was dead serious about this. If Patti's dad were alive, she might have appealed to him for support, the way her girlfriends were always turning to *their* dads. Like Stacey's father. He was a *real* pushover, giving her money for a new cashmere sweater last week when she didn't even wear half the sweaters she already owned.

Well, she didn't have a father. She didn't know why God had taken him from her, but she felt sure that there must be a reason. She still missed him a lot, though she hardly ever felt deprived. She'd been blessed with such a terrific mom. Patti had read somewhere that people with handicaps often develop amazing abilities that compensated for their losses. Blind people, for instance, could often hear with uncanny acuteness. Patti supposed that God had made up for the death of her father by giving her such a great mom.

Not that her mother was perfect. In fact, she could be a real pain sometimes, treating Patti like a five-year-old. But Patti didn't feel like a baby. Standing there, peering anxiously down Livingston Street for the school bus, she realized that she resented her mother's attitude.

After all, most of her friends had read *Slaughterhouse* and said it was great. Moreover, Patti strongly agreed with Mr. Grennart—her last year's social studies teacher—that books should never be banned. And what was her mother's "No, you may *not* buy it" but book banning?

Patti relaxed as she saw her school bus turn the corner at 86th. Before it pulled to a stop in front of her, she had already made up her mind.

She would buy *Slaughterhouse* without her mother's permission. It would be easy enough to hide. She would just keep it with all the other stuff in her book bag and take it out at night to read in bed.

Her mom was just being her old worrywart self, Patti thought as she moved down the aisle toward an empty seat in back.

After all, how much harm could a book do?

10

The first time he'd set eyes on the strange-looking gizmo sitting in the Kelloggs' rear yard, the Reverend Victor Hobart didn't know *what* the devil he was seeing. Some kind of new-fangled farming equipment, he expected—though for the life of him, he couldn't make heads or tails out of the confounded thing.

Later that day—a fine autumn evening back in October of '92—he had mentioned it at the dinner table. A robust septuagenarian, the Reverend Hobart had buried two wives. His third, a plump, pleasant-faced woman named Hannah, was his junior by twenty-five years. Their union had been blessed with a son Carl, who had just turned seventeen, a golden-haired boy with his father's strong, clean features and startlingly gray eyes.

It was Carl who had set the reverend straight at dinnertime. Laughing gently, the boy laid his hand lightly on his father's shoulder and said, "It's a satellite dish, Pop. To pull in cable TV channels."

The reverend placed his knife and fork down on his plate, put both hands on the table edge, and stared at his son.

"Well, I'll be darned," he said.

During the following week, the image of the big backyard antenna kept popping into the Reverend Hobart's mind. When he wasn't attending to his ministerial duties, he often found himself driving past the Kelloggs' property for a glimpse of the dish.

The seed of inspiration had been planted in his brain and was beginning to germinate.

A lifelong inhabitant of Plainfield, the Reverend Hobart knew the tribulations his fellow townspeople had endured. The village, settled in 1849, was located in a hardscrabble part of the state, an area so poor and unproductive that it used to be known as the "dead heart" of Wisconsin. But in agriculture, as in medicine, science had devised effective new means of mechanical resuscitation. Advanced irrigation machinery had pumped new life into the sandy soil, bringing prosperity to a fair number of local farmers.

None of Reverend Hobart's neighbors was rich. But folks in general were doing much better than ever before. Nearly everyone in town could afford color TVs, videocassette recorders, and cable hookups. Some, like the Kelloggs, could even indulge in fancier gadgets.

Except for the nightly news, the reverend never watched TV. He knew what sort of slop the networks offered—a vile stew of sex, violence, and profanity that the public, its taste corrupted by years of such rotten fare, gobbled up greedily. But surely a device as remarkable as television—a product of man's God-given technological genius—was meant for higher uses. The very appearance of the Kelloggs' new acquisition suggested as much.

Sitting under the wide Wisconsin sky, its hollow side tilted heavenward, the big receiver seemed to be listening for something, as though waiting for word from above. Gazing at it through the window of his '87 Chevy station wagon, the Reverend Hobart felt himself infused with a new sense of mission.

He would make the airwaves his pulpit, converting a vulgar medium into a tool of the Lord.

The reverend knew he was a compelling speaker. His congregants never failed to tell him so, and he could see it for himself in their rapt faces whenever he preached. Now, he would have a chance to bring his powers to bear on a much larger audience, to carry God's message into households throughout the state.

In truth, the reverend had another motive for trying his hand at televangelism. Not self-aggrandizement. Though he hoped to attract as many viewers as possible, he was largely devoid of personal ambition. But he was a deeply civic-minded person. His fondest dream was to repair the blighted reputation of his beloved hometown, to undo the damage wrought by the monstrous acts of a single, insane individual.

Years ago, the Reverend Hobart had known the Geins—as well, that is, as anyone could know that strange, reclusive family. He remembered the father, George, a sullen, shriveled, stoop-shouldered man whose very posture spoke of numberless hardships and bitter defeats. George Gein's shrunken figure contrasted sharply with that of his hulking wife. A fierce-willed, grim-faced woman, Augusta Gein was rarely seen in town. Fanatically religious, she considered the tiny farming community a hellhole of vice, shunned her neighbors as unregenerate sinners, and kept her offspring so tightly bound to her apron strings that she strangled whatever was normal within them.

And then there was Eddie himself.

Like almost everyone else in Plainfield, the reverend had always regarded the meek, slightly dim-witted bachelor as the village oddball, particularly during the dozen years Eddie lived by himself in the tumbledown farmhouse after the death of his mother. Still, he seemed totally harmless, what the younger generation used to call a kook.

To be sure, the reverend had heard all the stories about Ed: how he would sit for hour upon hour in the murk of his farmhouse, poring over his collection of lurid crime magazines. How his bedroom was decorated with shrunken heads, supposedly sent by a distant cousin who had procured them in the Philippines during the second world war. How, on moonlit summer nights, a grotesque figure with long, stringy hair and corpse-white skin could sometimes be seen capering in his overgrown front yard.

But no one gave much weight to these stories. They seemed like nothing more than schoolyard gossip—the kind of rumors children are always inventing about local haunted houses and neighborhood eccentrics who are really monsters in disguise.

When the hideous truth about Gein's farmhouse finally came to light—when its appalling contents, its skin masks and skull bowls and garments made of human flesh, were revealed to the world—the people of Plainfield felt as stunned as the rest of America. But these shocking revelations were only the start of their ordeal. Within days, the town was overrun by representatives of the nation's news media. Sensational stories about the Mad Butcher of Plainfield ran in papers from coast to coast and were splashed across the pages of *Life, Time,* and *Newsweek.* The peaceful little village became the focus of the whole country's morbid fascination. Its inhabitants felt like freaks in a carnival sideshow.

Their only hope was that the ghastly publicity would quickly die down, that the "Plainfield Horrors" would fade from public memory. But to their dismay, Gein's dark reputation continued to spread. First came the sick jokes, then the rumors that the atrocities uncovered in his farmhouse were only the tip of the iceberg.

Finally, there was Gein's metamorphosis into a ghoulish legend, a boogeyman who haunted the dreams of a whole generation of Midwesterners and who eventually became immortalized in a Hollywood classic.

It seemed as though the little town would never escape from the shadow of Edward Gein. It had gotten to the point where its inhabitants were reluctant to reveal where they hailed from. Tell some new acquaintances that you'd been born and raised in Plainfield and they looked at you as though you came from someplace accursed—Transylvania, Salem's Lot, the Village of the Damned. You half-expected them to make the sign of the cross: *Get thee behind me, Satan!*

But it was God, not the devil, who held dominion in Plainfield. The Reverend Hobart was determined to prove that to the world. And so, on a crisp fall morning less than two weeks after he'd first set eyes on the Kellogg's big antenna, he put in a call to the station manager of WKMP-TV, headquartered in Madison. The reverend had a commanding voice and a persuasive manner. The program manager's interest was piqued. He listened intently, then invited the reverend down to the studio for a talk.

Exactly one month later, *For Goodness' Sake with the Reverend Victor Hobart* began airing at midnight in a slot formerly occupied by reruns of *Gomer Pyle, U.S.M.C.* The program, a folksy half-hour of spiritual uplift, was a modest but immediate success. Within six months of its premiere, it had been picked up by a dozen local channels throughout the Midwest. It wasn't long before the reverend's campaign to improve Plainfield's image began showing results.

Though only the most minor of celebrities, he could count on at least a score of fan letters every week, generally from elderly insomniacs who wanted him to know how much comfort he brought them. Few failed to make some favorable reference to the reverend's hometown.

> And to think [wrote a typical viewer] that a righteous man such as yourself growed up in the same place where that inhuman fiend, Gein, come from. It only just shows how the light of God is so much more strong and powerful than Satan's evil darkness. As it says in the Good Book, "Ye were sometimes darkness, but now are ye light in the Lord: walk as children of light." I guess whatever darkness

there once was in Plainfield is gone now forever, or else there wouldn't be so much light
as you bring.

The Reverend Hobart had good reason to feel pleased
with himself. As a spokesman for the Lord, he was
spreading the word to a following far larger than any
he'd reached in all his years of preaching. And as a self-
appointed PR man for Plainfield, he was changing the
way people looked at his long-stigmatized town.

And then Paul Novak's book was published.

It was as if the nightmare had started all over again.

Not that there hadn't always been busybodies snooping around town from time to time: hard-core horror
fans looking for the spot where the "real Norman Bates"
had once lived; Milwaukee reporters assigned to do stories on the Plainfield Horrors whenever a major anniver-
sary rolled around (TEN YEARS AGO TODAY—THE CRIME
THAT SHOCKED A NATION!); even the occasional documentary filmmaker, shooting footage for a feature on
America's most celebrated ghoul.

When Paul Novak had shown up with his tape re-
corder and notepad, folks naturally assumed he was
some nosy East Coast journalist researching yet another
Sunday-supplement article on "the man who inspired
Hitchcock's *Psycho*," as every other story on Gein
seemed to be called. Almost everyone in town—the
Reverend Hobart included—gave him the ice-cold shoulder. But there were always a few publicity hounds eager
to see their names in print. (Even back in '57, at the
height of the nightmare, it wasn't hard to find folks who
would blab their heads off just to get their pictures in
Life.)

To most of Plainfield's citizens, the nationwide success
of *Slaughterhouse* was as welcome as a plague of potato
bugs. Some folks, of course, didn't mind all the publicity,
since they were able to find ways of exploiting it. Billy

Kolski, for example, owner of the Plainfield Café, did a land-office business on weekends, selling sandwiches and lemonade to the army of sightseers who trooped through the town on weekends. And an enterprising widow named Gilda Bladerfield had earned nearly three hundred dollars peddling hand-drawn maps that showed where Ed Gein's "death house" once stood before the outraged villagers had burned it to the ground.

But to most of Plainfield's inhabitants, the renewed notoriety brought upon them by *Slaughterhouse* felt like a profound violation—not just of their privacy but of their very sense of themselves as God-fearing, hard-working, law-abiding individuals.

Something had to be done. And with a growing audience of devoted viewers who hung on his every word, the Reverend Hobart felt primed for action.

It was time to strike back.

11

The set consisted of nothing more than a plaid-upholstered easy chair and a maple side table. The reverend sat cross-legged on the chair, his well-worn King James Bible resting on his lap. On the table stood an old-fashioned lamp with a fringed shade and a tall glass of water with which the reverend occasionally dampened his lips.

On Friday evening, September 18, however, regular viewers would have spotted another object—an unfamiliar one—lying beside the water glass: a hardcover book whose lurid jacket shone brightly in the warm glow of the table lamp.

After welcoming his "dear friends at home" to his show, the reverend announced gravely that he wanted to talk to them about a subject of vital and urgent concern. "I'm talking about the scandal-mongering, gossip-peddling, Peeping Tom members of the East Coast media establishment—babblers and meddlers who spend their days and nights poking into the private lives of others, sticking their long noses into other folks' business, and spreading their slander for their own dirty gain.

"Now this is a problem that affects me very personally. But it's also something that relates to every one of you good folks there at home, as citizens of this great and glorious country of ours. It's a problem that's growing like a cancer, a deadly cancer, eating away at the moral values of our whole society.

"You've heard the saying 'body politic'? It means that

our country—not just the government but our whole precious American way of life—is like a great human body, the strongest and most beautiful God ever created, but a body that can get sick like any other if you don't take good and constant care of it. And we've ignored this sickness for far too long, my friends. Oh yes. And unless we do something to cure it quick, it's going to carry us straight to hell and ruin.

"Now you might think that the Good Book wouldn't have much to teach us about this very modern problem, this disease spread by trashy television, by those prattling papers peddled in the supermarket. And, most vile of all"—here, the reverend's voice took on a particular edge of bitterness—"by those perverted books that feed like vultures off the poor dead victims of long-ago crimes, seeking to profit from the suffering of others."

Reaching down to his lap, the reverend patted his Bible. "But if you think the Good Book has nothing to say on this subject, well, my friends, you're in for another think. All truth, all knowledge, all the wisdom of the world is contained right here between these covers. And what does the Good Book have to say?" He flipped to a page he had marked off with a length of satin ribbon. "Listen here to the words of Leviticus."

Clearing his throat, he declaimed: "Thou shalt not go up and down as a talebearer among thy people."

The reverend looked up from his Bible and stared intently at the camera. "There you have it. God's commandment, spoken loud as thunder. *Thou shalt not go up and down as a talebearer,* spreading rumor, gossip, and slander among thy people like a lice-infested rat spreads the plague."

Balancing the open Bible in one hand, he riffled through the pages until he came to a second marked-off place. "Now, listen here to what it says in second Samuel, chapter one, verse twenty. 'Tell it not in Gath, publish it not in the streets of Askelon.'"

The reverend clapped his Bible shut and leaned forward on his seat. "My friends, could the message of the Lord be any clearer than that? The Lord is telling us, in language plain as daylight, that it is a sin and a crime not just to go prattling gossip among your own neighbors but to *publish* it in other places, where strangers will read about it, too. Oh, my friends, sin comes in all shapes and sizes. But this one here, this sin of talebearing and scandalmongering and publishing slanderous stories for all the world to read about, is among the very worst. And I'm here tonight to tell you why."

With that, the reverend launched into a diatribe about the damage being done to the social fabric by the media's "reckless irresponsibility, its lust for scandal and disgrace—the ranker the better. These money-grubbers in control of our national media have about as much sense of common decency as a bunch of wood ticks. They call themselves truth-seekers, my friends, but they lie. They're bloodsuckers is all. Latching onto other people, burrowing into their most intimate, private matters, then spewing out the nastiness for all the world to see. They call themselves journalists. But their real business is ruining people's lives. It's already got to the point where some of our most highly qualified men and women are terrified of running for public office for fear of what these leeches will do to 'em. It's a grave injustice, my friends. But it's worse than that. It's a growing danger to our whole American way of life as we've known it."

The reverend went on in this vein for fifteen uninterrupted minutes. He was not a fire-and-brimstone preacher in the usual sense. His charisma did not depend on florid gestures and dramatic flourishes of speech; rather, his strength lay in the intimate bond he was able to establish with his viewers, his way of making every one of them feel as if he or she were the most important person in the reverend's life.

He continued. "Now friends, I mentioned at the start of the show that this is a problem that affects me very personally. Let me tell you how. You all know where I come from—a quiet little town called Plainfield, right here in the middle of our beautiful badger state. It's a humble place, full of hard-working, churchgoing, law-abiding people. The kind of town where families pray together at mealtimes. Where parents can raise their children without worrying about drugs and violence and sinful diseases and all the other abominations of the modern world. Where the expression 'love thy neighbor' is more than just empty words—it's a way of life. Not too many places like it left in this country, let me tell you.

"Now I don't have to tell you about the terrible troubles that befell our little village many years ago. Amazing how much awfulness and tragedy one sick little man can create. Almost makes you think the Devil's hand was involved. Anyways, that's what lots of folks think.

"That was a hard time for us, my friends. It took us years to get over it. But through strength of character and unswerving faith in the Lord's everlasting support, our little town managed to pull itself back on its feet, put those terrible times behind it, and get life back to normal.

"And then what happened? Forty years later, along comes this *easterner*"—the reverend made the word sound like a curse—"and brings all that evil back to life. Before you know it, whole mobs of morbidly misguided strangers are swarming around our village like horseflies, turning our lives into a nightmare, stirring up the painful memories of those unfortunate folks whose loved ones were the victims of a monster. And why? Why has all this trouble descended on us again, years and years after we had managed to put it all behind us?" The reverend gave a snorting laugh. "Why else? Nothing but the greed of the East Coast media establishment and its money-grubbing lackeys."

The reverend's voice had risen as he spoke. Now he paused for a minute, as though to subdue his indignation. "So tonight, my dear friends, I'm asking for your help in standing up to this outrage. What can you do personally?" The reverend reopened his Bible and poked a forefinger at the page. "The answer, like all answers, is right in here." He turned his gaze to the passage and read: " 'Refuse profane and old wives' fables.' First Timothy, chapter four, verse seven."

Looking up, he repeated the injunction, this time speaking each word slowly and emphatically. " 'Refuse profane and old wives' fables."

Gently closing the Bible, he half swiveled in his seat and reached for the red-covered book on the side table. When he turned back to his viewers, his face wore a look of pronounced distaste.

'Tell you the truth, I couldn't decide whether or not to defile my show and your homes this evening by bringing this foul thing on the air. But Satan is cunning. He camouflages himself in all kinds of shapes and colors. And how can you do battle with him unless you know what to watch out for? So I want you all to take a good look at this." Holding the book with his fingertips, as though he were loath to touch it, he raised it high while the camera moved in for a close-up.

"See that cover? The same shameless color as the scarlet garb of the Babylonian whore. Now, listen here to its title: *Slaughterhouse.*" He laughed bitterly. "Sounds very literary, doesn't it? Now here's the name of the so-called writer who spawned it: Mr. Paul Novak." A world of contempt was contained in the reverend's tone as he pronounced the name.

The reverend dropped the book back on the table as though disposing some particularly offensive waste matter.

"What I'm asking you tonight is simple, my friends. I'm asking you to refuse to have anything to do with this foulness. Don't buy it. Don't borrow it. Don't so much as flip through its pages. If you've got a friend or family member who's thinking about reading it, let that person know just what kind of garbage it is. And if you happen to live in a place where there's a bookshop that sells it, you walk right in there and let that store owner know just what you think about him peddling such profanity where anyone, children included, can go in and buy it.

"I'm urging you tonight to join with me in my crusade and help put an end to this kind of moral and mental pollution that's threatening to bring ruin not just to one little town, as precious as that town is to me personally, but to our whole grand and glorious nation.

"Please lend me your support in this cause. For goodness' sake."

12

When she raised the remote control to turn off the TV, Agatha Cobb saw that her hand was trembling slightly. Normally, the Reverend Hobart's words were a great source of comfort to her.

Tonight, however, they had produced the opposite effect.

Carefully, she set the remote down on her glass-topped coffee table, taking a moment—even in her agitation—to make sure that it was lined up neatly with her stack of *National Geographics* (a simple bit of tidiness that her lunkheaded son could never seem to manage).

Then, tugging meditatively on the flaccid pouch of flesh beneath her chin, she settled back on the sofa and tried to figure out just how much of a threat she was facing. Agatha Cobb was not the sort who responded passively to a crisis. She believed in meeting trouble head-on.

For thirty-plus years, she had kept her secret hidden from the world. Only two human beings besides herself knew about it. Leon was one. Years before, when they'd been living together in that rathole on Glendale, she had broken down one night and whispered the truth in his ear. Later, she had even taken him home for a visit on the single occasion she had snuck back into town to say a final farewell to her disgraced, dying mother.

But Agatha wasn't much worried about Leon. The boy was a fool, but he wasn't a blabbermouth. *Who would he go blabbin' to anyways? Never known him to consort with another living soul. Just keeps to himself in that pigsty of a room, pawin' over his filthy treasures.*

Oh, yes—Agatha knew all about those shoe boxes stashed under the floor of her son's closet. No secrets from Mama. But men needed some kind of outlet for their hoggish desires, as she herself had learned to her everlasting regret. Better to let the boy defile himself with his collection of filth than to have him messing with living women.

No, Leon wasn't likely to go shooting his yap off to anyone, crowing like a rooster at sun-up. Agatha snickered at the image. *The boy ain't no cock of the walk, that's for damn sure. More like a dirty ol' turkey buzzard. Just like that stinkin', no-account father of his.*

That left just one other person who knew her shameful secret. She pinched harder at her dewlap as she considered the possibility of exposure from this second source. Finally, she gave her head an emphatic shake. *Not likely. He's kept his own counsel for better'n thirty years. Why would he do any different now?*

True, you couldn't be absolutely sure how folks might behave on their deathbeds. There were those who didn't like the idea of meeting their maker with a dark secret weighing on their souls. But from all visible evidence, that wasn't anything Agatha had to worry about just yet.

No, whatever troubles might be headed her way wouldn't come from those two places.

But it might well come from that goddamn book.

Tonight was the first time she had heard about it. *Slaughterhouse.* She let out a bitter laugh. *Imagine the damn gall of that easterner. Comin' out here where he ain't welcome. Stickin' his snoot into other folks' business. Makin' profit off the misery of others. What a world, what a world.*

She wondered if the book contained any information that would point in her direction. She assumed it didn't, or else there already would have been reporters knocking at her door.

Still, it was best to make sure. She would get hold of the book and read it for herself. Of course, she'd be going directly against the reverend's wishes. But she was sure he'd make an exception in her case.

With a grunt, Agatha heaved herself off the sofa and made her way toward the kitchen to fix herself a midnight snack—a nice slice of Drake's coffee cake topped with a scoop of pistachio ice cream and a big gob of Cool Whip. She already felt much better for having worked out the problem in her head.

Maybe no one would ever find out. It was hard to say exactly what she'd do if someone confronted her with the truth. As for what she would do to keep that from happening in the first place, well, that was easy.

Whatever she had to.

13

Hooked up to her Walkman, Patti Atkins lingered in bed until ten-thirty on Saturday morning, listening to her favorite Toni Braxton album. As soaring love songs filled her head, she thought about the guy who sat behind her in math, Andy Reichert. She was trying to decide whether she liked him. He was quiet and serious, and Patti tended to prefer boys with livelier personalities. Still, he *was* awfully cute.

Suddenly, her bedroom door swung open and her mother poked her head inside, mouthing something. Patti clicked the stop button and plucked off her earphones.

"You're going to make yourself deaf with that thing," Sheila said, stepping into the room. "I've been knocking on your door forever."

"What?" Patti said, cupping a hand behind one ear. "I can't hear you."

"Very funny," Sheila said. She was dressed in a white polyester blouse and gray pleated skirt and had her pocketbook slung over her shoulder. "I'm off to the church to help plan that charity supper. Then I have to run a few errands and do the grocery shopping. So you're on your own, kid. Don't spend all day in bed. It's gorgeous out."

"Don't worry," Patti said, stretching. "I won't."

Sheila blew her daughter a kiss and left the room.

Leaving her Walkman where it lay on the mattress,

Patti stuck her hands behind her neck, leaned back on her pillow, and gazed across the room at her *Beverly Hills 90210* poster. Now that she thought of it, Andy Reichert bore a faint resemblance to Jason Priestley.

A moment later, she heard the front door creak open, then close with a muffled slam. She waited another few minutes, then swung her legs off the bed and headed for the shower.

She had no intention of spending the day indoors.

She had other plans.

Forty-five minutes later, freshly showered and made up, she was strolling toward the Mayfair Mall. She was on her way to B. Dalton's to pick up a copy of *Slaughterhouse*.

The store had been sold out of the book since Tuesday afternoon. The manager, a middle-aged redhead sporting rhinestone-studded glasses shaped like cat's eyes, had promised Patti that a new batch would be in by the weekend.

Patti hoped so. She was baby-sitting that night for her neighbors, the Rostangs. Her plan was to put the kids to bed early, then snuggle up on the living-room couch with the book. The idea of reading it at night in a dark-ened house gave her a delicious thrill.

The mall was just under a mile from Patti's house, and she covered the distance quickly, enjoying the warm breeze and sunshine. She felt really good, and she knew she looked good, too. She was wearing a cream-colored T-shirt and her new leather skirt. The skirt looked shorter than she'd expected, but her legs were still very tanned from the summer, and they were the best part of her figure.

As soon as she stepped into the store, she saw that the shipment had arrived. A big pyramid-shaped stack was displayed on a table right up front. Snatching the topmost copy from the pile, she carried it straight to the checkout counter.

The clerk was a tall, pimply teenager—maybe seventeen or eighteen, Patti guessed—whose beaky nose, stringy neck, and bulging Adam's apple made him look unsettlingly like a vulture.

"Cool skirt," he said with a leering smile as she pulled the cash from her wallet.

Patti muttered a thanks and averted her eyes from his mottled face.

"Like your necklace, too," he said, handing her the change. Patti was wearing a silver peace symbol on a leather thong.

After bagging the book, the clerk leaned across the counter and fingered the amulet where it lay on her chest. "Just want to see it better," he protested as Patti jerked away from his touch.

Astonished, Patti turned on her heels and hurried from the store.

Creep, she thought.

She hung around the mall for an hour or so, window-shopping, checking out the new CDs at Music World, and treating herself to a chili dog and fries at the International Food Court.

It was nearly two when Patti headed for the exit. As she approached the doors that opened out onto the main parking lot (unusually empty for a Saturday, perhaps because of the beautiful weather), she decided to use the bathroom. She needed to pee and didn't want to hold it all the way home.

Fortunately, there was a restroom nearby, a little more isolated than the others in the mall. It was located at the northernmost end of the ground floor just behind the Jeans Outlet, the last store in the row.

The ladies' room was empty and had a vague air of disuse. The stainless-steel sinks were shiny and dry. A single brown paper towel lay crumpled at the base of the garbage bin, but otherwise the linoleum floor looked clean.

Entering the last stall in the row, Patti latched the

door behind her, yanked a length of toilet tissue from the roll, and gave the seat a quick swipe. She didn't really believe you could catch diseases from a toilet seat. Still . . .

Now that she was inside the stall, she became acutely aware of how full her bladder was. Quickly, she slung her purse strap over the metal hook, pulled her tight skirt up, drew her panties down, seated herself, and let go.

She was still holding the book. Slipping it out of the bag, she looked at the cover. It showed a spooky old house with a pair of big, crazy eyes looming above it. Superimposed over the picture was a bright red smear like a spreading bloodstain.

She ran her fingers over the embossed title, then flipped the book over. The back cover contained a portion of Ed Gein's official confession to the police:

Q. Now this item here, this skin vest, where did that come from?

A. That's from a person from the grave.

Q. What about the masks? You just peeled off the faces and disposed of the skulls, is that it?

A. That's right.

Q. And how did you preserve these body parts?

A. When I made those masks, I stuffed them all out with paper so that they would dry. On the vaginas, I sprinkled a little salt.

Q. Was there a resemblance in some of these faces to your mother?

A. I believe so.

Sick! thought Patti.

She opened the book and riffled through the pages, stopping at the glossy illustrations in the middle.

The first was a picture of Gein's ramshackle farmhouse, a grim, decaying place with a sagging roof and flaking paint. Icicles dripped from the porch eaves, and the frozen front yard was dotted with dead clumps of weeds. The house stood in a stand of barren trees. Above it, the sky was a ghostly gray.

Patti had never seen a house that looked so bleak. She shuddered slightly, imagining what it would feel like to live in such a god-awful place.

The next picture was a mug shot of Gein himself. Patti had never seen a photo of the Plainfield Ghoul and was amazed at his appearance. She'd expected a monster. Instead, he looked like a total dweeb. He was wearing a nerdy plaid hunting cap, his mouth was twisted into a sheepish little grin, and his watery eyes were full of melancholy—nothing like the maniacal orbs on the book jacket. Far from looking like a fiend, he reminded Patti of Mr. Hubbell, her high school's sweet, slightly dim-witted handyman.

Patti was still staring at the photo when she heard the restroom door swing open. Footsteps sounded on the linoleum floor and halted. An instant later, a faucet squeaked and water began to gush in one of the sinks.

Patti decided to look at one more picture. She flipped the page—and found herself staring at a police photograph of Gein's final victim.

The picture rattled Patti so badly that, for a second, her vision blurred. She squeezed her eyes tight, half opening them again after a moment as though afraid of what she would see. At the same time, she was aware of a terrible need to confront the horror.

On the page, a human body hung upside-down by its heels from the roof of a shed. You could tell it was a woman because of the breasts. Otherwise, it would have been impossible to say.

The head was missing, and the body itself was split from collarbone to crotch. There was a big hole between the legs where the genitals had been removed. There was nothing inside the body. It looked completely hollow, like the beef carcasses Patti sometimes saw as they were being wheeled into the supermarket meat locker.

Looking at the picture gave Patti the strangest sensation, a sick, queasy feeling combined with an electric thrill, as though she was seeing something horribly forbidden and obscene but—for that very reason—irresistibly exciting. She remembered having the same feeling once before, years ago in fifth grade, when Bobby Belsen brought in a book called *Freaks,* and, on a dare, Patti had looked at a picture of a person who was half man and half woman. There was a close-up shot of his—her—its—sex organs: a stubby penis poking through the hairy lips of a swollen vagina.

Just then, Patti heard a soft clattering sound at the sink, as though the other woman had accidentally dropped a plastic pocket comb. Patti closed the book quickly and stuck it back into the bag. Dabbing herself dry, she stood and rearranged her clothing. She left the booth while the toilet was roaring, still feeling a little shaky.

The woman at the sink was fiddling with her thick, coal-black hair. Approaching her from behind, Patti could see only the back of her dress. But that was enough to tell that it was truly ugly—one of those drab polyester things in a maroon color, with a lace collar and cuffs at the elbow. The dress was unflatteringly long, too. Why anybody below the age of sixty would want to wear such a long dress was a mystery to Patti.

As she stepped up to the faux-marble vanity, Patti cast a quick sideways look at the woman and saw that she was wearing thick-lensed eyeglasses. She looked like some kind of dorky school librarian. Yet her hair was unusually thick and glossy. Patti watched out of the corner of her eye while the woman fussed with it, frowning.

Setting her book bag on the counter, Patti washed and dried her hands, then checked out her face in the mirror. The sickly feeling was gone, but she looked slightly pale. She decided to use a little blush.

On went the Tawny Peach. Now she needed more lipstick for balance, the way *Mademoiselle* said. She pulled out her Maybelline True Heavenly Coral and carefully applied it. This part was tricky. She tried a quick smile, to make sure no lipstick was on her teeth.

The woman next to her was putting on lipstick, too—some awful cherry-red shade that didn't go with her dress at all. Suddenly, she stopped and looked at Patti.

"Now that's a pretty color," the woman said. "A pretty color lipstick you're wearing."

The woman's voice was surprisingly husky. The tone was weird, too, as if she was trying to be friendly but didn't have any practice at it.

"Thank you," said Patti.

"You look so much like my sister's youngest child," the woman went on. "I wish I had a camera to take your picture. You could be her twin. Her name's Carolyn. She's in high school, Carolyn is. Are you?"

Patti murmured a polite but evasive response. She didn't want to get into a pointless conversation with a complete stranger about some stupid niece. And anyway, there was something about the woman that made Patti feel uncomfortable, something about the way she was looking at Patti—like that creepy, pizza-faced clerk in the bookstore.

"Yes, I am," Patti said with forced cheeriness. "Well, I have to go." And she flashed the woman a bright, broad smile.

The woman caught her breath and stiffened a bit. Her heavily lipsticked mouth stretched into a jack-o'-lantern grin. Patti froze and, for the first time, took a hard look at the woman's face.

It was such a strange-looking face! Her smile was strange, too. But strangest of all were the words that came out of that red-smeared mouth as she took a step closer to Patti.

"Nice teeth," she said.

Part Two

—

In the Flesh

14

Around her, the world still stirred with movement—like a corpse that continues to twitch for a moment even after the heart has died.

Above her head, a song-sparrow flitted down from the sky and alighted on a tree branch. A speckled leaf drifted through air. In a corner of the yard, a squirrel scavenged for fallen acorns. From time to time, it lifted its head and looked around anxiously, pausing once to fix her with a shiny stare.

Huddled in a slatted chair on the small brick patio behind her house, Sheila Atkins gazed back blankly. *Life goes on,* said a bitter voice inside her head. But it did not feel like life—just a world of vacant, mechanical activity.

Life had ended for her two weeks before, the day her daughter's body had been found.

Patti is dead. She could hardly bring herself to form the words in her mind. She did not want to think about it—about the terror and pain and despair her child must have suffered. It was like approaching an abyss. A single glance into that blackness would send her plummeting over the edge into madness. They would have to lock her up in the county hospital, where she would spend the rest of her days shrieking in rage and sorrow.

She felt the wetness fill her eyes and slide down her face. *Remarkable,* she thought, pulling a tissue from the box clutched on her lap. She would not have believed she had any more tears to shed.

She lay in the chair for another long interval, her body full of pain, her mind's activity suspended. The squirrel came and went, busying itself with survival under the hungry eyes of the neighbor's tabby. *Everything feeds on something,* Sheila thought dully. *Life devours life. Nothing escapes.*

A sudden gust of wind sent a flurry of leaves across the patio. Sheila pulled her bathrobe tighter.

Must be almost noon, she guessed. Well, what did that mean? *It means,* she told herself, *that I should get out of this bathrobe and put on some clothes. And wash my face and comb my hair.* She tried to recall the last time she had bathed. It must have been—when?—the day before yesterday? But why bother to bathe? Why do anything?

Chaos reigned inside her house. The kitchen trash can overflowed with garbage; filthy dishes cluttered the sink. Her darkened bedroom had the reek of despair: sour sheets lay crumpled on the mattress, dustballs gathered in the corners, soiled stockings and underclothes spilled out of the hamper and littered the floor. Every room in the house was a mess.

Except for her daughter's.

Even as a little girl, Patti had always been exceptionally tidy. Unlike every other parent she knew, Sheila had never had to nag her child to clean up after herself. When Patti went off to school in the mornings, her room was always in perfect order: bed made, pillows fluffed, clothing neatly hung up or folded away. That was the way the room looked now, exactly as it had been the last time Patti—

Sheila let out a stricken cry as the world gave a sickening lurch. The ground seemed to fall away beneath her. She felt herself plunging toward the bottomless dark and fought to hold onto her reason. Squeezing her eyes tight, she willed her mind away form the horror of her child's death.

When she finally opened them again, the dizziness had abated; the world had steadied itself. Exhausted, she slipped into a kind of waking stupor.

How long she remained in that condition she could not have said. Five minutes? Ten? An hour? It was the insistent trilling of her phone that finally roused her back to an awareness of her surroundings.

Forcing herself out of the chair, she made her way into the house. "Hullo," she answered dully.

It was her friend Emily Drummond, who had lost her husband to cancer the year before. "How're you doing, hon?" Emily asked in a voice that exuded concern.

The question struck Sheila as so outrageous that she chewed on her lip to keep from screaming back: *"How am I doing? How in God's name do you think I'm doing, you stupid—"* Instead, she drew a ragged breath and muttered, "So-so."

"Listen, hon. I've been asking around, and there's this therapist. He specializes in grief management."

"Em, I know you're trying to help, but—"

Emily plunged ahead. "He does small groups or individual therapy. Everybody I talked to says he's very good. That he really helps you accept things and—"

Sheila could not contain herself. "Goddamn it!" she shrieked. *"Accept* things? Accept *what?* That my baby was murdered? *Tortured?* Do you know what . . . what that monster . . . ?"* Her voice was shaking badly now. Unable to see clearly through her tears, she fumbled the headset back onto the receiver, while Emily's tiny voice called out a desperate apology.

Hands clutched to her eyes, Sheila huddled on the living-room sofa, sobbing convulsively. After a while, her weeping subsided. She sat there, breathing heavily, her battered heart pricked by a sharp pang of guilt.

Emily meant well. All her friends meant well. Perhaps she should call back and apologize. She reached for the phone, then let her hand drop.

What did it matter? What did any of it matter?

Heaving herself off the sofa, she drifted into the kitchen. She felt so cold inside. Perhaps a cup of tea would warm her a little.

The silence in the house was oppressive. As the water heated up in the kettle, Sheila switched on the radio she kept on the countertop.

It was tuned to a classical station broadcasting from Madison. Sheila caught the last few minutes of Pachelbel's *Canon*. Then the music broke for the news.

As Sheila let a tea bag steep, the newscaster ran through the morning's top stories: another terrorist attack in Israel, a train wreck in Florida, a downswing in the national economy. Locally, the big news of the day was the gang-rape of a co-ed in a frat house a few blocks off the Madison campus.

Sheila reached for the radio before the announcer could provide more details. Her hand was trembling badly as she hit the off button.

She picked up her drink, sloshed a quarter of it onto the tabletop, and set the cup down immediately. By the time her nerves had steadied, the tea was lukewarm.

What in God's name is happening out there? she wondered. *Where is all this hatred coming from?*

Of course, even in her younger days, men and women often spoke about "the battle of the sexes." But there was a good-natured quality to it all back then. It was a kind of shared joke, something stand-up comedians built their routines around: "Take my wife—*please!*" The henpecked husband enslaved by a domineering wife was the stuff of Danny Kaye movies and *Saturday Evening Post* cartoons.

A long-obscured memory suddenly came into focus: a funny birthday gift Richard had received years before from a friend. It was a barbecue apron decorated with a drawing of two chickens. On top, a grinning rooster strutted proudly with a fat cigar jutting out of his beak. Below, his hen gazed at him wryly, a rolling pin clutched in her wing feathers. "He rules the roost—but *I* rule the rooster!" read the caption. For some reason, Richard had gotten a real kick out of the silly thing. Closing her eyes, Sheila could picture him wearing it as he stood out back on the patio, grilling hot dogs and burgers for his family.

A flood of longing for Richard surged through her. She thought of his natural courtliness around women, his ingrained desire to shelter and protect. From the first moments of their acquaintance, she had sensed this about him. It was there in simple things—the way he never failed to hold her chair for her at restaurants, or the times when they were strolling together in the fall and he would offer her his coat if she suddenly felt cold.

Well, he had been a good man, and yet not so very different in that respect from most of his friends—or his father, or Sheila's own father. Men used to be another breed.

When had it all changed? And why? Sheila had no answer besides some vaguely formed notion that it was rooted in the late 1960s, when all the old standards of behavior, morality, and civility seemed to go by the boards. Nowadays, people were not just exposed to more obscenity than ever before, they were *bombarded* with it. Wherever you turned, you saw the most horrifying images: women being raped and tortured, trussed up like animals and sliced to pieces with chainsaws. The horror was everywhere. Movies and television. Those awful music videos that were brainwashing the young with endless fantasies of sadism and violence. Not to mention all those disgusting books that glorified serial killers by turning them into media celebrities.

The whole thing was like a terrible malignancy that had popped up out of nowhere and was metastasizing at a frightening pace. No one could say where it came from or how it could be cured.

There was, however, one thing she knew with absolute certainty.

Her daughter was dead because of one of those books.

It was the first clue that police investigators had turned up—just a day after two teenage hikers had stumbled upon Patti's mutilated corpse lying in the undergrowth off Interstate 94.

A massive investigation had been launched right away. Using a list of names provided by Sheila, detectives had interviewed all of Patti's friends and classmates. One of them, a girl named Jennifer Uttley, had spoken to Patti on the phone Friday night. According to Jennifer, Patti had said something about making a quick trip to the Mayfair Mall on Saturday.

Fifteen minutes after talking to Jennifer, a team of detectives arrived at the mall. Moving from store to store, they quickly located the pimply clerk at B. Dalton's who identified Patti's photograph and even remembered the purchase she had made: *Slaughterhouse.* Someone else, a teenage boy who manned the hot dog counter on the ground level, thought he recalled seeing a girl who resembled Patti heading for the restroom on Saturday afternoon. Her leather skirt had caught his eye.

The detectives quickly got hold of the janitorial staff. Sure enough, one of the cleaning ladies had found the book, still inside its bag, lying on the washroom counter. She had taken it home to read. ("Piece of shit," was her considered opinion.) It was clearly Patti's copy. Only four copies of the book had been purchased that Saturday, three of them on credit cards.

During the week that followed, Sheila had been pounded by wave after wave of such overpowering anguish that she thought she would literally drown in her grief. When the tide finally receded a bit, leaving her in a state of numb exhaustion, her mind kept returning to the same tormenting question: what could she have done to prevent her child's death?

Only one answer came back at her: nothing. She had done what she could. She had expressly forbidden Patti to buy that book. Her daughter had disobeyed. Now she was dead.

In Sheila's mind, the book, Patti's unspeakable murder, the faceless monster who had committed it, and the woman-hating sickness that was spreading plaguelike across the land—all these things had coalesced into a single evil essence. Now, as she sat brooding in her kitchen, she felt her own outrage and fury solidify inside her chest, as if her shattered heart were being fused and hardened in a fiery kiln. When the moment passed, a fierce resolve had taken shape inside her.

She did not know precisely how she would go about it. Not yet. But her larger purpose was clear.

Sheila Atkins would not sit still any longer. She was going to strike back.

15

Naked and sweat-slicked, he lay in the murk of his bedroom, not even bothering to touch himself. The memory filled him with such powerful pleasure that he could get off just by thinking about it.

Not that he could recall everything. Past a certain point, his thoughts became very hazy. Still, there was plenty of good stuff to remember. Like that scared-shitless look she got when the chloroform wore off and the truth came crashing in on her. Man. He had never seen eyes bulge out that way before. It was like she had fucking Ping-Pong balls in her head.

He liked the noise that came out of her, too—that high-pitched gargling from way down in her throat. It was one of the few sounds she could make with the retractor in place.

Nowadays, he always made sure to insert the retractor while the sluts were still conked out. He had learned from his mistakes. The very first time he had tried it, he'd waited until the bitch was awake, thinking he'd have more fun that way. All he'd gotten for his trouble was a bunch of fucking bite marks on his hand.

No wonder they call them pussies. Rub 'em the wrong way and they sink their goddamn fangs into you.

Ever since then, he had finished prepping them while they were still in dreamland. Stripping them down, strapping them in, getting the retractor just right.

He wished he owned a real dentist's chair. That would

be so cool. Hard to come by, though. He'd had to settle for an old straight-back wooden chair he had salvaged from a curbside trash pile. He had spotted it while driving his truck around South Milwaukee one night and hauled it back to his room. It had its disadvantages—he would have preferred a recliner—but it worked all right.

He'd discovered, in fact, that the simplest things generally worked the best. Like his instruments. You didn't need any fancy surgical tools. A pair of Craftsman pliers right off the rack at Sears did the job just fine.

Or the chair straps—five webbed Cub Scout belts he had picked up for a few bucks at an army–navy store. One each for the ankles and wrists, another to keep the head from thrashing around.

You really needed the straps. Even the skinniest girl could get pretty worked up when she realized what was going to happen to her.

Funny how they freaked out at different things. With some, it was realizing they couldn't close their mouths. With others, it was feeling themselves naked beneath the disposable paper smocks (he didn't like seeing their bodies while he worked, especially those big hairy bear traps between their legs).

The latest one had gone completely bananas when she flicked her eyeballs over and spotted the stuff laid out on his mattress. The towels and pliers. The needles and floss.

She had begun making so much noise at that point he'd been forced to shove a dishtowel deep into her throat. That had quieted her down real quick. He'd let her gag on it for a minute, then yanked it back out.

"Feel like drowning in your own puke? Huh? That sound like fun?"

She shook her head.

"Then shut the fuck up."

She started crying then.

"Awwww. Little girl want her mommy?" Snicker. "Don't worry. This won't hurt a bit."

By then, he was pretty worked up himself. He'd have to hurry before he became too excited. There were delicate operations to perform.

He'd slipped into his clear-plastic surgical apron, belting it around his naked body. Worked his hands into the disposable latex gloves. Bent to her distended mouth.

It was scary but thrilling to be that close to it—the dark, wet hole, lined with so much danger. Like being a circus lion tamer and sticking your head into the jaws of the beast.

Quickly, he reached for his pliers. Working the handles with one hand, he moved the shiny tool toward her face. It came at her slowly, snapping like a living creature.

A new sound rose out of her—a gurgling whimper that seemed to form itself into a plea: "Ohhhnt. Ohhhnt."

He knew what she was saying. They all said it: "Don't."

He tittered in reply.

He liked to start with the top central incisors.

Making a small adjustment in his bed lamp to provide better light, he leaned down, clamped the pliers over Patti Atkins's front tooth, and went to work.

He wasn't sure when he had finally let her die. At some point, he had gotten so carried away with excitement that he'd lost track of everything—the time and place, who he was, and what he was doing. He must have strangled her when her screams got too loud. Only way to shut her up. A gag would've interfered with his work.

The next thing he remembered, he was sitting on his bed, panting like he'd just run a fucking marathon, his plastic apron all dripping with these big gooey clots. Her body lay spread-eagled on the floor, her mouth a sloppy red hole. There was a real mess between her legs, too.

Recalling it now made his climax come on without so much as a single handstroke. He lay there for a minute, savoring the afterglow. Then, wiping himself dry with his bedsheet, he swung his legs off the mattress and crossed the room to his bureau.

It was stupid to regret any part of the experience. Still, he wished he hadn't gotton *so* swept away that whole chunks of it were a blank. Sometimes, it made everything feel like a dream.

He knew it wasn't a dream, though. He had all the proof he needed.

A whole boxful of it, in fact, sitting right there on his bureau. Reaching his right thumb and forefinger into the box, he plucked out a single lovely specimen and carried it back to his bedside.

Seating himself, he switched on his lamp and held his treasure close to his eyes, examining its perfections— its flawless enamel, its graceful crown, its shapely roots (scrubbed clean of caked blood and gum tissue)—with the contentment of a true connoisseur.

16

"Leon! What the devil you doin' in there?"

Agatha Cobb stood outside her son's locked bedroom door, face flushed, hands clenched at her sides. Tightening her mouth into a lipless frown, she leaned an ear close to the door.

He was awake, all right. She could hear the creak of his bedsprings, then the shuffle of his shoeless feet as he made his way across the littered floor. Then a hollow bang, like the sound of a dresser drawer slamming shut.

Up to some nastiness. As usual. Keepin' his dirty secrets hid from his mama.

Outrage flared inside her. "Boy, you get your fat butt out here right this minute!" she roared, hammering the door with both fists.

An instant later, she heard a small metallic scrape as Leon flicked the metal hook from its eyelet. The door opened just wide enough to allow his big, shapeless body to pass through. Squeezing out sideways, he shut the door quickly behind him and stood there looking down at his toes. He was wearing a stained pair of flannel pajama bottoms and a T-shirt that showed a picture of a cowboy astride a sway-backed donkey. "Get Your Ass in Gear," read the caption.

Agatha gave him a squinty-eyed once-over, her gaze lingering briefly at the level of his crotch.

"Up to some of your filthy tricks again, eh, boy?" she growled. Her tongue darted in and out of her mouth, moistening her peeling lips. Suddenly—quicker than seemed possible, given her bulk—she shot out one spotted hand and pinched Leon hard on the exposed flesh of his left bicep.

Leon let out a yelp.

"Don't you *never* keep me standin' here waitin' again," she bellowed as Leon rubbed the sore spot on his arm. "You do like that shirt of yours says when you hear me callin'." She glared at him for a moment, as if debating whether to hurt him again. Then she grunted and turned on her heels.

"Come on here into the livin' room, boy," she said, lumbering ahead of him. "I got somethin' to show you."

Leon could tell how worked up she was from her tone of voice. His heart gave a fearful jolt. He must have done something terrible again. But what? He'd been extra careful lately to clean up after himself when *Aerobicize with Debbie* was over—to wipe off the coffee table, throw away his clotted tissues, check to make sure none of his jism had dripped onto the sofa.

Trying to figure it out was making him dizzy. Whatever it was, he knew he was in for trouble. He couldn't remember the last time he'd heard his mama sound so upset.

A gush of anger and resentment, caustic as stomach acid, rose up into his throat. *Damn old bitch! Wish to God she'd leave me be!*

Staring down at her back as he followed a few inches behind her, he spotted a scaly black mole sprouting on her dowager's hump, an inch or so above the neckline of her housedress.

Maybe it's cancer, he thought, his heart leaping. *Maybe she'll get real sick and die!*

Waiting for Debbie's show to begin the previous Tuesday, he had caught the last few minutes of a program on skin cancer. There was one kind—he couldn't remember what it was called—that could kill you quick as a wink. It looked just like that dark scabby growth on his mama's hump, too!

Suddenly, he let out a little whimper. *Sweet Jesus, no!* He didn't want anything bad to happen to his mama! *He* was the one who deserved to die for even thinking such a thing! He loved his mama! It was true what she always said—she was the only one in the world who cared a damn for his useless hide. He'd be lost without her.

He just wished she wouldn't be so angry with him all the time. He *tried* to be good—tried so hard to please her and make her happy. After all, like she always said, she'd devoted her whole life to taking care of him. Thinking of how hard she slaved in the cat food cannery so the two of them could have decent lives, he felt hot tears fill his eyes. He raised the back of one hand to wipe away the moisture.

They had reached the living room by then. Leon was so used to seeing everything in the same unchanging order that the unfamiliar object on the coffee table would have leapt out at him even if it hadn't been so brightly colored. It was a book with a lurid red-splashed cover.

"Your bottom clean, boy?" his mother snarled as she led him toward the sofa. "Then park it down there and keep your yap shut 'til you hear what I got to say."

He lowered himself onto the cushion while she reached down, snatched up the book, and thrust it at him.

"Go ahead. Take a gander."

Leon took it in his hands and read the title, his lips moving haltingly as he sounded out the words. *Slaughterhouse: The Shocking True Story of America's Most Infamous Psycho.*

Leon's eyes narrowed as he riffled through the pages. He paused at the glossy photo insert in the center of the book and stared at one of the black-and-white pictures. It took him a second to realize what he was looking at.

When the recognition hit him, his whole body gave a little jerk, as if the book were an electrical device that had just short-circuited in his hands.

Looming over him, his mama grunted. "Hard to believe, ain't it?"

Leon gawked at the photo. It was a mug shot of a meek-looking middle-aged man whose mouth was twisted into a silly little grin. He was wearing a denim work shirt and had a plaid deer-hunter's cap cocked on his head.

The caption below the picture read: "Official police photograph of Edward Gein, grave robber, ghoul, and collector of female body parts."

Leon gasped, "Damn."

He was staring into the face of his father.

Leon had heard lots of stories about his daddy, but except for a blurry photo that accompanied the newspaper obituaries when Gein had died back in 1984, he had never seen a picture of him. Now, he studied his father's face with an odd mix of emotions: curiosity and excitement combined with the bitterness he had picked up from his mama, whose loathing for Gein ("the mangy dog that ruined my life," as she generally called him) was fierce and unrelenting.

Leon was so deeply absorbed in the picture that he didn't feel the cushion sag when his mama plopped down beside him. Gradually, however, the piercing fish smell that clung to her from the cannery penetrated his awareness. He blinked and glanced in her direction.

"That's right, boy," she muttered. "Someone's gone and wrote a whole damn book about him." She barked a bitter laugh. "Can you believe it? What in the good Lord's name is this country comin' to when a creature like that"—she stabbed a stubby finger at the book—"comes to be as famous as a damn movie star?"

"Can I read it, Mama?" Leon implored.

" 'Course not, you fool," she said, snatching the book

from his hands. "You don't need to pick up no more bad ideas than you already got."

"Well, how come you brought it home, then?"

Agatha made a fist and rapped the knuckles hard against Leon's forehead. "That skull of yours completely hollow, boy?"

"That hurt, Mama," Leon whined, massaging his head.

"I'll hurt you a damn sight worse you don't shut up and listen."

Licking a thumb, she turned over the pages until she came to the passage she was searching for. "Listen up," she said, then began to read:

> After his mother's death, Gein became increasingly cut off. Always a misfit, he withdrew ever more deeply into his own secret world. More and more of his time was spent in the darkness of his decaying farmhouse. In the past, he would kill some time occasionally at the Plainfield ice-cream parlor or the new ice-skating rink in the neighboring town of Hancock. Now, except to do an occasional odd job or run an errand, he rarely went anywhere.
>
> By the early 1950s, he was in full retreat—from society, from reality, from sanity itself.

Agatha interrupted her reading with a dismissive snort. "Like to know how this writer feller knows so much 'bout what was goin' on in someone else's head. Hell, your daddy was dead four, maybe five years before this . . ." she turned over the book and studied the cover—"this *Paul Novak* even begun writing his damn book."

Shaking her head, she found her place again. "Now this here's the part I want you to pay real good attention to, Leon. Real good." She drew a deep breath as if steeling herself for something painful. Then she resumed:

Some people in Plainfield, however, claim that during the winter of 1956, Gein had a short-lived relationship with a local woman. According to reports, several residents of Main Street, peering through their windows late at night, spotted the couple strolling along the sidewalk when the town was otherwise deserted. There were even stories at the time that Eddie had impregnated his girlfriend, who subsequently fled town to avoid the disgrace of her situation.

These rumors, however, seem contradicted by Gein's later revelations. During the many hours of psychiatric evaluations that followed his arrest, Gein insisted that he had never had sexual intercourse—at least with a living woman. As for the possibility that he may have engaged in necrophilic acts with the female corpses he removed from local graveyards, there is good reason to believe that such unspeakable practices did indeed take place in the squalor of his lonely farmhouse. One of the psychologists who examined him offered this appraisal of Gein's sexual preferences: "Eddie's no queer. He likes women all right—as long as they're dead."

Perhaps the psychologist was right. Or perhaps, on one fleeting occasion, Eddie Gein did know the pleasures of normal love. If so, the misbegotten offspring of America's most monstrous psycho may be alive somewhere today.

It is a tantalizing—and unsettling—possibility.

Agatha raised her watery eyes from the page and turned them on Leon, who was sitting rigidly beside her, his own eyes round and shiny. She slammed the book shut with such force that Leon jumped at the noise.

Blinking rapidly as if snapping out of a trance, he glanced over at his mother. Her lower lip was quivering and little froths of spittle had gathered in the corners of her mouth.

"Mama?" Leon said nervously.

Cocking her right arm, she backhanded him across the side of his head. "You answer me straight," she hissed. "You ever shoot off that ugly yap of yours to anyone about *him?*"

"'Course not, Mama," he whimpered, tears rising. "You told me not to. Who'm I gonna tell anyway? I ain't got no friends—'cept you."

"That's for damn sure," she said. The book was still lying on her lap. She gazed down at it disgustedly. Suddenly, with a slap almost as savage as the one she had just administered to her son, she sent it sailing halfway across the room.

Looking up at Leon again, she said, "We got us some danger ahead, boy."

"How come?" Leon said, sniffling. The inside of his skull was still ringing from her blow. "You ain't done nothing wrong, Mama."

"It's like the saying goes, boy: the road to hell is paved with good intentions. Sometimes—only the Lord Himself knows why—good deeds ain't rewarded but punished. Here I felt sorry for that miserable creature, same way as you might for a stray dog. I let myself be nice to him in a moment of weakness." As she spoke, her voice grew tremulous with self-pity. "And look what I got for it. Look at the life I ended up with. The misery and sufferin' I had to endure. Well, I accepted it. I ain't never tried to shuck off the burden of my sin."

Her tone turned suddenly hard again. "But I ain't shoulderin' no more. I ain't about to let myself be made a public mockery of, let my shame be held up for all the world to laugh at."

She pointed a finger at him. "Ain't lettin' you be exposed, neither."

"Me?"

"They find out about you and that box of playthings

you got stowed in your closet, they'll lock you away forever like they done to your old man."

Leon felt his heart knocking against his breastbone like a mule trying to kick its way out of a burning stall. He licked his dry lips. "You been lookin' in my closet, Mama?" he managed to say.

" 'Course."

Leon shut his eyes as a bloodred wave swept across his mind.

"You think I didn't know?" she said. "What you was up to that day we drove out to your daddy's place?"

It had happened years before, the time Agatha—with twelve-year-old Leon in tow—had snuck back to Plainfield to visit her dying mother. Afterward, on an impulse, she had driven out to the old Gein farmstead. She wanted to gaze with her own eyes on the retribution that had befallen her betrayer. While she stood gloating at the charred remains of Gein's house, Leon poked around the rubble and explored the few rickety outbuildings that had survived the fiery wrath of the townspeople.

"Where'd you find 'em anyway?" Agatha asked now.

"In a box," he said quietly, "under the floor in that old chicken coop. I pried up one of the planks, and it was just setting there."

She shook her head. "And to think how the police went over and over that whole damn place with a fine-tooth comb. Well, you knew just where to look, didn't you, boy? Guess what they say is true." She snorted through her nose. "Like father, like son."

Leon swallowed hard. "You ain't gonna take 'em away from me, are you, Mama?"

"Not me. I know you got your needs—like all your kind. Leastways this might keep you from messin' with some slut, catchin' one of them diseases they all got nowadays." She looked hard at Leon. "But that's just *my* feelings, boy. Others won't see it that way. They'll take your toys away and lock you up so fast your head'll spin—if they find out about us."

"We won't let 'em," Leon said vehemently. "Nobody knows about us. Ain't that right, Mama?"

Agatha paused. "There's one other. But I believe we can trust him. Anyways, I'm keepin' my eyes peeled. And I don't reckon there's enough in that book to point anyone in our direction. Still, you can't never tell."

She laid a hand on Leon's left leg, high up. "Time come, we may have ourselves some trouble on our hands, boy. Anything like that happens, you're gonna have yourself some real dirty work to do. Maybe even some killin'. Think you're up to it, boy?"

"Yes, Mama," he said hoarsely. "I know I am."

Agatha looked at him appraisingly for a moment, then nodded slowly. Reaching her meaty right arm around his shoulders, she pulled him close.

Shutting his eyes with a grateful moan, Leon pillowed his head on his mother's vast, floppy bosom while she encircled him with her other arm and began rocking him gently from side to side. After a while, she could feel his tears seeping through the fabric of her housedress and dampening the skin of her unfettered breasts.

"Like father, like son," she said again—only this time with a soft, self-satisfied cackle.

17

Sticking his fists high into the air like Rocky Balboa after a triumphant title bout, Paul Novak stretched in his swivel chair and let out a loud, groaning yawn. Slumping back into his seat, he massaged the back of his neck and stared at the words on his computer screen.

Actually, he wasn't feeling very triumphant. Quite the contrary. He'd been wrestling in vain with the same paragraph for the past twenty minutes, cutting a word here, pasting it in there, undoing phrases, reshuffling sentences. He was struggling to put an idea into shape, but it just wasn't coming together.

He reached out, typed in a few words, and considered them skeptically for a moment before hitting the delete button. Though Paul had owned his computer for nearly ten years, its operations still struck him as magical. It seemed capable of doing almost anything.

Except writing this goddamn lecture for me, he thought dryly.

He had decided to accept the invitation at the University of Wisconsin and had started drafting his talk that morning. The beginning had come easily enough—a brief introduction that rehashed the grisly facts of the Gein case without sensationalizing them. It was when he had gotten down to the nitty-gritty that his trouble began.

He had been asked to speak about the "Gein phenomenon": why the deeds of a demented bachelor from Nowheresville, Wisconsin, who had spent his lonely hours digging up dead female bodies and turning them into human-flesh furniture, continued to fascinate millions of people more than thirty years after the ghastly crimes were uncovered.

Part of the answer, he knew, was simply the primal human appetite for gore—the same morbid hunger that had made public executions such a popular form of entertainment throughout the ages. But there was more to it than simple blood lust. Paul had some definite ideas on the subject, but he was having trouble expressing them in the right way. Some of his remarks—about Gein's symbolic significance as an embodiment of the "dark side of the American character"—sounded hopelessly pretentious; others, as if Paul was trying desperately to justify his own exploitation of an unspeakable crime.

Sighing, he sat there and stared at the screen until it abruptly went black and a large school of luminescent fish began floating past, interrupted by an occasional winged toaster.

He let out a little curse of frustration. People were always talking about writer's block, but to Paul it felt more like a form of impotence, as if his brain had suddenly gone limp. He knew there was no point in pushing it—he would only end up making himself frantic. He decided to take a break and try again later. Maybe his brain would perform better if he gave it a rest.

He shut down the computer and headed for the back door, grabbing a hooded sweatshirt from a wall hook as he passed through the rear hallway. "Melville!" he called. Before he could reach for the doorknob, the big black Labrador was at his side. Paul opened the door, and the dog scrabbled down the wood steps and went bounding away across the grass.

Standing outside on the lawn, Paul pulled on the sweatshirt and drew a deep breath of the crisp, fragrant air. His spirits lifted instantly. It was a spectacular day, sharp and bright. Not many trees had turned yet. The distant hills looked like mounds of green plush, splashed here and there with rich colors: cherry red, muted gold, burgundy, and burnt orange.

Paul decided to do some log-splitting—exercise his body while resting his brain. Just this last spring, not long after they'd moved in, a savage storm had ripped through Stoddard Bridge, the ragged edge of a major hurricane that had mauled the mid-Atlantic coast. The gale had toppled utility poles, flooded basements, uprooted trees. Paul's house had come through unscathed, though a towering maple had been wrested from the ground a hundred feet from his front door. It leaned at a precarious angle, half its roots jutting out of the earth like a knot of giant worms.

Paul had called a tree service. The next day, a pair of workmen finished the job the storm had begun. The tree was taken down and chainsawed into logs.

Since then, whenever he'd found the time, Paul had been converting the logs into fireplace wood. He had already split a sizeable stack. The pieces were neatly piled at the far edge of his lawn, where the grass met the woods at the top of the hill. But a sprawling heap of unsplit wood still remained.

Fetching his ax from the toolshed, Paul headed around to his chopping block, an ancient stump whose surface was scored with blade bites. He liked to split wood. He had learned the art from Wylie's dad, a retired real-estate lawyer, still vigorous at seventy, who grew up in northern Vermont and had built a little cabin near Rutland where he and his wife vacationed every summer. The work took precision—you had to strike the upended logs just right for a clean, even split.

It took muscles, too. Ten minutes after he started, Paul was sweating hard. He stripped off his sweatshirt and stood there for a moment in his gray, short-sleeved T-shirt, gazing at the birch trees and the meadow beyond. Carpeted with dried wildflowers and autumn-brown grasses, it sloped gently down to the bright winding river.

A sharp gust caused goose bumps to rise on his exposed arms. Stooping for a fresh log, he stood it upright on the shopping block, raised the ax high over his shoulder, and went back to work.

Paul was still going at it when he heard the approaching growl of a car engine, then the gravelly crunch of tires on the driveway.

That would be Wylie. Her classes were over by noon on Thursdays, so she used the free time to do their weekly grocery shopping, stopping off at a big supermarket in Torrington on her way home. She and Paul divided the domestic chores: she cooked dinner, he cleaned up the dishes; she put the kids to bed, he saw them off to school; she purchased the groceries, he unpacked them.

He split a final chunk of wood, then buried the ax in the chopping block. The blade made a satisfying *thwok* as it lodged deep in the stump. Snatching up his sweatshirt, which he had tossed onto the grass, he strolled toward the driveway.

"Hey, sweetie," Wylie called, her eyebrows flickering upward in surprise as she saw him round the corner of the house. "I expected to find you inside."

"Thought I'd split some wood." Paul said, pulling on his sweatshirt and brushing off a few bits of lawn debris that had stuck to the front.

Wylie was standing beside the open trunk, which was stuffed with bulging brown bags. Paul came up and kissed her on the lips. "You look radiant," he said. It was true. In the high midday sun, her face glowed as if lit from within.

"Thanks."

"Classes go okay?"

"Fine. What about you? How's the writing going?"

Paul shrugged. "I hit a wall."

"Oh, well." She gave his arm a consoling squeeze.

"It must be hard to get back to your stories after all this time."

Paul reached into the trunk for a couple of the bags. "I wasn't working on a story," he said over his shoulder. "I started that lecture I'm giving in Wisconsin."

There was a palpable pause behind him before Wylie said, "I see."

Something in her tone—a note of disappointment, even disapproval—made Paul bristle. He straightened up, a bag cradled in each arm. "Something wrong?" he asked.

"Uh-uh," she said without conviction.

"You knew I'd agreed to give that lecture."

"I know, I know. It's just . . ."

"Yeah?"

She sighed. "I was hoping you'd get back to something"—she hesitated, as if casting about for the most neutral words—"more serious."

He'd been feeling annoyed. Now he was angry. "Do we have to start this shit again?"

Wylie's features tightened. "Forget it. I'm sorry I said anything." She grabbed a bag from the trunk, turned, and made for the front door.

Paul followed close behind. "No. Let's not forget it. You brought it up."

She pulled up short and swiveled. "I'm not going to fight about this, Paul. Write whatever the hell you feel like."

"Damn right I will."

"Fine." She stomped up the front steps and disappeared into the house.

Paul stood there for a moment, seething, then hurried after her.

She was standing at the counter, yanking food cans from the bag and shoving them onto a cabinet shelf. Paul set his own bags on the counter a few feet away and began unloading them, casting sideways looks at Wylie.

He could see from the set of her mouth that she was

furious. Her lips were puckered tight, her cheeks sucked in. The expression made her fine facial bones more pronounced. Even through his anger, Paul was struck by her loveliness. He felt a surge of remorse. He hated to fight with her.

He heaved a loud sigh. "Look," he said. "I'm sorry I blew up. That comment of yours about my doing something 'more serious' pissed me off a little, that's all. You've got to understand—for me, this Gein stuff *is* serious."

For a long moment—so protracted that Paul assumed she was giving him the silent treatment—Wylie didn't respond. Finally, she said without looking at him, "That's the trouble, Paul. It's the only thing you *do* take seriously anymore."

"Not true."

"It *is* true." She turned to face him, eyes flashing. "It's taken over your life. It's what you write about and talk and think about. All that sick, disgusting, hateful—" She shook her head sharply and took a deep breath. When she spoke again, there was something different in her voice—not anger, but sadness. "It worries me, Paul. It's as if—I don't know—there's some dark, nasty part of you that really takes pleasure from this stuff."

He thought about that for a moment. "Well, that seems pretty normal. Most people have dark, nasty parts of themselves."

"Yeah. People like Ed Gein."

"Great," Paul said. "So now I'm a psychotic, necrophilic ghoul?"

The corners of her mouth twitched upward, as if she was amused in spite of herself. "Well, maybe not psychotic," she said.

Paul put down the Progresso soup can he was holding and took a few steps toward Wylie, who crossed her arms over her chest and glanced away from him. Very tentatively, he reached out his hands and placed them on her shoulders. She stiffened but didn't shrug him away.

"Come on, Wylie," he said. "Let's not fight. I apologize."

She looked up at him and their eyes locked. Tilting his head, he put his lips to hers. For a moment, she remained unresponsive. Then she kissed him back.

"I'll tell you one big difference between me and ol' Eddie," he said, brushing a strand of hair off her forehead. "I like making love to women who are more—how shall I put this?—"

"Alive?"

"Exactly. Also, I hardly ever get dressed up in women's clothes and parade around the house pretending I'm my mother."

"Thank God. One of her is enough."

"Hey—"

"Only kidding." She was grinning up at him now.

"I just had this terrific idea," Paul said. "The kids won't be home for another hour. Why don't we go upstairs and I can demonstrate my non-necrophilic tendencies?"

She kissed him lightly on the mouth. "Sounds delightful. But I've really got to do some writing of my own. And we should have lunch. I picked up some goodies at the little gourmet shop in Winsted."

Paul finished unloading the groceries while Wylie set out the lunch. They ate at the wooden kitchen table, chatting about the kids, Wylie's classes, their plans for the upcoming weekend. *Slaughterhouse* wasn't mentioned once.

"Want some coffee?" Paul asked when they had finished off the lemon chicken salad, marinated cucumbers, and pumpernickel rolls Wylie had brought home.

"Sounds great. Why don't you get it started? I left the mail in the car."

She was back in half a minute with an armful of envelopes, magazines, and mail-order catalogues. She tossed the pile onto the table and started sorting through it while Paul brewed the coffee.

When he returned to the table a few minutes later, the Melitta pot in one hand and a couple of white ceramic mugs in the other, he saw a fat brown mailer lying by his place. Wylie was leafing through the latest *New Yorker*.

"It's from your publisher," she said, looking up at him.

Paul went to fetch a container of milk and a package of Pepperidge Farm oatmeal cookies. Reseating himself, he opened the mailer, reached inside, and pulled out a fat packet of white envelopes, bound together by a thick rubber band.

Wylie glanced up from the magazine.

"Fan letters," Paul said.

Wylie gave him a faint half-smile, then went back to the magazine.

Every month or so, Paul's publisher forwarded the mail that had arrived for him. Even more than most authors, Paul was careful about guarding his private address, especially now that he'd achieved a modicum of celebrity. Not that he'd ever been the target of threats. For the most part, people wrote to tell him how much they liked his book. Still, the world was full of cranks— and worse.

Pulling off the rubber band, Paul thumbed through the envelopes. There were about thirty altogether. He stacked them on the table and started at the top.

The first dozen or so letters had nothing but nice things to say. One of the writers went so far as to call *Slaughterhouse* "the best crime book since Capote's *In Cold Blood*"—high praise indeed, as far as Paul was concerned. Another writer, a woman who described herself as "probably America's Number One Fan of Serial Killer Literature," enclosed a stamped return envelope and asked for Paul's autograph. Paul snorted with disbelief. Even so, he felt pleased.

The next letter was equally flattering. It was from a Milwaukee journalist named Stan Heckley, who identified himself as a "great admirer" of Paul's work. He had heard that Paul was coming to Madison and hoped to meet with him at some point during the visit. Heckley explained that he was planning to do some crime writing himself and thought he might "pick up a few pointers from a master such as yourself."

Though Paul's vanity was stroked by Heckley's letter, there was a wheedling, fawning quality to it that he found off-putting. He decided to drop Heckley a note, thanking him for his kind words but explaining—politely—that he'd probably be too busy for a meeting.

Paul reached for the next envelope in the stack and began to rip open the flap.

He paused, frowning. The envelope was in terrible condition—badly wrinkled and so smudged with fingerprints that it might have been handled by a grease monkey. There was no return address on the flap. Turning it over, he saw there was none on the front corner, either. Paul's name—care of his publisher—was scrawled in the middle. The ugly letters looked like the work of a semiliterate child wielding a blunt pencil.

Paul felt an icy trickle deep inside his chest. He tore open the envelope and shook out the letter.

It was printed in the same crude handwriting on a sheet of lined paper that had been sloppily torn from a spiral notepad. "Novak you slimy bastard," it began . . .

> Your nothing but scum. Your a filthy corupter of kids and decent people. Yet you and that bitch got kids of your own. O yes. I read all about you in that magazine safe on your hill in CT. looking down at everybody else. You only think your safe. I read you won't let your own kids read your sick shit. Only our kids right? I got two things to say to you stop writing. And 2: watch out for your own kids, maybe their not as safe as you think.

"What's wrong?" Wylie asked.

Paul glanced up quickly. "Huh?"

"You said, 'Oh shit.' "

"I did?" He hadn't even been aware of it.

Wylie's eyes narrowed. Her gaze shifted to the letter he was holding. Then—so unexpectedly that Paul had no time to react—she reached across the table and plucked the paper from his hand.

"Wylie!" His hand darted out but she turned away from him in her seat, her eyes flitting over the letter.

Paul sank back in his chair. It took Wylie only seconds to scan the letter. "Oh, God," she said, gazing up at him with a stricken look.

"Let's not overreact," Paul said, sounding calmer than he felt. The letter didn't frighten him; he assumed it was an empty threat. Still, its viciousness filled him with rage.

"He knows where we live," Wylie said hoarsely.

"He *doesn't* know where we live. All he knows is what he read in *People*—that we own a house somewhere on a hill in Connecticut. Connecticut's a big place, Wylie. With a lot of hills in it."

"I want you to notify the police," Wylie said.

Paul took a deep breath and tried his best to sound patient. "Wylie," he said. "I understand it's upsetting. I'm upset, too. But there's nothing to worry about. These assholes get their rocks off from writing, not from *doing* anything. They're like obscene phone callers: they just like to make a lot of sick, ugly noise."

"*Obscene* is the word for it, all right," Wylie said angrily. She held up the letter in a trembling hand. "You still think your book doesn't affect people? Huh, Paul?" Her tone was harsh and cutting.

All the anger Paul had been holding back exploded. His fist came down so hard on the table that some coffee splashed out of the mugs. "Bullshit!" he shouted. "You think that guy was just a perfectly normal, healthy individual until he read *Slaughterhouse*? That he finished my book and suddenly turned into a fucking psycho?"

They glared at each other for a long moment. Finally, Wylie said coldly, "Maybe you're right. But you can't tell me it's not having a harmful effect."

"What about all the other people who bought it?" Paul shot back. "The ones who made it a bestseller. I mean, it's being sold by the goddamn Literary Guild. You notice a mass outbreak of homicidal mania among Literary Guild members?"

"Is that all that's important to you anymore?" Wylie asked. "How many copies you sell?"

He gave a snorting laugh. "You're telling me you don't think the money is important? The things we can afford? This house? That nice sweater you're wearing?" His tone became nastier. "Those little gourmet shop 'goodies' you're so fond of?"

Wylie stared at him. "In the end, no. What's important is the effect it's having on our lives. What it's doing to you. To us."

He shook his head slowly. "I don't even know what the hell you're talking about. I—"

The phone in the family room shrilled. Neither one of them moved. Finally, on the third ring, Paul shoved back his chair and rose to his feet. "Here," he said, reaching down for a handful of the letters and tossing them onto the table in front of Wylie. "Take a look at these. You'll see who's reading my book and what kind of effect it's having."

He turned and disappeared into the family room. Wylie stared at the letters, then picked one up and began to read.

Paul was right about one thing: the letters did reassure her. Apart from a few oddballs (like the young fan who declared that *Slaughterhouse* would make a "really great interactive video game"), the writers seemed like intelligent, surprisingly literate people. From their comments, it was clear that they were all avid readers who recognized and appreciated Paul's literary skill. As an English professor, Wylie found it encouraging that there were still people in the world who took pleasure from books, as opposed to her own college students, whose cultural pastimes seemed limited to *Seinfeld,* gangsta rap, and Howard Stern. By the time Paul returned to the kitchen, she was feeling a little better.

Paul, however, seemed even more agitated than he'd been during their argument.

"Who was that?" Wylie asked.

"Keith," he said scowling. Keith Norris was Paul's literary agent. "Lional Lemmick wants me back on the show."

Wylie raised her eyebrows.

"Remember that minister out in Wisconsin, the one Keith sent me the clippings about?"

Wylie's brow furrowed for a moment. "Oh, right. That televangelist. The one who's been telling his viewers to boycott your book."

"The Reverend Hobart," Paul said sarcastically. "Seems like his crusade is picking up steam. Especially with that shit going on in Milwaukee. Those mutilation killings of—"

"I know, I know," Wylie said quickly, as if she could not bear to discuss it.

"Anyway," Paul said, "Lemmick's had this brainstorm. He wants to set up a televised debate between me and Hobart."

Wylie hesitated briefly before asking, "So what did you tell Keith?"

"I told him okay," Paul said, a trace of defiance in his voice.

Wylie's frown deepened. "Even after your last experience on his show?"

"Goddamn it," Paul said, his voice rising. "You think I'm going to let Hobart say whatever the hell he wants to and get away with it? That self-righteous asshole."

Wylie opened her mouth, then closed it again, as if there were no point in replying. Paul glared down at her, but the look she returned was devoid of everything but sadness.

Grabbing his sweatshirt from the back of his chair, he whirled and headed for the hallway.

"Where are you going?" Wylie called after him.

"Chop some more wood," he said over his shoulder. He could hear a quiver of fury in his voice. He wasn't sure what he was angrier at—Wylie's disapproval, Hobart's sanctimony, or the hateful crank letter he had received. All he knew was that he felt like smashing something.

He strode toward the tree stump where his jutting ax awaited.

18

"Hey, Arby." Franklin Turner rapped on Streator's half-open door, then poked his head inside the office. "Meeting's about to begin."

"Tell them I'll be right down," Streator said, looking up from the phone.

Turner waved and disappeared from the doorway.

"Task force?" Ellen asked on the other end of the line.

Streator nodded as if she could see him. "We're bringing in a shrink. Some prof from the university, specializes in male fantasies." Streator grimaced. "We'll be calling in the psychics next."

"Come on now," Ellen said soothingly. "Maybe he'll say something useful."

"Yeah." The word came out like a weary sigh. "Gotta go, hon. I'm running late."

"Arby?"

"Yeah?"

"You'll get the job done. There isn't the slightest doubt in my mind."

After dropping the handset back into its cradle, Streator sat motionless for a minute. Funny how marriages worked, he reflected. Ellen was a strong woman, tough as they came, but even so, there were times when what she needed most was to turn into a little girl and let Arby take care of her like a daddy would. At other times, just the opposite was true: it was Arby who

142

needed the comforting, needed Ellen to stroke his brow
and mother him and reassure him that everything would
work out just fine.

Right now, he thought grimly, was one of those times.

Rising from his chair, he grabbed his notepad from
the desktop, slapped his shirt pocket to make sure he
was carrying a ballpoint, then strode from his office
toward the elevator.

The "Cavity Killings" (as the papers had promptly
dubbed them) were the most sensational crimes to hit
Milwaukee since the cops had found a refrigerator full
of human remains in the apartment of a soft-spoken psychopath named Jeffrey Dahmer. The chief of police, still
smarting from accusations that his department had mis-
handled the Dahmer investigation, had immediately
called a press conference to announce the formation of
a multiagency task force. The city would spare neither
money nor manpower to put a halt to the latest scourge,
Chief Tylor declared. Heading the task force would be
Detective Sergeant R. B. Streator of the Homicide Division—"a much-decorated veteran and a man with a well-
earned reputation for his absolute composure in a
crisis."

As it happened, Streator needed every ounce of composure at his disposal. Between the pressure from his
boss (who was counting on a quick bust to boost the
department's image) and the clamorings of the public
(whose fears had been whipped to a frenzied pitch by
the relentlessly lurid press coverage), he had never felt
so harried in his life.

And then there was the urgency burning deep within
Streator himself.

To perform their jobs, homicide cops, like morticians
and medical examiners, have to build emotional barriers
against the horrors they confront every day. But the
atrocities committed on Carolyn Dearborn, Darlene
Redding, and Patti Atkins had broken down Streator's
defenses. The mutilation-murders of the three young

women were an outrage beyond endurance. Streator had never felt more desperate to find a killer in his life. The manhunt had become an obsession, and not just because he was determined to see the monster brought to justice. There was another, even more urgent motive driving Streator: the knowledge that unless he and his colleagues did something to stop it, the horror would keep on happening.

Other young women would die in the same unspeakable way.

That knowledge made the current state of the investigation all the more maddening. Though Streator did his best to project an air of confidence, offering upbeat sound bites every time a reporter shoved a mike in his face, the fact was that the police were no closer to nabbing a suspect than they had been six weeks earlier, when Patti Atkins's savaged corpse had been found. The few leads they'd pursued had gotten them nowhere. The physical evidence was negligible. The killer had left no fingerprints, body hairs, blood, or semen samples. The floss he'd used to suture his victims was a brand that could be found in any drugstore or supermarket.

Background checks of the victims had turned up nothing even remotely useful. Interviews with the young women's family, friends, co-workers, and acquaintances had been similarly fruitless. As in all highly publicized cases, the police had been innundated with tips. Every one had been checked out, no matter how far-fetched or slender. Every one had turned out to be a total waste of time.

Because of the killer's MO, the investigators had scoured their files for known sex offenders connected in any way with the dental profession: oral surgeons accused of molesting anesthetized patients, pedophiliac orthodontists, dental students arrested for rape. They came up with about a dozen names but no one who could possibly have been the killer. Some of the men were doing time; the rest had solid alibis.

After nearly two months of frantic pursuit, the manhunt had hit a dead end.

The only witness to come forward with a tangible clue was a twenty-five-year-old housewife named Kathy Kreutzer, who had arrived at the Mayfair Mall around the time of Patti Atkins's abduction. Kreutzer, the mother of a two-year-old boy, had just parked her van in a far corner of the lot and was unsnapping the buckles on her son's safety seat. Glancing up through the window, she had noticed a middle-aged woman helping a teenage girl—apparently her daughter—across the lot. The girl, who was leaning heavily against the woman, seemed barely able to walk, as though she had been stricken with a sudden illness while shopping. Kreutzer had caught only a glimpse of the pair. Her toddler had started fussing, and as she turned her attention back to him, the dark-haired woman and the woozy girl had vanished among the rows of parked vehicles.

Investigators hadn't known what to make of this clue. Could the killer be a woman? Or did he have a female accomplice? Perhaps the teenage girl hadn't been Patti Atkins after all?

So far, those questions—like all the other mysteries surrounding the Cavity Killings—remained unresolved. In spite of their efforts, Streator's team hadn't been able to turn up a trace of the dark-haired woman Kreutzer had spotted that day.

Now, riding alone in the elevator car, Streator watched the floor numbers tick down on the digital counter. The steady sinking was a fair reflection of his mood. Day by day, he was finding it harder to keep his spirits up. By now, with the killer's trail grown icy cold, it was going to take an extraordinary turn of luck for the investigators to find their man before he struck again. For Streator and his team, today's meeting was largely a matter of grasping at straws, a way of making themselves feel they were doing *something* concrete to earn their pay.

Inviting Dr. Rollins had been the brainstorm of a crime-scene technician named Janet Wagner, who'd taken a night course with the professor a few years before. Streator himself was willing to play along, although he was deeply dubious about all psychological "specialists."

Especially after his experience with the FBI.

The floor-counter hit *1* with a ping. Streator was through the shiny metal doors before they'd finished sliding open.

Outside the briefing room, Frank Turner, a Styrofoam cup clutched in one enormous hand, was chatting with Wagner, an attractive brunette in her midthirties. Both turned their heads as Streator approached.

"Sorry to hold things up," Streator said.

"No problem," Turner said, cocking his head toward the open doorway. "The prof's looking over his lecture notes."

"I'm going to grab a cup of coffee before we start," Wagner said. She looked up at Streator. "Can I bring you some?"

"Thanks. Milk, no sugar."

Turner watched her intently as she hurried down the hallway toward the coffee room.

"I think she's sweet on you," he said to Streator.

Arby gave him an incredulous look.

"No shit," Turner said. "Offering to bring you coffee like that. Hell, she didn't ask *me.*"

Streator looked down at the steaming cup in Turner's hand.

"Still," Turner said, following Streator's gaze. "I'm telling you, Arby, one thing I know is women."

Streator gave an amused little snort. "She's just got good manners is all. Wagner's a good person. Good cop, too."

"Good ass, too," Turner said.

"Why, Franklin—what a thing to say about a fellow officer."

"Hey, now," Turner said in mock alarm. "Don't you go telling *her* I said it, or she'll have *my* ass in a sling. Gotta watch every word you say nowadays, or these women'll have you up for sexual harassment." He pronounced the word with a heavy accent on the second syllable, so that it sounded like "her-*ass*-ment."

"Asses again," Streator said. "Trouble with you, Frank, you've got a one-track mind."

Frank's expression turned serious. "Look who's talking. It's no good, Arby, the way you're letting this thing eat you up. How much weight you lose anyway?"

Streator shrugged. "Couple of pounds." He shook his head slowly. "Just can't stop thinking about it, day and night. And you know the worst of it? We don't get a break soon, it's going to happen again."

Turner tilted his head toward the briefing room. "Maybe this guy'll give us something we can use."

Streator made a skeptical face. "Like those FBI hotshots, huh?"

After three futile weeks of searching for a suspect, Streator had put in an emergency request to the FBI's Behavorial Science Unit at Quantico, Virginia. In return, he had received a dishearteningly fat bundle of application forms, complete with the standard bureaucratic instructions. ("For *two* or more victims and *one* offender, you must complete and submit two or more Crime Analysis Reports, one for each victim. Do *not* duplicate the Offender Information, items 55 through 84, in the second and subsequent reports.") It had taken him the better part of a week—sitting at his desk after work from 6 P.M. until nearly midnight—to do all the paperwork.

He wasn't expecting miracles. He knew that the popular image of the BSU—an elite team of psychologically trained superagents matching wits with the likes of Hannibal Lecter—was pure Hollywood fantasy. Still, he had hopes that the Bureau might supply him, if not with a road map to the killer, then at least with something to jumpstart his stalled investigation.

The Bureau's response was prompt but disappointing. It had arrived only a few days before—a one-page criminal profile that drew a hypothetical sketch of the UNSUB (Unknown Subject). According to the FBI's psychological analysts, the UNSUB was probably "a white male between the ages of eighteen and twenty-nine, living within a thirty-mile radius of Milwaukee. He is of average intelligence or less. He is not overly educated, probably not beyond a high-school level. His employment would range from unemployed to employed in an unskilled capacity. He lives alone or possibly with a female relation. His interpersonal relationships are generally dysfunctional. Other people consider him strange. He is ill at ease socially, especially around women. He possesses a deep hostility toward the opposite sex and enjoys the suffering he inflicts on his victims, having no subsequent feelings of guilt. Almost certainly, he enjoys reliving his acts in his fantasies. These fantasies are fused with intense sexual impulses. He is probably an avid reader of pornography." The report went on in this vein for another few sentences before concluding: "In sum, the UNSUB possesses chronic sexual problems indicating deviance of a severe nature."

When Turner was shown the report, he had read it over, then looked up wryly at Streator and said, "Well, I guess that narrows it down to only a few thousand people. At most."

Now, Turner clapped Streator on the shoulder and said, "Never can tell when our luck's gonna change. Anyhow, no harm in hearing what the prof's got to say."

At that moment Janet Wagner returned with a Styrofoam cup in each hand. "Here you go," she said, extending her right hand.

"Thanks," Arby said, taking the cup. He puffed on the surface, sipped, and scalded the tip of his tongue.

"Better get this show on the road," he said, stepping aside so Wagner and Turner could precede him through the doorway.

"I think you'll like him," Wagner said as the three of them entered the briefing room. "He's got an interesting take on things."

Professor Rollins was seated alone in the first row of folding chairs, glancing down at some index cards through rimless half-glasses perched on the tip of his nose. Behind him sat a dozen members of the task force—ten men and two women. Nodding hello to their colleagues, Wagner and Turner took seats in the third row back, while Arby went over to greet the psychologist.

It was the first time he had set eyes on Rollins. Their contact had been limited to a single phone conversation. From the professor's soft, soothing voice, Arby had pictured a mousy little man in his middle years, the kind of stereotypical academic who smokes a pipe, wears horn-rims, and favors tweed sports jackets with leather elbow patches. He saw now that his mental picture had been completely off the mark.

Rollins was a big old man—seventy at least, Streator estimated—with the broad, ruddy face and physical bulk of a farmer. With his crinkled skin and unkempt white hair, he looked like Grandpa Walton or one of those backwoods codgers in TV commercials who sit around on porch swings, rhapsodizing over the good old-fashioned taste of Country Time Lemonade. He was wearing a rumpled blue suit, wrinkled white shirt, and a blue bow tie with white polka dots. His pants were held up by red-and-blue striped clip suspenders. Looking down at him, Arby thought that bib overalls would have suited him better.

Shaking hands with Rollins, Arby thanked him for coming. "It's all yours," he said with a nod toward the room, then went and sat down between Turner and Wagner.

Plucking off his glasses and sticking them into his shirt pocket, Rollins rose slowly from his chair, cleared his throat, and began to address the group. He spoke in a folksy Midwestern drawl, hooking his thumbs through his suspenders as he warmed to his subject.

"Ladies and gentlemen," he said, "thanks for asking me here today. I hope I can be of some service. Now, it's traditional for public speakers to begin with a little joke. So let me tell you one I heard a couple years back. Maybe some of you heard it, too. It's about that fun-loving couple, the Bobbitts. You remember them—John Wayne and Lorena, America's sweethearts. Another reason I'm partial to this joke is that it features one of our own local celebrities, the late and unlamented Jeffrey Dahmer."

Turner shot Arby a sideways look, as if to say, "What the hell is *this?*"

"Here's how it goes," continued Rollins. "What did Jeff Dahmer say to Lorena Bobbitt?"

Rollins gazed slowly around the room. Everyone sat silently, eyeing him back. Finally, Tom Rowe, a husky homicide detective with an open notebook resting on his crossed knee, piped up. "We give up, Doc. What'd he say?"

Rollins waited a beat before delivering the punchline. "You going to eat that?" he said in the tone of a gluttonous diner coveting a juicy leftover on his companion's supper plate.

There was a momentary pause followed by a loud guffaw from Rowe. The other responses were distinctly more muted: a scattering of titters, a few thin smiles, one loud female groan.

"Not exactly a knee-slapper, I admit," Rollins continued. "But from the point of view of someone like me, an interesting specimen of humor—very interesting. Why? Because of the way it connects two different ideas." He held out his hands and brought them slowly together so that the splayed fingers meshed like interlocking gears. "Castration and cannibalism. A dangerous woman chopping off a man's genital member and the act of eating— of devouring.

"Now what I'm going to say may be highly distasteful to you ladies, and I apologize for that. As for you men, I imagine you'll find it frankly incredible. The weirdest damn thing you ever heard. Fact is, though, that the ideas and feelings and fantasies I'm going to discuss are common, to one degree or another, to most, if not all, of us men.

"What I'm talking about is the way we males feel threatened, repelled, or just downright scared spitless by a woman's sexual organ. Now this is something that few men are willing to talk about. Hell, most of us don't even *know* we feel it. But it's there, all right, and it comes out clearly in all kinds of places. Like jokes. Or certain bizarre beliefs. Let me give you a for-instance.

"Back when I was a soldier during World War II, before some of you folks were even born, a bunch of us were stationed in Germany after the Nazis surrendered. Now being young and full of beans, it was only natural that we'd be tempted to discharge some of our . . . ah . . . excess energy in the local sporting houses. The army, of course, did its best to discourage such pursuits by showing us some highly educational films on the dangers of VD, and let me tell you people, those damn movies were enough to kill off anyone's sex drive. Still, a few of us boys remained undaunted.

"What really put a damper on our enthusiasm was a story that began circulating through the barracks. Seems like a young GI had gone off to a bordello and returned with a most grievous injury. His penis had been split lengthwise as clean as you would slice a carrot in two with a kitchen knife. How'd it happen? Why, it was one of those treacherous little fräuleins, taking her revenge on the American army by inserting a razor blade deep inside herself, so that when the poor fellow put his penis in there—"

"Hey," called out a detective named Norm Huertig. "I remember the exact same story making the rounds in 'Nam."

Rollins nodded. "That's right. It was also popular during

World War I and in Korea, too. Hell, for all anyone knows, Alexander the Great's troops used to spread the same rumor about Persian harlots. Needless to say, there's not a shred of truth to it. It's folklore, plain and simple."

Huertig leaned back in his seat with the look of a man who has just learned a surprising fact.

"And there're lots of other examples I could give you," Rollins said. "Stories about men getting their members stuck inside women during sex like creatures caught in bear traps. Or ones about women—forgive me, ladies; I know this is offensive—women with genitals big enough to swallow men whole. I assume, by the way, that's where the newspaper catchphrase comes from— the Cavity Killings."

Arby had wondered about that. Obviously the phrase had something to do with teeth—dental cavities—but there seemed to be a double meaning that eluded him. He half raised his hand and said, "Explain, please."

"It's from an old vulgar joke about the prostitute whose vagina was so large she put Colgate toothpaste up inside herself because she heard it reduced cavities."

Out of the corner of his eye, Arby saw Janet Wagner shift uncomfortably in her seat. He couldn't blame her. He was feeling pretty discomfited himself.

"Now all these nasty jokes and stories share a common theme. It has to do with men's perception of the female genitalia as a dangerous, insatiable, devouring organ. Not a source of physical pleasure, but of physical injury. Not a loving refuge but a hungry mouth—a mouth bristling with razor-sharp teeth, like the jaws of a man-eating shark.

"There's a fancy Latin name for this fantasy. Psychologists like me refer to it as the *vagina dentata*—the 'vagina with teeth.' Throughout the whole world, you find many examples of it—myths and superstitions and stories about women armed with genitals that'll chomp off a man's penis like a snapping turtle biting a bullfrog in two."

"Excuse me, Doctor," said one of the women, a detective named Susan Malverne. "You said before this fantasy is common to most men?"

"That's right."

"Where in the world does it come from?"

"Depends on which expert you listen to," Rollins said. "Dr. Freud says it starts when a little boy gets his first glimpse of a woman's privates and thinks she's been castrated and worries that maybe she'll do the same thing to him in revenge. Other psychologists believe it comes from the sex act itself—the fears that are aroused in a man by having to insert his most precious and vulnerable body part into some dark, mysterious place where anything might happen to it. And something *does* happen to it: it goes in stiff and strong and comes out all shriveled and lifeless."

Arby glanced over at Susan Malverne, who was shaking her head slowly. There was a wry, sideways twist to her mouth, as though she were thinking, *My goodness, but men are screwed-up creatures.*

"Then there's menstruation. That's something that produces a whole lot of anxiety in men—and always has: the notion of this sexual organ that gushes blood every month, like an open wound that never heals. No matter how much our modern, scientific minds understand it as nothing but biology, there's another, much more primitive part"—Rollins reached up one hand and tapped the base of his skull, as though he were indicating an area of the brain that was still rooted in prehistory—"that views it the same way our Neanderthal forefathers did. As women's magic. Something strange and taboo and mysterious. And *scary*."

Listening to Rollins's words, Arby suddenly flashed on a long-forgotten memory. It was something that had happened years before, not long after he and Ellen had gotten married. For months—like most young newlyweds—they couldn't get enough of each other. On this particular occasion, he and Ellen were making love on a Sunday morning, when he became aware of a change inside her, a sudden surge of liquid, as though a flood-gate had opened in her body. Withdrawing, he looked down at himself and saw his penis slathered with blood. The sight caused the room to go spinning; he had to clamp his eyes shut to curb the dizziness. He knew perfectly well that the blood was hers, that the sensation he had felt was the unexpected onset of her period. Still, on another, deeper level, he'd reacted as though he'd been mutilated. The experience had been so upsetting that, from then on, they had given up lovemaking during the week of her flow.

"Let me ask you another question, Professor Rollins." It was Susan Malverne again, leaning forward in her seat. "If this is something you find in all men, how does it help us with *ours?*"

Rollins nodded slowly. "Good question. The answer is this: with your average man, the fantasy I'm talking about is just a very tiny piece of his psychological makeup. It doesn't interfere with his adult functioning any more than, say, being afraid of the dark—which is something everyone's born with—would keep a normal, well-adjusted grown-up from going out at night.

"The individual you're looking for, though—well, he's a horse of a different color. In his case, you're dealing with a mind that's totally *dominated* by this fantasy."

Arby took a quick glance around the room. The people around him were listening intently. To his left, Frank Turner leaned back in his chair, frowning deeply, his massive arms crossed over his chest. Only Norm Huertig, who seemed to be doodling on his notepad, had his gaze averted from the speaker.

"Now, there're lots of things I can't tell you," Rollins said. "I can't tell you where to find your man, what his name is, what kind of car he drives. Wish I could. But there are a few observations I do feel confident in making."

Digging a dingy-looking handkerchief out of his hip pocket, the professor blew his nose with a loud razz.

"The first thing is, you're dealing with a virgin." He

gave his nostrils a few vigorous swipes, then stuffed the balled-up hankie back into his pants. "This isn't a Ted Bundy type, someone smooth and seductive and successful with the opposite sex. This is a fellow who's afraid to say 'boo' to an attractive woman. Why? Because the thought of normal sex with a woman scares him silly.

"You folks recall that motion picture a few years back? The title escapes me—my memory's not all it used to be. It's the one where that beautiful woman uncrosses her legs and turns a whole room full of police officers into jelly?"

"Hey, my favorite movie," said a detective named Mulford to the chuckles of the men seated around him. "I gave it two thumbs-up."

"Well, the man you're looking for would've had a very different reaction," said Rollins. "Because in *his* mind, what a woman carries between her legs is something completely terrifying."

"Something like this?" Norm Huertig raised his open notepad for Rollins to see.

The professor leaned forward, squinting. "Not bad."

Arby reached out and tapped Huertig's shoulder. "Let's see what you've got there, Norm."

Huertig turned in his seat and held up his notebook. Occupying the center of the open page was a simple line drawing:

"Looks like a damn zipper," Turner muttered.

"Hey," Tom Rowe called out. "Jack the Zipper."

"What's that?" asked Rollins, cupping a hand behind one ear.

"Jack the Zipper," Rowe repeated. "Guy we're looking for."

"Very good," Rollins said with a thin smile. "That nickname makes sense in more ways than one. Zipping up his victims' sex organs is just what the killer has in mind."

Streator wondered how long it would take before some reporter got wind of Rowe's quip and the whole city was buzzing about the hunt for Jack the Zipper.

"Okay," said the professor. "So what are we dealing with here?" His cheeks ballooned out, then deflated as he opened his lips with a *pop*. "A deeply psychopathic man who is driven, over and over again, to destroy the thing he fears most. First, he snares some good-looking girl. Carries her back home. Binds her up real tight. Then, he uses some kind of pliers on her teeth, not so much because he enjoys inflicting pain—oh, I'm sure he gets some sadistic pleasure from that, all right—but torture isn't his main objective. The real point is to render her harmless—the same way you might defang a rattlesnake.

"What does he do with the teeth? My guess is he keeps them locked up somewhere, nice and safe, in some kind of special box. Maybe he likes to take them out and handle them every once in a while. That way, see, he's establishing his power over them. They're not dangerous objects anymore—he's turned them into harmless little playthings.

"Of course, he doesn't save all of them. The scariest ones, the incisors, the ones that look most like animal fangs—he inserts those into the sex organ of the poor dead girl and sews the vaginal lips up tight. Why? It's a ritual act, see. He's driven to reproduce the image of his worst nightmare. Then he kills it, vents all his hatred and frustration on it. And just for good measure—as an extra added precaution, you might say—he stitches it shut."

Pausing, Rollins took a deep breath, as though his speech had suddenly winded him. A good fifteen seconds ticked by before he started speaking again. "About sixteen, eighteen years ago, I was asked to be an expert witness in a murder case. Nasty business. Some drifter named Buxton killed an eleven-year-old schoolgirl, then mutilated her sexually with a pocket knife.

"Anyway, I spent about five, six hours interviewing the defendant in prison, asking all kinds of questions, trying to get some sense of his psychological state at the time of the killing. Finally, I asked him point-blank why in the world he committed such a dreadful crime on a poor, innocent child. I still remember his exact words. He said—forgive the language, ladies, but this is what he said—he said, 'A dead cunt can't hurt you.'"

Rollins pursed his lips in distaste. "If you asked the man you're looking for the same question, I have no doubt he'd say something very much along those lines."

There was a dead silence in the room as Rollins finished talking. Raising his bushy white eyebrows, he gazed slowly around at his listeners, a conscientious teacher checking to see if his class has any questions.

It made Arby feel like a college kid again, sitting in his Psych 101 lecture hall back at Ohio State. When Rollins looked in his direction, he stuck a finger in the air and said, "One thing's bothering me, Professor. From the evidence we've gathered, it seems that the killer's last victim, a girl named Patti Atkins, was abducted from the Mayfair Mall by a woman. Now according to everything I've ever heard, serial killers are almost always lone males. The only major exceptions are a few cases of sicko couples who like to torture young girls as part of their sexual fun and games."

"That sounds about right," Rollins said. "Go on."

"Here's my problem," Arby continued. "If the guy

we're looking for is, as you were saying, a virgin who's scared to death of the opposite sex, how do you explain a female accomplice? She couldn't be his girlfriend."

"My guess is," Rollins answered after a moment, "that she's related to him in some other capacity."

"Like what?" Arby asked, surprised. "His sister? His *mother?*"

"I know it sounds incredible," said the professor with a rueful smile, "but let me tell you, Sergeant Streator. After fifty years of studying the countless aberrations and abnormalities of the human mind, there's one thing I can state with absolute confidence."

"What's that?' asked Arby.

"Weirder things have happened," said the professor. "Weirder things have most certainly happened."

19

Streator and Turner stood on the curb outside the police administration building, waiting for the traffic light to change.

"How about we head over to that new Bennigan's on Seventh, get us a regular sit-down lunch?" Turner asked.

"Nah," Arby said distractedly. "No time. Let's just grab something at Chuckie's."

A big yellow school bus rumbled by, spewing a dense cloud of black from its rear. Turner regarded it with a sour face.

"I'm telling you, Arby, your insides gonna get as messed up as that school bus's engine, you don't start eating better."

"Yes, Mother," Arby said as the walk light beamed and they started across the street. "So what did you think of Rollins's talk?"

Turner gave a noncommittal shrug. "Made sense, I guess. Hell, you hear guys talking crap like that all the time, calling women man-eaters and whatnot. Don't see how it matters much, though."

"How do you mean?" Arby asked, raising his eyes to glance at Turner. At nearly six feet one, Arby wasn't used to looking up at people. Franklin was the only man he knew who made him feel undersized.

"What I mean is, who gives a damn *why* this psycho's like he is? All this stuff about how seeing his mama naked turned him into a killer. Let's even say it's true. How's it gonna help us bag this maggot?"

"Yeah." Arby sighed. "Guess you're right. Still, you never know."

"That's a fact," Turner conceded.

In the bright autumn sunlight, Chuckie's wagon, with its shiny white paint and garish decals of ice-cream pops and sundaes, looked like a kiddie's dream: a delivery van from Willie Wonka's factory. As Turner and Streator approached, two other customers, a white-haired old lady and a boy who looked to be her grandson, stepped away from the counter, munching on foot-long hot dogs.

"Hey, Sarge. Detective Turner." Chuckie grinned. His white chef's apron, belted around the middle, was stained with assorted condiments. "How goes it?"

"It's going," Arby said. Inside his head, a little mocking voice added: *Nowhere.*

"What'll it be?" asked Chuckie.

"Gimme one of those foot-longs, heavy on the mustard." Frank said. "Big order of fries and a Coke."

"Sarge?"

"Make it two," said Arby.

"Coming up," said Chuckie, turning toward his grill. Less than two minutes later, the food was spread out on the counter. Chuckie took the ten-dollar bill Streator proffered and rang up the sale.

"Any hot leads?" he asked eagerly, handing Arby his change.

"We did, you'd be about the last person we'd tell," Turner said through a mouthful of hot dog.

Chuckie looked wounded. "Hey, I can keep a secret."

"Right," Turner said sardonically. "How come you're so interested?"

"Chuckie's a real crime buff," Streator said. He dipped a couple of soggy fries into his little paper ketchup cup and popped them into his mouth.

"You bet," said Chuckie. "And this is a big one, boy—the biggest since you guys nabbed Jeff the Chef."

"So tell us, Chuckie," Streator said, "you being such a first-rate amateur sleuth and all. What's *your* theory?"

Chuckie looked thoughtful for a moment. "Hard to say. Some guy who's got a problem with women. And, you know, with teeth." Chuckie grinned broadly. His own teeth were surprisingly big, almost horsey. "Maybe he hates women 'cause his mom forced him to brush after every meal when he was growin' up."

Turner looked at Streator. "Sounds about like what the prof was saying."

Streator expelled a little snort and took a big swallow of Coke. Gazing absently into Chuckie's truck, he spotted something that had never caught his eye before. It was a small, dog-eared print taped to the wall above the grill. The picture was so smoke-stained that Streator had to squint hard to make out the image.

It seemed to be a portrait of a dark-haired young woman, peering soulfully skyward, a halo framing her head. She was clasping something in one upraised hand. Arby couldn't tell what it was. It looked like an oddly curved candlestick with a little flame glowing on top.

"Didn't know you were such an art lover, Chuckie," he said.

"Huh?" said Chuckie. He looked around to see what Streator was staring at. "Oh, that." He laughed a little embarrassedly. "It's just a picture I tore out of a magazine. I don't know—something about her face . . ." He left the thought unfinished.

"Who is she?" asked Turner, peering into the truck.

Chuckie shrugged. "Some kind of saint, I think."

"You a religious guy, Chuckie?" Turner asked.

"Nah. Just like the picture is all." Suddenly Chuckie leaned forward on the counter. Craning his neck, he looked around as though making sure there were no other customers within earshot. "Hey, I got a good joke," he said, his voice dropping.

Streator groaned. "Not again."

Chuckie looked so crestfallen that Streator gave a weary sigh. "All right," he said. "Go ahead."

"Okay," Chuckie said, grinning wickedly. "How do you know the Cavity Killer is a funny guy?"

Streator let a few seconds tick by. "I give up."

"He always leaves his girlfriends in stitches," Chuckie said.

Turner lowered his Coke cup from his lips and muttered, "Jesus." His mouth was puckered in distaste, as though he'd just swallowed a mouthful of brine.

"Gotta go," Streator said, his voice tight. Plucking a napkin from the dispenser, he wiped the grease from his lips and tossed his trash into the basket.

"Wanna hear another one?" Chuckie asked.

Streator shot him a hard look, pivoted on his heels, and stalked away.

Turner caught up to him in a couple of strides. "Didn't like the joke, huh?"

Streator's face was grim. "Figured I'd better get out of there before I told Chuckie what I think." He let out a long, silent whistle like a pressure cooker blowing off steam. "Imagine laughing at what happened to those girls, turning it into a big joke."

"Hard to believe, ain't it?" Turner said.

"Yeah. But I'll tell you what's worse," Arby said. "This psycho we're looking for, he's somewhere out there laughing harder than anyone. And you know what he's laughing at? Me and you and the whole damn force."

"Come on, Arby," Turner protested.

"I mean it, Frank. He's probably busting a gut, watching us running around in circles."

A minute later, they were back at headquarters. They had just stepped into the building when a dark-haired woman in a gray suit and white blouse came hurrying across the lobby.

"Sergeant Streator!" she called.

There was something familiar about her features, though it took Arby a moment to place her, even when she was standing just a few feet away. When he finally did, he had to exert tight control over his own features to keep from conveying his shock.

It was Sheila Atkins. Arby hadn't seen her since the third week of September—a few days after her daughter's murder—when he had driven out to her home for a talk. He had spent about an hour in her company, gently prying whatever information he could from the stricken woman.

In the intervening weeks, she had undergone a frightening change. Hollow-cheeked and haggard, she looked like the victim of a malignant disease, as though her grief were a fast-spreading tumor. Her dark eyes were sunk deep in their sockets.

Staring into them now, however, Arby saw that she was not as feeble as she seemed. Her body might look ravaged. But there was something in her eyes that burned with a fierce determination.

Nodding in Turner's direction, Arby said, "Franklin, this is Mrs. Atkins, Patti Atkins's mother."

Sheila put out her right hand. Turner engulfed it in his own and gave it a gentle squeeze.

Sheila looked back at Arby. "Can we talk?" Her tone was urgent.

"Sure," he said, motioning toward the elevators.

The car stopped at the fourth floor to discharge Turner. Arby and Sheila continued up to six.

On the landing just outside the elevator was a little alcove containing a metal trash bin and two brightly lit vending machines, recently installed for the convenience of the clerical workers. One machine dispensed snack foods—corn chips and cashews, candy bars and cookies. The second was stocked with cans of soft drinks.

Emerging from the elevator, Sheila spotted the soda machine. "Do you mind?" Sheila asked Arby, cocking her chin toward the alcove.

"No. Of course not."

She stepped toward the alcove, rummaging through

her handbag. "Damn," she muttered, growing increasingly frantic as she searched fruitlessly for change.

"Here," Arby said, stepping to her side. He dug three quarters from his pants pocket and fed them into the machine.

"Thanks." Sheila sighed, hitting a button. Seconds later, a Diet Pepsi can clattered down the chute.

Sheila carried it into Arby's office. He gestured toward a chair, hung his jacket on a wall hook, and seated himself behind his desk.

Sheila, however, remained standing. Reaching into her handbag again, she removed a small plastic pill holder, snapped open its lid, and spilled a couple of capsules into her palm. Then she popped them into her mouth and chased them down with a swig of cola.

Arby watched her through narrowed eyes.

"Just Tylenol, Sergeant," she said with a humorless smile, setting the soda can down on his desktop and lowering herself into the molded-plastic chair. "No tranquilizers or antidepressants. My doctor wanted to put me on Prozac. But I refused. I don't want to feel *mellow.*" She spoke the word with bitter mockery.

"What *do* you want, Mrs. Atkins?" Arby asked in the kindliest tone he could muster.

She gazed at him with the same fierce look he had noticed downstairs. "I want to help find my daughter's killer."

Arby remained silent for a moment. "I appreciate how you feel, Mrs. Atkins," he said finally, choosing his words with care.

"Do you?" she said harshly.

"I think so, yeah."

"Nobody can know how I feel," Sheila said, closing her eyes. Her voice had dropped to a near whisper, but Arby had no trouble hearing the anguish in it.

"Maybe you're right," Arby said after a pause, "but that's just the point. You're too wrapped up in this to see things clearly." He shook his head. "I know it's hard, but you're just going to have to leave this in our hands."

"Why?" Sheila said simply.

Arby was slightly taken aback. "Because we know how to get the job done," he said.

"Really?" she said. "But you haven't done it."

The remark stung all the more because of its truth. "We're making good progress, Mrs. Atkins," he lied, "but it's slow going, tracking down this kind of individual. A random serial killer who—"

"How do you know it *is* a serial killer?"

Arby's brow furrowed. "What do you mean?"

"I mean, maybe there's something *you're* not seeing. Some connection between Patti and those other poor girls. Maybe the person you're looking for was a part of all three of their lives."

"Part of their lives?" Streater mused. "Like a boyfriend or something?"

"No—not a boyfriend. Patti didn't have a boyfriend."

"Then who . . . ?"

"I don't know," Sheila cried. "That's what I've been trying to find out. Look." She dug a hand into the side compartment of her handbag and extracted a folded yellow sheet. "I've interviewed almost three dozen people in the last few weeks. I spoke to Carolyn Dearborn's mother and father, her fiancé, two of her ex-boyfriends. Everyone was so kind, so helpful. No one refused to talk to me. I spoke to everyone in Darlene Redding's family, her co-workers, even a neighbor who said she dreamed about the murderer and could describe him. But there were so many possible leads, so many people to interview. And then I thought, what if the police have already questioned these people? Here, let me show you my list." She unfolded the sheet and passed it over to Arby. "I thought we could combine our investigations—pool our resources." There was a pathetic eagerness in her voice that pierced Arby's heart.

He glanced over the list, then emitted a sigh. "Mrs.

Atkins," he said gently. "We've covered these bases. We've done this work." He paused, searching for the right words, the right tone. "Believe me, we're doing everything we can do—"

"You're doing nothing!" she shouted, balling her hands into tight fists. "It's almost two months since my child was kidnapped and murdered. Where's the madman who did it? Where *is* he?"

"We don't know that yet," Arby said softly. "But this case is our highest priority. It's only a matter of time before we catch him."

Sheila glared at Arby for a long, tense moment. Finally, she said, "So you won't let me help you?"

"I think," Arby said slowly, "that the best help you can give is simply to trust us and—"

So abruptly that Arby's heart gave a jolt, Sheila sprang from her seat. "I won't sit around doing nothing!" she screamed. "I *won't*!" With that, she spun on her heels. As she did, her big leather handbag struck the Pepsi can perched on a corner of Arby's desk, knocking it over. Arby reached out to right it, but half its contents had already gurgled onto his desktop, sopping his papers in fizzy brown fluid.

Sheila stormed out of the office, leaving Arby to clean up the mess.

20

It was nearly 2 A.M. when Stan Heckley finally got home, his mood as black as the moonless sky. The hall light outside his apartment had burned out, and by the time he managed to unlock his door, he was nearly choking with frustration. Groping a hand along the inside wall, he flipped on the switch for the overhead fixture and staggered into the living room. A copy of the latest *Hustler* was lying on the carpet by the sofa. Blinking against the light, Heckley slipped on the slick magazine and went sprawling.

"Fuck," he yelled. Beneath him, the floor seemed to lurch like the deck of a foundering ship. He kept his eyes closed until the sensation subsided, then pulled himself to his feet and made his way into his cubbyhole of a kitchen. He was dizzy, depressed, and dog-tired, but the thought of retiring to his lonely bed seemed distinctly unappealing. Starting up his coffee machine, he perched on a stool at his tiny eating counter and, while the bitter liquid tinkled into the pot, watched the evening's most rankling moments replay themselves inside his throbbing head.

It had been a lousy night from start to finish. Hoping to pitch a few story ideas, he'd arranged to meet an acquaintance named Jim Tripper, an editor at *Milwaukee Today* magazine, at a popular downtown eatery called Penny's. Stan had waited at the bar for nearly an hour, nursing a double Scotch, but the asshole never showed.

Just as Stan was getting ready to leave, a hot-looking blonde with killer legs and dynamite tits came in and perched on the stool beside him. *Shit,* leered a voice inside his head, *I'd like to tear off a piece of that!*

For the next forty-five minutes, Stan had done his best to charm the panties off her, buying her drinks, laughing at her lame attempts at wit, listening to some boring bullshit about her job. Everything seemed to be going great. He had turned in his seat so that their legs were touching, and she hadn't moved away.

Just then, however, another woman showed up—some dark-haired bitch the blonde was obviously expecting. Immediately, Blondie turned her attention to her friend. The brunette seemed unaccountably immune to Stan's charms, rolling her eyes at nearly every crack he made. After a while, the two women got up and left.

"Fucking dykes!" he shouted after them. They strolled out of the restaurant without so much as a backward glance.

Some of the other patrons, however, shot him dirty looks, and the bartender informed him, quietly but firmly, that if Stan wanted to stay, he was going to have to control himself. Stan was tempted to tell the guy to go fuck himself, but he felt a sudden, desperate need for a drink. He muttered an apology and ordered another Johnnie Walker Red.

The Scotch made him feel a little better. If someone had asked him at that moment how things were going, Stan would have shrugged and said, "Can't get any worse."

Then Charlie Fuckhead Bernstein sauntered in with his ditsy little wife on his arm.

Stan and Charlie had started out as freelancers together. Now, Bernstein had his own syndicated newspaper column while Stan was still scrabbling for story commissions from editors who felt free to stand him up at restaurants. Bernstein's wife was a knockout, too—a bubblehead, maybe, but a grade-A certified prime piece of ass.

It was all too fucking much. Draining his glass, Stan settled his tab and shouldered his way out of the restaurant, pretending he didn't even hear when Bernstein called out a friendly greeting.

Now, sitting at his tiny kitchen counter, elbows propped on the Formica, palm heels supporting his chin, Stan struggled to put the whole depressing experience out of his mind. The coffee was ready. He poured himself a mug and wandered back into his living room.

Settling himself on the sofa, he grabbed his remote control and sampled the cable channels, stopping at some grade-Z gorefest. A trio of bimbos in Frederick's of Hollywood finery were being chased around a frat house by an ax-wielding psycho in a Frankenstein mask. Sipping his coffee, Stan wondered for the millionth time how it was that such garbage could end up on screen, while his own far superior efforts had met with nothing but indifference.

Over the past year, he had tried his hand at writing screenplays, sending a sample to a New York City agent who was listed in *Writer's Digest*. The agent had answered promptly, offering to represent Stan for a small retainer of five hundred dollars. Stan had scraped together the fee but to date, all he had to show for his investment was a shitload of rejection slips.

The turn-downs had baffled him. As far as he could tell, his scripts had all the right ingredients—maniacal killers, chainsawed chicks, plenty of T and A—everything the movie-going public wanted. The truth, he suspected, was not that his work sucked. Certainly it wasn't any worse than the crap he was watching now; it was just that he lacked the right connections.

It was the same with his journalism. Here he was, a first-rate investigative reporter (that's what his business card said; "Stan Heckley, Investigative Reporter"). His nose for news was as sharp as anyone's in the business;

no one could equal him at sniffing out the putrid truth beneath the perfumed surface, and yet he couldn't even get a goddamned junior editor at *Milwaukee Fucking Today* magazine to show up for a lousy drink!

At times, he suspected that there might be something more insidious involved than not knowing the right people—some dark conspiracy that kept guys like him from succeeding while lox-eaters like Charlie Bernstein made it to the top on considerably less talent.

Take the whole infuriating business with his current venture: his projected true-crime book on Milwaukee's latest sex-killer, the one everybody had started calling Jack the Zipper (a pun that, as far as Stan could determine, had originated with someone at police headquarters and was quickly picked up by the press). Stan had been on top of that case right from the get-go. He felt sure he could produce a book every damn bit as good as *Fatal Vision* or even *In Cold Blood*—a book that would bring him everlasting fame and fortune. Sometimes, just before he dozed off at night, he could picture the whole Heckley phenomenon with a fierce, Technicolor clarity: number-one nonfiction bestseller, guest shots on *Montel* and *Oprah,* book-signing parties packed with adoring young women who clutched autographed copies of his masterpiece to their succulent breasts . . .

The problem was, he just couldn't seem to generate any interest from publishers. All the book editors he had contacted had replied in essentially the same way. Since Stan was an "unknown quantity," they were reluctant to commit themselves unless he could guarantee some kind of exclusive cooperation from the principals in the case.

Stan had done what he could to secure that cooperation, but so far he had gotten nowhere. The families of the victims wanted nothing to do with him or his book. Even though he'd approached them with tremendous tact—explaining that his only concern was to see that their children's deaths were described in the most accurate and sensitive way possible—they treated him as if he was some kind of rank opportunist, seeking to profit from their misfortune. One of them—the mother of the Atkins girl—had gotten really nasty, calling him a "goddamn filthy vulture."

And the cops were completely stonewalling him. He had hoped to establish a pipeline to the investigation through that uptight asshole Streator, but the motherfucker wouldn't even return his calls anymore.

Meanwhile, some very big names in the writing racket had started sniffing around the story. *Shit,* thought Stan. *Next thing you know, that bastard Novak'll be doing a book on the case.*

Abruptly, Stan bolted upright on the sofa, mouth agape. *Oh, Christ. So* that's *why Novak's coming here! All that bullshit about lecturing at Madison. I betya anything he's really gonna be researching his next book—on Jack the Zipper!*

The thought brought a hot flush of anger to Stan's face. Just a week ago, he had received a three-sentence note from Paul, thanking Stan for his kind words about *Slaughterhouse* but informing him, with sincerest regrets, that they wouldn't be able to meet. Stan had really gotten his hopes up, too. He had the whole thing planned in his head—how he'd butter up Paul, tell him what a masterpiece *Slaughterhouse* was and how much Stan had learned about "the art of true-crime writing" from reading it. Then, after shoveling on the crap, he'd kind of suggest, very subtly and offhandedly, that maybe Paul could help put him in touch with some publishing connections in New York.

Instead, all Stan had gotten was the big brush-off—some phony bullshit about how busy Novak was going to be during his brief stay in Wisconsin, blah blah blah.

Arrogant son of a bitch, Stan thought, knocking back the last of his now-tepid coffee.

A sudden shriek from the TV screen diverted his attention. The mask-wearing psycho had bagged one of the bimbos and bound her to a chair. Stan's mind, dulled from drink and fatigue, suddenly felt very alert. He sat forward on the sofa. He knew what was coming.

Slowly, the psycho raised his gleaming weapon. The film cut to a tight close-up of the screaming bimbo, then back to the falling blade, then back to the bimbo just as the ax struck her squarely on the face, bisecting the bridge of her nose. Her eyeballs ruptured, squirting gooey fluid down her cheeks, while a geyser of blood, bone, and brain matter erupted from her cloven skull.

Nice effects, thought Stan with a grunt of admiration.

A sudden spasm deep in his bowels caused him to shift uneasily on the sofa cushion. Belching loudly, he heaved himself to his feet and made his way into the bathroom.

Switching on the light, he winced at the sight that assaulted him. He wasn't the most fastidious housekeeper in the world—hell, what bachelor was? Still, even by his own negligent standards, the john was an unholy mess.

A pair of his soiled undershorts lay crumpled in a corner, a fetid bath towel hung over the shower rod, the rattan wastebasket overflowed with used tissues. The floor was grimy, the bathtub was ringed with mold, the sink was sprinkled with whisker clippings. As for the toilet bowl, even Stan had trouble looking inside it.

Ah well, he thought, consoling himself as he undid his belt. *Guess it's just as well that blond cunt didn't succumb to my charms.* Stan pictured her coming back to his place and excusing herself to use the john. He didn't know the antonym for *aphrodisiac,* but whatever it was, his bathroom embodied it.

Dropping his pants and Jockey shorts, he lowered himself onto the toilet seat. On the floor at the base of the fixture lay his copy of *Slaughterhouse.*

Just the right place for that piece of shit. Stan sneered. In spite of the flattery he had laid on in his letter to Novak, the truth was that Stan hated everything about the book. Part of his aversion was simple jealousy—hey, he was a big enough man to admit something like that.

But there was another factor, too. Novak's temerity infuriated Stan. *Imagine that outsider coming here and writing that book! What the fuck did an* Easterner *know about Eddie Gein?*

Like many Wisconsinites, Stan took a certain perverse pride in Gein, having grown up hearing all kinds of legends about the Mad Butcher of Plainfield, the state's most notorious native son. Even now, Stan could recite verses from a poem he had memorized back in grade school—a takeoff on "A Visit from Saint Nicholas":

'Twas the night before Christmas, when all through
   the shed,
All the creatures were stirring, even old Ed.

The bodies were hung from the rafters above,
While Eddie was searching for another new love.

He sprang to his truck, to the graveyard he flew;
The hours were short and much work must he do.

He looked for the grave where the fattest one laid,
And started in digging with shovel and spade.

He shoveled and shoveled and shoveled some
   more,
'Til finally he reached the old coffin door.

He took out a crowbar and pried open the box;
He was not only clever but sly as a fox.

As he picked up the body and cut off the head,
He could tell by the smell that the old girl was
   dead.

He filled in the grave by the moonlight above—
And once more old Ed had found a new love.

Shit, Gein was the grandfather of gore. Every psycho from Norman Bates to the mask-wearing maniac who had just butchered the bimbo on TV sprang directly from old Eddie. He was a bona fide phenomenon, Wisconsin's contribution to twentieth-century American culture. And here was this nervy son of a bitch from *New York* coming out here and co-opting him!

Reaching down for Novak's book, Stan opened it on his lap and began riffling through the pages. He had forced himself to read it through several times, trying to figure out the secret of its success. The margins were full of Stan's hand-written annotations: "This sucks." "Dumbass sentence." "Bullshit!"

Flipping a page, he came across a passage heavily underscored in pen. In the margin, he had inscribed a big exclamation point and question mark. Stan squinted down at the passage. *Oh, yeah. That stuff about Ed's having a girlfriend, the one he supposedly got pregn—*

The brainstorm hit so suddenly that Stan's head gave a little jolt, as if lightning had literally crackled in his skull. "Holy shit," he whispered aloud. "What an amazing fucking idea."

Why hadn't he thought of it before? Probably because he had just dismissed the story as one of the countless crazy rumors the Gein case had generated. But what if it was *true?* What if Eddie really had produced a child—if some unholy offshoot of the Plainfield ghoul was living in secret, somewhere in Wisconsin?

Stan did a quick mental calculation. Assuming that the rumor had a basis, Eddie's girlfriend would have given birth around 1956. Stan tried to picture the possibilities: a forty-year-old female version of Gein, or (even better) an exact, middle-aged male replica. Eddie Gein, Jr. A freakish chip off the old, very warped block.

In that instant, as he hunkered on the bowl, Stan Heckley came to a momentous decision. He would put everything aside and commit all his energy and investigative know-how to a single goal. He would track down and expose Eddie Gein's secret love-child. Assuming Stan succeeded—and he felt sure that he would if Gein's bastard existed—his fortune would be made!

He imagined the sensation his story would create in Wisconsin. Every paper in the state—and probably beyond—would splash the story on page one. Given Eddie's reputation as the man who inspired *Psycho,* Stan's discovery might even get nationwide coverage—maybe even a story in *People!*

With his own reputation thus established, Stan was sure he'd have no trouble selling publishers on his Jack the Zipper project. Hell, he'd probably even nail down a movie deal. He'd be able to write his own ticket!

And to top it all off—the frosting on the cake—Stan would get to show up that arrogant asshole Novak, the big hotshot crime writer who hadn't been able to do what Heckley would—prove that Ed Gein really had fathered a child.

The fantasy made Stan laugh aloud. *Yeah!* He'd have it all; money, respect, as much pussy as he could handle. Reaching for the toilet paper, he thought of all the women who'd be after him once he hit it big.

Shit—he'd have to beat 'em off with a stick.

21

A fat, salty sweat drop trickled into Paul's eye, making him blink. He pulled out his hankie and dabbed at his brow. *Damn klieg lights,* he thought. He'd forgotten how hot they were.

"Looks like your opponent's starting to sweat a little, Reverend," said Lionel Lemmick. Standing in front of the audience section, cordless mike in hand, he shot Paul a big, friendly wink, as if to say, "All in good fun, old buddy." It was a classic Lemmick ploy—sucking up to both guests while sicking them on each other. If Paul weren't so pissed, he might have been amused.

"No doubt," intoned the Reverend Victor Hobart. He and Paul were seated onstage in matching chrome-and-leather chairs. "But it's not me that's making him sweat. He's feeling the heat of his own guilty conscience."

Paul felt his face flush—and not from the kliegs. "I don't need you to tell me what I'm feeling," he said, his voice tight with anger. "It'd be nice if I could get a word in edgewise, though."

There was a scattering of applause, and Paul felt a surge of gratitude for the sound. At least he had a few supporters in the house. But most of the audience seemed taken aback. They let out a sharp, reproachful noise, like a collective tongue-cluck of disapproval.

For the tenth time in as many minutes, Paul realized that he should have listened to Wylie. Agreeing to this so-called debate was one of the dumbest mistakes of his life.

Part of the problem was simply Hobart's demeanor. Paul had been expecting a wild-eyed Bible-thumper who would come across as a dangerous crank. But Hobart was a man to be reckoned with. Still powerfully built at seventy-two, he exuded a palpable air of authority. His voice was deep and arresting: he commanded attention every time he opened his mouth. For all his folksy mannerisms, he was an imposing figure, an old-fashioned man of the cloth, radiating quiet assurance and fatherly strength.

There was something else about Hobart that made him compelling: he seemed as wholesomely American as cornbread at Thanksgiving. This Norman Rockwell quality was partly a function of his homespun style and partly a matter of looks. With his craggy, weatherworn features, he resembled an early pioneer, a rough-hewn product of the country's heartland.

Paul found himself in a hopeless position—not only pitting *Slaughterhouse* against Scripture but debating a man who looked like a direct descendant of Abe Lincoln.

Not that Paul had done much debating so far. On top of everything else, Hobart was a natural showman who had managed to steal the spotlight even from such a master huckster as Lemmick. For the past five minutes, Paul had been relegated to the sidelines while Hobart held forth on his favorite bugaboo—violence in the media and its devastating effects on American society.

It was clearly a message that much of the audience wanted to hear. The reverend's jeremiad was regularly interrupted by wild bursts of applause. Paul was starting to feel like an interloper at a tent meeting. He wouldn't have been surprised to hear a few cries of "Amen, brother!" coming from the gallery.

Well, he had a few words of his own to say on the subject, and he was determined to speak his mind, come hell or high water, as the reverend himself would undoubtedly say.

"Let me ask you something, Reverend," said Paul. "Since you have such sincere convictions about how immoral the media is, why'd you agree to appear on this show? I mean"——Paul reached into his shirt pocket and plucked out a folded piece of newsprint——"I happened to come across this article a few weeks ago." This was not gospel truth. The clipping had actually come from his agent, Keith Norris, who had tried to provide Paul with as much ammo as possible for his showdown with Hobart.

"It's headlined 'Televangelist Takes Aim at Media Violence,'" said Paul, raising the news clipping high in the air like a prosecutor displaying a particularly damning piece of evidence to a jury. "I'd like to quote just a couple of sentences."

Locating a short paragraph halfway down the column——underscored in red ink by Keith——Paul began to read: " 'It's not just our air that's polluted, but our air-*waves*, too,' says the reverend. 'Turn on your television anytime, even in the middle of the day when the little ones are home from school, settled down in front of the TV set with their afternoon milk and cookies. Your senses will literally be assaulted with the foul fumes reeking from garbage like *The Lionel Lemmick Show.*' "

Even before he finished reading, Paul could hear rumblings of shock from the gallery. When he looked up, he was gratified to see half the audience glaring at Hobart. Clearly, their sympathies for the reverend's cause had its well-defined limits. After all, it was one thing for Hobart to denounce——as he'd done only minutes before—— the media for "wallowing in the most shameless orgies of sex and violence since the days of pagan idolatry." But it was something else entirely when he began bad-mouthing their own personal idol, Lionel Lemmick.

Paul refolded the clipping and tucked it back inside his breast pocket, feeling like a player who has just scored his first face-saving points in a contest that was shaping up to be a shutout.

Hobart, however, seemed completely unfazed. Nodding slowly, as though to acknowledge the gravity of the matter, he gazed directly at the audience and said, "I confess that those harsh words did express my views at one time. But after receiving an invite to appear on this program, I thought I'd better take a closer look-see before I made up my mind. And what I saw made me realize I had done Lionel here an injustice. Not that there weren't a few subjects that I found a mite distasteful."

No shit? Paul thought. *You mean you don't appreciate the educational value of that show on transsexual weddings?* Paul had been catching up on some recent *Lemmick* shows himself, in preparation for his appearance.

"But I arrived at the opinion," continued Hobart, "that Lionel is performing an invaluable public service, letting viewers see with their own eyes just how far off course our great country has drifted, demonstrating each and every afternoon that, with no moral compass to guide us, we are headed for the shoals of disaster.

"For my money," Hobart concluded, poking a finger at the floor, "there isn't a more important program on national TV than this one right here."

At this tribute to their idol, the audience exploded into a clamorous ovation. Lionel, wearing an "aw, shucks" expression, patted the air with one hand, as though to protest such undeserved adulation.

Paul had to hand it to Hobart. The man knew how to work a crowd.

A line of doggerel suddenly popped into Paul's head: *He was not only clever but sly as a fox.* He couldn't remember where he'd heard it. He had the teasing sense that it was part of a nursery rhyme or a nonsense poem of some sort, but beyond that, he couldn't say. Whatever its source, it summed up his feelings about Hobart.

"Thank you, Reverend Hobart," Lionel said humbly. "That means a lot to me, coming from someone like you."

A snatch of melody—the opening strain of *The Lionel Lemmick Show* theme music—drifted through the studio, signaling a station break.

"We'll be back in a minute, folks," Lemmick said into the camera. "Don't go away."

Occupying the stage between Paul's chair and Hobart's was a little round table holding a water pitcher, two glasses, and a pair of books: Paul's copy of *Slaughterhouse* and Hobart's leather-bound Bible. As the audience relaxed and Lemmick got a quick touch-up from the makeup woman, Hobart—without so much as glancing over at Paul—reached for his Bible and began to read. He couldn't have made it through more than a verse or two before a freshly powdered Lemmick appeared in front of him.

"Great job, Reverend. Looks like the audience is behind you one hundred percent."

"The truth is a powerful persuader, Lionel."

Paul felt an urgent need of some ice water—not to quench his thirst but to cool his anger. He couldn't have said which he found more outrageous—Hobart's sanctimony or Lemmick's smarminess.

Reaching for his water glass, Paul raised it to his mouth. He was still in midsip when Lemmick stepped to his side, bent to his ear, and whispered, "Hey, Novak, what the hell are you waiting for? When are you gonna stick it to this self-righteous asshole?"

Paul was so startled he nearly spat out his water. He was still trying to gather his wits when the theme music started again. Lemmick hurried back to his place at the front of the audience, grabbed his mike from an assistant, and welcomed the viewers back to the show.

"For those of you at home just joining us," he said. "Our topic today is 'Can books kill?' Our guests: Mr. Paul Novak, author of the bestselling true-crime book, *Slaughterhouse,* and the Reverend Victor Hobart of Plainfield, Wisconsin, who is leading a campaign—"

"*Crusade,*" said Hobart, interrupting.

"I stand corrected," Lemmick said. "A *crusade* against violence in the media. And in particular against *Slaughterhouse,* which, of course, deals with the notorious psycho Ed Gein, who came from Reverend Hobart's hometown.

"Paul," he said, "let me put it to you directly: in your opinion, is there any validity to today's question? *Can* books kill?"

Paul was prepared for this question—Keith's clipping wasn't the only card he had up his sleeve. Leaning back in his chair, he crossed a leg, folded his hands in his lap, and said, "Definitely."

The answer, as Paul had intended, caught everyone off guard. Lemmick raised his eyebrows in surprise, while Hobart frowned suspiciously, as though Paul was trying to pull a fast one.

"Let me give you an example," Paul said. "Back in the late 1920s, there was an infamous child-murderer named Albert Fish."

"Sure," said Lemmick. "We had a guest on the show who wrote a book about him. He chopped up some little girl and ate her. Fish, that is—not our guest."

The audience gave a nervous guffaw.

"Right," said Paul. "Abducted a twelve-year-old girl. Took her to a remote cottage, strangled her, butchered her body. Wrapped a chunk of her flesh in some newspaper, carried it home, and made it into a stew."

Some of the audience members gasped; others shifted audibly in their seats. Paul turned his eyes away from Lemmick and glanced at the faces in the first few rows. Their expressions were perfectly poised between fascination and revulsion—the look of spectators at a ghastly car wreck who cannot resist a peek at the sickening sight.

"Now, in Fish's case," Paul said, "there's no doubt that he was inspired by a book. Know which one?"

"Not *The Joy of Cooking,* I assume," Lemmick said.

"Not quite," said Paul. Turning in his chair, he extended a hand in Hobart's direction and said, "Reverend, may I?"

When Hobart realized that he was being asked for his Bible, his fingers clutched reflexively at the book, as though Paul had tried to snatch it from his lap. A few seconds ticked by before he grudgingly offered it up, holding it out over the interposing table.

"Thank you," said Paul. Setting the Bible on his lap, he opened it to the middle and flipped to the place he was looking for.

"Fish was a religious maniac," Paul said, glancing up again at the audience. "Had whole passages of Scripture committed to memory. This was one of his favorites. It's from the book of Jeremiah, chapter 19. The Lord is describing his vengeance on those who have forsaken him."

Gazing down at the open page, Paul read: " 'Behold, the days come that this place shall no more be called Tophet but the Valley of Slaughter. And I will cause them to fall by the sword before their enemies, and by the hands of them that seek their lives. And their carcasses will I give to be meat for the fowls of the heaven, and for the beasts of the earth. And I will cause them to eat the flesh of their sons and the flesh of their daughters, and they shall eat every one the flesh of his friend in the siege and straitness.' "

Paul shut the book and looked at the audience. "Fish claimed he was only listening to God's words when he cannibalized that little girl. 'And I will cause them to eat the flesh of their daughters.' "

In the momentary hush that ensued, Paul handed the book back to Hobart with a small, acknowledging nod. Taut-faced, the reverend grabbed it from his hand.

"Are you suggesting," he said with a slight, indignant quiver in his voice, "that the Good Book is a source of evil?"

"I'm saying," Paul answered, "that when it comes to psychopaths, *anything* can set them off. You can't blame the actions of a madman on a book. Or a movie. Or rock music. Hell, Charles Manson ordered his followers to go on a killing spree after listening to a Beatles song."

" 'Helter Skelter,' " said Lemmick.

"I admit I'm no expert on rock-and-roll singing," Hobart said. "Far as feel-good music goes, a few verses of 'Amazing Grace' will do just dandy for me. But I'd wager there's nothing the Beatles nor Elvis nor any of their kind ever wrote that'd match the immorality and horror that abound in what *you* wrote, Mr. Novak."

"But that horror you're talking about was *true*," said Paul. "It really happened. In *your* hometown, Reverend."

Hobart swiveled to face Paul. "You're right. It *is* my hometown. And I don't see why our good, God-fearing community should put up with the slanders of outsiders like you, someone interested in only one thing—filling your pockets with ill-gotten silver by appealing to the public's lowest nature."

"The only slander I'm hearing right now is coming from you, Reverend," Paul said evenly.

Hobart ignored him. "You know that every single weekend," he said, "there are dozens upon dozens of tourists traipsing through our village? Wanting to see where that Gein creature lived? To visit his unholy resting place? And all on account of you?"

"I'm not responsible for the public's behavior."

"You don't seem to take responsibility for anything," Hobart snorted.

Paul glared at Hobart. "I'll tell you what I'm responsible for. One thing only: discovering the truth, digging up the facts. That's what writers do."

"Digging is right," Hobert sneered. "Like digging manure."

Like a boxing ref breaking up a clinch, Lemmick cut in. "But Reverend Hobart, don't you think there may be some value in trying to understand a sick mind like Gein's?"

"Can evil of that magnitude ever be truly understood,

Lionel? Can any ordinary mortal ever comprehend such satanic cunning?''

Hearing the word *cunning*, Paul felt something click in his head. Suddenly, he remembered where that line of doggerel came from—a crude little poem about Gein that Paul had heard in Wisconsin, a parody of 'A Visit from Saint Nicholas.' *He took out a crowbar and pried open the box. He was not only clever but sly as a fox.*

"Let me ask you something," Paul said to Hobart. "You knew Gein, right?"

Hobart frowned deeply. He was silent for a moment, as though debating how to reply. Finally, he said, "No one *knew* him. He was a man of dark secrets. But yes, I was familiar with the man. That was many years ago, of course. A good half-century."

"And isn't it true that when I was out there doing my research—"

"Snooping's more like it," Hobart interjected.

Paul decided not to be provoked. "When I was out in Plainfield, trying to learn as much about Gein as possible, I asked you for an interview. But you refused. Isn't that right?"

"You bet," Hobert said. "Didn't want anything to do with you." He gave his head a regretful little shake. "Too bad there were some in our town who felt different, folks who'd sooner see their names printed in a book than bother about the welfare of their neighbors."

"But don't you see how inconsistent you're being?" Paul asked. "You talk about Gein's 'dark secrets.' That's exactly the point. Evil like that *needs* darkness to flourish. It can't exist in the daylight. It's like Dracula—shine a few sunbeams on him and he dissolves. All I did was try to shed a little light on those dark places. But you wouldn't have any part of it. Why?"

Hobart looked squarely at Paul, his gray eyes so full of ill will that Paul was momentarily taken aback. He knew that Hobart was his adversary, but he was unprepared for such intense hatred from a man who professed the gospel of peace.

"Since you're such a big one for the Bible," Hobart said with a sneer, "let me throw some Scripture back at you. 'A talebearer revealeth secrets. But he that is of a faithful spirit concealeth the matter.' Proverbs 11:13. That answer your question, Mr. Novak?"

Paul looked puzzled. "Are you saying . . . ?

He never finished the question. "What I am saying," Hobert snapped, "is that books like yours are tools of darkness. You claim to be rooting out evil, but that's a lie and you know it. You're *cultivating* it—fertilizing it—tending it like a garden of vile weeds that's overrunning our glorious civilization, choking out all that's good and healthy and beautiful. . . ."

Before Paul knew it, Hobart was on a roll again, sermonizing up a storm, evoking another chorus of cheers from the audience.

But Paul was barely listening. He was still brooding over the proverb Hobart had quoted. "He that is of a faithful spirit concealeth the matter." There was only one way he could make sense of it. He finally understood what lay behind Hobart's bitterness—his fury at Paul for "snooping" into the secrets of Plainfield.

Up until a minute ago, Paul had been convinced that, in researching his book, he had managed to uncover every significant fact about Ed Gein's grotesque life. But now, a new conviction overcame him. He was sure that there was at least one more dark mystery to be solved.

And the Reverend Victor Hobart knew what it was.

22

The instant the program ended, Hobert rose to his feet and unclipped his lapel mike. He was desperately eager to leave. Heading straight to the green room, he grabbed his hat and coat from the metal tree and made for the elevators, without even bothering to scrub off his makeup.

He knew he should have taken a moment to shake hands with Novak. Simple good sportsmanship demanded it. His religion demanded it, too. To be sure, he couldn't bring himself to *love* his enemy. But he always tried his best to show Christian compassion. To hold out a hand to a sinner like Novak would have been the right thing to do.

By a bitter twist, however, it was he, Hobart, who felt like the sinner—the one in sore need of forgiveness. All through the latter part of the show, he could sense his opponent's searching gaze upon him, as though Novak were peering into the innermost recesses of the reverend's troubled soul.

It was a particularly galling irony, as far as Hobart was concerned. He should have been savoring this victory. He had won the debate hands down. The ovation he'd received as he hurried from the studio proved that plainly enough.

But instead of basking in his triumph, he was running—no, *slinking*—away, fleeing to the solitude of his hotel room, where he could fall on his knees and implore God for strength.

He had accused Novak of suffering from a stricken conscience, but Hobart could no longer hide from the truth. *He* was the one harboring a guilty secret. And now, after so many years, it was beginning to devour him from within, like a cancer that comes raging to life after decades of remission.

The elevator seemed stalled on seven. Hobart poked the button impatiently, then glanced around for a stairwell. As he did, the studio door swung open and Lionel Lemmick emerged, trailed by a retinue of female assistants, each with the flawless looks of a cover girl.

"Hey, Reverend," Lemmick called, "what's your hurry?"

As Hobart murmured something about a pressing appointment, Lemmick clapped him on the shoulder and began enthusing about the show. "You're a charismatic guy, Reverend," he said, "like me."

Hobart was so taken aback at being likened to Lemmick that his mouth actually fell open. Lionel, however, seemed not to notice. He kept prattling away, proposing that Hobart appear on an upcoming show. "It's about Christian gays who've come into conflict with the church because of its intolerance for the homosexual lifestyle," Lemmick explained. "We've got some fascinating guests lined up. A minister who was defrocked because he condoned same-sex weddings. A former nun who's become the founder of a lesbian church. A transvestite preacher who calls himself Father Mary."

Hobart stood there wordlessly, trying to figure out a civil way to refuse. Though he'd been happy to use *The Lionel Lemmick Show* as a soapbox, he had no intention of ever being part of it again. In spite of what he'd said during the program, he regarded Lemmick as a clown. Still, he saw no reason to be rude to the man.

Just then, he heard the elevator *ping* behind him. *Saved by the bell,* he thought.

"I'll sleep on it, Lionel," he said, stepping into the empty car and reaching for the "lobby" button.

Lemmick was still pitching his program on Christian homosexuals. For an instant, Hobart thought that Lionel might actually stick his foot in the door to keep it from closing, like a traveling salesman who won't take no for an answer. But that didn't happen.

"Great," Lionel said, beaming. "We could use a real straight-arrow like yourself to balance the program. My people will—" The sliding metal door chopped off the end of his sentence.

Downstairs in the lobby, a dark-skinned guard in gray slacks and a blue blazer offered to hail Hobart a cab. Hobart declined. Sightseeing the day before, he had taken a taxi to the World Trade Center. The fare had left him shaking his head in wonderment. Even with his per diem, a cab seemed like a crazy indulgence. He could walk to his hotel in ten minutes.

Shrugging on his overcoat, he pushed through the revolving door, then paused on the teeming street.

At a few minutes after five on that wintry Thursday, night had already arrived. The sky—or what little of it was visible above the soaring towers of midtown—was solidly black. Hobart had been cooped up inside one building or another for nearly twenty-four hours, and he was starving for air. That was another reason he wanted to walk—to breathe some air. Not *fresh* air, of course. To Hobart's countrified nose, there was a charred, noxious smell to the city's atmosphere, as though it were suffused with incinerator ash. But at least he was outdoors. To a lifelong resident of the Wisconsin hinterlands, the cold, blustery night was a tonic.

He had just reached the corner, however, when he began thinking that he'd made a mistake. In the darkness, the city seemed far more unsettling than it had in the daytime. Not that Hobart felt physically menaced. As far as he could tell, the biggest danger came from the countless pedestrians rushing down the street with their heads bowed against the wind. One burly fellow bumped into him so hard that Hobart was almost knocked off his feet. On the whole, however, New York seemed far safer than he'd expected.

But in the nighttime, the sheer turbulence of the city— the blaring horns, swirling lights, swarming bodies— made him profoundly uneasy. He felt trapped in the midst of chaos. It was as though the surrounding world had assumed the aspect of his own inner confusion. For the first time in his life, he felt like a lost man.

He decided to go ahead and hail a cab, but every vehicle in the endless yellow stream that flowed past him was occupied. Perhaps he should make his way back to the network building and ask the guard for help after all.

Suddenly, he felt a sharp tug on his coat sleeve. Someone spoke his name. He turned to see a woman at his side.

She was wearing a gray wool coat and a matching ski hat pulled low on her brow. Hobart couldn't tell her age. The eyes that gazed up at him had a youthful intensity. But her face was sunken and lined. She might have been in her sixties. Or she could have been considerably younger: a middle-aged woman, perhaps in her forties, made prematurely old by hardship or disease.

"Reverend Hobart," she said breathlessly. "I'm so glad I caught up with you. You slipped away so quickly. I didn't know where you'd gone."

"Did you come from the studio?" he asked. He assumed she was one of his admirers, seeking a private word of counsel or possibly (it had happened on several occasions before) his autograph.

"I was in the audience," she said, nodding. "But I've come even farther than that. All the way from Wisconsin." She extended her gloved right hand. "I'm Sheila Atkins."

It was clear from her tone that she expected him to recognize her name. But it meant nothing to Hobart.

"Patti Atkins's mother," she explained, her voice trembling slightly. "My daughter was killed by the monster."

* * *

They were sitting in the coffee shop adjoining the lobby of Hobart's hotel. Sheila had managed to flag down a cab. In the crawl of the rush-hour traffic, the twenty-block ride took nearly ten minutes—time enough for Hobart to discover that, compared to Mrs. Atkins's sentiments, his own outrage over Paul Novak's book was positively mild.

Three weeks earlier, Sheila had spotted a squib on the TV page of the *Milwaukee Journal* about Hobart's scheduled debate with Novak. By the next afternoon, she had express-mailed a ticket request to *The Lionel Lemmick Show,* made a flight reservation to New York City, and booked a midtown hotel room.

She knew that Lemmick devoted the last ten or fifteen minutes of his program to audience questions. Her intention was to condemn *Slaughterhouse* before all of America, to stand up and testify, as the mother of a horribly murdered daughter, that Paul Novak's book was directly to blame for her child's death.

Ironically, if inadvertently, it was the reverend who ruined her plan. He had proved to be such a crowd-pleaser that Lemmick had been loath to cut him off. Then Novak had angrily insisted on having his say, launching into a lengthy spiel on the "social benefits" that stories of horror and bloodshed provide by giving people a way to discharge their "uncivilized impulses." Needless to say, Sheila regarded this argument as a bunch of self-serving bullshit.

By the time Novak finished speaking, the show had nearly run its course. Lemmick had been able to call on only one audience member. Sheila had done her best to attract his attention. But Lemmick, who was standing on the opposite side of the gallery, ignored her frantic waves.

Bitterly disappointed. Sheila had resolved to accost Novak after the show and let him know exactly what she thought of him and his vile book. Berating him in private was a poor second to the public denunciation she had planned. But at least it would offer her the satisfaction of venting her feelings, of spitting figuratively in Novak's face.

Before she had a chance to descend from her twentieth-row seat, however, Novak had already disappeared backstage. She attempted to follow, but a studio employee, posted by the door, blocked her way. She had argued vehemently with the young man, trying to make him understand how urgent it was that she speak to Novak. But the young man just kept shaking his head and saying, "Sorry. No unauthorized personnel backstage."

Swallowing her fury and frustration, Sheila had turned on her heels. Through the porthole of the swinging studio door, she had caught a glimpse of Reverend Hobart stepping onto an elevator. She needed desperately to talk to him. She made for the main exit, hurrying to catch up.

Now, as they sat across from each other in a little booth, nursing mugs of hot chocolate, she was addressing him in fervent tones.

"It's true I don't belong to your church, Reverend. I'm a practicing Catholic."

"We are all His children, Mrs. Atkins," he said softly.

"Yes. And I want to help you accomplish His work."

Hobart stared into his half-empty mug for a moment. "But our faith demands forgiveness, not vengeance."

Sheila looked surprised. She had expected Hobart to greet her offer enthusiastically, but the reverend seemed beset by qualms. He appeared troubled, uneasy. Sheila couldn't tell why.

"You're right, of course," she said, trying with only partial success to keep the bitterness out of her voice. "I'd love to see Paul Novak in pain—the kind of pain I suffer every day of my life because of—" She shut her eyes and clamped her lips, as though struggling to assert self-control. When she spoke again, her voice was a raw whisper. "I fight against it. I know it's un-Christian."

Hobart nodded. "We must strive to put hatred from our hearts," he said softly, speaking as much to himself as to Sheila. " 'And forgive us our trespasses, as we forgive those who trespass against us.' "

Sheila looked at him questioningly. She was having trouble making sense of his responses. Onstage, he had seemed so forceful and confident. Now, he appeared vaguely unfocused, as though only half paying attention to her.

"My personal feelings are secondary, Reverend," Sheila said, leaning forward on her arms. "The important thing is your mission. I want to help, to work alongside you. Think of how effective I can be—someone who knows from firsthand experience the truth of what you're saying, who can stand up and be a living witness to the terrible destruction caused by people like Novak. I can be a very powerful weapon in your crusade."

"Weapon?" Hobart asked pointedly, as if to say, "See, it *is* a matter of personal vengeance for you."

"Tool, then," she replied hastily. "I have administrative experience, too. I can help you expand your movement. Start a newsletter. Generate nationwide support. Create a real organization."

"I've certainly dreamed of such things," he said.

She reached across the Formica table and laid her hand on his forearm. "Then let me help make the dream real!"

The reverend stared into his mug. He seemed to be searching for guidance, as though hot cocoa had replaced tea leaves as a medium of divination.

As his silence stretched on, Sheila found it impossible to contain herself. "Don't make me beg you for this, Reverend Hobart," she urged. "I begged the Milwaukee police to let me help them, and they told me to shut up and go home. Don't *you* turn me down."

Finally, the reverend looked up at her. "All right, Mrs. Atkins," he said in a relenting tone. "I'll see what I can do. Come visit me in Plainfield at the end of next week."

Sheila exhaled a long sigh of relief. "Thank you, Reverend Hobart," she whispered. Reaching for her purse, she unsnapped the latch and fished out her wallet.

"No, no," Hobart said quickly. "I'll get it. My way's being paid."

Sliding out of the booth, Sheila reached down for her coat. "I'll let you get some rest. I'm sure you can use some after the excitement of the last few days."

"Yes," he said with a grim smile. "Peace and quiet have been in short supply. Can I help you get a taxicab?"

"I'll be fine," Sheila said, slipping into her overcoat and pulling on her wool cap. "Next week, then."

Hobart raised his right hand in good-bye. Sheila noticed that his fingers were trembling. *Poor man,* she thought. *He must really be exhausted.*

She turned and headed for the lobby.

He was still feeling shaky when he rode the elevator up to his room. His hands were quivering so badly he had trouble fitting the plastic key-card into its slot. It took him nearly a full half-minute to open his door.

Dropping his hat and coat onto the bed, he crossed to the bathroom, making his way to the sink. He splashed some cold water on his face, then checked himself in the mirror. In the flat, fluorescent glare, his skin looked dead-white and clammy.

His encounter with Sheila Atkins had been a trial from start to finish. He'd been dumbstruck with shock when she first materialized beside him on the street. Coming straight on the heels of his confrontation with Novak, her sudden appearance seemed like a message from God—a divine rebuke, as though the good Lord were reaching down a finger, poking Hobart hard in the chest, and saying, "Did you think you could conceal your sins forever?"

Every second he'd spent in her company—first in the taxicab, then in the coffee shop—was an agony for him.

Listening to her pour out her poisonous hatred of Novak was especially painful. Hobart could barely look her in the face. His guilt was too overwhelming.

After all, Novak wasn't really to blame for the Milwaukee horrors.

Hobart was.

If it weren't for him, Sheila Atkins's daughter—and two other innocent young women—would still be alive.

He dried his damp hands on a towel, then replaced it on the rack. If the nubby white fabric had been stained brownish red, he wouldn't have been surprised. He felt like a man with innocent blood on his hands.

Shuffling from the bathroom, he turned off the overhead light and then stretched out, fully clothed, on the mattress. He hadn't bothered to close the drapes. Seeping through the uncurtained window, the night lights of the city gave the room a spectral glow.

Hobert saw nothing. Staring sightlessly upward, he felt moisture leaking from his eyes and spilling down his cheeks. It was a sensation he hadn't experienced in so long—not since his mother's funeral, nearly forty years earlier—that it took him a moment to realize he was weeping.

How had he caused so much evil and suffering? He had only been trying to do the right thing, to protect one of his flock, a devout young woman he had known since her childhood, to spare his hometown further notoriety at a time when the prying eyes of the entire country seemed riveted on Plainfield.

Good intentions, he thought bitterly. *The paving stones of hell.*

He still recalled every detail of that night in the winter of '57 when he had been awakened from an untroubled sleep by the insistent buzzing of his doorbell. Throwing on his bathrobe, he had hurried downstairs, assuming that he was being summoned to a deathbed. That was usually the reason people roused him in the middle of the night—though, as he reached for the cut-glass knob, he couldn't think of anyone who was mortally ill at that moment.

Yanking open the door, he was startled to discover a young woman shivering outside in the cold. He knew her very well; her family had lived in town for generations. Her name was Agatha Roberts. She was a singularly ill-favored female, homely enough to sour milk (as the folks around Plainfield put it), with a disposition to match. There seemed little doubt that she was doomed to a life of spinsterhood. Her hatchet face seemed fixed in a perpetual scowl.

On that night, however, panic was etched onto her face. Casting fearful looks over her shoulder, she pushed her way into Hobart's living room and collapsed on the sofa, clutching her coat around her body with trembling hands.

Once she'd calmed down enough to communicate, she spilled out the most astonishing confession Hobart had ever been made privy to. In a voice choked with warring emotions—revulsion, self-pity, terror, confusion—she told him all about her brief but fateful relationship with the monster Eddie Gein.

She recounted the course of their affair: how, about six months earlier, the strange little bachelor who lived on the outskirts of town had shown up at her home late one evening and asked if she'd care to "keep company" with him. Agatha had been flustered—but also flattered. No man had ever displayed even a modicum of interest in her before. Eddie wasn't much to look at, but Agatha had no illusions about her own physical charms, either.

Mostly, their "dates" consisted of long strolls along dark country roads in the depth of night, while the rest of the village slumbered. Both of them felt shy and self-conscious enough not to want to be spied on by their neighbors.

They didn't do much talking as they walked. Eddie wasn't much of a conversationalist. Occasionally, he'd regale her with the details of some exciting story he'd recently read in a *Men's Adventure* magazine. Agatha remembered one in particular—about a sailor who was shipwrecked on a South Seas island and ended up as a captive of head-hunting cannibals, who ate his brains raw and used his belly skin to make tom-toms.

Things had gone on this way for a couple of weeks when a powerful feeling began to stir within Agatha. Returning from one of their midnight walks, she had invited Eddie into her parlor. Her aged parents, both of them semi-invalids, were sound asleep in their second-story bedroom.

Seated on the couch beside her blushing, bewildered boyfriend, Agatha had taken the initiative, Eddie being notoriously shy in such matters. She threw her arms around his neck and gave him a big, slobbering kiss. Eddie didn't seem to like it very much, wiping his lips with the back of one hand like a little boy who's been forced to swallow castor oil. But Agatha just kept on going—she was in the grip of something she didn't have the power to resist.

With frantic hands, she began fiddling with the buttons of his bib overalls. He turned crimson and stammered and tried to push her hands away. But Agatha was a woman possessed.

Somehow, she had managed to consummate the affair. When it was over, Eddie—sweaty, slack-mouthed, a wild look in his eyes—had thrown on his clothing and rushed out the door. Strangled gurgling noises were issuing from his throat, as though he'd been subjected to an unimaginable ordeal that had reduced him to a state of babbling idiocy.

Agatha had never laid eyes on him again—in person. The next time she saw him, he was staring out at her from a front-page photo in the Milwaukee *Journal Sentinel* under a banner headline that read: CORPSE FACTORY FOUND IN HOME OF PLAINFIELD FARMER.

That was one month before she learned she was pregnant with Eddie Gein's child.

By the time she finished relating this incredible tale, Agatha was blubbering uncontrollably. Liquid spilled from her eyes and bubbled from her nostrils. Hobart went off in search of some tissues, his brain spinning.

His immediate response to Agatha's story was that the young woman was a victim of the mass delirium that had gripped the entire community for months, ever since the police had first broken into Ed Gein's charnel house. The horrors that had been brought to light—the flesh furniture and face masks, the soup bowls made from human skulls and shoe boxes full of preserved vaginas— had caused a collective outbreak of hysterical delusions.

Every housewife in Waushara County suddenly recollected a time when she'd peered through her bedroom window and seen Ed Gein's lust-crazed face pressed up against the glass. Every farmer seemed to have the same story to tell: about the day Ed had dropped by with a gift of fresh-killed "venison." Fortunately for the farmer, he had politely refused—something about the meat just didn't look right. It was only later—when the butchered remains of various women were found inside Gein's summer kitchen—that the farmer realized exactly what kind of flesh he'd been offered. . . .

Handing Agatha the tissue box, Hobart couldn't conceal his skepticism. Even through her tears, she could see what he was thinking. She quickly dispelled his doubts.

Undoing her overcoat, she grabbed the reverend's right hand and pressed it to her rounded belly. When something inside gave a little twitch, Hobart jerked away his hand as though a creature he'd been petting had suddenly turned and snapped its jaws at him.

It took him a few seconds to regain his composure— or at any rate, an appearance of composure. Beneath his facade of fatherly assurance, he felt nearly as frantic as Agatha. Seating himself beside her on the sofa, he gave her hand a comforting pat and tried desperately to think of a solution.

Even under ordinary circumstances, Agatha's condition, once it became public knowledge, would have created a scandal in the little community. But at that particular point—less than two weeks after *Life* magazine ran a twelve-page spread on Ed Gein's "horror house"—the ill-fated young woman would have attracted the ghoulish interest of the entire nation. The last thing Plainfield needed was another horde of journalists descending on the town, seeking interviews with the pregnant paramour of the "Wisconsin fiend."

Aborting the fetus was out of the question. Hobart knew that there were disreputable practitioners who would perform the vile operation for a price, but he himself would never be a party to such a crime.

As far as he could see, there was only one way to deal with the crisis. Speaking with all the authority he could muster, he told the trembling young woman what she must do.

She must seek refuge in the anonymity of the big city, take on the identity of a widowed wife and mother and start a new life with the product of her sin.

Agatha listened—and heeded. By noon the next day, she had disappeared from Plainfield. A few weeks later, Hobart learned from her parents that she had found an apartment in Milwaukee.

For years, he had lived in anxiety, especially after hearing that Agatha had given birth to a boy. That the son of the monster was roaming free in the streets of the city made Hobart deeply uneasy, but as the years passed without incident, his apprehensions slowly subsided.

And then, the hideously violated corpse of a young woman named Carolyn Dearborn was found.

When he first heard the news on the radio, Hobart had felt a little alarm go off in his breast, but he'd quickly disarmed it. *After all,* he told himself, *the world is full of horrors.*

Only later—when the other victims were found, each mutilated in the same unspeakable way—did the reverend face up to the truth. By then, Agatha Roberts's child would have been in his midthirties—exactly the decade of life at which Ed Gein himself had embarked on his insane spree of corpse mutilation and murder.

The facts seemed to point to an inescapable conclusion.

The monster's spawn had come of age and was loose in the city of Milwaukee.

Why Hobart hadn't alerted the police right away was a question even he couldn't answer entirely. Part of it had to do with ethics. After all, Agatha Roberts had confessed to him in secrecy, and Hobart believed that as a man of the cloth, he was bound by the same standards of confidentiality that applied to lawyers and physicians.

But there were other, less high-principled reasons, too: denial, guilt, a fear of bringing further notoriety to his town.

Whatever the explanation, the consequences of his behavior were clear.

Because of his silence, three innocent young women had met appalling deaths.

Now—as he lay in his darkened hotel room—Hobart felt a pain in his chest sharp enough to jolt him upright. At first, he thought he was having a coronary. A full minute passed before he realized that there was nothing wrong with his heart. It was his conscience that was stabbing him.

Sliding off the mattress, he knelt at the bedside and prayed. For mercy. For courage. For the chance to make amends.

Not that he could bring back the dead. But there were other young lives at stake—future victims whose blood would be sacrificed to the maniac's lust, unless Hobart did something to stop him.

His plane left first thing in the morning. By tomorrow afternoon, Hobart would be back on his native soil. As soon as he was safely home, he would do what he should have done right from the very start.

Once upon a time, evil had lived in Wisconsin—just a few miles down the road from Victor Hobart's front door. Its name was Gein. Now it was back.

But not for much longer.

Hobart—as God was his witness—would make sure of that.

23

Even through the thick partition of bullet-proof Plexiglas separating him from the driver—a Mr. Rajeev Kalra, according to the cabbie permit riveted to the rear of the driver's seat and facing the passenger seat—Paul could hear the exotic plunking of the sitar emanating from the tape deck. It made him remember just how much he disliked Indian music.

Of course, Paul had to admit that his knowledge of Indian music was exceedingly slight. His entire exposure to it, in fact, had been through the Beatles. Though Paul had only been a kid during the heyday of the counterculture, he knew the Beatles' canon by heart. His older brother, David—like virtually every other teen of the time—had played their albums in more or less continuous rotation. *Sergeant Pepper* was the soundtrack of Paul's childhood.

He could vividly remember lounging in Davy's bedroom, staring at the psychedelic wall posters while George Harrison strummed a sitar and droned on about peace, love, and Krishna. Paul had always hated those Oriental-flavored cuts. To his ears, the sitar sounded like some kind of weird, out-of-tune banjo. Harrison's transcendental ditties were the worst parts of any album, as far as Paul was concerned—tuneless filler he had to suffer through until the good stuff came on: "Yellow Submarine," "Ob-la-di, Ob-la-da," "Rocky Raccoon."

The memory of "Rocky Raccoon" made Paul shake

his head in bemusement. Nowadays that song seemed as quaint as "How Much Is That Doggie in the Window?" Just two days before, he had overheard his ten-year-old son, Matt, blithely singing a snatch of a Nirvana lyric that went, "I wish I could eat your cancer."

Seated in the rear of Mr. Kalra's cab, Paul had plenty of time for these reflections. Stuck in the cross-town gridlock, the taxi hadn't budged for the past five minutes. Paul shoved back his coat sleeve and raised his left wrist, angling it so that his watch dial caught the light of the street lamp directly outside his window. He was dismayed to see that it was almost 6:15. In another few minutes, he'd be a half-hour late for his dinner with Wylie.

She had spent the day in the city doing research at the Forty-second Street library. Her essay on Emily Dickinson had been accepted by *The Dickinson Quarterly,* and she was expanding it into a book. She and Paul had arranged to meet at their favorite East Side restaurant for a post–*Lemmick Show* dinner.

Glancing at the taxi meter, which kept ticking steadily higher though the cab itself remained perfectly stationary, Paul gave fleeting consideration to finishing his journey on foot. But the prospect of a twenty-block walk in the frigid, windy night was seriously unappealing.

Ah, well, he thought. *Wylie'll be okay.*

Paul had been raised by a world-class worrier, a mother who always imagined the worst when her loved ones were late. Disaster was never far from her mind. Paul could still recall the day, during his freshman year at BU, when he'd driven home for winter break. He had promised to arrive around noon but had partied pretty heavily the night before and forgotten to set his alarm clock. When he walked into his parents' house at around 1:15 P.M., he'd found his mother on the phone with the Massachusetts State Police. She had called them to see if her son had been reported dead in a traffic accident.

Wylie, on the other hand, was refreshingly casual

about such matters. It was one of the things Paul liked best about her. If he didn't show up at the restaurant on time, she would simply assume he'd been delayed for some reason—not that he'd been mugged, murdered, or horribly mutilated in a car crash. She would study the menu, read a book, relax with a drink.

Still, Paul was impatient to get to the restaurant. He was eager to see Wylie and have a drink himself. Maybe order a really nice bottle of wine. Somewhat to his surprise, he was in a celebratory mood.

Part of it was simple relief that his head-to-head with Hobart was finally over. The looming debate had been giving him butterflies for weeks. In the end, he was pretty satisfied with the way things had turned out. That was another reason for his upbeat mood. Though Hobart had dominated the program, Paul had managed to have the last word, and his closing argument had been force-ful, even eloquent (if he did say so himself). Though he would have preferred a little more air time, he felt he had acquitted himself well, all things considered.

True, most of the audience had taken Hobart's side. Some of them had seemed frighteningly hostile to Paul. There had been one woman in particular, seated in an upper row, who'd spent the entire program shooting him murderous looks. During the closing minutes, when the audience was allowed to ask questions, she had tried desperately to get Lemmick's attention. Thank God, he hadn't called on her. Paul didn't want a replay of his last appearance on *The Lionel Lemmick Show,* when that pissed-off feminist had begun lobbing balled-up pages of his book at him.

The instant the program was over, the woman had scooped up her belongings and headed for the aisle, clearly intending to confront Paul face-to-face. He had hurried backstage to avoid her. For nearly twenty min-utes he had lingered in the green room, unwinding with a cup of coffee, removing his TV makeup, chatting with Lemmick's producer. Paul wanted to make sure that the angry-looking woman was gone when he emerged. That was largely why he was running late now.

Still, even if the studio audience had been stacked with Hobart supporters, Paul knew that they represented only part of the larger viewing public. He felt sure that among the millions of people who had seen and heard him that afternoon, there were a sizable number who agreed with him—maybe even some whose minds he had managed to change. Even Hobart had seemed a little less sure of himself by the end of the show.

There was a sudden easing of traffic. The taxi began to crawl forward. It was still moving more slowly than the passing pedestrians, but at least it was moving. Paul settled back in his seat and thought about Hobart.

Though he had nothing beyond intuition to support his belief, he remained convinced that the reverend was hiding something. That would certainly help explain Hobart's fury at Paul. It wasn't just a matter of principle. Hobart had a personal stake in keeping people from "snooping" around Plainfield—Paul felt sure of it.

Needless to say, he was burning with curiosity. If Hobart had skeletons stashed in his closet, Paul definitely wanted to know about them—not for any reason as petty as personal revenge. *Well, yeah . . . okay,* he thought in silent concession. *So maybe that* is *a small part of it.* But there were other, more important factors involved.

After all, Paul had his own emotional investment in the case. He had devoted two full years of his life to researching his book. He liked to think that he had written the definitive account. But now it appeared that he had missed something significant. Were there other, even darker secrets in Ed Gein's appalling life?

Well, Paul would have a chance to find out soon enough. His Wisconsin lecture was coming up in a few weeks. He hadn't planned to stay very long, but maybe he'd extend his visit by a few days, possibly even take a quick trip to Plainfield.

The more he thought about it, the more intriguing the

idea seemed. Of course, he couldn't share his plans with Wylie. She might not worry when he showed up forty minutes late for dinner, but an undercover trip into the dark heart of Gein country was a different matter entirely.

By the time the taxi finally pulled up in front of the Metropolitan Café, Paul had made up his mind.

He would go to Plainfield. He would do a little digging around (to use a metaphor that Eddie Gein himself would surely have appreciated) and see what turned up.

24

Leon almost dropped his paint brush when the panic hit him. What if he'd forgotten to lock his bedroom door? He shot a terrified glance at the door hook. When he saw it stuck securely in place, his gut unclenched and he heaved a loud sigh.

His mama was moving around out there—he could hear the heavy shuffle of her slippered feet—and he sure didn't want her barging in on him right then. He could just imagine what she'd say: "Jesus Christamighty! You turnin' queer on me, boy? Sitting around in your little panties, playing with a *doll!*"

Well shit on you, you stinking old bitch, Leon thought, making a face at the door. *I ain't playing. I'm making something special. Just like my daddy used to do.*

Seated cross-legged on his mattress, stripped to his yellow-stained undershorts, Leon reached over to the night table and made a small adjustment to his Tensor lamp. His work in progress was at a delicate stage, and he wanted the light to be just-so.

Leon had always had a creative bent, of course. He loved working on his corkboard collage, making new and imaginative combinations out of the female body parts he scissored from assorted porno mags. Gazing across the room right now, he could see his latest creation—a spread-eagled blonde with a big, hairy caterpillar (secretly clipped from one of his mama's old *National Geographics)* slithering from her snatch. Like his other designs, this one had just popped into his mind when he closed his eyes; he didn't have to think hard or anything. Though he would have been embarrassed to admit it aloud, Leon considered himself something of an artist.

And now he knew where his talent came from.

Though his mama had expressly forbidden him from reading it, Leon had lost no time in rooting *Slaughterhouse* from its hiding place in her bedroom bureau. For the past several weeks, he'd been reading it in private every chance he had. He knew his mama detested the book and the "shitty little snot-nose" who'd written it, but Leon was enjoying every sentence. For the first time in his life, he was learning the complete truth about his daddy.

Living such a sheltered life, Leon had picked up only a few scattered facts about his daddy over the years. He knew that Ed Gein was a well-known figure—hell, there'd been people on TV that very afternoon arguing about him. Still, Leon had never realized just how *much* of a celebrity his daddy was. Probably the most famous so-called psycho in the whole United States!

Movies had been made about him. Songs had been written about him. Believe it or not, there was even a damned opera based on him! Up until now, Leon hadn't been aware that his daddy had made such a deep impression on people; now he couldn't help but feel a touch of filial pride.

True there were certain things about his daddy that Leon couldn't quite relate to—his taste in women, for example. Ed had preferred them much older than normal, generally in their sixties or even seventies. He'd also liked to obtain his female companionship fresh from the grave. It was a concept that made even Leon, a person whose own sensibilities were not overly fastidious, wrinkle his nose in distaste.

Still, Leon could only shake his head in admiration at the uses to which his daddy had put his raw materials. The man had truly been an artist. Of course, this didn't come as a complete surprise to Leon. After all, among his own most treasured possessions were several of his daddy's hand-crafted artifacts, including a bracelet made of nipples and a toothpick carved from a finger bone.

Slaughterhouse, however, provided a complete, highly detailed inventory of Ed Gein's output. Until reading the book, Leon had never known about the face masks or titty vest or skull bowls. Not to mention the lampshades, chair seats, and wastebaskets, all crafted from female flesh.

There was no doubt in Leon's mind that his daddy had been a man of unusual gifts—and that he himself had inherited some of that talent.

Of course, Leon knew that he had a ways to go to match his daddy. For all their originality, his collages couldn't compare to the amazing creations he had learned about from *Slaughterhouse.* Neither could the object he was presently occupied with—though he was still having a whole lot of fun working on her.

Laying her lengthwise across his lap, he opened her legs to their fullest extent, then reached his slender art brush into the little jar of red enamel paint that sat, along with eleven other bottles, on an inverted shoe-box lid atop his mattress.

Her name was Krystal. He had acquired her the day before at a big discount drugstore where he'd gone to buy some ointment for his hemorrhoids, which had been playing hell with him lately. As he had been standing on the checkout line, his eye had fallen on a nearby metal bin with a big FOR SALE sign taped to it. The bin had been piled with pink cardboard boxes, each with a little cellophane window in it. Through each of those windows Leon could see the same vixenish face staring out at him.

It was as if she had been beckoning him to her side. Stepping from the line, he had shuffled over to the bin, pulled out one of the boxes, and squinted at the label, his lips moving as he'd read the big yellow words.

CHEERLEADER KRYSTAL! it said. AMERICA'S PERKIEST PLAYTHING!

He had opened the flap and removed the doll from its package.

She was a leggy, blue-eyed blonde, about one foot tall and dressed in a wildly provocative cheerleader outfit—teensy white skirt and tight white sweater with a big letter *K* on the bust. She looked like those Barbie dolls Leon was always seeing advertised on TV, but with a sluttier face and even bigger tits.

Leon had been all in a sweat to peek under her skirt and see if she was wearing panties, but there had been an awful lot of people milling around. He'd stood there, debating whether to invest the $2.99. What had finally decided him was the printing on the side of the box. AMAZINGLY LIFELIKE! it said.

Leon had told the checkout girl he was buying her for his niece—not that the checkout girl had seemed to give a shit one way or the other.

As soon as he was back in his truck, he'd ripped open the package, yanked out the doll, and torn off her clothes. When he'd seen her body, a featureless hunk of molded, flesh-toned plastic, he felt like crying with frustration. *Amazingly lifelike, my ass!* he'd thought bitterly.

Then a sudden inspiration had hit him.

Right in the same shopping center was a hobby shop with a big display window full of plastic airplanes and battleships and racing cars. Leaving Krystal propped on the passenger seat, Leon had hurried into the store. A few minutes later, he had emerged with a plastic sack. Inside was a complete set of paint for model-builders—twelve little bottles of brightly colored enamel—plus a pair of fine-tipped art brushes.

Now, with his paints all neatly laid out on the mattress beside him, he was in the process of turning Cheerleader Krystal into the girl of his dreams.

He'd already redone her face to make her look more

like the whore she really was. The formerly fresh-scrubbed co-ed now sported purple eyeshadow, tattooed cheeks, and leering red lips like the grin of a demented clown. A fat, flesh-pink tongue lolled obscenely from her mouth.

He had devoted the same loving attention to her tits, providing each with a network of navy-blue capillaries and a huge orange nipple. Out of the center of each nipple flowed a stream of white paint that was meant to represent milk. The dumb-ass whore had forgotten to take her birth-control pills! Krystal was going to have a baby.

He'd gone ahead and painted the fetus directly onto her belly. It was a little lump of brown that was supposed to represent a German shepherd puppy.

That's what you get for fucking dogs, Leon had snickered as he'd dabbed a tiny paw onto the fetus. Truth to tell, he wasn't very satisfied with the fetus. Try as he might, he just couldn't get it to look like a curled-up puppy. As a matter of fact, it didn't look like much of anything—just a little brown smear, as though Leon had accidentally set Krystal belly-down on one of the slices of peanut-buttered Wonderbread he'd been snacking on for the past few hours.

Oh well. He shrugged. *He* knew what it was supposed to be. That was all that really mattered.

Now, with Krystal cradled in his lap, he was ready for the best part. His red-tipped brush was poised between her wide-flung legs.

He'd been waiting for this moment all day.

Though it was already close to 4:00 P.M., it was only within the last hour that Leon had finally found a chance to work on Krystal.

When he'd risen at noon and shuffled from his bedroom, he'd been startled to hear his mama puttering in the kitchen. For some unknown reason, she had played hooky from the cannery. He had hurried back into his bedroom and thrown on some decent clothes—a pair of drab work pants and a T-shirt that said: "If you don't like my attitude, call 1-800-EAT-SHIT"—before venturing out to speak to her.

He'd found her hunched at the little Formica table, slurping up a bowl of Frosted Flakes and poring over the *TV Guide*.

When Leon had asked her why she was home, she had grabbed him by the wrist, yanked him closer to the table, and jabbed her dripping spoon at the open page.

Bending, Leon had squinted at the entry she was pointing to. *"The Lionel Lemmick Show,"* it read. "Today's topic: 'Can Books Kill?' Guests: the Reverend Victor Hobart and best-selling author Paul Novak."

"You and me got a show to watch, Leon," his mama had muttered through a mouthful of milk-sodden flakes.

Leon hadn't been pleased with this unexpected turn; he didn't like spending any more time in his mama's company than he had to. But his curiosity had been piqued. He didn't give a shit about the Reverend Hobart, that Scripture-spouting gasbag his mama was so fond of—but he *was* interested in getting a look at the author of *Slaughterhouse*.

Hell, maybe they'd even talk about his daddy!

By five minutes to two, he and his mama had been seated together on the plastic-covered sofa. Leon had squeezed himself into one corner, trying to keep as far away from her as possible. But his mama, who was wearing a sleeveless cotton housedress, occupied so much space that his left elbow kept rubbing up against her blubbery arm. The pungent fish stink that clung to her from all her years in the cat-food cannery seemed to fill the whole room.

Leon tried to ignore her presence by focusing as intently as he could on the TV. The trouble was that he had a difficult time concentrating on the show. All that jabber about "media violence and its effects on American society" was hard for him to follow. His attention kept drifting in and out. The only times he really perked up were when they spoke about his daddy. But even those parts of the show turned out to be disappointing. Neither Novak nor Hobart ended up saying anything about Eddie Gein that Leon didn't already know from reading *Slaughterhouse*.

Much to his surprise, he realized that he seen Paul Novak before. It took him a while to figure out where and when. Finally, he remembered catching a glimpse of the curly-haired writer a few months before on this very program. Some braless slut in a tank top had been winging paper balls at him.

When the program was over, his mama sat there for a long time, tugging at the little whiskers sprouting from her chin and staring off into space. Leon could tell she was thinking. He took the opportunity to creep back to his bedroom.

As soon as he was inside, he began rummaging through one of the mounds of printed matter—mostly porno magazines and tabloids—that lay heaped on his floor. The TV debate, which had included a few heated exchanges about Milwaukee's latest serial killer, had reminded him of some newspaper articles he hadn't gotten around to yet.

Leon loved reading stories about Jack the Zipper and saved every one he could find. He had already built up quite a collection. Every newspaper in the city seemed to publish at least one article a day on the case, talking about the progress of the police investigation or speculating about the killer's motives.

Some of these articles were so boneheaded they made Leon laugh out loud, like the one he had happened to turn to right then. It was some kind of "personality profile" offered by a local professor of psychology, who claimed that Jack the Zipper thought women had teeth in their vaginas!

Leon had guffawed loudly. What kind of damn-fool notion was *that*? There weren't any teeth down there;

Leon knew that for a fact. After all, he'd had plenty of opportunity to study the matter.

Just thinking about the subject of vaginas had made him feel so hopped up that he couldn't wait another minute to begin working on Krystal. Stripping down to his undershorts, so as not to splatter paint on his good clothes, he had set about his work.

Now, he was about to supply Krystal with her own red-painted privates. It was a delicate operation. He didn't want to make it too big. He knew from reading magazines like *Beaver* and *Gash* that the best ones were 'tight." At the same time, it had to be wide enough to accommodate the German shepherd puppy when it was ready to be born. Holding his breath, he placed the edge of the red-tipped paintbrush against the blank space between her legs.

At that very instant, there came a pounding on his door, so loud and unexpected that Leon started with a yelp. His brush hand jerked wildly.

"Leon!" his mother hollered. "You haul that useless carcass outta there right now!"

Leon gaped down at Krystal. There was bloodred paint smeared all over her crotch. She looked like a man who'd been castrated. Just seeing her made Leon sick to his stomach.

She was ruined! Tears springing to his eyes, he threw her so hard against the opposite wall that all four of her limbs came flying from her torso.

"Leon!" his mother bellowed again.

Leaping from his bed, he threw on his clothes, stumbled to the door, and flung it open.

His mother reared back her right hand, ready to box his damn ears for making her wait out there so long. Suddenly, her eyes narrowed. She unclenched her fist and studied him intently.

"What the hell you bawlin' about, boy?"

Leon wiped his eyes with the back of his right hand.

There was a splotch of red paint on his thumb where he'd accidentally dabbed himself when his mother knocked. Leon noticed it through his tears.

"Just cut myself is all," he said, sniffling, holding out his thumb for his mama to see.

"Aw," Mama said with a sneer. "Did the little sissy boy hurt hisself playing?" Her voice turned hard and mean. "If you got trouble with blood, boy, you better get over it right quick."

"What'd you mean, Mama?" Leon said.

"You're gonna be seein' a whole lot more of it pretty soon."

Leon felt a sudden tremor of alarm. "My blood, Mama?"

"No, you idiot," she said, turning toward the living room and nodding for him to follow. "That no-good, big-mouth preacher's."

Seated beside her on the couch again, he listened in amazement as she told him the whole story about herself, Ed Gein, and the Reverend Hobart. And about how worried she'd become that after all these years of keeping mum, the old man was finally losing his stomach for the whole business.

"Sure as you're sittin' there, Leon, he's gonna spill his guts."

"But he didn't say nothin' about us on TV," Leon said in protest.

"No. But he come close. I could see it in his face. He'll spill it one of these days, Leon. Maybe on his dyin' bed."

"Is he gonna die soon, Mama?" Leon asked, surprised.

"I expect so, Leon." She reached for his right hand and laid it on her lap, so high up that he could feel the warmth emanating from between her legs. "That is," she said, turning his hand palm upward and stroking it with a stubby index finger, "if you're half the man your daddy was."

25

The parking lot of Deane's Steak House was packed to overflowing, but a ruby-red Taurus slid from its space just as Stan Heckley arrived, as though the driver were deliberately making room for him. Seated behind the wheel of his '89 Honda, Heckley let out a low, self-satisfied cackle. He was on a roll, all right. It was as if the whole world were doing its best to make him happy.

And this is just the beginning, babe, said a gloating voice inside his head. *From now on, everything's coming up Stanley.*

He eased his car into the vacated spot. Switching off the engine, he sat there for a moment, listening to the sputtering cough of the after-run. Ordinarily, the sound grated so badly on his nerves that he wanted to punch out the windshield. Tonight, however, as he slid from the seat, he felt a twinge of nostalgia for the little jalopy.

Well, ol' hoss, he thought, giving the roof a playful pat, *you'll be headed for the glue factory purty soon.*

In another couple of weeks, he'd be tooling around town in a brand new—what? Infiniti? Lexus? BMW? He couldn't quite make up his mind.

Tossing his key ring into the air, he caught it with a quick sideways snatch and dropped it into the pocket of his snappy gray trousers. *Guess I'll just have to test-drive them all.*

Whistling a jaunty tune, he strolled across the parking lot to the canopied entranceway and pulled open the big wooden door.

Inside the candlelit restaurant, he paused to check out the bar scene. As usual, the joint was jumping. Among aficionados of saloon decor, Deane's was famous for its antique mahogany bar, an elaborately carved, richly polished beauty dating back to the Gilded Age. But on most nights, the bar was completely invisible, buried beneath the mob of chattering singles.

Compared to the city's other popular nightspots, Deane's attracted a more upscale crowd: prosperous, slightly older men—either unmarried or pretending to be—and eye-catching women who aspired to the status of trophy wife or, at the very least, expensively kept mistress. Like the women, the steaks and lobster tails were arguably the most succulent in the city and came with a price tag to match.

Truth to tell, Stan was a bit out of his financial league in the place. Indeed, the two hundred bucks crammed into his wallet should have gone to settle his long-overdue phone bill. For the past month, he'd been living off the last of his savings while turning down a number of money-making assignments. He was determined to let nothing distract him from his mission.

Now, his single-mindedness had finally paid off.

In a matter of days, maybe a week at most, he'd be rolling in dough from peddling his story to the highest bidder, probably one of those TV tabloid shows that paid top dollar for such sensational scoops. He could already picture the segment on *Hard Copy* or *A Current Affair*—Milwaukee supersleuth tracks down son of *Psycho*. Then the other deals would start rolling in—the quickie paperback, the made-for-TV movie. Hell, maybe even a full-length theatrical feature!

He'd given some thought to hiring a hotshot Hollywood agent, then decided against it. Why throw away ten percent of his hard-earned money when he could handle the negotiations himself?

Shit. No one was going to best him at the bargaining table. He was Stan-the-Man Heckley, soon to be the most famous investigative journalist in the whole Midwest. That's why he didn't feel any qualms about blowing the last of his bankroll tonight. He was determined to celebrate big time.

And he didn't plan on doing it alone.

He swept his eyes across the bar crowd, checking out his options. A few of the women were obviously there with dates, but most of them seemed up for grabs. There was one in particular, a languid, leggy blonde in a skin-tight black minidress, who caught his attention. Her hair had that tousled, wavy look, as if she'd toweled it dry after a quick postcoital shower. She was seated sideways at the bar, one sleek, shiny leg crossed over the other. Her dress was so short that Stan could almost see all the way up to her crotch without even squinting. The punchline to an old Jeffrey Dahmer joke popped into his head: *Don't bother wrapping it, ma'am; I'll eat it right here.*

After passing his coat to the coat-check woman, a chipmunk-cute brunette with the professional pertness of an airplane attendant, he strolled to the bar area, shooting the blonde an appraising glance as he passed. She eyed him back openly, as if to proclaim her availability. Up close, she looked a little older and harder than he'd expected. Stan kept walking. He wasn't about to settle for secondhand merchandise. Not tonight.

Though every seat was occupied, Stan didn't have the slightest doubt that he'd find an empty spot before he reached the end of the bar. *Come on, world,* he thought. *Make room for Stanley.*

As if on cue, a clipboard-toting maître d' appeared and called out the name of a couple; they rose from the stools directly in front of Stan and headed for the dining area.

Stan could barely contain a chuckle as he seated himself. He hooked his arm around the back of the neighboring stool, as though reserving it for a companion he expected momentarily.

"Scotch and soda," he told the bartender. "Make it a double." Cocking an eye toward the entranceway so he could check out the arriving talent, he reached a hand into the little bowl of goldfish crackers and popped a few into his mouth.

Stan, m'boy, he thought gleefully, *today is the first day of the rest of your life.* He had always detested that motto. It was one of those chirpy, inspirational sayings that inspired him with an overwhelming desire to puke. All of a sudden, however, it struck him as surprisingly apt, even profound.

It really was a watershed day in his life.

Just a few hours before, he had finally located Agatha Roberts Cobb and her bouncing boy, Leon—or, as Stan liked to think of him, Eddie Gein, Jr.

And what an amazing stroke of fortune to find them living right here in Milwaukee! Of course, that really wasn't so surprising when you thought about it. Hicks like Agatha Roberts commonly spent their whole lives in their tiny hometowns without ever venturing farther than the county seat. Moving to Milwaukee, a place that must have struck her as a sprawling metropolis, would have required all the courage she could summon.

Stan was very grateful to find her living right under his nose. He was prepared to follow her trail wherever it led, but a long-distance trip would have really put him in hock, given the sorry state of his finances. Lady Luck had been smiling on him, no doubt about it.

Hell, he thought, *she did a lot more than smile. She flopped on her back, hiked up her skirt, and spread those firm, silky thighs!*

Of course—to give himself the credit he deserved—tracking down Eddie Gein's girlfriend and bastard kid had taken a lot more than luck. It had taken smarts, determination, and professional know-how—certainly a lot more know-how than that asshole Novak possessed.

Stan had to laugh just thinking about it. All the clues

to Agatha Roberts's identity had been right there in Novak's book! But Mr. Bigshot Best-selling Author had obviously been too lazy—or dumb—to follow through on them.

Stan had started with the most basic piece of information—the rumors floating around Plainfield that Ed Gein had nailed an actual living woman shortly before his arrest.

At that time, Eddie would have been closing in on fifty. Obviously, the woman must have been younger—she was fertile enough to get pregnant during their ephemeral fling. Still, it was impossible to believe that she was any spring chicken. Eddie wasn't exactly the kind to pursue—or attract—a nubile farmer's daughter. Stan figured that the mystery woman must have been some pathetic loser like Eddie, well on her way to a life of lonely spinsterhood. Someone in her late twenties to midthirties, say.

That was a fairly broad age range. But in a town as minuscule as Plainfield, whose population had never risen higher than roughly eight hundred in all the years since its founding, there couldn't have been more than a few dozen possibilities. The question was how to locate them.

Again, Stan found the key in Novak's book. Many people in Plainfield—especially the older folks who had lived through the Gein trauma in the 1950s—remained bitterly resentful of the world's undying interest in the case. But there was a younger generation who regarded it as a colorful part of their local history. Some of these had assisted Novak in his research—and one of them, who had received a special acknowledgment in *Slaughterhouse*, was the town librarian, a woman named Joan Larkin.

Posing as a psychology professor from the University of Wisconsin, Stan had phoned Mrs. Larkin and explained that he was researching a scholarly article on the role which Ed Gein's early environmental influences, particularly his schooling, had played in his psychosis. Inviting him to Plainfield, she had given him free access to her files, including the little archive that contained a complete set of yearbooks from the local high school.

Stan had left Plainfield with photocopies of the senior photos for every graduating class from 1934 to 1948. Back home, he had taken a red Magic Marker and circled the names and faces of every girl in the pictures.

One of them, he felt sure, had grown up to be the woman Ed Gein had knocked up.

Stan's quest had taken him next to Madison, where he'd spent four full days at the Wisconsin State Historical Society, studying microfilmed back issues of the village newspaper, *The Plainfield Sun*. It was one of those small-town publications whose pages record every trivial occurrence, from church rummage sales to the weekly minutes of the local 4-H Club.

In the issue dated December 12, 1957, Stan had found a most intriguing item. Agatha Roberts, the twenty-nine-year-old daughter of Mr. and Mrs. Floyd Roberts of 24 Main Street, had moved away from Plainfield to "seek her fortune in the wider world. Her friends and neighbors wish her well." No destination was listed.

As soon as he happened upon this item, Stan felt a little drumroll of excitement in his chest. Pulling out the photocopied yearbook pages, he had quickly shuffled through them until he came upon the photos for the class of '46. There, scowling out at him, was the grim visage of Agatha Roberts. She was only eighteen at the time but already had the looks of a Gorgon. All that was missing was the reptile hairdo. Even so, Stan felt like planting a big sloppy kiss on that gruesome countenance.

It was the face of his quarry. Stan would have bet his life on it.

There was one sure way to find out. He'd phoned a woman he knew named Mona Leary, a good-natured butterball who worked at the Milwaukee Register of

Deeds. They'd met at a bar a few years back. When he found out where she worked, he started cultivating her friendship, figuring she might come in handy one day. He even threw her an occasional fuck—strictly out of pity for the poor, love-starved skank. The funny thing was, she was a terrific lay. Too bad she resembled Miss Piggy. No way Stan would ever get seriously involved with a porker like that and risk the ridicule of his friends.

Stan had called Mona at work and given her the information. For the past few days, she had stayed overtime at the office, checking through the birth certificates for 1958. He'd heard back from her yesterday afternoon. That was why he was sitting in Deane's right now, toasting himself with a big glass of Johnnie Walker Black.

"Hey, Heckster," Mona had said excitedly. It was her favorite pet name for Stan and always filled him with the passionate urge to take her in his arms and throttle her. "Guess what? I found her for you! Agatha Roberts Cobb. Gave birth to a bouncing boy named Leon. Father: E. G. Cobb, deceased."

Stan had to stifle the impulse to let off a deafening whoop into the mouthpiece. *So Eddie Gein's squeeze made up a fictitious daddy for her unholy bastard! Thought up some real clever initials, too—E.G.*

There was an address listed, but when Stan checked his street directory, he found that the building didn't exist anymore. It had apparently been razed and replaced by a shopping center sometime in the mid-1960s. Finding the current address, however, had posed no problem. He had simply called in the markers from another friend, an IRS clerk named Bob Spitalny who owed Stan a favor and did a quick computer check on Agatha Cobb.

Spitalny had called with the info that very afternoon. Printed on a little slip of paper folded inside Stan's wallet was the current address of Mrs. Agatha Cobb. And the man who would soon be revealed to the world as Eddie Gein, Jr.—son of *Psycho*.

Tomorrow, Stan intended to pay them a visit.

He knocked back the last of his drink and ordered another. As he did, he glanced toward the entranceway and was transfixed by a vision in blue.

She was wearing a low-cut silky number that clung to her body like an undergarment, as though she'd gotten distracted partway through the dressing process and left her house in her slip.

Handing her coat to the coat-check attendant, she paused at the far end of the bar and casually surveyed the scene. Stan caught her eye and flashed her his most rakish grin. She gazed back indifferently, but Stan could tell that she had noticed the empty seat beside him.

That's right, sweetmeat, he thought, beaming out telepathic vibes. *Step right this way. Don't fight the inevitable.*

Reaching a hand to his throat, he separated the open collar of his canary-yellow shirt to reveal an extra inch of chest hair. He hadn't worn a tie—he was an artist, not some boring, tight-ass businessman out to cheat on his wife.

The next thing he knew, the blue-wrapped cupcake was sliding her sweet ass onto the seat beside him. Stan snapped his finger at the bartender and pointed to the lady. She ordered a Vermouth—half sweet, half dry—as Stan turned to face her.

Up close, he could see that her titties were smaller than he'd expected. But they bulged like a double scoop of French vanilla from the top of her dress, creating an impressive display of cleavage. He guessed she was wearing a Wonderbra. The thought that he'd find out for sure before the evening was over sent a liquid charge through his groin.

"I gotta tell you," he said, lying, "you look just like a girl I wrote a piece about in *Cosmo* a few years ago."

She cocked an eyebrow. "You a writer?"

"Investigative journalist," he said, holding out his right hand. "Stan Heckley."

The bartender slid a glass in front of her. She raised it to her luscious lips, sipped, then made an unimpressed sound. "Never heard of you."

Stan felt a surge of irritation that only fueled his determination to get this babe in the sack and give her an evening she'd *never* forget. He leaned a notch closer and smiled.

"You will," he whispered.

26

As the plane began its descent into Madison, the fellow in the passenger seat, a florid-faced computer salesman named Roy Kawin, waved a stick of Doublemint in Hobart's direction. "It'll keep your ears from plugging up, Reverend," he said between vigorous chews.

When Hobart muttered a curt, "No thanks," Kawin shrugged, stripped the foil from the gum, and popped it into his own mouth. Watching him out of the corner of his eye, Hobart felt a twinge of disgust. Kawin already had so much Wrigley's stuffed into one cheek that he looked like a mumps patient.

In spite of his distaste for the man's gum-chewing habits, Hobart felt a little bad about the salesman. As soon as their flight had lifted off from O'Hare, Kawin, who had actually caught part of the previous day's *Lemmick Show* and recognized Hobart immediately, had tried to engage the reverend in a conversation. Normally, Hobart would have been happy to chat. He was a naturally gregarious man and a terrific listener: he had a gift for making people feel that their stories (no matter how stupefyingly dull) were not just interesting but important.

At this moment, however, Hobart couldn't even manage a pretense of polite interest. After fifteen futile minutes of trying to coax a response from the reverend, Kawin had slumped back into his seat and contented himself with occasional complaints about the bumpiness of the flight and the crumminess of the food.

The lack of conversation suited Hobart just fine. He was sorry to have snubbed the salesman—he could see that the man's feelings had been hurt—but he had too much on his mind right now to bother with idle talk.

Even after arriving at his resolution the night before, Hobart had found it impossible to sleep. He kept turning his options over in his mind, trying to figure out the best way to proceed. Finally, fatigue had overtaken him. He had dropped off to sleep around 2:00 A.M., still in a state of indecision.

When his wake-up call roused him four hours later, he discovered that his mind was made up. It was as if the Lord, perceiving his uncertainty, had settled the matter for him as he slept.

As soon as he got home, he intended to contact the head of the Jack the Zipper investigation, set up a meeting, and reveal the whole ugly story of Ed Gein's misbegotten son, who (as far as Hobart was concerned) was the prime suspect in the case.

Hobart realized that he could have taken more immediate action simply by picking up the phone and calling the Milwaukee PD. But as he knew from the papers, the police received dozens of outlandish phone tips every day, and he was afraid of being dismissed as just another crank. He believed he stood a better chance of persuading them at a face-to-face meeting.

He had another reason, too, for waiting until he got home. Before taking such a momentous step, he wanted to talk the matter over with Hannah.

For the past twenty years, Hobart's wife had been his dearest confidante. He relied on her for comfort, counsel, and wisdom in precisely the way that the members of his congregation relied on him. In all their years together, there was only one significant secret he had ever withheld from her—the truth about Agatha Roberts and Eddie Gein. Now that he was about to reveal it to the world, he wanted her to hear it first from his own lips.

* * *

After retrieving his bag from the conveyor, Hobart took a minute to seek out Mr. Kawin and apologize for his rudeness. "I just have a good deal on my mind right now is all," he explained. "No offense intended."

"None taken," said the computer salesman. Fishing out his billfold, he handed Hobart a business card embossed with a colorful corporate logo.

"I know what you're thinking," he said as Hobart studied the card. "Apple—the very thing that caused all our troubles to begin with, according to the Good Book. But let me tell you something, Reverend. I can fix you up with an Apple that'll make your life so trouble-free you won't believe it. Why—"

Hobart quickly cut him off. Why, yes, he said. As a matter of fact, he might be in the market for a computer pretty soon, and he would surely like to hear more about Mr. Kawin's product when he wasn't in *quite* so much of a hurry. . . .

"I'll give you a call in a week or so," he said, extending his right hand. He didn't mean it, of course, but it made the salesman happy, so where was the harm?

After giving Kawin's hand a firm farewell shake, he turned and headed for the exit.

Before leaving the terminal, he stopped at a pay phone and dialed his home number. He wanted to let Hannah know that he'd arrived safely and would be home around seven-thirty. The phone rang again and again—ten times in all before Hobart replaced the handset with a frown. He was surprised that his wife hadn't answered. She generally stuck pretty close to home when he was away.

Well, he told himself, maybe she'd gone off to fetch a few provisions for a welcome-back dinner. Or perhaps she was just indisposed and holed up in the bathroom. Though you wouldn't know it from her ample physique, his wife had a delicate digestive system that had been giving her more and more trouble lately.

He grabbed up his suitcase, then exited through the automatic door, heading for the parking lot.

Ordinarily, his son Carl would have been there to pick him up. But Carl was no longer living at home. He had left for college in the fall. Hobart had hoped that his son would enroll in a local religious school. But Carl, though a dutiful boy, had a mind of his own and had insisted on going off to study mathematics at Ann Arbor. After many bitter arguments, Hobart had grudgingly accepted the boy's decision, though he wasn't happy about it—especially after a recent telephone conversation during which he had distinctly heard a young woman giggling mischievously in his son's room.

The very idea of co-ed dorms made the reverend cringe.

Try as he might to reconcile himself to Carl's departure, Hobart continued to feel bitter about it. Among other things, he would have preferred to have the boy living closer to home. Hobart hardly saw Carl anymore and missed him badly. His house seemed surprisingly dreary with his only child gone.

Even so, the yellow lights burning through the windows of the house were a comforting sight when he pulled into his driveway nearly two hours later. The three-bedroom ranch, built in the late 1950s, was situated in a thickly wooded area five miles outside of town. The nearest neighbor lived just over a quarter-mile down the road. It was already a few minutes past 8:00 P.M. when Hobart arrived. In the cold, moonless night, the glowing yellow lights looked as welcoming as a hearth fire.

Removing his suitcase from the trunk, Hobart slammed the lid shut and trudged to the front porch. He let himself in without a key. City folk might feel the need for deadbolts and chains, but people still slept with their doors unlocked in this neck of the woods.

Stepping into the darkened hallway, Hobart set down

his suitcase with a little groan. His limbs felt like sand-bags. It had been an arduous return trip, with an unscheduled three-hour delay at O'Hare, caused by a storm off Lake Michigan. The reverend couldn't remember ever feeling wearier.

"Hello," he called. "I'm home."

Silence.

He raised his voice and called again. Still no answer.

His wife must be shut up in the bathroom again. His heart went out to her. He'd have to take her back to the clinic in Wautoma and get her a different prescription. The antidiarrheal medicine she'd been guzzling didn't seem to be doing her much good.

He was sure she was home. Her car was parked in the driveway. And as he moved into the living room, he could see that it had recently been occupied.

The table lamp was on, its fringed shade glowing warmly. The seat cushion of the chintz easy chair showed a deep indentation. The *TV Guide,* opened to the middle, had been placed facedown on the ottoman, as though Hannah had been interrupted in the middle of her reading—probably (Hobart assumed) by a sudden attack of the runs.

And no wonder! Sitting on the floor at the foot of the chair was a half-empty bag of barbecue-flavored potato chips. Hobart's wife had always had a weakness for such unwholesome fare; it was one of the reasons she weighed as much as she did. But he believed she'd managed to abjure junkfood forever, since it played such havoc with her guts.

He clucked his tongue as he crossed the living room. He'd have to give her a stern talking-to about her dietary habits.

Heading down the corridor, he passed the brightly lit kitchen. The smell of frying meat wafted from inside. Glancing in at the stove, Hobart caught a glimpse of something sizzling in a pan—a reddish-brown lump of meat.

His wife must have been taken ill very suddenly to leave it cooking like that. He picked up his pace toward the bedroom, wondering vaguely what the frying meat was. It looked a little like liver, but not exactly.

As he approached the bedroom, he saw that it was dark. Reaching in a hand, he groped for the wall switch and turned on the overhead light.

The sight that struck his eyes made him freeze. On the double bed he and his wife had shared for twenty years, Hannah lay absolutely motionless. Only her head was visible. The flower-patterned comforter was drawn all the way up to her chin. Her eyes were shut; her face was a ghastly white.

Hobart felt the blood drain from his own face as he gaped at her. She looked like a corpse.

"Hannah!" he gasped as he hurried to the bedside.

The comforter lay motionless over her lumpish body. He grabbed the edge, close to her chin, and yanked the covering back.

For a flash, he stood paralyzed, uncomprehending. There was simply no way to assimilate what he was seeing.

When the realization hit him, he opened his mouth to its widest extension and let out a roar. Had any of his neighbors heard that sound, they would have paused in whatever they were doing and wondered what sort of creature had made it. It certainly didn't sound human. Still, it sounded so agonized that someone might have suggested calling the sheriff.

But none of his neighbors heard it.

Eyeballs straining in their sockets, hands flailing wildly, Hobart staggered back a few steps, still bellowing in terror. Suddenly, he felt a crushing blow to his chest, as though someone had smashed him in the breastbone with a mallet. He clutched at his shirt collar, tearing it open, a choking man struggling for breath.

Collapsing to his knees, he fell sideways to the floor, then rolled onto his back. White froths of spittle formed at the corners of his mouth. Blackness spread like squid ink across his vision.

Then, as his sight began to fade, something swam into focus in front of him. It was a face, one he had not seen in many years—except, of course, in his nightmares. It was altered slightly from the way he remembered it—a little pudgier, a little more pasty.

But the features were essentially the same. They were the features of Edward Gein.

Hobart opened his mouth, as though to speak, but all that emerged was a gurgle.

The Gein-thing leaned closer. Frowning in disappointment, it reached out its hands and shook the dying man's shoulders.

Then, as Hobart's eyes fluttered open for the final time, the Gein-thing began to talk.

27

Heckley snapped on the map light and peered at the little slip of paper, double-checking the address.

Ta-da! he trumpeted silently. Carefully, he refolded the paper and slipped it back into his shirt pocket. This was the place, all right.

Cranking down his window, he put his head outside and squinted at the house.

What a dump, he thought. Not that he'd expected to find Agatha Cobb and her son living in luxury. The old lady worked in a cat food cannery, for Chrissake! And God only knew what—if anything—Eddie, Jr. did for a living.

Even so, the house was a lot crappier than he'd imagined—a ramshackle bungalow adjoining an empty, garbage-strewn lot.

The darkness didn't help, of course. Stan had deliberately waited until nearly 8:00 P.M., when he felt reasonably sure the old lady would be home from work and finished with her supper. There was a street lamp on the corner, but it seemed to be on the fritz. It buzzed like an insect, and its dim, sickly glow barely trickled down to street level.

All in all, the place gave Stan a serious case of the creeps. Reaching behind the passenger seat for his attaché case, he wondered if he should have waited a couple of days. He could have caught her at home on a weekend morning.

Nah, he thought. *He who hesitates . . .* Anyway, what difference would it have made? The whole neighborhood was a shithole. It would have looked just as desolate in the daylight.

As he stepped from his car and locked the door, he felt the nape of his neck prickle. Just turning his back to the street made him nervous. Driving onto the block, he had passed a trio of sullen teens in army jackets and ski caps, huddled on the corner. It was the kind of neighborhood custom-made for a mugging. Stan owned a Colt .38 that he kept in a drawer in his nightstand. At the moment, he wished he hadn't left it at home.

Starting toward the house, he suddenly froze, his heart thumping. He was sure he'd seen something move in the lot. He peered nervously into the blackness.

Seeing nothing, reminding himself of the enormous good fortune waiting on the other side of the door at number 2716, he crossed the street, made his way along the badly cracked walkway, and hopped onto the sagging little porch.

He rang the doorbell. From inside, he could hear the muted sound of a laugh track. Someone was watching TV.

He let a few seconds tick by, then rang again, keeping his finger on the button. Tilting an ear to the door, he could hear the insistent chiming of the bell.

With a suddenness that made him jerk back with a gasp, the door was yanked open. A hulking form filled the entranceway.

Stan's first thought was *It's her!* His second: *Jesus, she's ugly!* Even uglier than she'd been in her yearbook picture, and that was saying something. Back then, she'd seemed prematurely wizened. If her high school had staged *The Wizard of Oz,* she would have been a natural for the Wicked Witch of the West. In the intervening years, she'd added about fifty pounds of bulk. She had a bull neck, ham-size biceps, and a body as big as a sumo's. Her enormous breasts, unfettered beneath her housedress, drooped all the way down to her belly.

Her facial expression hadn't changed, though. The look she gave Stan could have stopped a clock.

"Whatever it is you're selling," she snarled, "I ain't interested."

Heckley shoved a hand against the door before she could slam it in his face.

"I'm not here to take your money," he said. "I'm here to make you some."

Her pig eyes narrowed. "What the *hell* you talking about?"

"You and I are going to make a bundle, Mrs. Cobb," Stan said with a sharkish grin. "Or should I say . . . *Miss Roberts?*"

Something flickered in the old lady's eyes. *Fear,* he thought—and the realization quickened the predatory instinct in him.

"I know all about you, Agatha," he said, gloating. "Where you come from. Why you ran away from Plainfield. Who your *boyfriend* was." He had to struggle to keep from laughing right in her gargoyle face. He felt so full of triumph he wanted to crow. He had this ungodly bitch *cornered.*

Agatha opened her mouth as if to protest, then clamped it shut again. With a sharp little jerk of her head, she summoned Stan inside. He followed her into the brightly lit living room.

For twenty-five years, Agatha had been bringing the stink of her workplace home with her, and—in spite of her liberal use of Airwick—it pervaded the house. To Stan's nose, the living room smelled like dead fish doused in toilet water. Apart from the unpleasant odor, though, the room, with its plastic-covered furniture, dust-free surfaces, and cheap but spotless carpeting, seemed perfectly, even weirdly, neat. The *National Geographics* stacked on the coffee table might have been arranged with the aid of a T-square. Agatha was obviously a finicky housekeeper.

Her personal appearance was another matter. Her ratty housedress was splotched with old food stains, and her fuzzy gray slippers resembled dead animals, as though her feet were shod in roadkill.

She jabbed a stubby finger at the sofa. "Sit down if you want," she growled.

My, thought Stan, *what a charming hostess.*

He lowered himself onto the vinyl-covered cushion. Agatha lumbered over and plopped herself down at the opposite end—still too close for comfort as far as Stan was concerned. He placed his attaché case between them. It wasn't much of a barrier, but it made him feel a little better.

She fixed him with her Gorgon's gaze and said, "State your business."

Stan had been debating what tack to take with the old battle-ax. He knew he had her under his thumb: the shameful secret of her past was about to be exposed to the world, whether she liked it or not. Still, there was no sense in antagonizing her; it would be best to have her full cooperation. Honey, he concluded, would work better than vinegar.

He would lay on the old Heckley charm. How could she resist? After all, repulsive as she was, Agatha Cobb was still a woman.

Forcing himself to look her deep in the eyes, Stan mustered his most seductive tones and began laying out his scheme. Before he had gotten very far, however, Agatha cut him off.

"You one of them bullshit artists, writes for those trashy newspapers?" she demanded.

Stan looked wounded. Without a word, he snapped open his attaché case, removed a handful of articles, and passed them over to Agatha. "Check 'em out. Top-of-the-line stuff. *Milwaukee Journal. Wisconsin Today. Milwaukee Magazine.*" He tried not to sound too arrogant—

he wanted to put the old bitch at ease, not intimidate her. "You're dealing with a serious journalist, Agatha. One of the best in the business."

Agatha's expression remained sullen as she thumbed through the clippings.

"But that's just small potatoes," Stan continued. "We're about to hit the big time, you and me. *People. Us.* Not to mention the TV talk shows. *Geraldo. Oprah. Lionel Lemmick.*

Once again, he launched into his spiel. It was the perfect time for Agatha to step forward with her story. The country would gobble it up. Psychos were the new celebrities, and in the realm of psychodom, Agatha's former lover was one of the greats!

Sure, Agatha might feel self-conscious at first about being exposed to the limelight. But as long as she had someone like Stan to present her story with taste and sensitivity, there would be nothing to worry about. The great American public would open its collective arms and clasp her to its heart. She would be seen not as a sinner, but as an innocent female who had fallen under the hypnotic spell of a fiend. What a story!

Agatha's baleful expression remained unchanged. Apparently, Stan wasn't getting through to her.

"Think about it," he urged. "About what a relief it would be to step out of the shadows and into the sunlight. To live your life openly for the first time in forty years. No more lying, no more hiding away your real identity." He flashed her a conspiratorial wink. "And think about the *money.*"

For the first time, Agatha betrayed a glimmer of interest. "Money?"

"A shitload, if you'll pardon my French," Stan said. "We're talking major bucks here." He ran through his master plan, ticking off the steps on the fingers of one hand. "First, we sell an exclusive interview to one of the big tabloid TV shows, probably *A Current Affair.* Then we auction the book. We're looking at a six-figure advance, *minimum*. Next come the movie rights. Maybe a theatrical feature, maybe a miniseries—I haven't decided yet. But hey, that's not for you to worry about. You just gotta worry about spending your share."

Agatha said nothing. Stan could see the wheels spinning inside her head.

"It'll be a whole new life for you," he said. "Nice new clothes. Big new house. Not"—he hastened to add—"that this isn't a real cozy place you've got here. But I'm sure you'd appreciate a little more living space for you and your son." Stan glanced around the room. "Where is he, anyway?"

"Leon?" said Agatha. Stan thought he saw a nervous little flicker in her eyes. "Working," she said quickly. "Won't be back till the morning."

So that's his name, thought Stan. *Leon.* "Well," he said. "I'll come back and see him in a day or so."

Agatha still wore a look of deep suspicion. She was a tough nut to crack, all right.

Leaning a bit closer, Stan resumed his pitch, his voice growing more fervent by the minute. At one point, he got so carried away that he actually reached out to touch her hand. Fortunately, he caught himself just in time. After all her years of factory work, Agatha's hands looked as raw and scabby as a leper's.

All in all, it was a source of wonderment to Stan that *any* man could have brought himself to have sex with a monstrosity like Agatha Cobb. For the first time, the true depth of Ed Gein's madness became real to him. He knew that Gein was a necrophiliac. But Stan could imagine corpses that were more appealing than Agatha.

"How'd you find out about me, anyways?" Agatha said abruptly. "You read that piece of shit—*Slaughterhouse?*"

Stan was surprised. Agatha didn't look like a reader. "Yeah," he said, a little defensively. "It gave me a couple of clues. But mostly it was my own detective work." He made a hitchhiker's fist and poked himself in the chest with the thumb. "I'm an investigative reporter, Agatha," he declared proudly. "They don't come any better."

Agatha glared at him. "You tell anybody else?"

"You kidding?" said Stan. "This is a Stan Heckley exclusive."

Agatha fell silent. She seemed to be giving Stan's proposition serious thought. Her liver-spotted brow was deeply furrowed, and she chewed meditatively on her rubbery lower lip.

She was going to say yes. Stan could see it! Reaching into his attaché case, he extracted a typed sheet of paper—a letter of agreement he had prepared for the occasion.

When Agatha finally spoke up, however, her words caught Stan off guard. "You want some lemonade?" she growled.

Lemonade? he thought. *In November? Oh, well, what the fuck.* "Sounds great." He smiled. "We can toast our new partnership." Shutting his attaché case, he laid the letter of agreement on the Naugahyde top.

Agatha ignored it, though. Rising from the sofa with a grunt, she clomped across the room and disappeared into the kitchen.

Stan shook his head as he watched her go. *What a behemoth!* he thought. *Too bad Spielberg didn't know about her when he was making* Jurrassic Park. *Put her in a dinosaur costume, she could have played the T-rex, saved a fortune on special effects.*

Leaning back against the sofa, he glanced around the room, taking in every pathetic detail. It was going to be *fun* to describe this craphole in his magazine articles. He particularly liked the sappy inspirational sampler hanging over the TV. "Why let a lousy past spoil a perfectly good future?" it read.

Gimme a break, sneered his inner voice. Still, he had to admit there was a kernel of truth to it, at least as far as his own future was concerned. Things were definitely looking bright.

He let out a self-satisfied sigh and wondered what the rest of the house looked like.

Rising quietly from the sofa, he stole across the room and peered around the corner. There was a closed door halfway down the narrow hallway—someone's bedroom, Stan guessed. Immediately, his curiosity was piqued. He cocked an ear toward the kitchen and heard the clattering of glassware. Maybe he'd take just one little peek.

Tiptoeing down the hallway, he paused at the threshold. He reached down for the knob, turned it, and pushed open the door.

Instantly, he was assaulted by a stench so intense that he had to pinch his nose to keep from gagging. The last time he had smelled anything that foul was way back in his high-school science lab, when the guy standing next to him accidentally dropped a jar containing a noxious old biological specimen—a decaying pig fetus imperfectly preserved in some kind of brine. Compared to the miasma emanating from the room, the rest of the house smelled like an alpine meadow.

Keeping one hand over his nose and breathing through his mouth, he opened the door a little wider. It was dark inside, but the light spilling out of the living room provided some illumination, enough for him to see that the floor was a wall-to-wall carpet of trash.

For a moment, he seriously wondered whether crazy old Agatha and her weirdo son were too lazy to dispose of their garbage by the usual means and just dumped it into this spare room instead. That would certainly account for the smell!

Squinting into the murk, however, he saw that he'd been right to begin with. It *was* a bedroom. He could make out a sagging unmade mattress, a little night table, a cheap-looking bureau. The few tacky furnishings seemed to be floating in a sea of refuse.

It was hard to believe that anyone actually lived in

such a shambles. Squinting into the room—which he assumed belonged to Leon, since the narrow bed couldn't possibly have accommodated Agatha's bulk—Stan was reminded of something. It took him a minute to recall what it was: the old newspaper photos of Ed Gein's living quarters that were reprinted in Paul Novak's book. Gein had sealed off his dead mother's bedroom, preserving it as a kind of shrine. Otherwise, the house was in a state of absolute, unholy squalor—very much like the condition of the room Stan was looking into right now.

Like father, like son, Stan thought. Given the evidence of Leon's bedroom, Ed Gein's bastard must be every bit as sick as his fath—

Stan went suddenly rigid, as though a bolt of electricity had just coursed through his body.

Jesus! he thought, his heart pounding so hard he could feel it smack against his breastbone. *Jesus!* He clamped his hands over his mouth, as though to keep from exclaiming aloud.

Could it possibly be true? Why hadn't this occurred to him before?

Of course! It made perfect fucking sense!

Leon Cobb—aka Ed Gein, Jr.—was Jack the Zipper!

Standing there, eyes wide but unseeing, he tried desperately to think straight. No way was he going to call in the cops and let them grab all the glory. He had to handle this just right—in a way that guaranteed maximum credit and publicity for *him.* He was going to be a fucking hero! The man who single-handedly accomplished what the entire Milwaukee PD had failed to do—track down the city's most notorious serial killer since Jeff "the Chef" Dahmer!

So much for that self-righteous asshole, Streator, and his so-called elite task force!

The first thing was to find some solid evidence. He was trying to figure out a way to search through Leon's bedroom when he heard Agatha's voice calling out from the kitchen: "Hey, mister. C'mon in here and give me a hand."

He needed to get hold of himself—fast. Very carefully, he drew the door shut, took a few deep breaths, smoothed back his hair, and walked—very calmly—toward the kitchen.

His brain was still spinning from his recent revelation. For that reason, he failed to register something peculiar as he walked into the kitchen—Agatha was nowhere to be seen. All at once, he sensed her presence behind him, as though she had stepped out of the room for a moment, then quickly reentered as soon as Stanley appeared. Something dug into the flesh beneath his jaw, then skimmed across his throat.

There was no pain at first, just a strange stinging sensation. He started to speak and heard an awful gurgling wheeze. *Where did* that *come from?* he wondered. The ghastly sound continued, and he realized with a shock that it was coming from *him.*

Something hot was spilling down his shirtfront. The stinging in his throat had turned into a lacerating pain. He raised a hand to his neck and it came away coated in red.

A surge of terror dizzied him. He thought, *She's cut my throat.* He could not believe this was happening.

He wanted to flee, but his muscles had jellied. He staggered, knees buckling. Powerful hands grabbed him beneath his armpits, supporting him. Blood was spurting everywhere. He heard Agatha's reproving voice behind him: "Now don't you go bleedin' all over my fresh-waxed linoleum."

He was being dragged across the floor toward the kitchen sink. Through the dimming light, he saw the basin beneath him, felt a firm hand on his forehead, glimpsed the brightness of his arterial blood as it splattered against the white enamel.

Just before he died, a perversely tender voice whispered into his ear.

"There, there," Agatha said comfortingly. "You just go to sleep now, little man."

28

Seated behind the wheel of his delivery van as it barreled through the blackness of I-94, Leon felt so good he wanted to sing. Clicking on the radio, he spun through the dial but got nothing except static.

That was strange—the radio had worked just fine on his way *up* to Plainfield. He couldn't figure out what was wrong until he glanced at the dashboard clock and saw the time: 3:37 A.M.

No wonder there was nothing on the air! He hadn't realized it had gotten so late.

He let out a high, manic giggle and thought, *Time sure flies when you're having fun.*

It had been the best damned night of his whole life, no doubt about it. Nothing he'd done before even came *close*. Just thinking about all the fun he'd had made him giddy with pleasure. Now he knew how his father must have felt.

Daddy, he thought, *I wish you'd've been there. You would've been proud of me tonight.*

The funny thing was, he'd been real nervous during the whole drive up to Plainfield. He was worried that he'd screw everything up. So was his mama, that smelly old shit. "Try doin' something right for a change," she had said to him just before he left. There was a real funny look on her face—not anger, but sadness, as if she might burst into tears at any second. "Oh, Leon," she had moaned, shaking her head as she looked at him.

"You're all I got to depend on in my old age. Try actin' like a man for once in your sorry life."

"I will, Mama," he'd said, his voice full of emotion. He'd meant it, too. He wanted desperately to please her; he could just never seem to manage it somehow.

During the whole drive up to Plainfield, he kept thinking about what his mama had said. By the time he crossed over into Waushara County, around five in the evening, he had worked himself into a real lather about it. He had just about convinced himself that he was going to make a big mess of things. He had to chew on his thumb to keep from whimpering out loud.

Then something weird had happened.

As soon as he saw the sign—PLAINFIELD, POP. 642—something came over him. He could feel it deep inside. He couldn't describe it exactly—but it was almost as if he became like his daddy. That was it! It was like that rhyme he suddenly remembered having heard somewhere, the one about his daddy: "He was not only clever, but sly as a fox." That's exactly how Leon felt now—sly as a fox!

Driving a few miles out of town on a rutted dirt road, he'd found a nice concealed spot to park his truck, behind a little clump of trees, a few hundred yards away from the Hobart place. Then he'd crept across the snow-crusted field toward the house. It was already fully dark by then, but he'd been able to find his way just fine by the lights that were burning through the windows.

"Now don't go gettin' any damn-fool notions in that pea-brain of yours, or you'll screw up for sure. Just knock on the door, and when he opens it—bam!—you just shove that pigsticker right into his chest and skedaddle." That's what his mama had told him to do. She'd even bought him something to do it with—a big hunting knife with a real sharp point and a jaggedy edge. He was carrying it in a leather sheath in his coat pocket.

And that's just what he'd been planning to do, too—walk right up to the front door, ring the bell, and when the old man answered, stab him right in his shitty heart. But as Leon approached the house, he suddenly got another idea. He figured that as long as he'd traveled all that distance, he might as well have a little fun.

So instead of proceeding up the walkway, he'd snuck around the whole house, peeking through the windows.

As it turned out, the old man was nowhere to be seen. But Leon saw something even better.

He saw his fat old wife, watching some crappy TV show in the living room while she munched like a sow on a big bag full of potato chips.

Spying on her through the window, Leon felt his heart start to go a mile a minute. He knew he was ignoring his mama's orders. But Hobart hadn't gotten home yet. Why not have a little fun like his daddy used to do until the old man showed up?

Getting into the house was easy. He'd just shoved open the bedroom window and clambered inside. The TV was on so loud, the old bag never heard him. She didn't even hear him as he tiptoed up behind her and looped his belt around her neck.

She had a mouthful of half-eaten chips that went spraying all over the rug as he tightened the belt around her throat. It had taken Leon a hell of a long time to clean up the mess before the reverend got home. Killing the old lady, though, took no time at all.

That's when the real fun started.

Tell the truth, he couldn't recollect every little detail of what happened next. He remembered dragging the corpse back into the bedroom and stripping it naked. But as soon as he had all its clothing removed, he got so crazy-excited that he just sort of went blank. There was something about it—the fat dead old lady, just lying there, helpless and naked and in his power. He finally understood why his daddy had preferred his women like that.

The rest was kind of a blur. He had gotten so hot and bothered that he just tore off his own clothes and threw himself onto the dead old sow. Next thing he recalled, he was lying there beside her, all wrung out and breathless and sweating like a hog.

After a while, he'd lugged the body into the bathroom and used his knife on it. Did all kinds of things to it. He knew his mama would disapprove. He could almost hear her ugly voice, yapping at him, as he sliced away at the old woman's flesh. "What the *hell* you doing, boy?"

But Leon didn't give a shit. He was having too much fun. He intended to have more fun, too. Just as soon as the reverend got home.

As it turned out, that had been the only disappointing part of the evening. Leon hadn't expected the old man's ticker to give out like that. He looked so strong and healthy on TV! It was a real letdown for Leon, especially since he had spent so much time arranging the surprise: first, sawing off the old lady's head, then searching all through the house and garage to find something to stick under the bedclothes—something that would look like her body.

Guess it had been too much of a shock for the old man, pulling back the blanket and seeing his wife's sawed-off head balanced on a big sack of lawn fertilizer.

The reverend had gone ghost white and keeled right over. It had been kind of funny, seeing him stagger around that way, foaming at the mouth like a sick dog. As soon as the old man began to black out, Leon had shaken him by the shoulders and managed to rouse him back to consciousness for a while, long enough to let him know exactly what had happened to his wife during those long, intoxicating hours when Leon had been alone with her. That had been fun.

But mostly he was real angry at the old man for dying on him like that. Leon'd had all kinds of things planned. He had put the old lady's heart in a frying pan, just like his daddy used to do, and cooked it up nice and juicy. He had wanted to make the reverend eat some of it. But the old fart had gone and died on him!

Oh, well. At least Leon had accomplished the job. Reverend Victor Hobart wouldn't be shooting his blabbermouth off on TV anymore, that was for sure. Leon's Mama would be real proud of him for that.

Leon had even brought back a souvenir. It was sitting beside him on the passenger seat, wrapped in a plastic trash bag. Leon reached over and lifted it. He was surprised at its heft; it felt as heavy a bowling ball. He couldn't wait to get it back home.

Humming with pleasure, he gave the truck a little more gas.

Funny thing about the reverend. Just before he died, he mumbled some awful crazy stuff. Leon had to bend an ear all the way down to the old man's mouth just to hear it. The old man kept calling Leon a monster and accused him of killing those girls in Milwaukee!

Leon made a clucking noise. *Crazy old coot. Seeing his wife's chopped-off head must've discombobulated his brain.* Imagine thinking that Leon was Jack the Zipper!

Now where in hell do you suppose he got that *idea?* Leon wondered.

29

Her name was Samantha Bulger. She had turned sixteen exactly one week before, on November 23. Her best
friends, Cindy Dolan and Marcia Weitz, had chipped in
to buy her a set of Prismacolor art pencils. It was not
only the best birthday present Samantha had received,
it was the only one.

Her mother hadn't even bothered to get her a card.
"Hey, birthday girl," her mom had said, suppressing a
belch. She was sprawled on the living-room couch,
watching a rerun of *Roseanne.* "How about running
down to the luncheonette and getting me a carton of
Camels?" That had been her single acknowledgment of
her daughter's birthday.

No wonder Samantha's dad had walked out on the
family when she was only ten. She still missed him terri-
bly, still felt tremendous anger at him, too, but she could
certainly understand it. Who in his right mind would
want to stay married to her?

In fact, Samantha herself intended to follow in her
father's footsteps. She daydreamed about leaving home
all the time. She had it all planned out. That's why the
pencil set was such a wonderful gift.

Samantha loved to draw. She doodled all the time.
She was a really good artist, too. She had even been
accepted in an art school—not a school, exactly, but a
study-at-home program. She had seen the ad in the back
of *Teen Beat* magazine: a picture of a clown under a
caption that said: "Draw me!"

Samantha had spent over an hour copying the clown. She had done a really good job, too. Two weeks after mailing in her drawing, she got back a letter from the president of the institute, telling her how talented she was and accepting her into the program!

Unfortunately, she hadn't been able to start her lessons yet. She was still saving up money from her after-school job at Denny's. Most of her salary had to go toward her share of the household expenses. The pitiful money her mother earned as a checkout lady at the A & P couldn't support both of them. But Samantha managed to squirrel away a few dollars each week. Pretty soon, she'd be able to enroll.

That was her plan: to earn her art degree from the institute, then move to New York City and get a high-paying job as a commercial artist. She liked to imagine herself standing at the front door, suitcase in hand, saying good-bye to her mother. *I'm out of here.* Just picturing the look on her mother's face made Samantha smile. It was one of her favorite parts of the fantasy.

Of course, the thought of living on her own in New York City was pretty cool, too. It would be so glamorous. She had seen this movie with Sharon Stone—what was it called? The one where Sharon Stone played this successful single woman, living in this cool high-rise in Manhattan? And she got involved with whatsisname—you know, that hot-looking actor? Actually, Samantha didn't remember too much about it. But living in New York City looked like it'd be really neat.

Of course, Samantha knew it was a dangerous place. But, shit, Milwaukee was becoming dangerous, too. Things had gotten really scary lately, what with the druggies and street gangs and drive-by shootings. Not to mention that awful serial killer that everyone was so frightened of—Jack the Zipper.

Actually, it wasn't strictly true to say that *everyone* was frightened. Most of the guys Samantha knew treated the whole thing like a big joke. In fact, they were always *cracking jokes* about it. Larry Pittman had told her one just a couple of days ago. How did it go again? Oh, yeah: What did Jack the Zipper's girlfriend say when people asked her how he was in bed? *"Sew-sew."*

Samantha had let Larry Pittman know what she thought of him *and* his joke. *The big asshole.* As far as she was concerned, there wasn't anything even slightly funny about Jack the Zipper. Cindy and Marcia felt the same way—all the girls at school did. They talked about Jack the Zipper all the time—how fucked-up he must be, how he must really *hate* women to do those kinds of things to them. They figured he must be some kind of homo.

Samantha didn't know or care whether he was a homo or not. All she knew was that it creeped her out completely to even *think* about the sicko stuff he did.

Even now, hurrying down Stark Street—alone, in the dark—she felt a little uneasy, even though she'd walked this route a zillion times before. The bus she took from work dropped her off on Appleton, six blocks from where she lived, and cutting through Stark Street was the shortest way home.

Not that she'd *ever* liked Stark Street. Even as a kid, she always found it slightly creepy—even worse than the seedy block she lived on. It was lined with a dozen shabby houses, half of them empty and shuttered. There was something intensely forlorn even about the ones that were inhabited, with their sagging porches, scaling paint, and littered, chain-linked yards. The mounds of old snow edging the sidewalk were ice-hard and grimy. In the yellow glow of the street lamp, they reminded Samantha of the clumps of old soap caked onto the porcelain dish above her bathroom sink. Her mother wasn't much of a housekeeper.

Shivering in her thin leather jacket, Samantha hugged herself tightly and picked up her pace. Except for the muffled din of a Nirvana song, pulsing dimly from a basement, the clopping of her boot heels was the only sound on the desolate street.

She was halfway down the block when she heard another sound—a vehicle approaching from behind. She expected it to drive past, but it must have been going very slowly because it remained out of sight right behind her.

She felt something squeeze in her chest—a little spasm of alarm. Quickly, she shot a look over her shoulder.

Instantly, her fearful heart eased. There was something so harmless, even reassuring, about the vehicle that she felt slightly abashed by the momentary panic that had seized her.

True, there was something vaguely peculiar about the vehicle, though Samantha couldn't put her finger on exactly what was wrong. Maybe it was simply the fact of seeing it *here,* on this dismal street, in the dead of winter, with no one around. It was a sight she associated with daylight and groups of people—children mostly—gathered for a treat.

The guy who drove it must live around here, she decided. That was the only logical explanation.

She looked straight ahead and kept walking.

Sure enough, before she had covered another two yards, the vehicle sped up slightly, pulled ahead of her, and parked at the curb. Samantha assumed she'd been right. The driver must live in one of the darkened houses. Certainly, he wouldn't be stopping for any other reason. Obviously, there was no one around to buy anything.

As she came up alongside the vehicle, she glanced over at the pleasing images that decorated its sides. One picture in particular made her smile. She couldn't remember the last time she had tasted one. It used to be her favorite childhood treat, too. Orange-coated Creamsicles with vanilla ice cream inside.

It was only then that she realized what was so odd about the vehicle. It had been driving with its lights out.

Maybe the driver had just forgotten to switch them on. Or maybe they were broken. Why else—?

Suddenly, another possibility hit her. But by then, it was too late.

The driver's door flew open and a scrawny figure leapt out. Before Samantha could scream, he hooked an arm around her throat and clamped a damp cotton cloth over her nose and mouth. A thick chemical smell clogged her airways. She struggled, flailed her arms, tried to fight him off.

Then blackness overcame her.

Grunting softly, the man known as Jack the Zipper hauled the limp teenager into the cab of his van, then dragged her into the rear.

He had made his preparations earlier. Sitting on a shelf was a lantern-style flashlight. He clicked it on. By its dull yellow glow, he trussed the girl's wrists and ankles with two lengths of nylon rope he had left on the countertop. He had also scissored off a piece of duct tape and placed it within easy reach, dangling from the drawer of his cash register. He plucked it from its place.

Before he stuck it over her mouth, he decided to sneak a look. He knew he shouldn't take the time, but he couldn't resist. Using his thumbs, he peeled back her lips, exposing the ivory treasures.

Instantly, he was shaken with such a paroxysm of rage that he had to clamp a hand over his own mouth to keep from screaming. There was a terrible flaw on her left incisor—a dark, ulgy blotch right at the gumline! He felt like a collector of rare porcelain who had just acquired an expensive *objet*, only to discover a nasty chip he had overlooked when he'd bought it.

Suddenly, a thought pierced the black fog of his fury. Using a thumbnail, he scraped at the offending spot. It came off instantly. It was just a particle of food—a tiny scrap of lettuce from the BLT Samantha had eaten for lunch.

As it happened, it was the last food she would ever taste. By daybreak, the maniac's work would finally be done. Oddly, given Samantha's feelings about her mother, the final word to bubble from her savaged mouth would be *Mommy*.

It was time to get under way. The girl had let out a muted moan, probably in response to the small but stinging injury he had inflicted. He had snagged her gum with his thumbnail while scraping at her tooth. A bead of blood, dark and shiny as a cranberry, had emerged from the cut.

He needed to make tracks before the chloroform wore off—and before he got carried away. He was already so stiff that he felt like unzipping. Driving around with his cock poking out didn't seem like such a hot idea, though. He didn't want to take a chance on being stopped by a cop for indecent exposure.

Pressing the duct tape over the girl's mouth, he rose from his knees and made his way to the front of his van.

Then, sliding behind the wheel, Chuckie Frewer put his truck into gear and disappeared into the night.

Part Three

—

Nobody

30

His seventy-fifth birthday was only two weeks away, but it would have taken a blizzard to keep Lewis Stimpson inside. Milwaukee had, in fact, been hit by a brutal storm that dumped nearly four inches of new snow on the city. But that had been five days before. Today—Saturday, December 10—the sun was high, the sky was clear, and the day seemed to sparkle.

Peering through the window of his first-floor apartment, Stimpson could tell it was frigid outside. Two heavily bundled-up children—boys or girls, it was impossible to say which—were puffing out thick clouds of smoke as they made their way down the shoveled path between the snowbanks on the sidewalk. But a little cold never stopped Lewis Stimpson. He knew people ten years younger who kept themselves shut up inside their houses for the better part of the winter, barricading themselves against the cold. The very idea made Stimpson snort with derision. The time wasn't far off when all of them—himself included—would be shut up in snug little boxes forever. As long as he was above ground, he intended to *live*.

Rubbing his hands like a man anticipating a treat, he made his way across the mess of his living-room floor and into his cramped and equally unkempt bedroom.

The clutter of his living quarters suited Stimpson just fine. His late wife, Nelda, had been (as Lewis used to complain to his friends) a real "neatness bug," constantly tidying up their home and stashing his things in places—drawers and shelves and closets—where he could never find what he was looking for. When she had passed away of Hodgkin's disease fifteen years ago, he had promptly moved into a little one-bedroom apartment. Before very long, his stuff—almost all of it connected to the one real passion of his life, photography— had overrun the place like some kind of living organism. It reminded him of the kudzu that used to take over his backyard when he was growing up in Georgia.

The living-room carpet was barely visible beneath his dusty stacks of photography books, piles of bedraggled camera magazines, and precarious heaps of old contact sheets and prints. In addition to his narrow bed, a maple bureau, and a twelve-inch TV on a rolling cart, the only furnishings in his bedroom were four gray metal filing cabinets stuffed with his work—some of it dating back to his days as the official photographer for the Wisconsin Crime Lab, the rest of more recent vintage. The walls throughout the apartment were hung with his Lucite-framed photos, all of them taken since his retirement— radiant flowers, rolling landscapes, horses grazing in placid fields, and the beaming faces of children.

Even his john did double duty as a darkroom. Every nook and cranny was crammed with chemical jars and developing equipment. On almost any given day, two or three drying strips of negatives dangled from the curtain rod like shiny black ribbons.

Living alone in this congenial chaos, Lewis Stimpson— though he still felt a little guilty about admitting it—was happier than he'd ever been before in his life.

His afternoon constitutional was vital to his happiness. To this daily ritual he attributed his continuing soundness of body and soul. For thirty or forty minutes every day, he took a brisk stroll through some section of the city. "Good exercise," he would say to his friends, "for my heart *and* my art." He would pause and snap pictures whenever the spirit moved him—pictures that were the polar opposite of the ones he had taken for nearly forty years of his life.

Now, rummaging through a mountainous clothes pile, Stimpson located his warmest winter garments. It took him several minutes to get into the outfit—thermal underwear, fleece-lined pants, turtleneck sweater, two pairs of wool socks. He laced on his duck boots, struggled into his parka, pulled on a ski hat, and then worked his hands into his insulated gloves.

By the time he was finished, he felt as tightly swathed as a mummy. But then, he didn't require much flexibility—just enough to put one foot in front of the other and raise his camera to his eyes.

Stimpson's Nikon FTN was his single most precious possession. He kept it in the top drawer of his dresser, along with his collection of lenses. Carefully removing the camera from its storage place, he managed, with a little grunt of effort, to lift his arms high enough to loop the strap around his neck. Then, after staring thoughtfully into the drawer for a moment, he reached in for a telephoto lens, fitted it to the camera, and headed for the front door.

Outside in the stinging air, he let his eyes adjust to the dazzle. He thought briefly of taking a bus to the lake shore but abandoned the idea. Stimpson hated riding buses in the winter; they were stuffy and overheated and generally occupied by at least half-a-dozen passengers who sounded like recent discharges from the TB ward. He decided to settle for a stroll in the neighborhood park, three blocks away.

The air was so cold that it froze the moisture in his nostrils, but the sensation only made Stimpson feel more alive. Inside the little park, the trees poking out of the snow-covered ground looked as fragile as blown glass. As Stimpson made his way along the narrow, shoveled pathway, something zipped across his vision—a bright, crimson flicker. Pausing, he squinted at a spindly tree and spotted a brilliant cardinal. Almost immediately, it swooped from its perch and alighted on the back of a wrought-iron bench, about five yards away.

Pulling off his gloves and removing the lens cap, Stimpson raised the camera to his face and clicked. The bird cocked its crested head and regarded him warily; through the viewfinder, Stimpson could clearly see its bright, dancing eye. Stimpson managed to get off a half-dozen shots before the bird flitted from the bench and into the sky. Lowering his camera, he watched it streak out of sight.

"Lovely," Stimpson muttered aloud. "Absolutely lovely."

After replacing the lens cap, he drew on his gloves—his fingers were already burning from the cold—then continued on his way.

For many years, ever since his retirement in 1974, Lewis Stimpson had taken pictures of only things that brought him joy: lovely things. He regarded himself as a serious photographer—an artist, in fact. His work was represented by a gallery called Contempo Art, Ltd., located in the Grand Avenue Mall. The gallery managed to sell about two dozen of his prints every year—mostly soft-focus close-ups of butterflies, birds, and flowers.

Stimpson, who subsisted on a modest pension plus his monthly Social Security checks, didn't earn much from these sales. But the income was vital to his very existence. Without it, he would have been hard pressed to afford his photography supplies—film, developing fluid, printing paper. And photography was the only thing that gave his life purpose and meaning.

To Stimpson, creativity was its own reward. He wasn't looking for fortune and fame. He took pictures to please himself. His photos were sunny and sweet and uplifting, qualities that seemed to have fallen out of fashion in the modern world. Stimpson couldn't care less about fashion. If the simple beauties of life had become hopelessly passé, that was the world's problem, not his.

As a lifelong reader of camera magazines, Stimpson

kept up with the work of those so-called artists whose photographs ended up in museums and commanded prices that made him shake his head in disgust. As far as Stimpson was concerned, most of it was sheer, unqualified crap—almost a form of pornography, full of ugliness and debasement and horror.

Stimpson had no doubt that he could have made a name for himself by photographing the same sordid subjects. Hell, he could take disturbing pictures with the best of them. After all, that was how he'd made his living for nearly thirty years. During that time, he had seen and recorded enough horror and degradation to last a lifetime.

Correction, he thought as he made his way along the pathway toward the far end of the park. *Several lifetimes.*

It had, in fact, been one of those pictures that caused him to quit his job with the crime lab. In July 1974, he had been summoned to photograph the corpse of a murder victim, a nine-year-old girl who had been raped and strangled by an unknown assailant. Her name was Sarabeth Terry. Even after all this time, Stimpson still remembered it. Searchers had found her body dumped in the woods not far from her home, the day after she'd disappeared while riding a bike back from her best friend's house.

When Stimpson had arrived on the scene, the police were busy keeping gawkers away from the pale, naked body that was lying face-down on the forest floor. Quickly setting up his equipment, Stimpson shot about a half-dozen photographs. Then the coroner gently rolled the body over on its back.

For the first time, Stimpson gazed upon the features of Sarabeth Terry. She was an exceptionally lovely child, but her face was disfigured by dozens of ugly black marks. A layperson might have assumed that she'd been afflicted with a dreadful skin disease. But Stimpson, who had seen such marks before, knew exactly what they were.

The little girl's face, pressed against the ground, had been nibbled on by ants throughout the night.

Raising his camera to his eye, Stimpson proceeded to photograph the child's pockmarked face with the cool detachment of the highly skilled professional that he was.

It was only later, after he'd developed the photo of Sarabeth's face, that the full horror hit him. Why that particular image should have affected him so profoundly, he could never say. He'd certainly seen more gruesome sights in his career—car-wreck victims, tortured infants, human bodies subjected to every variety of mutilation and decay.

Not to mention the unimaginable sights he had witnessed on that long-ago night inside Ed Gein's charnel house.

It must have been the expression on young Sarabeth's face that had set off his reaction. It wasn't a particularly agonized look, but rather one of wounded surprise, as though she could not understand how her safe, familiar world had suddenly turned so cruel.

Whatever the reason for his response, as he stared at that image of ravaged innocence, Stimpson suddenly felt his bottom lip start to quiver. A whimper rose up in his throat—and then the dam broke. The bottled-up emotion—the outrage and terror and pity—of thirty long years seemed to erupt all at once from his heart. Doubled over in his chair, he wept so convulsively that by the time his outburst subsided—almost twenty minutes later—he did not have enough strength to move. Finally, he managed to pull himself out of his seat and make his way across the office to his typewriter.

The next morning, he handed in his letter of resignation.

Sarabeth Terry's murder was the last outrage Stimpson would ever photograph. He had seen enough of life's dark, tragic depths. From that day on, he would focus only on the sunlit side.

Even so, it had taken him a long time to put his bad memories behind him. The specters of the past kept rising up before him. He would aim his camera at a child's laughing face and see, through the viewfinder, the death grimace of a bludgeoned infant. Or start to shoot a clump of flowers and see the mottled viscera of a disemboweled boy. Or photograph a budding maple branch that became, even as he pressed down on the shutter release, the withered arm of an exhumed skeleton.

And then there were the bad dreams that, night after night, jolted him awake—the harrowing, chaotic horror films, full of maimed flesh and mangled limbs and mummified remains.

But eventually all of these terrors had passed. Over the years, the ghastly images simply faded from his consciousness, the way long exposure to sunlight will bleach a discoloration from a blemished white cloth.

Stimpson finally began to sleep as sweetly as a child. By now, he couldn't even remember the last time he had been awakened by a nightmare.

The day was even colder than he'd expected. In spite of his heavy layers of clothing, Stimpson felt chilled to the core by the time he reached the far end of the park, and his nose was going numb. There was a shopping plaza with a luncheonette in it only two blocks away. He decided to warm himself with a cup of hot cocoa before tackling the trip home.

A short time later, he was hunched over a big, steaming mug, breathing in the chocolate aroma like a bronchitic patient inhaling healing fumes from a vaporizer. He stayed at the counter for a full twenty minutes, savoring every creamy spoonful and sugared sip. The drink suffused him with pleasure and warmth, but his finger joints remained stiff and achy. Though in good shape for a man of his age, Stimpson suffered from a touch of arthritis. As he headed for the cash register, he remembered that he was running low on analgesic. Fortunately, there was a big discount drugstore right next door to the luncheonette where he could replenish his supply.

Stimpson, who had fond memories of the musty pharmacies of his childhood, had never gotten used to these newfangled warehouse-size drugstores that seemed to stock everything from aspirin to electric blow-dryers to stationery. As he wandered up and down the broad, brightly lit aisles, peering overhead for the sign that said PAINKILLERS, he approached a big, doughy man who was standing in the cosmetics section, examining a display rack of Revlon lipsticks. There was something nervous in his manner, as though he were engaged in a vaguely illicit act.

As Stimpson moved passed him, the big man suddenly glanced up and shot him a dark, glowering look. Staring into his face, Stimpson was so startled that his upper body gave a sharp backward jerk, as though he'd been yanked by invisible strings. Quickly lowering his head, he hurried past the man to the far end of the aisle, where he paused to catch his breath. The shock of what he'd seen had set his heart galloping.

Pretending to examine a shelf full of cough medicines, Stimpson cast a cautious glance over his shoulder. The big man had turned his attention back to the lipstick. Abruptly, he plucked a shiny tube from the display rack and headed to the front of the store, walking with a hunched, furtive gait.

Stimpson, whose mind was spinning with fright and confusion, stood frozen for a moment. Then, as though willing himself out of his paralysis, he turned and hurried back down the aisle, stopping several feet behind the man, who was standing at the checkout counter, his back to Stimpson.

"Hope this is the right color," Stimpson heard the man say with a strained, nervous laugh. "My girlfriend'll kill me for sure if it ain't." The checkout girl's expression remained utterly indifferent as she rang up the sale and bagged the purchase. Then, grabbing his change and the little white sack, the man lumbered toward the automated doors.

Plucking off his camera's lens cap with quivering fingers, Stimpson made for the big plate glass window that overlooked the parking lot. As the man clambered into the cab of a dirt-caked delivery van with MIDWEST MAGAZINE DISTRIBUTORS, CO. painted on the side, Stimpson shot a picture of the vehicle, then swung his camera in the direction of the driver's window. As if on cue, the glass slid down and the pasty-faced man stuck out his head and glanced behind him as he backed up the van.

Doing his best to control the shaking of his fingers, Stimpson aimed at the man's face and snapped the camera.

31

That evening, Stimpson sat bent over a magnifying lamp, staring down with wide eyes at the contact sheet he had just printed.

He had half convinced himself that his afternoon encounter had been nothing but a delusion—an old man's tired brain playing tricks on him after a long, taxing walk on a glacial day. There was obviously no way he could have seen what he *thought* he'd seen, not unless he'd tumbled down Alice's rabbit hole while strolling through the park. *Lewis, ol' buddy, looks like senility's finally settlin' in. . . .*

That, at any rate, was what he'd come to half believe by the time he reached home. But now, seated at his kitchen table, he could not protect himself from the truth. *The camera never lies.* That was a favorite saying of Stimpson's long-deceased father, a self-described photography nut who had bought Lewis his first Kodak Brownie.

It seemed wholly inexplicable—even insane, but there was no getting around it: the picture Lewis was staring at right now was of a face he had photographed before. Almost forty years before. It was a face that had been plastered across the pages of newspapers and magazines throughout the country. Lewis himself had once spent a good twenty minutes studying that face through the bars of a county jail cell, seeking some visible sign of its owner's appalling depravity.

Turning away from the glow of the magnifying lamp, Lewis rubbed his eyes wearily with his right thumb and forefinger. His mind continued to struggle against the evidence of his senses. The whole thing must be some kind of bad dream.

And yet, when he looked down again, there it was, amid the other images he had taken that afternoon. The bright, crimson bird. The branch shimmering with icicles. The fat-tailed squirrel. The sledding children.

And Edward Gein.

The Wisconsin Ghoul. The Mad Butcher of Plainfield. The Original Psycho. The single sickest mind ever to spring from the soil of Stimpson's adopted state.

How in the name of all that was holy could this be possible? The dead could not walk the earth—and cancer had ended the monster's life almost two decades ago!

Placing his palms on the tabletop, Stimpson shoved himself upright and made his way into the bedroom. Seating himself on the edge of his rumpled bed, he bent to the bottom drawer of the corner filing cabinet, slid it open, and—after a bit of searching—plucked out a thick manila file, which he carried back to the kitchen table.

The folder, labeled GEIN, contained several dozen eight-by-ten prints. Shuffling through them, Lewis was swept back to that bleak, moonless night when he'd first journeyed out to Gein's lonely farmhouse. Having worked as a crime photographer for over twelve years at that time, he was sure he'd already seen it all—every horror imaginable. But the Gein atrocities were something else entirely. Stepping into the farmhouse was like crossing the threshold into a radically new realm of experience.

The realm of the wholly *un*imaginable.

Even now, it would seem impossible to believe—except that Stimpson had the documentary proof right in front of him. There it was, in glossy black and white. The dressed-out corpse of Gein's final victim, dangling from the rafters like a butchered deer. The kitchen chairs with their human-flesh seat covers. The soup bowls made from skullcaps. The shriveled faces decorating the bedroom walls. The skin suit with its dried-up breasts. The shoe box full of salted vaginas. The belt fashioned from nipples. And more.

And then there were the other shots Stimpson had taken. The brooding, haunted farmhouse. The local graveyards that Gein had plundered on his ghastly midnight raids. And the photos of Eddie himself, gazing at the camera with his goofy lopsided grin while flanked by grim-faced sheriffs.

It was a curious thing. Virtually all of the pictures Stimpson had taken in the course of his career had the cold, clinical quality of autopsy photos. They could have served as illustrations in a forensics textbook. By contrast, his shots of Gein's living quarters possessed an eerie power, a baroque, macabre quality, as though Stimpson had managed to capture not just the interior of Gein's home but the inside of his *mind*. Viewed in a certain way, they were the best work he had ever done. And yet they had been taken when Stimpson was teetering on the very edge of shock—if, indeed, he had not already slipped over it.

Removing a close-up of Gein from the stack, Stimpson set it on the table beside the contact sheet. Then, peering back and forth between the magnifying lens and the photo, he compared the two faces.

He could see immediately what his reason had already told him—that the man he had encountered that afternoon was not Ed Gein. Gein's face was harder, more weathered and hollow-cheeked than that of the man in the drugstore. And yet their features were so similar! The thin lips, the heavy-lidded, vacant eyes, the crooked nose. The resemblance was uncanny. Stimpson struggled to make sense of it. He picked up the file folder and began leafing through the other pictures, searching for a different shot of Gein.

As he did, something slipped from the folder and fluttered onto his lap—a single sheet of stationery. Curious,

Stimpson reached down and held it to his eyes. It was a letter he had received a year ago and forgotten about. A handwritten thank-you note. From Paul Novak.

Several years earlier, when Novak was working on *Slaughterhouse,* he had contacted all the living eyewitnesses to the Gein horrors, including Stimpson. "I'll be making a research trip to Wisconsin next month," he had explained on the phone, "and I'd be grateful if you'd agree to an interview." Lewis's first response was a flat refusal. He wasn't interested in dredging up the past or in contributing to a book that, as far as he was concerned, would be nothing but a piece of cheap exploitation.

Still, Novak had sounded like a serious, intelligent fellow. He was a persistent one, too. By way of establishing his legitimacy, he had sent a few of his published stories to Stimpson. One of these, a bittersweet tale about a little boy who finds a magic camera that photographs his playmates as they'll look in middle age, had struck a responsive chord in Stimpson. In the end, Stimpson had not only granted Paul an interview but given him permission to reprint about a dozen photographs from his Gein file.

As soon as *Slaughterhouse* had been published, Paul had mailed Lewis a copy. The stationery that had fallen from the folder was the accompanying thank-you letter. Stimpson, who had no desire to immerse himself in the Gein horrors again, had never bothered to crack the book. He couldn't even say where it was—probably buried in one of the piles scattered all over his living room.

Still, he retained affectionate memories of Paul, with whom he had kept up a sporadic correspondence over the years.

Now, as he glanced over the letter, an idea struck him. First thing in the morning, he would make enlargements of the photos he had taken in the drugstore and mail them to Paul. If anyone would be interested in Stimpson's discovery, Novak surely would.

Fetching a notepad and ballpoint from the drawer of his nightstand, Stimpson returned to the table and wrote:

Dear Paul,

Hope all's well with you and yours. I've been doing fine myself—until this afternoon, that is, when this old frame received a shock from which it has not yet recovered. That's the reason I'm writing. I'm hoping you'll tell me I'm going crazy and just seeing things. I swear that would be a comfort—compared to the alternative.

As I'm sure you've noticed, this letter comes attached to a couple of pictures. Go ahead and take a look at them. Recognize that face? I'll bet you do. And I'll bet you're saying to yourself right now, "Why's ol' Lewis sending me more pictures of Crazy Ed? I already published my book." Well, hold onto your hat. Those pictures you're looking at weren't taken back in '57. No sir. They were taken this very afternoon, in a Buy-Rite Drugstore not more than a mile from my front door! *Now* you know what's got me so worked up.

At first I thought maybe those stories were true and Eddie Gein wasn't human after all but some kind of supernatural creature who can never die. But then, looking closer at the two faces, I saw that this fellow is too pudgy to be Ed. Still, the features are almost identical. Now, what the devil do you make of *that*? I suppose it might be true that everyone in the world has an exact double walking around somewhere. But hell, I sure haven't ever run into *mine*. Have you?

No. Something else is going on here. Remember when you and I spoke about those stories that used to circulate around Plainfield—about how Eddie once had a girl and maybe even knocked her up? Given Ed's— what's the word I'm looking for here?—*predilections,* that always struck me as so much bull. But suppose it was true, and this fellow in the pictures is Ed Gein's grown-up son—a chip off the ol' warped block, on the loose right here in the city of Milwaukee? Now *there's* a scary thought—almost as bad as Eddie himself coming back from the dead.

Let me know what you think.

Your friend,
Lewis Stimpson

By the time Lewis finished the letter, his finger joints were burning. He'd been so unnerved in the drugstore that he'd hurried away without buying his painkiller. Switching off the living-room light, he shuffled into his bedroom, changed into his flannel pj's, and crawled under his heavy blankets. The apartment was heated to the point of stuffiness, but Lewis felt almost as cold inside as he had near the tail end of his walk.

For the first time in many years—more than he could remember—Stimpson couldn't fall asleep. Shivering under the bedclothes, he stared up at the ceiling until the blackness of the room dissolved into a murky gray. He was glad he felt so wakeful. He was afraid to doze off—afraid of what he'd dream.

All at once, an old memory popped unbidden into his mind. It was a rumor that had made the rounds in the wake of Gein's arrest—one of those bizarre, apocryphal stories that seem to spring up out of nowhere and take on a life of their own. Eventually, it became a kind of local legend, creepy enough—in spite of its wild implausibility—to cause recurrent nightmares in successive generations of schoolkids.

According to the story, Gein had been in cahoots with

a young man named Otis, who worked in the local funeral home and served as Ed's perverted procurer. For a fee of twenty-five dollars a pop, Otis allowed Eddie a half-hour of privacy with every female cadaver brought in for embalming.

Most of the bodies were those of middle-aged or elderly women. One day, however, Otis found himself with a remarkably lovely specimen on his hands—a nineteen-year-old young woman who had died of congenital heart disease. He immediately notified Eddie. So smitten Ed was with the lifeless beauty that he offered to buy her outright for four times his usual fee. Otis readily agreed, and Eddie spirited the body back to his ramshackle home. There, in the unspeakable gloom of his bedroom, he fulfilled his necrophiliac lusts upon her, experiencing a frenzy of feeling he had never known before.

Ordinarily, Ed would have disposed of the body the moment his passion was spent. But in this instance, he couldn't bear parting with her. Applying his taxidermic skills to the body, he managed to stave off its inevitable decay. For the next few months, she shared his bed. And every night, Ed had his way with her.

Then one morning, almost half a year later, Eddie awoke to discover that an unaccountable change had taken place in the body of his beloved. Her belly was starting to swell. Horrified at the sight—and at the phenomenon it seemed to suggest—Ed let out a whimper and sprang from the bed. Dragging the body out to his backyard, he buried it as far down in the unyielding soil as he was able to dig.

But it was too late. Insane as it seemed, the conclusion that Ed had leapt to was true. Somehow, the seed he had deposited into the belly of the corpse had taken root.

Several months later, a monstrous parturition occurred. An undead thing, sparked by Gein's seed and bred in the womb of a corpse, emerged from its subterranean birthing chamber. Its eyes were blank, its skin was maggot white, and its breath reeked of the grave. Over the years, it grew to adult size.

And ever since, the son of Gein had stalked the Wisconsin countryside.

32

The fourth time she found herself rereading the sentence, Wylie clapped the book shut in disgust. True, it wasn't a very good sentence: "The problematic of 'meaning' in all of these poems may derive, at least in part, from an untenable definition of this concept as *terminal* (the slumber of a determinate signification) rather than *limnal* (a vital, energetic process)."

Still, the problem wasn't the prose. Wylie was fully fluent in academese and could decipher such critical gobblygook with the best of them. Now, however, she was having trouble concentrating. She had too much on her mind.

She let the book—Porter Wallenburg's *The Mutilated Muse: A Psychoaesthetic Study of Emily Dickinson's Poetry*—drop to the floor and reached for the snifter on the side table.

Outside the uncovered windows, the world was frigid and black, but Wylie was encapsulated in comfort. The living-room lamps glowed warmly; the splits of seasoned hardwood crackled and popped in the fireplace. At her feet, Melville lay snoozing on the burgundy Bokhara, while the lilting strains of Dvořák's *American Quartet*— a piece of music that never failed to move her—flowed from the CD speakers. Her children lay asleep in their bedrooms upstairs. Directly above her head, she could dimly discern the muffled slam of a closet door. Paul was up there packing.

Under these circumstances, Wylie would normally have felt suffused with contentment—"glad to the brink of fear," to quote her favorite line from Emerson. But tonight, she was troubled with a vague sense of unease.

Part of the problem was her usual pre-Christmas anxiety. The thought of the approaching holiday filled her with pleasure, but also with something like dread. There was just so much work to be done! This year, for example, she was planning to invite the Hellers and another couple over to the house for a holiday lunch. Wylie had found a recipe for a spectacular turkey gallantine in *The New York Times* and was seriously tempted to make it. Presently, however, she was torn between two conflicting fantasies. In the first, she pictured the beaming faces of her guests as she brought the dazzling dish to the table. In the other, she saw herself trapped in the kitchen for an entire day, cursing herself for having undertaken such an insanely complicated task.

Even while having these thoughts, Wylie was aware that they were really a way of distracting herself from a deeper concern. Paul was leaving in the morning, and she was worried about his trip.

For most of her life, Wylie had thought of Wisconsin as a friendly, folksy place—the home of Clydesdale horses, cheddar cheese, and "the beer that made Milwaukee famous." Lately, however, she had come to associate it with far more sinister things—madness, murder, mysterious abductions. She kept telling herself that her fears for Paul's safety were exaggerated: after all, he was only going out there to deliver a lecture! But she could not shake her forebodings. She felt like the young woman in *Dracula,* whose beloved is about to depart on a business trip to darkest Transylvania.

On the rug, Melville let out a muffled whimper and twitched in his sleep. Wylie lifted the glass to her mouth and sipped, savoring the Courvoissier for a bit before letting it slide down her throat.

The living room was full of things she loved—posters

and prints and assorted artifacts that she and Paul had collected in the years of their marriage. A few were quite costly. Occupying the center of the mantel, for example, was a handcarved statuette from New Guinea— a squatting woman with a headdress like a spike—that she and Paul had purchased with his first royalty check from *Slaughterhouse*.

For the most part, however, the objects had a strictly sentimental value. Right now, for instance, Wylie was gazing at an African tribal mask that hung on the opposite wall. Paul had bought it for a song at a big outdoor flea market in Paris during their honeymoon trip to Europe, twelve years before. Just looking at it now brought back happy memories: Paul trying to bargain in his fractured French, while the dashiki-garbed vendor struggled to hide his amusement.

Cheap as it was (Paul and the vendor had finally settled on fifty francs), the wooden mask was an elegant object. Wylie had always regarded it as a piece of pure sculpture, abstracted from any practical function. Now, however, as she stared at the stylized features, she became acutely aware that she was looking at something uncanny: the face of a god—or a demon.

In that instant, the long-familiar mask became a living presence. Its hollow eyes seemed to stare back at her; its puckered mouth appeared to be shaping a word, as though preparing to deliver an augury.

When she caught herself listening intently—as though truly expecting the spirit to speak—Wylie let out an incredulous snort. *Get a grip,* she scolded herself silently.

She was raising the snifter to her mouth again when something spidery skittered down the back of her neck.

With a loud cry, Wylie jolted half out of her seat, sloshing brandy all over her lap.

"Jesus!" Paul exclaimed behind her.

Wylie squeezed her eyes shut and sank back in the chair, her heart thudding. She exhaled forcefully. "God. You scared me half to *death*."

"Scared *you?*" Paul said, stepping around to the side of the chair. "You almost gave me a heart attack, screaming like that." He glanced down at her lap. "Hope that wasn't the Courvoisier your dad gave us."

Wylie nodded. "Yep. Got a hankie?"

"Hold on." He strode out of the room, returning a few moments later with a wad of paper towels. Perching himself on the arm of the chair, he reached down and blotted up the brandy on Wylie's jeans.

"Think we can squeeze it out of here?" he asked, holding up the dampened wad. "Maybe salvage a few drops? I hate to see it go to waste."

"Don't blame *me*," said Wylie. "You're the one who snuck up on me."

"I didn't sneak up. I walked in the way I always do and gave your neck a little tickle. You must have been lost in the clouds."

Wylie glanced up at the wooden mask. "I was just—" She shook her head and glanced at Paul. "Finished packing?"

"Yup. All ready to go."

She reached for his right hand. "I kind of wish you weren't."

"You and the kids'll be fine," he said, brushing a wisp of hair from her forehead. "Melville'll protect you."

She glanced down at the slumbering dog. "Right," Wylie said sarcastically. "Just looking at him fills me with a profound sense of security." She gave her head an amused shake. "Good-for-nothing dog," she said fondly.

"I wouldn't say *nothing*. You could always lay him across the driveway. He'd make an outstanding speed bump."

Wylie smiled, then looked up at Paul, her expression growing somber. "It's not me and the kids I'm worried about," she said.

"Wylie—"

"I know, I know," she said quickly, shaking her head. "It's just . . . I guess I'm still shaken up about Hobart."

Paul ballooned out his cheeks and gave a sputtering sigh. "Yeah," he said, his voice barely audible. The news of Hobart's death had hit both of them hard. "But remember—the guy had his own TV show. Nowadays, people like that attract all kinds of weirdos."

Wylie gave him a skeptical look. "You don't think it's a funny coincidence? That he was murdered right after your debate?"

"Who knows?" said Paul. "But the way I figure it is, if *that's* why he was killed, the murderer must be a *really* big fan of my book."

"Somehow," said Wylie, "I'm not comforted."

Paul bent down and kissed her widow's peak. "You're beautiful when you're worried."

"Thanks," she said, smiling wanly. "And what about this other guy—whatsisname, the journalist—?"

"Heckley," said Paul.

He had gotten a call two days earlier, from a Milwaukee police sergeant named Streator. Some friends of Stan Heckley's had reported him missing. When questioned by the cops, they had revealed, among other facts, that Heckley had been obsessed with Paul Novak and *Slaughterhouse.* Paul had told Streator everything he knew, which wasn't much—that he had received a flattering letter from Heckley a few months before and had sent a polite response.

Now, Paul gave a weary shrug. "Look, no one knows for sure if something's even happened to the guy. I mean, he's a bachelor—no wife, no kids, no family ties. Maybe he just decided to pick up and get out of town for a while. Take a tropical vacation. Research a story. Whatever."

"Without telling *anyone?*"

Paul rose to his feet. "Come on, Wylie. Stop fretting. I'll be fine. I'll give my talk, maybe do a few newspaper interviews, look up a couple of acquaintances. The way I figure it, the biggest danger I face is freezing my butt off."

"That would be too bad. I'm very fond of your butt."

"Believe me, the feeling's mutual," he said, holding out his right hand. When she reached out and grabbed it, he pulled her to her feet and into an embrace. She pressed her cheek against his chest while he held her close.

"Look who's decided to wake up," he said after a moment.

Wylie moved her head away from Paul's chest and glanced around him. Melville was on his feet, staring at them expectantly.

"Hey, mutt," Wylie said, "you going to take care of me while Daddy's away?"

"You know," said Paul, "I saw a movie like that at a frat party once. Only the dog was a Great Dane, and this young woman was—"

Wylie silenced him with a poke to the solar plexus, then moved across the living room, switching off the lights.

Hand in hand, they headed into the big kitchen. It was still fragrant from the gingerbread cookies she and Diana had baked that afternoon. Rinsing out her snifter, Wylie placed it upside down in the Rubbermaid drain, while Paul got the dishwasher going. Melville trotted in a few seconds later and paused at the back door, tail wagging impatiently.

"Okay, okay," said Wylie, stepping to the door and pulling it open. The big Labrador bounded down the steps and across the snow, a dim shape receding into the darkness of the encircling woods. Wylie pushed the door closed again as a frigid draft gusted into the room.

Paul came up beside her and put an arm around her shoulders, drawing her close. They stood there for a while, looking silently through the glass panes of the door. Outside, the moon gave the world a silvery sheen. That afternoon, glancing out the kitchen window, Wylie had been struck by how much the silent, snow-blanketed scenery resembled a black-and-white photograph, as though it were an Ansel Adams landscape. Now, in the moonlit darkness, it looked like the negative from which the print had been made.

Suddenly, Paul stirred beside her. "You know," he said pensively, "it *is* pretty isolated here. Maybe my mom's right. Maybe we *should* think about putting in an alarm system."

She glanced up at him, surprised. *"Now* who's being the worrywart?"

"I guess," he sighed. Then, after the briefest pause: "Did you remember to enter the police department's number into the autodialer?"

"The police, fire department, county hospital. Everything but the National Guard." She rose on her tiptoes and kissed his cheek.

"Let's see," said Paul, as though trying to get hold of a fugitive thought. "There was one more thing I wanted to—oh, yeah. Just dump all my mail on my study desk. I'm not expecting anything that can't wait 'til I get home."

Melville was finished now and ranging back and forth over the snow, sniffing busily at it, the very picture of the eager hunter with nothing to hunt. Pulling open the door again, Paul let out a sharp whistle. Melville took a big mouthful of snow and trotted reluctantly back to the house.

Kneeling, Wylie rubbed him down with an old towel she kept in the wood box near the back door. Then she and Paul crossed the wooden floor, he switched off the fluorescent light, and they stepped into the hallway, the kitchen door swinging shut behind them. Melville was always banished to the kitchen for the night. Even after all these years, he still couldn't be trusted not to chew up their living-room furniture. Besides, on an icy winter night, the kitchen was the warmest place in the house.

Climbing the carpeted stairs ahead of Paul, Wylie felt a hand on her blue-jeaned behind.

"I guess this is why a gentleman is supposed to *precede* a lady upstairs," she said over her shoulder.

"Gentleman?" said Paul. "You talking to *me?*"

"Apparently not," Wylie said, feeling his hand slide along her bottom.

On the landing, they paused briefly and kissed, then went to check on their children.

Diana, who would turn eight in February, was surrounded by so many stuffed animals that in the dim light that spilled in from the hallway, it was hard to distinguish her head from the collection of teddy bears, puppies, and pussycats that crowded her pillow.

"You sure she's there?" whispered Paul.

"I hope so."

"Oh, yeah. Now I see her. For a minute, I thought we had a changeling situation on our hands—you know, our kid abducted by goblins and replaced with a Gund animal."

Moving to her bedside, they each kissed her sweet-smelling head in turn, then crossed the hall to their son's room.

Littered with dozens of toy mutant warriors—Z-bots and X-Men and Power Rangers—Matt's floor looked like a battlefield strewn with doll-size casualties. Stepping gingerly over the sprawled plastic figures, Paul and Wylie moved to the side of the slumbering boy.

"Sweet dreams, pal," Paul whispered, lightly stroking his son's cheek. Wylie bent and put her lips to Matt's forehead, feeling a pang as she did so. Bedtime was one of the few remaining occasions when she was still permitted to kiss her son. He had already reached the age when he cringed from more public displays of maternal tenderness.

Softly closing the door behind them, Wylie and Paul walked down the hallway into their thickly carpeted bedroom.

"Brrr—it's *cold* in here!" Wylie said, shivering. The automatic thermostat had shut down the furnace at eleven—twenty minutes earlier—and their big, airy room was always the first to cool down.

Pulling what Paul called her "Grandma Moses special" from her bureau, Wylie tore off her sweater and jeans and slipped into the plaid flannel gown. As she hurried toward the bathroom, she saw that Paul, who was changing into his own checkered pj's, looked slightly disappointed.

Probably, she thought, he had pictured something else on the last night before their separation: his lovely wife slowly stripping off her clothes, then climbing into bed in some silky little getup with spaghetti straps and a plunging front.

Well, it was too cold for sexy lingerie. But she would make it up to him.

She was patting herself dry when Paul entered the bathroom. "Don't take long," she said, rising from the seat and kissing him lightly on the mouth. He was back in the bedroom two minutes later. When he slipped under the blankets, her body had already generated a welcoming heat.

They lay in each other's arms, discussing a few last-minute matters. Wylie loved to snuggle under the blankets with Paul on a cold winter night. There was a coziness about it that made her feel like a child again. He stroked her back while they talked—another sensation she loved. She regarded her back as a major erogenous zone and often wondered if other women felt the same way.

After a while, his hand slid down the curve of her spine and worked its way under her nightgown. She parted her legs for his fingers. She and Paul hadn't made love in a week—their schedules had kept them apart. When he touched her, she could feel how wet she was.

She reached between his legs. "Mmmm," she whispered. "You're hard." She liked how easy it was to arouse him.

He nuzzled her neck. Placing a hand against his chest, she nudged him onto his back.

"Just lie there," she whispered, rising to her knees and pulling away the comforter. "Here," she said, tugging at the waistband of his pajama bottoms. "Let's get these off."

She worked them down and off his legs and tossed them over the bedside. Then, holding back her hair with one hand, she bent over him and took him in her mouth.

"Let me lick you for a while," he pleaded hoarsely after a few minutes.

"Not yet," she said, looking up. Puling up her nightgown, she straddled him, guiding him into herself. She slid up and down—slowly at first, then faster and harder—until she was afraid he was going to come. "Does it feel good?" she whispered, bending to his ear.

Reaching up, he clutched her arms and pulled her onto her side. She made a soft, protesting noise as he drew himself out of her. Yanking up her nightgown, he buried his face between her legs.

He made her come twice that way. "Come back inside me," she said breathlessly, reaching down for him. He plunged himself inside her and put his open mouth to hers. She could taste herself on his lips. She slid her tongue around his mouth until she could tell by the violence of his movements that he was ready to come. Reaching a hand underneath herself, she cupped his contracted balls. Instantly, he came so hard that they both ended up half off the mattress, Paul lying limp, Wylie stroking his damp hair and murmuring softly, "Did you like that, baby? Did you like it . . . ?"

Snow fell that night. Though the storm had petered out by the time Paul and Wylie awoke, it left a treacherous glaze on the roads. Switching on the radio at 6:30 A.M., Wylie heard the expected announcement: the local schools had been shut for the day. Paul spent the morning fretting about his flight, afraid that it, too, would be canceled. By 10:30, however, the sun was out, the day had warmed, and the ice had turned to slush.

At 10:45, Wylie was on the phone with a neighbor, Emily Perlin, whose family lived half a mile away. Of course, Emily said. She'd be happy to entertain Matt and Diana while Wylie drove Paul to the airport. Her own children were going a little stir-crazy from all the recent snow days and would welcome the company.

Hanging up the receiver, Wylie gazed out the window at the deep, silent woods and the glittering fields of snow.

Just before noon, Paul, Wylie, and the children—who were bearing a gift of yesterday's gingerbread cookies on a foil-wrapped Styrofoam plate—climbed into their Cherokee. At the Perlin place, just across Stoddard Bridge, Paul got out to give his kids a good-bye hug and kiss. Then he and Wylie headed off for the airport, forty miles away.

His plane left precisely on time. At approximately 1:30—while Wylie was driving away from the airport—the mail carrier deposited the day's delivery in the Novaks' white-painted mailbox: four bills, an alumni newsletter from Wylie's college, three mail-order clothing catalogs, and a big manila envelope addressed to Paul from Mr. Lewis Stimpson of Milwaukee.

Sorting through the mail after arriving back home, Wylie tossed the newsletter into the garbage, saved the catalogs for recycling, filed away the bills for future payment, and placed Lewis Stimpson's envelope—unopened—on Paul's study desk.

33

Like a drumbeat in the far distance, the pain was so faint at first that he was only dimly aware of it. Gradually, it grew stronger, like an approaching parade. Two minutes later, Streator felt as if a whole regiment of jackbooted troopers were tromping inside his head.

Yanking open the top right-hand drawer of his desk, he fished around for his aspirin bottle, praying it wasn't empty. He'd been devouring several pills a day for the past week or so, and he kept forgetting to replenish his supply.

Exhaling a breath of relief at the feeble rattle inside the bottle, he thumbed off the lid and spilled the three remaining pills into his palm. Then, pushing himself out of his chair, he headed for the hallway water cooler.

He filled a little paper cup and popped the aspirins into his mouth. The water tasted great—cold and sweet. So did the second cup, and the third. The Chicago pan pizza he and Frank Turner had shared for lunch had left him with a savage thirst.

Crumpling the empty cup, he aimed a foul shot at the trash can in the corner. The little paper ball bounced off the wall and landed on the floor.

"Do me a favor," growled a voice behind him. "Don't try out for the Bucks. Their season's for shit as it is."

Turning, Arby saw Donald Ryan lumbering down the hallway, bulging gut, florid face, thick crop of graying hair that looked as if it had been trimmed with a hedge clipper.

Stopping an arm's length from Arby, Ryan peered at him through slitted eyes. " 'S matter, Streator? You don't look too hot."

I don't feel *too hot* Arby thought. The troops in his head had started marching at double time. Squeezing his eyes tight, he massaged the sockets with the heels of his hands.

"Damn headache," he muttered.

"No surprise," Ryan said, reaching for the cup dispenser. "I keep tellin' you, Streator, you're gonna pop a fuckin' vein, you don't lighten up."

Arby gave a little grunt. He didn't much care for Ryan. The man had all the social skills of a roadhouse bouncer and couldn't seem to formulate a sentence without at least one four-letter word.

Still, he was a capable cop. Among other assignments, he was currently handling the Heckley business. Arby himself—after remembering the phone call he had received from Heckley right after Darlene Redding's murder—had taken a brief interest in the journalist's disappearance, thinking it might have something to do with the Zipper case. But after satisfying himself that there was no apparent connection, he had passed on the matter to Ryan.

"Turn up anything on Heckley?" asked Streator.

Ryan balled up his paper cup and tossed it at the trash can. "Swish," he said as it dropped through the hole. He looked at Arby with an arrogant smirk. "All in the fuckin' wrist."

"I'm impressed. What about Heckley?"

"Zilch so far. Spoke to his landlady. Talk about being hit with the ugly stick. Wooo-eee, this is one skaggy-looking broad. Thing is, I'm pretty fuckin' sure this Heckley was playin' hide the kielbasa with her."

"Why's that?"

"Just a feelin' is all," Ryan said. "Claims she's pissed 'cause he skipped without payin' the rent, but I think there's more to it. I think he was boinkin' her. Probably the first time she's been laid since fuckin' D-day. Now that he's split, she's steamin'.' "

"Hell hath no fury."

"Whatever. Point is, she don't act like Heckley ripped her off for a couple months' rent. She acts like he dumped her—hard."

"She have any bright ideas about where loverboy might be?"

Ryan shrugged. "All she knows is, he was hot on the trail of something. 'Biggest story of his life.' That's what he told her."

Streator looked intently at the detective. "What story?"

"Something to do with this writer guy, Novak."

Arby shook his head. "Amazing how that name keeps popping up."

"Howdaya mean?"

Arby counted off on the first three fingers of his right hand, beginning with his thumb. "First Patti Atkins. She buys this guy's book in the mall; an hour later, she's snatched from the rest room and killed. Then Hobart. He's on that TV show with Novak; next day, him and his wife are chopped into pieces. And now Heckley disappears."

"What kinda book is it, anyways?" Ryan asked. Pulling out a grimy-looking hankie, he blew his nose with a honk.

"It's about Ed Gein."

"You're shittin' me," Ryan exclaimed, peering into the hankie before stuffing it back inside his pocket. "The Geiner!" He gave a little guffaw. "I still remember my old man scarin' the livin' crap out of me when I was a kid—tellin' me how crazy ol' Ed was gonna come creepin' into my bedroom at night, turn me into burger meat if I didn't behave." He looked at Arby, eyebrows raised. "Hey, maybe *he's* one you're lookin' for."

"Your father?" said Arby.

Ryan let out a single explosive "haw!" "Wouldn't put

it past the old bastard if he was still livin'. But naw, I meant ol' Eddie. Maybe he's come back from the grave—just like my old man used to say."

"Maybe he has, Donald," Arby said wearily. "Maybe we're chasing a ghost." He drew a deep breath and let it out in a slow, silent whistle. "Sure as hell feels that way sometimes."

By the time Arby got back to his office, the aspirins had started to kick in. Hands shoved into his back pockets, he strolled behind his desk and stood by the window. It was sunny outside and warm enough to make the shoveled sidewalks below glisten with the runoff from the piled snow.

Waiting for the walk signal at the corner of West State Street, a businessman in an unbuttoned winter coat hopped backward as a passing bus splashed puddle water onto the curb. A mother pushing a baby stroller stopped to loosen the hood of her infant's heavy parka. And at Chuckie Frewer's wagon, which occupied its spot on Seventh Street every season of the year, a half-dozen people lined up for their hot dogs, cheeseburgers, and coffee.

Streator, lost in thought, stared down at these sights without seeing them.

Suddenly, he stepped over to his desk and seated himself. Flipping open his notepad, he grabbed a pencil and wrote three names across the top of the sheet: HOBART, ATKINS, HECKLEY. In the center of the page, he printed NOVAK, then drew three lines radiating from the writer's name to the others.

Brow furrowed, he stared down at the page for a long time. It just didn't make sense. What possible relationship could there be between Novak and the others? Arby sat there, tapping the eraser against his chin and trying to figure out a connection.

He was jarred from his thoughts by the trilling of his phone. It was the desk sergeant. Frowning, Arby listened for a moment, then said, "Send her right up." Replacing the receiver, he leaned back in his chair and thought back to the last painful visit he had had with the woman. What could she want this time?

He was still pondering this question when Sheila Atkins appeared at his door.

Arby got to his feet. "Mrs. Atkins," he said, motioning toward the molded plastic chair at the side of his desk. "Please."

Unbuttoning her overcoat, she shrugged it off her shoulders and seated herself. She was dressed in a gray cotton turtleneck, black wool skirt, and ankle boots. A plain gold cross hung around her neck. Her appearance hadn't changed since he'd seen her last. If anything, her face looked even more angular and gaunt, as though grief were a blade that had whittled away every ounce of superfluous flesh.

"I see from the newspapers," she said, dispensing with formalities, "that my club will be welcoming a new member."

"Club?"

"You know. Bereaved Mothers of Milwaukee. Very exclusive—though the roster's getting bigger all the time."

Arby looked at her without saying anything. He didn't know what to say.

She smiled bitterly. "Well, I won't take up too much of your time, Sergeant Streator. I'm sure you're hot on the trail of the culprit."

In spite of himself, Arby felt his ire rise at the woman's tone. "Did you come here just to bust my chops, Mrs. Atkins?"

"Not at all," she said, crossing a leg. "I've come to talk about the Reverend Victor Hobart."

Arby looked surprised. "That's not within my jurisdiction, Mrs. Atkins. If you have any information, you should be telling it to the police up in Waushara."

"Oh, but this concerns *your* investigation, Sergeant."

Arby nodded slowly. "Go ahead."

"I was with the Reverend Hobart the day before his . . ."—her voice cracked slightly—"his murder."

Arby leaned forward on his elbows. "Where was this?"

"New York City. I went out there to see him debate that awful man."

Arby gave her a quizzical look.

"Novak," said Sheila, looking as though she were tasting something vile.

Arby shook his head in amazement.

"What is it?" asked Sheila.

"No. Nothing. It's just—I was just thinking about this Novak character when you arrived."

"Yes?" she said eagerly. "Then you believe that he might be to blame in some way?"

"No," Arby said. "I don't. No matter which way I figure it, it just doesn't add up."

"But don't you see?" Sheila said, clenching her fists and leaning forward in her chair. "The Reverend Hobart saw the evil unleashed by that man. And he tried to defeat it. He was like a knight, a glorious knight, armed with a flaming sword of righteousness. One brave man, going forth to fight a monster. Only the monster was too powerful. It devoured him." Her voice faltered and Arby saw the moisture in her eyes. "Just as it devoured my child!"

"Mrs. Atkins," Arby said gently, "I'm not sure I—"

"It's that book!" Sheila exclaimed, her voice rising to a near shout. *"Slaughterhouse!"* Her expression had turned suddenly fierce, almost fanatical. To Arby's eyes, she looked—there was no other way to describe it— slightly crazed. "It killed the Hobarts! It killed my child! And it will keep on destroying and destroying and destroying until you do something to stop it!"

Trying to gather his thoughts, Arby said nothing. When he finally spoke, he kept his voice soft. "Mrs. Atkins, I have to tell you I just don't see how a book can kill people."

"But it can!" she cried. "You have to be blind not to see it! There is something evil about that book!" She squeezed her eyes and lips tight, as though struggling to get hold of herself. When she looked at Arby and spoke again, her voice was more subdued, though it quavered slightly from her efforts to control it. "Here's my question, Sergeant Streator: can you think of anything or anyone else with a direct link to both my daughter and the Reverend Hobart?"

Arby opened his mouth to reply—he intended to say that there seemed to be no link at all between the two killings—when he was struck by a thought so unexpected that his head literally gave a little jolt.

Sheila, noticing his strange expression, narrowed her eyes. "What is it?"

"Huh? Oh, n-nothing," he stammered. "Sorry. I just . . . Can I ask you a question, Mrs. Atkins?"

"All right," she said, still peering at him with a puzzled look.

"Did you ever hear of a man—a journalist—named Heckley? Stan Heckley?"

Sheila's brow wrinkled. "Not that I—" Suddenly, she raised her eyebrows. "Wait. A journalist? Why, yes—"

Arby ran his tongue over his lips. His mouth had gone suddenly dry. "Yes?"

"Now I remember. Yes, yes. He telephoned me right after Patti . . ." Her expression was undergoing a striking change—from deep concentration to sudden realization to something like absolute contempt and loathing.

"Yes?" said Arby. "What did he want?"

"Want?" Sheila said in a voice charged with disgust. "To batten on the corpse of my child. Like all his kind. *Vultures.*"

Though Arby was staring at Sheila, she seemed not to notice. Finally, she stirred from the hateful recollection. "Why do you ask?"

"It's not important, really," he said, trying to sound nonchalant. Then, clearing his throat, he said, "Mrs. At-

kins, tell you what: I haven't read Novak's book yet."
He shrugged. "Maybe I'm missing something. I promise
you I'll get hold of a copy and give it an honest look."

Sheila regarded him silently, as though trying to decide whether he was just humoring her. Finally, as though giving him the benefit of the doubt, she gathered up her coat, rose from the seat, and extended her hand. Arby stood up and shook it.

"Thank you, Sergeant, for hearing me out," she said. "You know where to find me if you have to." Turning on her heels, she walked briskly from the office.

For a long moment after she was gone, Arby just stood there, gazing at the empty doorway. His head was spinning. *No way!* he told himself. *You've gone completely nuts! Hell, it makes as much sense as Ed Gein's damn ghost!*

And yet . . .

It was Sheila's own question that had brought the wild idea to mind. *Can you think of anything or anyone else with a direct link to both my daughter and the Reverend Hobart?*

As a matter of fact, Arby could: a person who—it turned out—also had reason to despise Heckley.

Dropping back into his seat, Arby grabbed his pencil and erased the name NOVAK from the center of the page.

Then, in its place, he printed: SHEILA ATKINS?????

34

Pushing through the revolving door, Sheila emerged onto the sidewalk. It was an unusually mild day for that time of year in Milwaukee—almost balmy compared to the Siberian cold that had gripped the city for the past two weeks. In the sunlit plaza across the avenue, people moved along the shoveled walkways like promenaders on a Sunday stroll in June.

Sheila stood in the shadow of the police administration building and wondered which way to go. By now, of course, that was a depressingly familiar feeling to her. She was often at a loss nowadays.

She wasn't even sure what to make of her meeting with Streator. True, he hadn't dismissed her out of hand, the way he'd done last time. That was an improvement. But it was possible that he'd simply been humoring her. She certainly hoped not. She was sure that if he kept his promise and read Novak's book, he would come to see the truth that was so clear to her.

What now? she wondered, checking her wristwatch. Perhaps she should walk over to the Milwaukee *Journal Sentinel* building or the headquarters of the *Milwaukee Today* TV show and try to interest someone in her theory.

A sudden grinding pang in the pit of her stomach settled the matter. Before she did anything else, she needed some food.

She hadn't eaten a bite since daybreak, when she'd

nibbled on a slice of blackened toast and force-fed herself a few spoonfuls of cottage cheese. Her appetite—not only for food but for all physical pleasure—had perished along with her child.

Sometimes, when she stared at her gaunt, hollow-eyed face in the bathroom mirror, Sheila recalled with a kind of wonder the trouble she used to have with her weight—her constant struggle to resist the temptation of a midmorning Danish or an extra serving of mashed potatoes at dinnertime. But that was in a different lifetime. In this one, the one she had entered the day Patti's body was found, Sheila suffered from the opposite problem: taking in enough nourishment to keep herself going.

Spotting the white refreshment van parked along Seventh Street, Sheila headed across the plaza and took her place behind two middle-aged men who were engaged in a heated chat about the NFL playoffs. While she waited, Sheila checked out the offerings printed on the menu board affixed to the side of the truck.

She was still undecided when she reached the counter.

"How's your chili?" she asked the scrawny young man who grinned down at her. With his shaved skull, enormous square teeth, and cadaverous skin, there was something almost comically grotesque about him. He looked like one of those cartoon skeletons that decorate store windows around Halloween.

"Best in the Midwest," he answered. "But I just sold my last bowlful. Sorry."

Sheila made a "no problem" gesture. "Makes life easier," she said. "I'll have a bratwurst, please, with sauerkraut. And a small coffee. Black."

"You got it," Chuckie said, turning away from her.

Not much later, he set a steaming Styrofoam cup in front of her. The coffee gave off an acrid smell, as if it had been sitting in its big metal brewer all day. Sheila didn't care. Nothing she ate or drank had much flavor anymore. Perhaps if the coffee was bitter enough, she might actually have the sensation that she was tasting something.

"Some weather, huh?" said the skeletal young man, laying her lunch on the counter.

Sheila smiled thinly and nodded. Answering seemed like too much effort. She had no patience anymore for meaningless chitchat. She lifted the sausage and bun from its long paper boat and took a bite.

Immediately, she knew that she'd made a dreadful mistake. How could she have forgotten? Patti had always loved bratwurst. Whenever the two of them were out shopping at the Grand Avenue Mall, they would invariably stop for lunch at the International Food Court and buy a couple of brats at the Bavarian Sausage Haus.

The recollection caused Sheila's throat to constrict. She began to choke.

"You okay?" said the counterman, leaning forward on his hands.

Eyes watering, Sheila grabbed for her coffee and washed down the food, burning her tongue in the process.

"Yes," she said hoarsely. She felt like a fool. "I just—" she coughed into a fist, shook her head, cleared her throat. "It just went down the wrong tube."

"Had me worried there," said Chuckie, looking at her intently. "Thought I'd have to do a Heimlich on you."

Pulling a napkin from the metal dispenser, Sheila blotted her eyes. "I'm fine," she said. As she dropped the balled-up napkin into the boat that held her bratwurst— *so much for lunch*—her eye was caught by something on the rear wall of the truck: a strange picture taped above the grill.

The image was so smoky and grease-stained that its details were hard to make out. Even so, there was something very familiar about it—a dark-haired young woman, crowned with a halo. Her eyes were trained fervently skyward, and she clutched a strange object in one hand: a candlestick perhaps, or—*no*—*some sort of implement . . . ?*

"That picture," said Sheila, pointing with her chin. "Who is that?"

Chuckie glanced over his shoulder, then back at Sheila. "Got me," he said with a shrug. "Don't even remember where I found it."

"She's a saint," Sheila said, frowning. "I just can't remember . . ." Unconsciously, she raised her right hand and absently toyed with her crucifix.

"So familiar," she said, half aloud. "So familiar."

"You know," said the counterman, "you look kinda familiar, too."

Sheila tore her gaze away from the tantalizing picture and looked at the young counterman, who was staring at her with a strange intensity. Suddenly, his pale eyes widened. "Wait a sec. Aren't you . . . ?"

Quickly, Sheila unclasped her handbag, fished out her purse, removed a five-dollar bill, then pushed it over the counter. "How much do I owe you?" she said tautly.

But the cadaverous young man wasn't listening. "I seen your picture in the papers," he said excitedly. "You're one of their moms, right? That Atkins girl, right?"

Sheila had experienced this kind of thing before, though it always came as a shock when it happened. It was a source of amazement—and utter abhorrence—to her that there were people in the world who regarded her as a celebrity because her daughter had been murdered by a fiend. *So sick! So sick!*

Mustering every shred of self-control, she shoved the bill an inch closer to Chuckie and barked, "Here!" She was reluctant to leave without collecting her change. She would feel as if she had tipped the loathesome young man.

Finally, however, she could stand it no longer. A few other people had appeared at the van, and Sheila was afraid that if she remained there for one more second, all her outrage would erupt and she would make an embarrassing scene.

Shooting the counterman a murderous look, Sheila turned on her heels and stalked away. As she marched down the sidewalk, she thought she could feel his prurient gaze boring into her back.

And she was right.

What she didn't know, of course, was that as Chuckie Frewer stared at her receding form, his whole body had begun to quiver with excitement.

35

Mrs. Charles Edward Frewer hadn't intended to get pregnant. At the age of fifty-one—with her "monthlies" occurring at increasingly irregular intervals—she was surprised to discover that she was still fertile enough to conceive.

Her husband was equally surprised—and not the least bit pleased. As the president of Veri-Best Paper Goods, Inc.—a company that supplied cups, containers, and carry-out packages to some of the nation's leading fast-food chains—he had never had much time for a family life. When his only child, Catherine, had graduated from college ten years earlier, he had celebrated with a bottle of Dom Perignon—not because his daughter had earned a *cum laude* degree but because his own parenting duties were finally over. Or so he'd assumed.

Still, an abortion was out of the question. Both parents were practicing Catholics. And so, on a frigid night in March 1965, Charles Edward Frewer, Jr.—to be known as "Chuckie" to the few acquaintances he would make in his life—came into the world.

His father, nearing sixty at the time, had little use for his namesake. He was too preoccupied with his business affairs as well as with the upkeep of his twenty-eight-year-old mistress, a former table dancer at the X-tasy Lounge, now luxuriously ensconced in a condo on Milwaukee's Gold Coast. But Chuckie's mother doted on her change-of-life baby. That was the sweetest time of

Chuckie Frewer's life, although he could never recall it with any clarity. It lived on in his mind less as a memory than a sensation—a warm, blissful feeling, like a sunbath on a honeyed summer day.

Unfortunately for Chuckie Frewer—and for the victims who would someday pay for his sufferings—that idyll did not last very long. Precisely one week before her fifty-ninth birthday, when her cherished little boy was just entering third grade, Madelaine Frewer died of ovarian cancer.

Five days later, Frieda Poole came to live with him.

Though she'd worked as a professional nanny for a number of years, she was still very young—a slender twenty-five-year-old with a pleasant face and a brisk, no-nonsense manner. In his own no-nonsense way, Chuckie's father had secured her services from a local agency less than forty-eight hours after his wife's demise. All his life, Chuckie could clearly remember the day his father had introduced him to Frieda.

"Now that your mother's dead, you'll need someone to care for you. I wish I could do it, but you know how busy I am. That's why I've hired Miss Poole. I'm not saying she can love you like your mother did. Nobody'll ever do that. But she'll take good care of you."

It was the longest speech his father ever made to him.

She stayed with him for almost five years—right up until the night of the burning. The elder Frewer must have lived at home some of that time, but so infrequently that Chuckie had only the dimmest recollections of his father.

During the time that he and Frieda shared the big house by themselves, Chuckie was subjected to the greatest extremes of pleasure and agony he would ever experience. Nothing—not even the ecstasies he would know later on in his life with his bound and anguished victims—could ever match the intensity of those years with Frieda Poole. She made him what he was, what he became.

Later, immediately after Frieda's sudden death—during that period of his life when Chuckie was in and out of state mental institutions—the examining psychiatrists learned some of the truth. But not all of it. There were things Frieda did to him that Chuckie never told anybody, things too wonderful to share—or too excruciating to reveal.

There were those nights when, as he lay in the darkness, weeping for his lost mother, Frieda would come to him, slide into his bed, and stroke him with her fingers until he subsided in exhaustion. There were his evening baths, when she would kneel at the tubside and soap him until he whimpered, even wept, with pleasure. And the lazy weekend afternoons, when she would dress him in her underwear and giggle and applaud as he minced around her room, then reward him for his performance by kneeling before him and taking him in her mouth.

But then there were the punishments, when he'd done something to displease her. She had done bad things to him, things he made a desperate effort to forget. Those places on his body—his penis, his anus, his nipples—that were, under her loving ministrations, a source of such exquisite pleasure now became the site of unbearable pain. She used simple things to hurt him—wire, tweezers, sewing needles.

At school, Chuckie's behavior became increasingly erratic. He was subject to violent outbursts in class. His father was called in to speak to the guidance counselor. "It's the trauma of my wife's death," the old man insisted. "The boy was very attached to his mother."

Chuckie said nothing about Frieda; he had become too dependent on the pleasures she provided. Nor did he say anything about the voices he had begun to hear, or the strange visions that sometimes came to him, even while he was wide awake.

He was sent to a child psychologist twice a week, but his behavior remained too disruptive. Eventually, his father was forced to withdraw him from public school and send him to a private one for "special" children. Things went on this way for over four years.

Then one afternoon, just before Chuckie's twelfth birthday, he heard strange noises emanating from Frieda's bedroom, and when he climbed the stairs and swung open her unlocked door, he found her in bed with a man.

It took him a while to understand what he was seeing—the tangled limbs, the hairy male backside heaving between Frieda's wide-flung legs, the grunts and gasps and groans. He had never seen people fucking, though Frieda had described it to him many times.

A minute later, the man let out a shuddering cry, gave a few violent thrusts, then sank heavily onto Frieda's body, burying it under his sweaty bulk. After a short time, he rolled off of her. Frieda lay there as though lost in a pleasant dream, her face damp and flushed. Suddenly, her eyes fluttered open and she spotted Chuckie in the doorway. She sat up lazily and leaned her back against the headboard, cushioning her neck with a pillow. Planting her feet on the mattress, she opened her legs and stared at Chuckie over her knees.

Her companion followed her glance. Seeing Chuckie, he broke into a leering grin and sat up beside Frieda.

"That the nutcase you take care of?" he said in an amused voice.

Frieda snorted. "Yeah." She moved her knees wider apart.

Chuckie stood there open-mouthed, gaping at the sopping place between her legs. He had seen her naked many times before, of course—she liked to parade around him with her clothes off. But the sight of her body never failed to transfix him.

"Hey, kid," the man said. "Whaddya think? Nice-looking snatch, huh?" The big, hairy-bellied man draped his arm right around Frieda's shoulders, cupping his hand over one breast. "Ever fuck her?"

Freida had laughed. "With *his* little dick?"

Turning toward Frieda, the man had reached his left hand between her legs. Frieda closed her eyes and made a little purring sound as the man slowly worked a finger in and out of her.

Glancing toward the doorway, the big man beckoned to Chuckie. "Come on over here, kid. Maybe she'll give you a piece." Then, when Chuckie remained motionless, he added: "What's the matter—'fraid it'll bite?"

Chuckie felt dizzy, paralyzed. Suddenly, the man removed his hand and held it up to his face, regarding it with a mixture of surprise and amusement. The middle finger was slick with bright red fluid.

"Hey, whaddya know!" he cried out. "It *did* bite me!"

Frieda shot him a look, then reached a hand between her legs. Her fingers came up coated with blood. "Shit," she cried. "My period's started. What a fucking mess."

She scurried from the bed, clutching herself between the legs.

The big man roared with hilarity. "Hey, kid," he called to Chuckie, holding up his bloody middle finger. "Look what she did to me. Better watch your dick. These cunts'll eat you up alive."

Frieda dashed by Chuckie, leaving a trail of scarlet drops on the floor. Chuckie could barely see through the tears that had gushed into his eyes. Anguish rose up inside him and exploded from his throat in a long, piteous wail. Turning, he fled to his bedroom.

It was dark outside by the time he regained his self-control. By then, he had decided what to do.

Creeping down to his father's long-unused basement workshop, he found several suitable pieces of scrap wood. From the three-car garage, he took the big can of spare gasoline. Then, he crept silently up to the second floor.

The door to Frieda's bedroom was shut. Wedging the scrap wood under the door, he splashed the gasoline all over the landing and down the stairs.

Pausing in the front entranceway, he struck a safety

match, tossed it onto the gasoline, and stepped calmly outside. He sat down on the wide front lawn in his pajamas, watching the house ignite and listening hard for Frieda's shrieks.

Much to his disappointment, he never heard any. Thoroughly depleted by her afternoon's exertions, she perished of smoke inhalation without ever emerging from her sleep. That wasn't how Chuckie liked to remember it, though. In the years that followed, whenever he fantasized about her death, he always imagined that she was fully conscious, shrieking in torment while her seared flesh melted from her bones.

Because of his youth and obvious mental derangement, Chuckie escaped prison, though he spent the next nine years in and out of various institutions. During that time, Charles Frewer, Sr., died, leaving the bulk of his wealth to his daughter. Chuckie was left with a pittance.

Even so, he was not entirely unprovided for. Discharged from Mendota in 1991 by a panel of experts who declared that he posed no further threat to society, he was able to purchase a ramshackle bungalow on the outskirts of the city. With the remnants of his meager inheritance, he acquired and equipped his refreshment truck.

Both of these possessions suited his needs perfectly. Chuckie's tumbledown home was the only residence in a desolate area of derelict factories and warehouses. There were no neighbors to take note of Chuckie's strange comings and goings, the limp, unconscious figures he periodically smuggled inside, or the muffled screams that occasionally issued from its flaking walls. And his business allowed him to cruise the city without ever arousing suspicion.

Trolling the streets, of course, was only one way Chuckie located his victims. He had other methods, too. Sometimes, for example, he dressed up in female clothes—the way Frieda had taught him—and cased the women's rooms in big department stores and malls.

He did not select his victims entirely at random. Each one possessed a common trait.

An avid reader who maintained an interest in his religious heritage, Chuckie liked to pore over books about the Spanish Inquisition, the martyrdom of saints, and other instances of religious sacrifice and torment. Once, years before, as he leafed through a copiously illustrated volume on hagiography he had stolen from the local library, he was riveted by an eighteenth-century painting of a female saint. It was not simply the means by which she had been tortured that he found so transfixing; there was something else about her—something about her face. He had not at first recognized what it was: her eyebrows, which were unusually thick and dark and almost formed a single line above her nose.

Frieda Poole's eyebrows had looked like that. It had been one of her most distinctive features—before Chuckie's retributive flames had scorched all her features from her skull.

Each of Chuckie's victims had the same kind of eyebrows. Detective Sergeant Streator, in his endless, frustrated search for a common link among the victims, had never noticed that particular similarity. After all, coroners' reports seldom mention the size and shape of corpses' eyebrows. Streator himself had spent many hours gazing at the faces of the victims, in snapshots and high-school photographs provided by their survivors. He had been struck by many things—the youth and glow and fragility of these doomed children. But he had never been struck by that feature.

But Chuckie had been struck by it. It served as a kind of trigger, setting off responses in him that could be stilled only when he had completed his ghastly work on the savaged corpses of his victims.

Like the others, Patti Atkins had possessed eyebrows that resembled Frieda Poole's.

It was a feature—as Chuckie had just discovered, much to his excitement—that she had obviously inherited from her mother.

36

As she stepped to the kitchen sink with her plastic breakfast bowl—scraped clean of every dab of her favorite cereal, Quaker Instant Oatmeal with artificial Peaches 'n' Cream flavoring—Agatha spotted a small reddish brown stain on the pea-green linoleum beneath the counter. Muttering an imprecation, she hiked up her flowered housedress and knelt to the floor with a grunt. Then, with the edge of her thumbnail, she scratched away at the caked substance—about the size of a rat turd—until she had reduced it to a fine powder.

My Lord, she thought, dusting away the particles with her fingertips, *how much blood did that peckerwood have?*

In spite of her efforts to get Stan Heckley to gush neatly into her basin, the spray from his severed jugular had ended up all over her kitchen, and even now—almost three weeks after she had slashed his throat—Agatha was still finding occasional traces of his dried blood. Still, though she resented the mess he had left in her house, she couldn't really complain. All things considered, the whole potentially disastrous episode had turned out just fine. All that existed of Mr. Stan Nosy-Parker Heckley were a few clotted specks on her linoleum. She had taken care of the rest of him with her usual efficiency.

Even Leon—to give the Devil his due—had acquitted

303

himself respectably for the first time in his good-for-
nothing life. . . .

It had taken a surprisingly long time for the journalist
to die. His blood kept spurting, his body jerking like a
man with St. Vitus's dance. Finally, when his twitching
ceased and the fountain from his gaping gullet ran dry,
she had dragged his worthless carcass into the bathroom
and dumped it into the tub. Then, gathering up her supplies—bucket and mop, sponge and yellow Rubbermaid
gloves—she had set about cleaning up her bespattered
kitchen.

She was still working hard at 4:30 A.M. when she heard
the front door creak open and Leon come creeping in.
He was surprised to find her awake at that ungodly hour.
He was cradling something in one arm, an object roughly
the size and shape of a small pumpkin, wrapped in a
black plastic trash bag. In spite of his efforts to keep the
bundle concealed from her view, she could guess what
it was, especially after he began to prattle excitedly
about what he'd done to the Hobarts. Ordinarily, she
wouldn't have let him bring the nasty thing into her
house, but she was too tired to argue. Let him keep his
damned souvenir! The lunkhead was becoming more
like his no-good father every day.

For the first time, Agatha could even see certain ad-
vantages in that similarity.

When Leon finally got around to asking his mother
why she was scrubbing the kitchen at that time of night,
Agatha instructed him to go look in the bathroom. He
came running back a few seconds later, so excited he
could barely stammer out a question. Agatha had told
him to shut his yap and go to bed. She'd explain everything in the morning. She wanted him to get some rest.
She had another job for him to do.

She let him sleep until half past noon. By the time he
crawled out of bed, she had already gone to the local
hardware store and purchased a box of Hefty extra-

strength trash bags and a hacksaw. The saw alone set her back nearly twenty dollars. She wasn't very happy about that, but she didn't see what choice she had. She didn't own another tool that could cut through human bone.

When Agatha had explained to Leon precisely what he must do, his face had assumed the strangest expression. His eyes got a shiny, faraway look and his mouth curled up into a hungry little grin. At that instant—even with his extra bulk—he looked so much like his shitpoke of a father that the resemblance was truly uncanny.

After instructing him to fetch his hunting knife from his bedroom—the one he had brought with him to the Hobarts'—Agatha had handed Leon the box of trash bags and the hacksaw and left him alone in the bathroom, while she retired to her own room to get a little rest. He was in there until midafternoon. He was such a mess when he emerged—his arms coated in bloody slime up to the elbows, and his face, even his hair, smeared with gore—that she ordered him to turn right around and take a long, hot shower while she disposed of his unspeakable clothing.

They waited until it was good and dark outside before loading up Leon's delivery truck with the big, lumpy bags. Then Agatha went over the instructions carefully, explaining to her lamebrained son exactly what he must do, how he must drive to the outskirts of the city and beyond, depositing each of the bags in a different Dumpster, behind big supermarkets and fast-food restaurants and factories and highway rest stops.

While he was gone, she set about cleaning the bathroom. As she knelt on the tiled floor, scrubbing the leftover gore from the bathtub, she thought for the thousandth—no, *ten* thousandth—time just how much better life would be without men. *Hell, the only thing they're good for is squirting their slime between your legs to make babies!* Why in hell hadn't the good Lord made it so that women could conceive children by themselves?

Even as she framed the question in her mind, Agatha felt a twinge of unease, as though she were on the brink of blasphemy. It wasn't for her to question God's will. Still, it seemed inexplicable that the Lord would make procreation such a vile business. Especially when the end results were jugheads like Leon.

He'd returned a few hours after daybreak, pleased as all get-out with himself. Everything had gone without a hitch, he declared. Agatha didn't rest easy, though. As the days passed, she waited in a state of constant anxiety, expecting the cops to come knocking at any time. . . .

But here it was, three weeks later, and no police officers had appeared on her doorstep. Maybe Leon wasn't such a hopeless loser after all. Maybe he was finally coming into his own. She certainly hoped so. There was one last job for him to do before she could rest easy, and it was the most ticklish one of all, far more difficult than silencing that blabbermouth minister or disposing of Heckley's body parts. She prayed that Leon would be up to the task.

Grabbing hold of the kitchen counter, she rose to her feet with a groan and plodded over to the stove. Striking a wooden match, she lit the back burner and put a pot of water on to boil, then walked over to the cupboard and removed Leon's special mug. It had a little cartoon on it—two naked children, a boy and a girl, standing by a toilet. The boy was clutching himself between the legs and looking nervously at the girl. "No, you can't touch it!" read the words emanating from the boy's mouth. "You already broke yours off!"

Spooning in some instant coffee, she placed the mug on the Formica table, then took an unopened box of Hostess whole-wheat doughnuts from the cupboard and set it down beside the mug. Then she left the kitchen and headed down the hallway to Leon's room.

"C'mon out, boy," she shouted, pounding on the locked door. "I fixed your breakfast."

"Be right out, Mama," came the muffled reply.

Proceeding down the hallway, Agatha entered her bedroom. In contrast to the pigsty her son spent his days in, her own room was tidy as a pin and pretty as a picture in a magazine. The mattress was covered with a frilly, flowered bedspread, the pillows had matching shams, and the window curtains looked like genuine hand-made lace. There were doilies on her dresser top and night table and a multicolored scatter rug on the floor beneath her bentwood rocking chair. Hanging on the walls were framed pictures with inspirational sayings. Her favorite was the one that showed a female cherub with bright blue eyes and shiny yellow hair. It was hovering outside a partially opened window. "Open up," read the caption, "and let an angel into your life!"

Crossing the room, Agatha pulled open her closet, stooped, and removed something sitting just inside the door. Then she trudged back out to the kitchen.

Leon was hunched in his chair, his back to the doorway. He was still in his pajamas—the blue flannel ones covered with little duck decoys. She had bought them for him at Kmart last Christmas.

As she lowered herself into the chair across from him, Leon held out his half-eaten doughnut and shook it accusingly. "Why'd you buy *these?*" he whined. "You *know* I like the powdered kind."

"These here are healthier for you. *Good Housekeeping* says."

"Taste like shit," he grumbled, then took another sullen bite.

"Watch your yap in my house, boy," she said darkly. Then, reaching down beside her chair, she raised the object she had taken from the closet and laid it on the table. It was an attaché case, covered in black imitation leather.

Leon's eyes narrowed. "What's *that?*"

"It's for you."

Leon grinned so broadly that a few doughnut crumbs spilled from his mouth. "Where'd you get it?" he asked excitedly.

"Heckley. He brought it with him to the house."

"Nice," said Leon, running his hand over the top. Suddenly, he shot his mother a wary look. "How come you're givin' it to me?"

"To pack your things in. You're goin' on a little trip."

Then while Leon gaped at her in astonishment, Agatha told him about the arrangements she'd made. She explained about the airplane ride and the rental car and exactly what he must do once he reached his destination. Reaching out to stroke his hand, she described such a perfect future for the two of them that Leon felt his throat constrict with happiness. Once this final threat was removed, they would be safe for the rest of their lives.

"Don't that sound nice, Leon?" she crooned. "Just you and your mama, together forever?"

Leon nodded eagerly. "But, Mama," he said after a moment, "Connecticut's a whole state, ain't it? How'll I know exactly where to go?"

Raising the lid of the case, Agatha reached in and removed a small sheet of stationery. "Found this inside," she said, passing the paper across the table to Leon. "Along with a whole buncha other crap—magazine articles and whatnot, all of it about that damned book about your daddy."

Leon took the paper from her hand and began to peruse it, mouthing the words silently as he read. It was a brief, handwritten note to Stan Heckley—just a couple of sentences—thanking him for his "flattering words about *Slaughterhouse*" but declining his request for an interview.

When Leon finally looked up, his brow was furrowed in puzzlement. "But how's this gonna help—?"

Agatha smiled. " 'Cause that letter come in this," she said, reaching out her right hand.

She was holding a small envelope. Leon took it from her fist and looked at it carefully, a big smile spreading across his face.

Printed in the upper left-hand corner was Paul Novak's home address.

37

While his mama tidied up the kitchen after breakfast, Leon carried his handsome new attaché case into his bedroom. Locking the door, he laid the case on his unmade bed, unsnapped the latches, and raised the lid.

His heart felt like an inflated balloon, he was so excited and proud. After all these years, his mama was finally beginning to treat him with respect. Well, why shouldn't she, the stinking old bitch? He'd proved that he could get the job done. *Twice*—first with the Hobarts, then with that dead lump of shit, Heckley. That was all he wanted: to show his mama he was worthy. To please her and make her proud. To win her love.

A lump came into his throat as he thought about how much he loved his mama, and before he knew it, he was crying again. *Sniveling,* she would call it. She was right about him. He wasn't a man at all, just a weak, spineless little sissy boy. Well, he'd show her. He'd show that fat old sow she was wrong about him.

Grabbing the front of his pullover pajama top, he raised the duck-patterned fabric to his face and wiped his eyes and nose. Then he glanced around his room.

He wouldn't have known exactly what to take with him—he'd never traveled so far from home before!—but his mama had gone over the list, item by item. One pair of underpants. One pair of socks. One change of clothing—T-shirt and pants—in case he got blood all over the outfit he was wearing and had to dispose of it somewhere. And, of course, his toothbrush and dental floss. His mama was a real pain when it came to personal hygiene.

He couldn't bring his hunting knife, of course. He'd asked about it, but his mama had explained about the security at airports. He'd just have to find something to do the job with once he snuck into Novak's house. That shouldn't be a problem, though. Everyone had butcher knives and whatnot in their homes.

Rubbing his palms together in anticipatory pleasure, he bustled about the room, rummaging through his various clothes piles. He took the least fetid underpants he could find, a pair of grubby cotton socks with a little orange stripe running around the ankles, his gray sweatpants, and his newest novelty T-shirt. It showed two speeding cars, one following directly behind the other. The driver of the car in front was leaning out the window, giving the finger to the tailgater. "Unless you're a hemorrhoid," read the caption, "keep off my ass!"

He had to shove the clothes down real hard to fit everything inside the case, but he finally managed. There was a problem, though. There wasn't an inch of space left—and Leon had one more item he was determined to bring along. His mama would have frowned on it, but he thought it would add to the fun.

He'd have to remove something from the attaché case to free up some room. He stood there for a moment, tugging pensively on his lower lip, then reached down, plucked out the stained cotton briefs, and tossed them into a corner.

Hell, for the amount of time he'd be gone, he didn't need a change of underwear.

Getting to his knees, he reached under the bed and brought out an old shoe box. He laid it beside the ataché case, then sat down on the mattress and removed the lid.

Inside lay the thing he'd been working on for the past three weeks. He had fashioned it from the trophy he'd brought back from Plainfield. It had been surprisingly tricky to make. He had gotten the idea from that *Slaughterhouse* book, which gave all kinds of helpful information about his daddy's old tanning methods.

Not that Leon was totally satisfied with the results. For all the tender loving care he had put into it, it looked pretty crude. Still, it was just his first try. He assumed he'd get better with practice. And it didn't look all *that* bad. The lipstick he had bought at that big discount drugstore and applied to the mouth made the thing look almost alive. Sort of.

Reaching into the shoe box, he carefully removed the item, then carried it across the room. He had punched a little hole on either side of it and attached shoestrings, so he could tie it around his head.

He put it on in front of his wall mirror. It felt kind of itchy against his face and didn't smell very good. But as he gazed at himself in the mirror, a jolt of pure sexual electricity hit him right between the legs, so powerful it made his pajama bottoms bulge.

The thing on his face looked so weird, all dark and wrinkled—more like cow leather than human skin. Still, he had managed to preserve enough of the features to make the thing recognizable.

Someone who had known the victim well would have had no trouble identifying the ghastly mask as the face—flayed, cured, and oiled—of Hannah Hobart.

38

The days had been sunny since he'd arrived in Wisconsin, but Paul knew that the weather was too lovely to last. Sure enough, he had awakened that morning to a raw, dismal day. Now, as his rental car raced northward on Route 51, he stared ahead at the lowering sky.

On the radio, a disk jockey named Skeeter was predicting a winter storm by midnight. Skeeter droned on. "Three to five inches of white stuff before it lets up sometime tomorrow morning. Gonna make those country roads and highways a mess. But here's Ray Stevens to remind us that 'Everything Is Beautiful' in its own way. . . ."

Spare me, thought Paul as the mawkish ditty began to play.

Reaching for the radio, he hit the scan button but found nothing except static. Skeeters' *Sounds of Gold* appeared to be the only offering on the airwaves, at least in that neck of the woods.

Better the sounds of silence, Paul thought.

Clicking off the radio, he listened to the engine whine and prayed that the snow held off until he got back to Madison. He didn't relish the thought of being stranded in Plainfield, not even overnight. Years before, while researching *Slaugtherhouse,* he had been compelled to spend nearly a week at Plainfield's only hostelry, the Whispering Pines Motor Lodge. The "lodge"—actually a collection of ramshackle bungalows on the outskirts of town—had all the charm and comfort of the Bates Motel; every time Paul stepped into the shower, he felt like Janet Leigh. It wasn't an experience he cared to repeat.

Unfortunately, the situation didn't look very promising. Since setting out from Madison just before 8:00 A.M., he'd already driven through a few flurries. Outside his windshield, the world looked as dull and grainy as an old Movietone newsreel.

Well, Paul thought, *that's appropriate.* Though Paul's only previous visit to Plainfield had been made during the summer, Gein's hometown existed in his imagination as a realm of wintry gray—the somber tone of the old police and newspaper photos that had documented the story back to the 1950s. Paul always thought that if *Slaughterhouse* were ever made into a movie, it would have to be shot in black and white. "Living Color" just wouldn't seem true to the ghoulish horrors of Ed Gein's unspeakable life.

His lecture on Gein, delivered the evening before, had gone well. The audience had listened raptly for nearly an hour and made appreciative noises at several points, particularly when Paul described Gein as "the Walt Whitman of horror—the man who had given the genre a distinctly American face." Paul had explained that before Ed Gein and *Psycho,* movie monsters were invariably alien beings—either foreign-born creatures like Dracula and Frankenstein or invaders from outer space. Ed Gein's atrocities—as mythicized in the dark deeds of Norman Bates—had initiated a uniquely American form of Gothic horror.

"Even as a necrophile, there was something quintessentially American about Ed," Paul had said, standing at the lectern in the big auditorium. "After all, the famous Continental ghouls—like the nineteenth-century French graverobber, Sergeant Bertrand—dug up female bodies in order to make love to them. Eddie, on the other hand, took the corpses home and used them as the raw material for his various do-it-yourself handyman projects.

Turned them into wastebaskets and wall ornaments and kitchen chairs. His crimes were a kind of nightmare version of *Home Improvement.*"

Though he'd been gratified by the audience's response—he had gotten an enthusiastic ovation at the end of his speech and was thronged by people who wanted him to sign their copies of *Slaughterhouse*—Paul felt vaguely dissatisfied with his lecture. In the end, there was something superficial, almost glib, about it. He had failed to get at the heart of the Gein enigma: how did it happen that this nondescript Midwestern farmer had ended up performing such ghastly rituals in the murk of his private chapel of horrors? It was as though Gein were the priest of some archaic religion that practiced human sacrifice, cannibalism, and the worship of the dead. There was a dark, tantalizing mystery in the case that Paul hadn't even begun to solve to his own satisfaction.

It was just after 10:00 A.M. when he drove past the road sign that read PLAINFIELD, POP. 642. Cruising through the "downtown" area, Paul was unsurprised to see that it hadn't changed at all since he'd seen it last. It was nothing but a single street lined with a few modest houses, two white-painted wooden churches, a post office, and a handful of businesses, including a funeral home, a tavern, a hardware store, a gas station, and a café. Plainfielders liked to joke that their town never had trouble with teens hanging around on street corners because there *weren't* any street corners.

Some joke, thought Paul. He'd always wondered what people—not just the adolescents but the grown-ups as well—did for fun around there. Bingo at the VFW hall? Roller skating at the indoor rink in Wild Rose? 4-H meetings in the basement of the Methodist church?

Well, at least he knew the answer in one case: sneaking off to the graveyard and digging up corpses. Maybe the real mystery wasn't why Eddie Gein had been driven to madness. Maybe it was why more people didn't go crazy living in such a place.

His stomach gave a growl as he rolled along Main Street. Having skipped the motel's free "Continental breakfast"—which consisted of coffee and an assortment of Hostess snack cakes set out on a card table in the lobby—Paul was starting to feel a serious need for sustenance. Pulling up to the curb in front of Plainfield's only restaurant, a boxlike eatery called Bob's Café, he slid out of his Ford, crossed the sidewalk, and climbed the three concrete steps to the doorway.

The inside was dimly lit and redolent of cigarette smoke, bacon grease, and burned coffee. Two men wearing winter jackets and hunters' caps with ear flaps were perched at one end of the counter, sipping from mugs. They were chatting with the waitress, a wiry-looking woman of indeterminate age who lounged behind the counter, right fist on hip, cigarette dangling from the corner of her mouth. Her mousy hair was pinned up in a disheveled pile.

As Paul seated himself at the opposite end of the counter, she squinted in his direction, plucked a coffee-stained menu from behind the cash register, and approached.

"Mornin'," she muttered. "Need a menu?"

Paul shook his head. The refrigerated display case on the opposite wall held a single dehydrated grapefruit half, two parfait glasses of yellow glop that Paul assumed was vanilla pudding, and a sorry-looking cherry pie.

"That pie homemade?" he asked.

"Oh, yeah," one of the men said with a sneer. "Rose here's quite the little baker, ain't you, Rose?" The other man let out a cackle.

Without turning toward the pair, the waitress snapped a hand in their direction, as if to say, "Shut your yaps." "I wouldn't recommend the pie," she said to Paul.

Paul nodded. He briefly considered bacon and eggs,

but the griddle looked as if it were coated with axle grease. "Coffee and toast'll be fine."

"Think you can manage that, Rose?" the first man said in the same sneering tone.

"Better'n you been managing your farm, Earl," she shot back. At this riposte, the second man cackled again, this time even louder.

Rose was back in a minute with Paul's order. Reaching beneath the counter, she came up with a little metal milk pitcher and a small plate holding two foil-wrapped slices of butter. The milk curdled into yellow lumps when Paul poured it into his coffee, and the frozen pats tore holes in his toast when he attempted to spread the butter. Paul was starting to regret that he had turned up his nose at the motel's complimentary breakfast.

As he began to eat, he noticed that the waitress was studying him through the smoke curling up from her Camel. Suddenly, she clipped the cigarette between the first two fingers of her right hand, plucked it from her lips, and said, "Have I seen you before?" She spoke in a harsh, raspy voice that reminded Paul of Marge Simpson's sullen, chain-smoking sisters. One of Paul's favorite family rituals was watching *The Simpsons* with Wylie and the kids every Sunday night in their TV room.

He swallowed the toast he was munching and said, "I spent a little time around here a few years back." The toast left an odd bitter aftertaste. *How can you mess up toast?* he wondered.

All at once, the waitress began waving her cigarette excitedly at Paul. "Wait just a minute," she exclaimed. "You're him. That writer fella."

Oops, said Paul's inner voice.

"Who?" growled the more talkative of the two locals, the one named Earl. Both men swiveled on their stools to stare at Paul.

"You know," said the waitress. "The one who wrote that book about ol' Eddie Gein."

Glancing over his shoulder at the men, Paul smiled

pleasantly and nodded hello. From under the peaks of their caps, they regarded him through slitted eyes. They did not appear happy to meet him.

The waitress, on the other hand, seemed genuinely thrilled. "'Well, I'll be damned. Saw you on TV that time with poor Reverend Hobart." She stubbed out her cigarette in a tinfoil ashtray on the counter. "What brings you to these parts?"

Paul had already begun asking himself the same question. He raised his mug to his lips and sipped the sour-tasting coffee. "Just passing through."

"Hope you ain't plannin' to write another damn book 'bout us," snarled Earl. "You done enough harm as it is."

"Oh, hush," said the waitress with a dismissive wave at the man. "Don't you listen to that jackass," she said to Paul. "Your book's done plentya good, too."

"Done *you* good," Earl snorted. "Feedin' all them outsiders come to see Ed Gein's grave." He shook his head slowly. "Goddamn sickos. Turnin' our cemetery into some kinda damn tourist attraction."

Planting her fists on her hips, Rose turned on Earl. "And what's so bad about that? Just makes our town a little special, is all. Like that place I was readin' about, in Kansas or wherever, where Lawrence Welk was born. Brings a little excitement to this godforsaken place."

"Kind of excitement we don't need," growled Earl, sliding off his stool and dropping some change onto the counter. "C'mon, Lyle," he said to the other man, who had not spoken a word. The two men stalked out of the café, casting dark looks at Paul as they exited.

"Morons," muttered Rose. Fishing her pack of Camels from the pocket of her uniform, she extracted a cigarette, stuck one end between her lips, and lit the other with a disposable Bic. "Guess some of the folks around here don't feel too friendly to you. Sorta blame you for what happened to the reverend and his missus."

"Me?" Paul said, alarmed.

Drawing deeply on the cigarette, Rose exhaled the smoke through one corner of her mouth and nodded. "They think maybe some nutcase who's a big fan of your book didn't like what the reverend was sayin' about it."

Paul put down his coffee mug and looked at Rose. His heart was thumping, as though he'd overdosed on caffeine. But it wasn't the caffeine that was agitating him. It wasn't even the fact of finding himself in Plainfield, though his visit here suddenly seemed intensely ill advised. No. What was really causing the quaking in his chest was the notion that his book might have provoked the Hobarts' murders.

"How about you?" he said to Rose. "What do you think?"

Leaning forward on her elbows, Rose took another drag of her cigarette and said. "I don't think it had anythin' to do with your book. I think it was that psycho, the one they're callin' Jack the Zipper."

Paul's brow furrowed. "But he's down in Milwaukee."

Rose looked at him as though he were a simpleton. "Guess even psychos know how to drive."

"But why would he murder Hobart? All his other victims have been women."

Holding her cigarette between the first two fingers of her right hand, Rose plucked a shred of tobacco from the tip of her tongue with her thumb and ring finger while keeping her pinky cocked at a ladylike angle. It was an incongruously delicate gesture in a woman who looked as leathery as a ranch hand. "Maybe he didn't cotton to all the names the reverend called him on that show."

Paul frowned as he tried to recall what Rose was referring to. After a few seconds, the memory came back to him. At one point in their debate—while attacking Paul for having instigated the Zipper murders—Hobart had referred to the unknown perpetrator as a "loathesome abomination," "a filthy degenerate who has doomed his soul to eternal perdition," and "a piece of human foulness."

"Anyways," Rose said, "what happened to the reverend wasn't nothin' compared to what that psycho done to poor Hannah.''

"Hannah?"

"Mrs. Hobart." Leaning closer to Paul, Rose lowered her voice to a conspiratorial whisper, as though the café were packed with eavesdroppers. "Betcha didn't know," she confided, "that he cut off her head and took it with him."

Paul's heart flopped in his chest like a hooked fish. "Jesus."

Rose nodded slowly. "Wasn't in the papers. But that kinda thing don't stay secret in a town like this for long." She sucked on her cigarette, one eye squinting against the smoke. "Way I figure it, that Jack fella carried poor ol' Hannah's head home with him so he could take his time playin' dentist on her."

Paul stared down at his plate. He had managed to consume only a few nibbles of the inedible toast. But the problem wasn't the food; he couldn't have eaten another bite if it had been blini and Beluga caviar.

" 'Course," said Rose with a shrug, "coulda been some completely different psycho did 'em in. One of them celebrity stalkers, say. Saw a show about it on TV. All your movie stars got bodyguards nowadays. And the reverend sure had a taste for the spotlight."

"That occurred to me, too," said Paul.

Rose cocked her head and looked at him thoughtfully. "You know, you're kinda a celebrity yourself."

"Me?" He gave a self-deprecating snort. "Hardly."

"Hey!" she exclaimed. "*I* recognized you, didn't I? Hell, you been on *The Lionel Lemmick Show*. Had your picture in *People* magazine. Got copies of your book with your face right on it in stores all over the country."

"So what exactly are you saying, Rose?" Paul asked.

She reached out and gave his forearm a pat, as though she were his oldest friend. "What I'm sayin' is you better watch your ass, hon."

39

Opening the connecting door from the kitchen, Sheila flipped on the light switch just inside the stairwell and descended into the basement. According to the forecasts, there was a snowstorm on the way, and she wanted to check on her supply of rock salt. Her front walkway, which ran down to the street on a gentle decline, turned treacherous in icy weather, and Sheila didn't want to risk breaking her neck. Not that she gave a damn about her life. But she still had a job to accomplish. She wasn't ready to die. Not yet.

She found a brand-new bucket of rock salt, the receipt still stapled around the wire handle, sitting on a storage shelf. *Of course.* She had bought it just a week before. Made a special trip to Ace Hardware. How typical of her to forget! More and more, she was having trouble keeping certain things in mind.

Other things—the sound of her daughter's voice, or the radiance of her smile—she could not keep out of her mind, no matter how desperately she tried.

Her memory, once so retentive, had become completely unreliable. Take that odd religious picture she had glimpsed yesterday afternoon, the one taped inside the refreshment van. It was so naggingly familiar. And yet, she couldn't place it for the life of her. Not that it mattered. Why she was still mulling over the thing, she couldn't really say. Probably just a way of distracting herself from her misery. Still, the question continued to vex her. Where had she seen that picture before . . . ?

As she turned back toward the staircase, she bumped into the barbecue grill. The big, red-painted Weber had been Richard's pride and joy. He had bought it only a month before his accident. Something prompted her to lift the lid. There was nothing inside but a scattering of ashes.

Sheila felt a terrible pang as she peered inside the grill. Her heart, her home—each was like that dark, hollow bowl: something that had once glowed with warmth, now dead and empty and cold.

No. Not her heart. Not completely. There was still one living ember that continued to burn in her chest: her desire for revenge.

Replacing the dome, she wondered how the grill came to be in the basement. She could not recall carrying it down from the patio. Perhaps one of the friends who had rallied to her side in the dreadful time after Patti's death had decided to store it away for her.

Oh, well. What difference did it make? She would never use the thing again. It had become just one more useless object among the dozens that cluttered the basement: the camping equipment and fishing gear, the ice skates and cross-country skis, the rolled-up hammock and golf clubs. And, of course, Richard's tools, still neatly laid out on his worktable: the hammers and screwdrivers and wrenches and pliers . . .

It was the sight of pliers that did it, but not immediately. Sheila was already halfway up the staircase when the realization hit her—hit her so hard that her vision swam and she had to grab onto the banister to keep her balance. When the vertigo passed, she bolted to the top of the stairs, dashed through the kitchen, and made for the living room, where Richard's religious volumes were stored in one of the built-in bookcases that flanked the bay window.

He had been born and raised a Lutheran but had converted to Catholicism—Sheila's religion—when they were married. Like many converts, he had become intensely devout—even more so than Sheila. Over the years, he had amassed a sizable collection of books on Catholicism. The one she was looking for now was an old encyclopedia of saints. She pulled it from the shelf with a trembling hand and carried it to the easy chair. Opening it on her lap, she flipped rapidly through the pages.

She found the entry on page 42: Saint Apollonia. *Of course!* Now she remembered. When she was twelve, her parents had sent her to a Catholic summer camp in Michigan for three weeks. Hanging in the infirmary had been a faded reproduction of a medieval miniature depicting the martyrdom of Saint Apollonia before a crowd of jeering onlookers.

Running her eyes down the entry, Sheila read:

> In the year 249 A.D., during the reign of Philippus Arabs, the pagan masses of Alexandria rose up in fury against the followers of Christ. Apollonia—"a virgin of advanced years," according to the account of Dionysus, Bishop of Antioch—was seized, her jaws were crushed, and all her teeth were knocked out. The mob built a pyre in front of the city and threatened to burn her alive unless she recanted her religion and embraced their heathen practices. She asked for breathing space, and when they undid her bonds, she leapt into the flames, joyfully accepting martyrdom.
>
> In later centuries, this story underwent numerous elaborations. The "virgin of advanced years" and daughter of obscure parents was transformed into "a girl hardly ripe for wedding," the "offspring of ancient kings, excelling in beauty the nymphs of the Nile." Her mother was forced to watch her daughter, whom she had educated to piety, dragged to the pyre. Apollonia's teeth were pulled out and she was

thrown in jail, where several saints and angels appeared to her and strengthened her soul. The flames had no power over her. This is the story as retold in the late fifteenth century by the Latin poet, Battista Spagnuoli Mantuano.

Given the nature of her torture, it is no surprise that of the 13,825 martyrs spoken of in the Roman Martyrology, Apollonia was chosen as the protector and intercessor of those afflicted with toothache and that she became the patron saint of dentists. An invocation recorded from Bavaria is characteristic:

Apollonia, Apollonia,
Thou the holy saint in heaven,
See my pain in yourself,
Free me from evil pain,
For my toothache may torture me to death.

At the bottom of the page were two Renaissance illustrations of Saint Apollonia. The first showed the bound and helpless woman gazing up at a hovering angel, while a muscular young man raised a long-handled tool, a torture implement, to her mouth.

The second, by the seventeenth-century painter Carlo Dolci, was a portrait of the martyr. She, too, was staring heavenward with a look of intense supplication. A golden halo crowned her head. One delicate hand clutched her bosom. In the other, she held a pair of antique pliers with elegantly curved handles. There was a tooth clasped in the jaws of the pliers—a single shining molar, its roots pointing upward like the peaks of a flame.

It was the same picture Sheila had spotted on the rear wall of the lunch wagon in the plaza across from police headquarters.

She didn't know how long she sat paralyzed, eyes wide, heart knocking in her chest. "My God," she whispered, her throat so tight the words came out like a croak. Knocking the book from her lap, she leapt from the chair and bolted to the phone.

Her hand was trembling so badly that she had to try three times before she hit the right buttons. It seemed to take forever before someone answered—a gruff-voiced man who sounded vaguely bored.

"Detective Streator, please," said Sheila. Her voice was shaking as badly as her hands.

"Hold on," said the man. The line went silent for an instant, then the man came back on. "He's in a meeting."

"Damn!" She felt like screaming with frustration. "Is he . . . can you interrupt him?"

"Sorry, lady. He should be done in about ten minutes. Wanna leave a message?"

"Yes! Please. It's very urgent. Tell him to call Sheila Atkins. The instant he gets out."

Slamming down the phone, Sheila clamped a hand over her mouth and tried to think clearly. Perhaps she should jump in her car and drive over to headquarters. But what purpose would that serve? Streator would be out of his meeting before she arrived. What if he called while she was en route? He might decide her message wasn't so urgent after all and disappear on some business.

What to do? What to do? She stood in the living room, staring down at the floor and gnawing on a thumb.

The doorbell buzzed.

Sheila froze. Who . . . ? Suddenly, she remembered. Her friend, Emily Drummond, had called to say she would be dropping off a church mailing around six, after finishing her volunteer work at the hospital. But it couldn't already be six, could it? Outside the living room windows, the leaden sky was just going black. Maybe Emily had left the hospital early.

Hurrying to the front hallway, Sheila pulled open the

door. It wasn't Emily at all. It was a skinny young man. He was leering at her, and he had something clutched in one hand.

Even before Sheila could register his features—his lipless grin and yellow teeth, his waxen skin and raving eyes—Chuckie Frewer was upon her.

40

By three in the afternoon, Paul knew he was pushing his luck. So far, the snowfall had been limited to a few feathery flakes, drifting out of the sky as though from a pillow fight in heaven. But the clouds had grown considerably more ominous in the past half-hour or so. Driving cautiously along the deserted country road—a narrow strip of blacktop, booby-trapped with potholes and ice patches—Paul could see that if he lingered in Plainfield much longer, his worst fear would be realized and he'd end up having to spend the night at the Whispering Pines Motor Lodge.

There was certainly no reason to stick around. As far as his main objective was concerned—unearthing the secret he had sensed Hobart was concealing—the trip had been a total bust.

Before leaving Bob's Café, Paul had asked his new buddy Rose if she'd ever heard any nasty gossip concerning Hobart. She had begun shaking her head before he'd even finished the question. The reverend was "a straight arrow—as fine and upright as they come." Not a whiff of disgrace had attached itself to him in all the years he had ministered to the town.

Paul had chewed this over for a while before asking, "Any other kind of rumors going around? Something Hobart might've learned too much about for his own good?"

Rose had raised her eyebrows. "Like what—sex stuff?"

"Whatever. Anything scandalous."

Rose had barked a laugh. "Lemme tell you something about this town, hon. Biggest scandal 'round here was when the Peters girl come home from college last summer with a gold ring through her nose. Believe me, this ain't no Peyton Place. Hell, far as that stuff goes, this town's deader'n one of Eddie Gein's girlfriends."

From the café, Paul had driven a few short blocks to the town's only gas station. As he stood by the self-service pump, feeding fuel into his tank, he watched the comings and goings at the hardware store across the street. To aficionados of the Plainfield horrors, the store was a grim landmark. Nearly forty years before, it had been the site of Ed Gein's final murder.

The date was Saturday, November 16, 1957—the first day of deer-hunting season, when Plainfield was largely depleted of its male population. Early that morning, Gein drove into the deserted town and parked his beat-up Ford alongside the hardware store. As he'd expected, there was no one inside except the owner—a fifty-eight-year-old widow named Berenice Worden who vaguely reminded Ed of his own long-departed mother.

After explaining that he was thinking of purchasing a new rifle, Ed removed a .22-caliber Marlin from a display rack, loaded it with a shell he had brought with him expressly for this purpose, and when Mrs. Worden's back was turned, shot her in the skull. Grabbing the corpse by its feet, he dragged it out to his car and sped back to his farmhouse.

There, inside his dismal summer kitchen, he disrobed the corpse, shoved a sharpened stick through its ankles and hauled the body up to the rafters with a block and tackle. Then he proceeded to dress the body out like a slaughtered game animal.

It was Mrs. Worden's gutted and headless body that horror-struck searchers had first encountered when they broke into Gein's charnel house. Later, while sifting through the unimaginable contents of the house, they came upon her head. Gein had bent a pair of ten-penny nails into hooks, stuck one into each ear, and connected them with a two-foot length of twine. In this way, the widow's head could be hung from the wall of his bedroom like a trophy or wall ornament—the latest acquisition in his monstrous collection of human *objet d'arts*.

After topping off his tank, Paul had stuck the nozzle back into the pump and stepped into the attendant's shack. Immediately, his eye was caught by a small cardboard box sitting on the counter between the cash register and a plastic canister of barbecue-flavor beef jerky. ED GEIN TOUR—$1.00, read the hand-printed label taped to the front of the box.

Stacked inside were a dozen or so mimeographed sheets, folded into fourths. Paul fished one out and opened it. FOLLOW THE FOOTSTEPS OF AMERICA'S MOST FAMOUS PYSCHO! read the block-printed headline. Below was a crude, hand-drawn map of the Plainfield area, showing the "major milestones" of Ed Gein's "career of horror": the hardware store, the site of the old Gein farmstead, the neighbor's house where he had been arrested following the discovery of Mrs. Worden's body, and more. Printed on the bottom was an unattributed quote that Paul instantly recognized as a line from his own book: "If there can be such a thing as a seminal psychotic, that dubious honor surely belongs to Eddie Gein, the patron saint of splatter, the grandfather of gore."

Returning his credit card to his wallet, Paul removed a dollar bill and handed it to the teenage boy behind the counter, whose eyes—beneath his low-pulled woolen cap—were full of a strange and inexplicable hostility.

Paul wasn't especially paranoid, but he was beginning to feel like one of those *Twilight Zone* characters who, while traveling through the boondocks, finds himself in a quiet little town that turns out to be populated by cannibalistic country folk who feast on wayfaring strangers.

Back in his car, Paul refolded the Ed Gein guided tour and tucked it into the breast pocket of his plaid flannel shirt. Then, from the inside pocket of his Patagonia parka, he withdrew another map. Rose had drawn it for him on a greasy paper napkin, using the ballpoint she kept stuck behind one ear.

Seated behind the wheel, Paul studied the directions briefly, then started the engine and pulled out of the gas station.

It took him about ten minutes to reach his destination. The house was even more modest than he'd expected— a little white-painted ranch, planted on a gentle rise about five miles outside of town. Barren trees grew all around. There must have been a driveway leading up to the garage, but Paul couldn't see it. Like the front walkway, it was completely buried in ice-crusted snow.

Parking as far to one side of the little road as possible, Paul sat in the car and stared at the dead, silent house. Everything about it—from the darkened windows to the strip of yellow police tape strung forlornly across the doorway—filled him with a terrible sense of bleakness. He felt as if he were gazing at a sepulchre or mausoleum. In a sense, he was.

It was the house where Victor Hobart and his wife, Hannah, had been slaughtered by an unknown fiend.

Exactly what had brought him to this desolate place, Paul would have been hard put to say. Certainly he had no intention of entering the house and snooping around. He knew it was a sealed crime scene. Besides, he was no detective. Even if he managed to get inside, he'd have no idea what to look for.

Through the sealed windows of the car, he could hear a muffled caw. An instant later, a pair of enormous crows swooped down from the trees and lighted on the undisturbed whiteness of the snow-buried yard. With the motor shut off, the temperature inside the car was dropping fast. Even with his parka zipped, Paul was beginning to shiver.

In spite of what the waitress had said, Paul remained convinced that Hobart had been hiding something. But whatever that dark secret was, he was obviously not going to find any clues to it here.

Reaching for the steering column, he turned over the engine with a twist of the key and pulled away from the funereal house.

He spent the next forty minutes or so driving to some of the places he had visited years before while researching *Slaughterhouse*. The crude map he had bought at the gas station turned out to be a good investment. Without it, he would have had trouble finding his way around, it had been so long since his last trip to Plainfield. Not that there was much to see at any of the stops he made.

The old Gein farmstead was nothing but a big empty field with some scraggly undergrowth poking up from the snow. Of course, even when Paul had been there five summers ago, there hadn't been much left of the place. The house itself had been destroyed back in 1958, when a bunch of outraged townspeople—like the frenzied mob in an old Frankenstein movie—had torched it. When Paul had toured the infamous site during his research expedition, only the charred foundation was visible. Now, even that last barren fragment of the unhallowed place was concealed beneath the snow.

A quarter-mile down the road from the farmstead stood the house of Gein's nearest neighbors, the Armstrongs. The family matriarch—a shriveled, half-blind old lady named Sarah Jane Armstrong—had been very kind to Paul years before, inviting him in for tea and spending the better part of the afternoon sharing her memories of the pathetic little bachelor who had led his appalling secret life "within two whoops and a holler" (as she put it) of her front door. Paul had thanked her profusely in the acknowledgment section of his book, sent her an inscribed copy as soon as *Slaughterhouse* was published, and received a kindly thank-you note in return. That had been their last communication.

On this afternoon, he had parked in her driveway and knocked on her front door, which was cracked open by an unfamiliar, middle-aged woman—still dressed at that hour in a pink terrycloth bathrobe—who regarded him with the undisguised wariness Paul had come to expect of the locals. When he inquired about Sarah Jane Armstrong, the woman told him brusquely that the old lady had died six months before. The rest of the family had sold the house and "cleared out." Before Paul could get out another word, the door was shut in his face.

A few miles outside of town, he had stopped beside another landmark highlighted on his map—an old boarded-up Quonset hut that had once functioned as a roadhouse. Its proprietress, a dumpy, notoriously foul-mouthed woman named Mary Hogan, had been another of Gein's victims, her flayed and lipsticked face ending up among his collection of wall-mounted death masks, her preserved vulva in a shoe box along with a dozen other specimens.

As Paul sat inside his car, gazing out at the derelict structure, a sudden sense of confusion overtook him. What had impelled—no, *driven*—him to make this morbid sightseeing trip? The longer he mulled over it, the more perplexed he felt at his own purposes.

The sky was growing grimmer by the minute, the flurries coming thicker and faster. It was nearly three o'clock. The thought of getting back to Madison and holing up in his warm motel room for the rest of the day seemed profoundly appealing. There was just one more stop he needed to make. After that, he would go.

Double-checking the directions on his macabre little map, he had pulled the car onto the blacktop and headed back in the direction of Plainfield.

* * *

He parked the car beside the chain-link fence and stepped out into the cold. Heavy flakes quickly speckled his face and dampened his hair. Tugging his collar up around his neck, he hurried beneath the wrought-iron sign that spanned the entranceway: PLAINFIELD CEMETERY.

The silence was so heavy that he imagined he could hear the tumbling of the snow. The thickening gloom made the scattered pines look black. Like the town itself, the graveyard was utterly nondescript—a collection of plain, stubby tombstones sticking out of the snow. Paul paused just beyond the gateway, gazing around. Then he spotted them—a pair of headstones about five yards off to the right. Even in that dismal light, they looked brighter, less weatherworn than the rest.

Shoulders hunched against the wind, he tromped through the snow and stood at the foot of the graves. As he gazed down at the headstone of the Reverend Victor Hobart, Paul struggled to sort out his feelings. Though the news of Hobart's murder had shocked him, he couldn't pretend to be grief-stricken. He had detested the reverend too much. Still, he felt no satisfaction at the man's death. He hadn't come there to dance on the grave of his nemesis. Mostly, what he felt was defeated. The secret he had traveled so far to unearth seemed lost to him forever, buried in the frozen ground beneath his feet.

The sheer bitter dreariness of the place was beginning to make Paul feel slightly unwell. His nose and ears were burning from the cold. Still, he wasn't quite ready to leave. With one gloved hand, he wiped away the heavy flakes that had settled on his eyelashes, then turned and headed deeper into the graveyard, to pay his final call.

He did not need his map to find the grave. He recalled its location from his last trip. The tombstone, like all the others in the cemetery, was a simple marker, inscribed with nothing more than the name and dates of the deceased: EDWARD THEODORE GEIN, 1906–1984. The remains of the Plainfield Ghoul lay in the most appropriate place, side by side for all eternity with the corpse of the woman in whose thrall he had lived—his overmastering mother, Augusta.

As Paul approached the plot, he spotted something dark sticking up at the foot of the headstone. Stooping, he scooped away the hard-packed snow and removed the object. It was a hand-carved wooden coffin, perhaps six inches long. It was painted entirely black, except for a message printed across the length of the lid in small blood red letters. MY HEART BELONGS TO EDDIE, it read. The miniature coffin had clearly been left as a tribute by one of the many devotees who made regular pilgrimages to the gravesite of the legendary ghoul.

Paul shook his head in wonderment. What was it that people found so compelling about Gein, a backwoods nonentity who had transgressed every boundary, broken every taboo, plunged himself into a black, abhorrent pit where sex and death and horror seethed in some unimaginable brew? Studying the grotesque offering in his gloved hand, Paul felt not revulsion, but a kind of vertigo, as though he were poised at the brink of an abyss.

All at once, he remembered Lewis Stimpson, the former crime lab photographer he had gotten to know while researching *Slaughterhouse*. He recalled what the old photographer had told him—how, one day many years ago, Stimpson had been so overcome by all the ghastliness he had witnessed that he simply walked out of his job, never to return. *Just had my fill of horror is all,* was the way the old man had put it. At the time Stimpson had related the story, it had seemed slightly abstract to Paul. Now it seemed viscerally real.

Tossing the miniature coffin onto the grave, he turned and hurried toward the entranceway. By now the sky was nearly drained of light. There was too much darkness in this place.

And way too much death.

41

Streator had carried his topcoat with him into the briefing room so that he could leave work right after the meeting. He had awakened that morning feeling achy and flushed. After pressing her mouth to his forehead, Ellen had insisted that he stay in bed for the day. "I knew you were going to make yourself sick," she had scolded. "You're not burning up, but it's definitely a fever. I'd say a hundred and one."

Arby was sure she was right; Ellen could determine the body temperature of a loved one so accurately that her lips seemed equipped with a built-in thermometer. Or as their younger son Bobby used to pronounce it when he was in kindergarten, a "ther-mommy-ter."

Even so, Arby had forced himself out of bed and into the shower. He couldn't stay home, he had explained over her objections. The psychologist—Professor Rollins—was scheduled to consult with the task force again, and Arby felt duty-bound to be there. In the end, he and his wife had reached a compromise. Arby would go to work for only half a day, driving to the office after lunch and returning as soon as the meeting was over.

Now, as he emerged from the briefing room and held the door open, Frank Turner stepped out behind him. "More banana oil," Turner muttered.

"Banana oil," Arby said with a weary chuckle. "Haven't heard *that* one since I was a kid."

"My daddy used to say it all the time," said Frank.

He reached into his jacket for his Marlboros and shook the last one out of the pack. "So what'd *you* think?"

"About what Rollins was saying?"

Frank nodded. Extracting the cigarette with his mouth, he lit it with a snap of a Bic.

Arby made a "who the hell knows" face. "Guess it makes some sense."

The psychologist had suggested that because of the serial killer's obsession with mouths and devouring, the stymied investigators should check their files for sex offenders who might work in the food industry. Perhaps as a restaurant employee.

Turner blew smoke from his nostrils. "How many short-order cooks and waiters you figure there are in Milwaukee?"

"Not to mention waitresses," said Arby, shrugging on his topcoat.

Turner gave him a questioning look. "How's that?"

"I've been thinking," Arby said. "Maybe our Jack is really a Jill."

Turner's eyebrows arced in surprise. "Now *that's* a new one." Half his mouth twisted sideways. "You really think that could be?"

"Frank," Arby said with a sigh, "I don't know *what* the hell to think anymore."

As they headed past the station desk, the sergeant on duty, Gerry O'Dell—a bullet-headed man with a badly pocked face, shiny dome, and thick black moustache that looked like a pocket comb pasted above his mouth—called out to Arby. "Got a message for you, Streator. Urgent."

"Thanks," said Arby, plucking the yellow memo page from O'Dell's outstretched hand. He scanned the message and looked up quickly at the sergeant. "When'd you get this?"

"Ten, maybe twelve minutes ago. Sounded really weird."

"How do you mean?"

"Voice was shaking. *Bad.* Like she was having trouble controlling herself."

Frank came up beside Arby. "What's up?"

"Hand me the phone book, will you, O'Dell?" said Arby, reaching out his hand. His fever-fogged head felt suddenly clear. Turning to Frank, he said, "Your coat in your office?"

Turner nodded. "What's going on?"

"Get your coat, I'll tell you in the car," said Arby, as he riffled through the directory, looking for Sheila Atkins's address. "We're going for a ride."

42

He knew it was going to be tricky—nice residential neighborhood, the old bitch standing right there in the doorway. He'd have to put her out of commission immediately, before she could let out a scream and alert the whole block. Knocking her out with a quick haymaker would've been the easiest. *Just wait 'til she opens the door, then—bam!—smash her right in the fucking face.*

He could've done it, too—he was a lot stronger than he looked. The problem, of course, was the risk to her hole. He wanted to take his own sweet time with her teeth, not knock 'em down her fucking throat.

The best way, he figured, was to go for her windpipe—which was exactly what he'd done. The second she'd opened the door, he had lunged for her throat, cutting off her scream with his choking right hand while, with his left, he clamped the chloroform-soaked rag over her snout. She had put up quite a struggle. She was surprisingly strong for such a dried-up old bitch—much stronger than her teenybopper daughter, that was for sure.

Sprawled on her back in the foyer, she had clawed and squirmed and kicked while he straddled her chest and pressed down on her face with the chloroform. She managed to give his cheek a pretty nasty scratch before her muscles went limp. He kept the rag over her face for another thirty seconds, then scrambled to his feet, slammed the front door shut, and leaned against it, panting.

He had parked his wagon a few blocks away, beside a darkened schoolyard, where it would be less conspicuous. His plan was to put out the old bitch's lights, then return to his van, pull it into the driveway, and smuggle her out through the garage. The way he figured it, the whole thing—from arrival to getaway—would be over in a matter of minutes. *Quicker than you could say "Jack the Zipper"!*

Then back to his house for a slow, sweet night of fun and games.

Standing there now in the entranceway, however, a peculiar desire began seeping through him. *Why not do her right here?* It struck him as such a crazy idea that, for a few moments, he simply stood there and tried to make sense of it. A full minute passed before the answer came to him.

It was the house itself. Something about it—the ivory walls, beige carpet, mellow lighting—reminded him of *her. Frieda.* Her warm, perfumed bedroom. That fantasy chamber where so much had been done to him. Where rapture and pain became forever entwined in the pit of his soul.

The minute *her* image swam into focus, like a nixie emerging from a black, fetid pond, a torrential desire overwhelmed him. *What a trip—to do it right here in her own house. The way I took care of Frieda in her bedroom!* He was sure he'd be safe. The old bitch lived by herself. And he was certain that no one had seen him enter.

He stared down at the woman, sprawled on her back on the carpet. She was breathing noisily through her mouth—a loud, liquid gurgle. In the light from the overhead fixture, he could see the gleam of her teeth in the round, moist hole. The sight was so arousing that he thought he might shoot off right in his pants.

No way! No way can I control myself until I get her back home!

He'd need some tools, of course, but nothing that couldn't be found in almost everybody's house.

Stepping over the old bitch's prostrate body, he made his way down the carpeted hallway and began to explore.

"I gotta tell you, man." Turner turned in the passenger seat. In the intermittent glow of the passing street lamps, Arby's face seemed to pulsate with a dull, sickly light. "I think those headaches you been getting are starting to affect your brain."

"Parents kill their kids all the time, Frank. Beat 'em. Burn 'em. Toss 'em out of windows."

"Yeah, but you ain't talking about some fifteen-year-old crack addict."

"How about that woman down South a few years back? The one who strapped her kids into their car seats and rolled them into the lake?"

Turner made a derisive noise. "One in a million."

Arby chewed that over a few seconds before replying. "Maybe Sheila Atkins is two in a million."

Arby slowed his car to a stop behind several other vehicles at the intersection off Mitchell and 20th. He could've stuck his dome light onto the roof and made it to the Atkins house in half the time, but he wasn't in that big of a rush. He wanted a chance to talk out his theory with Turner, who was facing the windshield again, his lips screwed into a pucker of pure skepticism.

"Anyways," Turner said after a pause. "That sicko down South—Smith, I think her name was—even she didn't *torture* her kids."

The light went green. "Remember Gertrude Baniszewski?" Arby asked, putting his foot to the gas pedal.

"Hell, yes," said Frank. Even thirty years later, most people in that part of the world had vivid recollections of the notorious Indianapolis housewife—the "baby-sitter from hell"—who had supervised the torture-murder of her sixteen-year-old boarder, Sylvia Likens. The girl had been systematically beaten, scalded, and mutilated with a white-hot sewing needle, which had been used to inscribe the words *I am a prostitute and proud of it* on her stomach.

"But that poor gal wasn't her own daughter," Turner protested. "And even ol' Gertrude wasn't a serial killer. Let's say you're right and this Atkins woman offed her own child. Why would she go around killing those other girls?"

"Throw us off the track."

Turner snorted. "I'll say this for you, Arby. You got answers for everything."

"The problem is I don't have *any* answers," Arby said, swinging left onto Beloit. "Eight goddamn months without anything like a solid suspect."

"So what—you hit on Mrs. Atkins by a process of elimination?"

"Look. *She's* the one put the idea into my head. Coming to my office. Dropping hints about how I should be looking for someone connected to all these different people. Then it turns out *she's* the one with the connections."

"So why would she want you to know?"

"If I'm right, for the same reason she wants to talk to me so badly right now."

Turner looked over at Arby. "Which is?"

"She can't live with it anymore. She needs to confess."

Sure enough, it took him only a few minutes to locate everything he needed for the operation: pliers and twine in the basement, needles in the bottom drawer of the sewing-machine cabinet. He had taken a couple of wooden spools, too. Not for the thread—he was counting on finding some of his preferred suturing material—but to jam into the corners of her mouth as makeshift wedges.

That only left one thing—dental floss. But when he checked the medicine chest in the bathroom adjoining the big master bedroom, he let out a whimper of frustration. Clearly the old bitch wasn't big on dental hygiene. He stood by the sink, gnawing furiously at his lower lip. In a pinch, of course, he could always use some of the thread from the sewing cabinet. *Still . . .*

Suddenly, his eyebrows arched as a radiant image crystallized in his mind—the pristine perfection of her daughter's little treasures. *Of course!*

It was situated at the end of the hallway—a second, smaller bathroom, decorated with framed prints of kittens and daisies. As soon as he pulled open the door of the mirrored medicine chest, he let out a whoop of delight. There it was, the little plastic dispenser, exactly as he'd expected. He snatched it from the shelf and examined it under the white fluorescent light. Unwaxed, too. *Perfecto!*

Time to get to work.

Heading back along the corridor toward the entranceway, he passed a darkened room and paused, peering curiously into the murky interior. He could tell it was another smaller bedroom. Reaching inside the doorway, he slid his hand along the wall until he felt the switch plate and flipped on the light.

Yes! It was *hers*—the little cunt's bedroom!

As soon as he stepped over the threshold, a powerful sexual charge surged through his loins. He had never been inside the bedroom of one of his victims before.

Stepping to the dresser, he yanked open the drawers until he found the one stuffed with her underwear. He reached inside and began removing the items one by one. The little panties with their tiny flowered prints. Her delicate satiny bras, some with underwiring, which made him picture the swelling of her pert, pink-tipped breasts. The small silken half-slips, and the panty hose in Ever-So-Light and City Beige.

Pressing a pair of panties to his nose and mouth, he stood there, luxuriating in the sweet smell that suffused the little cotton crotch. It was only then that the sight of her bed registered forcefully on his intoxicated awareness.

It was an old-fashioned four-poster with a fluffy white comforter and two fat pillows plumped against the headboard. His heart began to knock against his chest. It was the ideal place to perform his operation! He could just picture the old bitch lying there—stripped, spread-eagled, her wrists and ankles bound to the wooden posts. The way her blood would look against the whiteness of the comforter!

Something stung his eyes, making him blink. He was so excited by now that he was sweating like a fucking pig. Mopping his eyes and forehead with the panties, he reached down and cleared off the side table with a single backhanded sweep of his hand. All the little cunt's shit—her crystal animals and clock radio and reading lamp—went crashing to the floor. Then, like a nurse setting up the surgical tray in an operating room, he carefully laid out his tools, side by side.

He hurried back down the corridor toward the entranceway. As he approached the body, the old bitch let out a moan and stirred. Stepping close to her head, he took careful aim with the toe of his left boot and let her have a good sharp kick right in her fucking temple.

She moaned, quivered, and lay still again.

Stepping around to her feet, he stooped, grabbed her ankles, and began dragging her along the hallway to her dead daughter's bedroom.

Turner flipped open his Marlboro box and stuck a finger inside. "Shit," he muttered.

"What's up?"

"Out of smokes." He peered out the window. "Hey, pull up at that Quik Shop, okay? It'll just take a sec."

"Jesus, Frank."

"Hey, man, if she's so hot to confess, a couple minutes won't make a damn bit of difference."

With a relenting sigh, Streator slowed down and

turned into the little parking strip alongside the convenience store. Even before the car came to a complete stop, Turner was out the door.

There were no other customers inside the brightly lit shop. Through the plate glass window, Arby could see his partner step up to the counter and say something to the female clerk, a chunky brunette in tight jeans and a purple sweatshirt. The woman was too far away for Arby to make out her features. But even from that distance, he could tell that she was equipped with what Turner would have called "killer globes." As she slid the red-and-white pack across the counter, Turner said something that made her toss back her head and let out an open-mouthed laugh.

Waiting impatiently behind the wheel, Arby had time to wonder if his partner was right. Maybe he *had* gone off the deep end. Why assume that Sheila Atkins had called him to confess? Why assume she was guilty at all?

Ever since her last visit to him, he'd been mulling—or rather *obsessing*—over the bizarre possibility that Sheila Atkins was the psycho he was seeking. He'd even done a computer search of cases involving women responsible for the torture-murders of their own children, just to check on the prevalence of such an unthinkable phenomenon. The most striking case was a relatively recent one—that of a forty-one-year-old British housewife named Rosemary West, who had been arrested in 1994 and charged with ten counts of murder. Her victims had been hideously tortured before being killed and dismembered. One of them was her own sixteen-year-old daughter.

The West case confirmed one thing at least—that no crime was beyond the scope of human depravity. A middle-aged mother could not only be a serial lust killer but commit the most unspeakable atrocities on her own child. Even so, the likelihood that Sheila Atkins was a monster on the order of Rosemary West seemed extremely remote. Watching Frank stride out of the Quik

Shop while the counterwoman eyed him, one hand on a big outthrust hip, Arby felt his heart sink. His own self-delusion suddenly seemed painfully clear. It was bullshit, plain and simple, the notion that he would arrive at Sheila Atkins's home and have the solution handed to him on a silver platter. Pure wish-fulfillment fantasy.

Well, he thought with an inner sigh. *We're—what?—two minutes away from her house? Might as well see what's so goddamn urgent.*

The car door swung open and Turner squeezed inside. "Let's roll," he said, taking a deep drag of his freshly lit Marlboro.

"Yeah," Arby said, feeling so beaten down and weary that just uttering the word cost him an effort.

The unwieldiness of a limp female body never failed to surprise him. The old bitch was just a dried-up bag of skin and bones. Even so, hauling her carcass up onto the four-poster turned out to be a struggle. He'd had to reach under her armpits, grab her around the upper back, and wrestle her upright. For a minute there, he'd felt as if he were doing the foxtrot with a corpse.

Clutching her like that, her tits pressed up against his chest, he'd experienced that strange, shivery mix of repulsion and desire he had felt in the entranceway, when the image of Frieda floated into his mind. By the time he got the old bone-bag laid out on the comforter, he was panting like a dog—partly from exertion, partly from excitement.

It took him just a couple of minutes to strip off her clothes and bind her spread-eagled limbs to the wooden posts. He hovered by the bedside, staring down at her. She wasn't much to look at. Saggy skin. Jutting bones. Brown, shapeless nipples. Bush all wiry and threaded with gray. Very different from his other victims, who had looked like living confections, with their vanilla flesh and bubble-gum nipples and snatch hair soft as cotton candy.

Her own daughter, for example. True, she could've stood to lose a few pounds of baby fat. But otherwise, she was a hot-looking little slut. Plump, juicy body. And a sweet, sexy face. Until *he'd* gotten done with it, that is.

The thought made him snigger.

Well, at least the old bitch had a full mouth of teeth—even if a bunch of the back ones were marred by ugly black fillings. He'd have to dispose of those. They weren't fit for his collection. But the front ones were okay, especially the incisors. He decided to start with the wisdom teeth and work around to the front. *Save the best for last.*

Quickly, he peeled off his clothes and dumped them in a pile on the floor. He was already so aroused that his rampant cock looked almost purple against the whiteness of his belly.

The bitch's head had lolled to the side. Drool was running from the corner of her slack mouth, dampening the pillow.

He reached down, took her bottom lip between his thumb and forefinger, and pinched. Hard. Her eyelids fluttered and she gave a deep, tremulous moan. But she didn't come to. Maybe he'd used too much chloroform. Or maybe that kick in the head had been harder than he'd intended. Either way, the old bitch was out for the count.

He felt a twinge of disappointment. He liked having them conscious while he worked on them. On the other hand, they could get pretty noisy—and this house was a whole lot less isolated than his own. All things considered, it was better to keep her unconscious. He'd just have to do without the extra added pleasures—the sound of her screams, the look of hopeless terror in her eyes.

Ah well. Life's full of sacrifices.

Climbing onto the bed, he straddled her body, then reached down with both hands and straightened her head on the pillow. "Good doggy," he said aloud, patting her hair. "Now don't move." Reaching over to the end table, he picked up one of the spools, then opened her jaws and wedged the wooden cylinder all the way back into the left corner of her mouth. "Nice," he said hoarsely, running a finger over her exposed teeth. He was beginning to shiver, although the room was close and warm.

Quickly, he stretched a hand to the end table again and snatched up the pliers. Bending low, he inserted the head of the tool all the way back into her mouth, grabbed hold of a rear molar, and grunting with the effort, began to pull.

The tooth came out without much trouble. The old bitch's brow furrowed and she let out a whimper from deep down in her throat, but she did not wake up.

Removing the tooth from the jaws of the pliers, he held it up to the light for minute. Then, sticking the root end into his mouth, he sucked off the blood and tissue, like a man nibbling the last bits of fruit off a cherry pit.

Carefully, he set the tooth down on the end table. He wiped the pliers against the pillow to clean off the spit. Pre-cum was leaking from the tip of his cock. He reached down with his free hand and massaged the juice over the head and shaft. Then he bent to the old bitch's mouth again.

At that moment, the door buzzer sounded.

The noise was so startling that he almost flew off the mattress. *Jesus!* He froze atop the old bitch's chest, hardly daring to breathe. Inside his own chest, his heart was thumping like crazy.

Beneath him, the old bitch moaned and shifted her head to the side. Spit mixed with blood leaked from her jammed-open mouth onto the pillow. He reached down and clamped a hand over her yap, praying that whoever it was would just go the fuck away.

The door buzzer sounded again.

*   *   *

"Weird," said Frank. "Sure it's working?"

Arby, finger on the button, leaned his ear close to the door. "I can hear it."

"Maybe she's in the crapper."

Arby straightened up and tugged his coat collar tight around his neck. Though the forecasted blizzard had never materialized, it had begun snowing lightly—a gentle flurry of big wet flakes. "Who the hell knows."

"Could be she had to run out for some reason."

Arby thought that over. "Why don't you radio headquarters, see if she called again? I'll take a look-see around the house."

Nodding, Turner hurried to the car, while Arby tramped around the north side of the house, shoes crunching on the frozen crust of month-old snow. He paused at every window and peered inside, hands cupped around his eyes. Most of the rooms were dark and empty. A few had lights burning behind drawn blinds. Arby banged on the illuminated windows but got no response.

Rounding the garage, he came to a little wooden gate, which opened onto the backyard. As he stepped through the gate, a neighbor's dog barked twice, then stopped abruptly.

Amber light spilled from the sliding glass doors at the back of the house and fell on the snow-blanketed patio. Climbing the little wooden porch, Arby made his way around a few forlorn pieces of outdoors furniture and crossed to the doors. Through the glass, he could see clearly into the living room, which was bathed in the warm glow from a table lamp. No one appeared to be home. He pounded on the glass, then tried the handle. The door was locked.

He shivered. In spite of his raised collar, icy flakes were settling onto the back of his neck. Banging on the door one more time, he listened hard for a bit, then turned and headed back around the house.

Frank was waiting by the front door, hands thrust inside his coat pockets, shoulders hunched, dark coat speckled with white.

"Any luck?" Arby asked.

Turner shook his head. "You?"

Arby pulled out a hankie and wiped his leaking nose. "Nada."

"Guess it wasn't all that urgent, huh? Let's get the hell outta here, Arby. I'm freezing my butt off."

Arby nodded without saying anything, then muttered, "Right."

Inside the car, Arby fired up the engine and pushed the heater control to full blast. Beside him, Frank sat shivering.

"How 'bout dropping me off at home?" Frank said. "Got my car in the repair shop."

"No problem."

Switching on the headlights and wiper, Arby backed the car out of the driveway and into the street, then threw it into drive. As they cruised down the block of modest split-levels, Turner said, "I'll show you a short-cut. Swing left at the next corner."

"You got it," said Arby. His insides felt numb. He was beyond disappointment. By this point, failure was nothing more than what he expected.

He almost lost control of his bladder when he heard the pounding on the glass door. Beneath him, the old bitch was beginning to stir and moan. He could feel her jaws working beneath his hand. Grabbing one of the big feather pillows from the headboard, he shoved it over her face to muffle the noise.

He stayed that way for a full half-minute, straining to hear the sounds from outside. Finally, he pulled the pillow from the old bitch's face. She sucked in a few quick, raspy breaths, then subsided into a stupor again.

Climbing off the bed, he tiptoed to the bedroom door, cracked it open, and poked his head outside, listening intently.

Silence. Then deep muffled voices just outside the front door. Then the slamming of car doors, the roar of the engine, the crunch of tires on the driveway.

They were leaving—whoever the fuck they were. *Yaaay! Adios, assholes!*

He waited until he was sure they had driven away, then pranced back to the bed. His deflated cock flopped against his thighs, but it sprang back to ramrod stiffness as soon as he climbed aboard the old bitch's body again.

He was glad she hadn't suffocated. He didn't like working on corpses, though it probably wouldn't have made that big a difference in this case, since she was stone-cold unconscious anyway. Still, just knowing she was alive while he worked on her was nice.

He'd have to work faster, though, in case the old bitch got another unexpected visitor. That was a pity—he preferred taking his own sweet time. Maybe he should have hauled her back to his own place after all. Oh, well, he'd made his bed; now he'd have to lie in it. As his old daddy used to say.

Grabbing up his pliers, he bent to his work. His excitement built quickly. He could feel it wash over him—that overwhelming sensation of sheer, mindless abandon.

He had no idea how much time had passed. It could have been hours; it could have been days. In truth, it was only a few minutes. But he was so lost in his ecstasy that he was no longer aware of the outer world at all. By the time the noise registered on his consciousness—the pounding and crashing and exploding of glass—Streator and Turner were already inside the house.

With a furious shriek, Chuckie leapt off the bed and flew out of the room, toward the source of the noise. He burst into the living room, brandishing the pliers in one quaking hand . . . and froze.

It took a few seconds for his lust-fogged brain to make sense of what he was seeing—the two big men gaping at him as they half crouched inside the shattered sliding door, their arms extended in his direction.

What the fuck? *How did those two loser assholes . . . ?*

He stood there, sweat and blood and semen dripping from his skinny naked body. Slowly he turned the pliers in his hand and raised it high above his head like a stabbing weapon.

Then with a maniacal roar, he launched himself at the two men—and in that very instant, to the accompaniment of an even more thunderous roar, something hot and white and blinding blossomed in Streator's hands.

43

By 6:20 that evening, every radio and TV station in Milwaukee had interrupted its regular programming to break the news. The first reports were sketchy: the serial killer known as Jack the Zipper had been slain by police while committing his latest atrocity. More details to come.

It wasn't until the eleven-o'clock news that the public learned the full story. By then, the police were already completing their search of Chuckie Frewer's torture lair, as reporters had dubbed it. Video footage showed dozens of investigators swarming into and out of the floodlit bungalow. Nearby, a crowd of gawkers, undaunted by the tumbling snow, strained at the sawhorse barricades that had been erected around the property.

Though officials were obliged to refer to the suspect as "the alleged serial killer," the contents of his "horror house" left no doubt about his guilt. Among the items reportedly discovered were a straight-back "killing chair," complete with web-belt restraints, a blood-caked pair of pliers, and a supply of dental floss. One burly detective was captured on videotape leaving the house with a small wooden box "believed to contain," in the words of one breathless newswoman, "the maniac's grisly collection of dental 'trophies.'"

According to anonymous witnesses, the walls of Frewer's squalid bedroom were hung with dozens of pictures of the same religious scene, tentatively identified as the martyrdom of Apollonia, the patron saint of dentists.

Other footage showed Mrs. Sheila Atkins—"mother of one of the teenage victims of the killer and herself the target of his final assault"—as she was carted out of her home on a stretcher and loaded into a waiting ambulance. A physician on the scene described her condition as serious but stable. "She's suffered quite a shock, as you can imagine," the doctor intoned for the microphones. "He really did a number on her mouth. But we can expect a full recovery. If you can use the word in a case like this, she's a lucky lady. If those detectives had showed up a few minutes later . . ." He finished the thought with a meaningful look.

Sheila's saviors, Detective Sergeant R. B. Streator and his partner, Detective Franklin Turner, were mobbed by reporters as they emerged from her house. Speaking into the bank of microphones shoved into his face, Turner explained that it was Streator who had noticed Chuckie's van parked in the shadows as they headed out of Mrs. Atkins's neighborhood.

"Soon as he spots the wagon, it was like everything clicked. What the hell was Frewer doin' *there?* A block away from Mrs. Atkins's house?" Suddenly, all the peculiarities of Chuckie's behavior—his obsessive interest in the Zipper case, his constant grilling of Streator for details of the investigation—fell into place. "Man," Turner said, laying a hand on his partner's back, "I could almost *see* the lightbulb going off in his brain."

Arby said nothing. When one of the newsmen called out to him, "How does it feel to be a hero?" he just grimaced and made a dismissive little wave. He seemed oddly subdued for a man who had just purged the city of one of the most depraved killers in its history.

"Well, when you've given so much of your life to achieving something," one local anchorman said, "you sometimes feel a little bit of a letdown when it finally happens."

"Good point, Brock," his coanchor concurred. "And don't forget—from what we're hearing, Detective Streator was actually acquainted with the suspect, who, as you know, operated a food concession just two blocks away from police headquarters."

Chuckie Frewer's background had, of course, been thoroughly dredged up by then. Milwaukeeans watching the late news that night (nearly eighty percent of the city's households, according to subsequent estimates) learned all about Chuckie's pathological past. His involvement in the arson death of his young governess, Frieda Poole. His nine-year internment in various mental institutions. His discharge by state psychologists, who had deemed him "harmless." And, of course, his life as the operator of a food van, that was regularly stationed just a short distance from police headquarters and patronized by numerous officers—including Detective Streator.

Though it seemed remarkable that a killer as cunning as Frewer would deliberately place himself right under the noses of his pursuers, such behavior was not at all uncommon, according to Professor Sam Rollins, one of the experts interviewed that night on TV. On the contrary, Dr. Rollins observed, it was characteristic of serial murderers to "inject" themselves into the investigation of their crimes.

"Sometimes, they'll send letters to the media, bragging about their crimes and hinting at where and when they'll strike next," he explained. "Or they'll make taunting, 'catch me if you can' phone calls to the police. Believe it or not, they'll even show up at the crime scene, oftentimes right after the murder, while the investigation is still going on. There've been cases where a serial murderer has actually approached a police officer, pretending to be a bystander and offering helpful suggestions."

"Why in the world would they do something like that, Professor?" asked the interviewer. "Are they trying to get caught?"

"Some of them," said Rollins. "But it's also a kind of

power trip, a way of toying with the police, proving their superiority. Plus, it allows them to stay close to the action. They like to see all the attention they're getting. Makes 'em feel important.''

As for the final tally of Chuckie's victims, the newscasters that night reported that police were still uncertain about the total number of his victims. There was much speculation that Frewer had been responsible for the savage murder of the Reverend Victor Hobart of Plainfield and his wife, Hannah, whose decapitated head had been removed from the murder scene by her killer. Professor Rollins tentatively theorized that Chuckie might have subconsciously identified the stern, censorious Hobart with his own hated father. "Plus, the killing of the reverend and his wife might have had something to do with Frewer's religious mania, which we've been hearing reports of."

In any event, the police would certainly know the answer before long—just as soon as their forensic experts finished comparing the teeth in Frewer's gruesome collection to the dental charts of all his known and suspected victims, including Hannah Hobart.

44

The debate on the proposed new curriculum was so heated that the faculty meeting ran almost twenty minutes late. As a result, it was nearly 4:00 P.M. by the time Wylie pulled her car into the driveway.

By then, the children had been home for over an hour. She found them both in the family room—Diana sprawled on the floor with a drawing pad, Matt on the sofa, transfixed by the TV. Draping her coat over the easy chair, Wylie sat beside Matt and put her arm around him, while Diana came over and snuggled on her lap. Together they watched the final minutes of the *Power Rangers,* a climactic, kung-fu battle between the costumed heroes and some kind of giant robotic dinosaur.

Afterward, they chatted happily for a while, telling one another about the events of their day. Then Wylie got up and went into the kitchen to remove a package of boneless chicken breasts from the refrigerator.

It was almost 4:30 by the time Wylie headed upstairs to change into casual clothing and check the answering machine, which was hooked up to the bedroom phone.

There were messages from her mother, her friend Susan Schlanger, a salesman offering high-yield investment opportunities, and, finally, a long one from Paul. Wylie was sorry she had missed her husband's call. They hadn't spoken for two days and she missed him badly. She couldn't wait to have him back home. The house seemed very empty without him. So did their bed.

Ah well, she thought. *Soon, soon.* He was scheduled to fly home the next evening.

His voice sounded excited on the tape. He was calling to tell her the news about Jack the Zipper. As it happened, Wylie already knew about it. The slaying of the infamous serial killer had made the papers from coast to coast. Even the *Times,* which normally sniffed at sensationalism, had devoted a full column to the story.

"Looks like I'm off the hook," Paul had said dryly on the tape. "As far as I can tell, this Frewer guy never even heard of *Slaughterhouse.* Apparently, he was some kind of religious nut. The cops think that's why he killed Hobart."

Paul went on to send hugs and kisses to the kids and tell Wylie how much he missed her. He was just saying good-bye when a final thought occurred to him.

"Oh, yeah," he said. "On my way through Milwaukee, I'm going to stop off and see Lewis Stimpson. Remember? That old police photographer who supplied me with all those pictures of Gein? I thought I'd drop by his place and say hello. Can't wait to see you, Wy. Love you."

For a few moments after the message beeped to an end, Wylie sat on the edge of the bed, frowning. Something was tugging at her memory. Finally, it came to her.

Heading back downstairs in her sweatshirt and jeans, she went into Paul's study and switched on his desk lamp. By now, there was a sizable stack of mail on his desk. She sifted through the pile until she found what she was looking for—the big manila envelope that had arrived just after he'd left. Just as she remembered, the return address bore the name Stimpson. She stood beside the desk, debating what to do, then decided to go ahead and open the envelope. Perhaps there was something inside that Paul ought to know about before he saw Stimpson.

Sliding open the center drawer of his desk, she removed the letter opener she had bought him years before during their first trip to Cape Cod, right before their wedding. It had a daggerlike blade and a scrimshaw handle engraved with a whaling scene. She inserted the point under the flap and slit open the envelope.

She read the letter first. By the time she looked at the pictures, her heart was already beating anxiously. She held the photos close to the light and studied them.

For the past few years, Ed Gein had been so much a part of their lives that he sometimes seemed like a distant relative—a kind of Charles Addams character, the ghoulish great-uncle mentioned only in whispers. Even so, Wylie—who had done her best to distance herself from Paul's preoccupation—had only the vaguest impression of his appearance.

As a result, she couldn't say whether the man in Stimpson's pictures resembled Gein. All she knew was that there was something intensely creepy about him. Flaccid and beady-eyed, with a doughy complexion and a look of low cunning, he resembled an overgrown, slightly moronic schoolboy. His mouth was twisted into a sniggering half grin, as though he were smirking at some private joke.

Returning the photos to the envelope, she stood by the desk, nibbling worriedly on her bottom lip. Suddenly, Paul's innocuous message about visiting Lewis Stimpson seemed extremely disturbing. She knew her husband well enough to foresee exactly what he would do once he learned about Stimpson's discovery. He wouldn't rest until he had determined if the man in the photos was really Ed Gein's son. The prospect of confirming such a startling discovery would be too exciting to resist. In a sense, Wylie could empathize with Paul. After all, if one of *her* acquaintances had supplied her with her a tip about an unknown Emily Dickinson poem, Wylie would have pursued the lead with equal alacrity.

On the other hand, Emily Dickinson—so far as anyone knew—had never been involved with necrophilia, dismemberment, and serial murder.

She decided to telephone Paul.

He had left her a detailed itinerary of his trip. It was hanging on the refrigerator door, attached by a magnet in the shape of a miniature eggplant. Carrying the cordless phone over to the fridge, she ran her finger down the list until she found the Milwaukee hotel he was staying at, then punched in the number. The desk clerk who answered confirmed that Mr. Novak had checked in that morning.

But when he rang Paul's room, nobody answered.

45

"**W**hat the hell you doin' *here?*"

The question was uttered in a tone of such bitter dismay that Paul was startled into a momentary silence. Clearing his throat, he began rattling off the reasons for his trip—the invitation to lecture at Madison, his urge to travel to Plainfield, the chance to see a few old acquaintances from his previous visit.

"So," he said, raising his hands, then letting them drop back into his lap. "That's why I'm here. Summer would've been a better time to come, I guess, but I didn't have much choice. I knew your winters were cold, but I hadn't realized jut *how* cold. Much worse than where *I* live, that's for sure. Still, at least we weren't hit by that blizzard everyone was predicting." He laughed. "I was afraid I'd be snowed in and *never* get back home."

He could hear how strained and unnatural his laugh sounded and realized he was prattling, partly from nerves, partly from excitement, partly from the discomfort of trying to make conversation with someone who was treating him with all the warmth and hospitality the average person would lavish on a leper.

The room they were seated in wasn't helping. There was something distinctly, if indefinably, creepy about it—something that had to do with its disconcerting blend of sterility and uncleanliness. On the one hand, there was an air of extreme, almost fanatical tidiness about the place. It was there in the fastidious arrangement of the stacked magazines. In the high polish of the glass-topped coffee table. In the spotlessness of the cream-colored rug. In the smoothness of the clear plastic slipcover Paul could feel beneath his ass as he sat forward on the sofa, hands clasped between his knees.

On the other hand, the air was suffused by a sickening odor—a foul blend of stale sweat and decaying fish. It was hard to pin down the source of the stink, though it seemed to be emanating from the person seated on the easy chair catercorner to Paul—a person who, just then, was regarding him with all the wariness of a longtime fugitive who suspects that the smooth-talking salesman who has just shown up at the door is really an FBI agent in disguise.

Agatha Cobb.

Seated a few feet away from the hulking woman, Paul had to force himself to look directly at her. Excluding a troupe of sideshow freaks he had once seen in a small upstate carnival—a human skeleton, a seal-boy, a pin-head, an armless wonder, and a "morphodite" named Roberta—he had never been face-to-face with a more grotesque human being.

Squeezed into the chintz-covered easy chair, she resembled something out of the dreamworld of fairy tales: an enormous, flabby toad, mottled with warts and decked out in a flower-printed housedress. That Gein had been capable of sexual congress with such a woman was—Paul couldn't help thinking—only further confirmation of his extreme psychopathology. True, their liaison had occurred forty years earlier, when Agatha was presumably a less repellent figure. Even so, it was hard to imagine that she had ever been much to look at.

But if the sight of her was unsettling to Paul, he appeared to be having the same effect on her. From the instant he showed up at her doorstep, she'd seemed profoundly discomposed. Her eyes kept shifting, her fingers twitching, her tongue flicking nervously over her cracked lips. Of course, his unannounced appearance must have come as a shock. He hadn't telephoned in advance. He was afraid she would refuse to see him—and he was determined to, at the very least, get a look at her. Ever since his visit to Lewis Stimpson that morning, he'd been burning with curiosity about her and her son.

As it happened, she had recognized him as soon as he told her his name. "You're that writer feller!" she had said with a gasp as he stood on the cracked concrete porch.

She had gaped at him briefly, then invited—or rather, ordered—him inside. Paul, taking this as a hopeful sign, assumed she was willing to talk with him. But much to his chagrin, she had hardly said a word since they sat down in the creepy living room.

Now, curling her lip into an ugly snarl, she jabbed a stubby finger at the floor and growled. "That ain't what I mean. I mean what're you doin' right *here?* In my house."

"I wanted to come meet you," Paul said with what he hoped was a winning smile. "And your son."

Her eyes narrowed and her tongue darted over her lips. "Leon?"

"That's right."

"Whatchyou want to talk to *him* for?" Her eyes kept flicking back and forth, as though she was engaged in some frantic silent calculation.

Paul breathed out a sigh. "Look, Mrs. Cobb, I'm not here to interview you for an article or a book or anything like that. I'm just here to satisfy my own curiosity. You've got to understand—I spent years researching the life story of your . . ."—Paul paused, frantically fishing for the appropriate phrase—"your former companion."

"Researchin'?" she said with a sneer. "That what you call it? Pokin' your big nose into other folks' affairs?"

In a sense, Paul could understand—even sympathize—with her attitude. After all, she'd gone to great lengths to conceal her existence from the world. And who could blame her? Being Ed Gein's ex-lover—and the mother of his illegitimate son—wasn't exactly the kind of accomplishment you'd want to trumpet. And then suddenly, after years of total anonymity, some presumptuous stranger shows up at your door and announces that he's discovered your secret. How else would *anyone* react except bitterly?

"How'd you come to find me, anyways?" the woman asked suddenly.

There was something in her voice that made him wary. "A man I know," he said after a moment. "A retired police photographer. He happened to catch sight of your son, and he recognized the face."

Agatha Cobb snorted through her nostrils. "Just a whole damn tribe of you Nosy Parkers, ain't there?" Abruptly, she shifted her bulk forward in the seat. "Who is he? What's his name?"

Paul was taken aback by the fierceness of her tone. Though they were separated by a yard or more of floor space, he found himself reflexively sliding back on the sofa cushion, as though to put himself farther out of her reach.

"Look," he said, "it doesn't matter. He's not going to bother you, Mrs. Cobb."

Staring at the woman, Paul saw that she was clutching the chair arms so tightly that her knuckles were white. She lowered her gaze and began mumbling under her breath, as though conducting a whispered debate with an unseen companion.

Well, thought Paul. *Might as well forget it.* Clearly, he wasn't going to get any information out of the woman. Or even so much as set eyes on Ed Gein, Jr.

Still, he decided to give it one last shot. He felt something like a connoisseur of post-Impressionist art who had heard rumors of a previously unknown work by Van Gogh. All he craved was a glimpse of the remarkable thing, just to confirm its existence and know that he, virtually alone among men, had actually viewed it.

"Look—would it be possible for me just to meet your son?"

"He ain't here," she answered gruffly.

"Ah," Paul said. "Will he be back soon?"

She glowered at him. "Not soon enough for you."

"Right," he said, with a gentle slap of his palms. "Guess there's no need for me to hang around, then." He placed his hands on the cushion and began to rise.

"How 'bout some lemonade?"

Paul, who was already halfway off the sofa, stopped and stared at her. "Excuse me?"

"I said, you want some lemonade?"

Trying hard not to show his astonishment, Paul lowered himself back onto the sofa. He studied the woman closely, trying to divine what had prompted this unexpected turnabout. But her expression—a kind of lame simulation of friendliness—was completely unreadable. Though she had contorted her flaccid lips into something approximating a smile, her eyes were as dead as the coal lumps on a snowman.

Did this sudden display of rudimentary etiquette signify a real change of heart? Or was it just some kind of ploy? But if the latter, what was she hoping to accomplish? Paul couldn't make heads or tails of the whole thing. But on the off chance that she had decided to relent and share a few recollections with him, he decided to accept the offer. After all, what harm could it possibly do to share a glass of lemonade with the old lady?

Perhaps she might even confirm what he had come to suspect about the late Victor Hobart.

"Sure," Paul said. "Sounds great."

With a grunt, Agatha Cobb squeezed herself out of the chair. "You just set right there," she said. Then she turned and lumbered out of the living room.

As soon as she was out of sight, Paul, who had been sitting rigidly on the edge of the cushion, sank back on the sofa and glanced around the sterile room. Hanging on the opposite wall, directly above the console TV, was a small grouping of framed photographs. Getting to his feet, Paul stepped around the glass-topped coffee table, crossed the floor, and peered at the pictures.

They were hanging in cheap wooden frames, the kind sold in stores like Kmart and intended for 8" × 10" photographs. Each of the pictures showed a beaming young couple or, in several cases, a whole family—mother, father, two young children. The faces were different in every picture, but all the people were as perfect as the models in a toothpaste ad.

Paul couldn't imagine what relation these glowing specimens had to Agatha Cobb. It took him a moment to realize that the pictures weren't authentic at all. They were the phony make-believe portraits that are routinely prepackaged in photo frames. Apparently, Agatha Cobb hadn't realized that she was supposed to throw away the dummy pictures and replace them with real ones of her own. Either that or there was something so appealing to her about these sugary, idealized images that she was moved to display them in her living room.

In either case, the sight of the pictures struck Paul as simultaneously funny, pathetic, and indescribably weird. He didn't know whether to laugh, cry, or get the hell out of there as quickly as possible.

Wait'll Wylie hears this *one,* he thought. He glanced at his watch. His flight wasn't departing for another four and a half hours—plenty of time to get to the airport and to call Lewis Stimpson. He had promised to phone the old man before leaving and report on his meeting with the Cobbs.

Paul had been a little shocked the previous evening when he'd gone to Stimpson's apartment. Just a few years before, when Paul had first met him, Stimpson was hail and hearty and taking full advantage of his retirement to indulge his passion for photography. This time, however, he seemed strikingly older, as though he'd been hit by a wasting disease. His body was stooped and shriveled and his face deathly pale, as though he hadn't ventured outdoors in weeks.

He seemed only mildly surprised to see Paul. "Guess you're here about those pictures," he had said. Paul had no idea what Stimpson was talking about, and Stimpson, in turn, seemed puzzled by Paul's ignorance. It took a few minutes to straighten things out—to establish that Stimpson's package must have arrived after Paul's departure for Wisconsin. Paul explained the reason for his visit—how, during his brief expedition to Plainfield, he had thought about Stimpson and decided to stop by and say hello before returning home.

Seated in the amiable wreckage of his living room, Stimpson went on to tell Paul about his startling encounter with the man who looked like Ed Gein's pudgier twin. In one of the photos Stimpson had snapped—of the man in the cab of his delivery van—the company's name was clearly visible on the driver's door. Using his contacts in the police department, Stimpson had been able to trace the identity of the Gein lookalike.

Leon Cobb. Son of a woman named Agatha Cobb.

With a little more digging around, Stimpson had learned a fact that, as far as he was concerned, absolutely confirmed his suspicions. Agatha Cobb was, in reality, the former Agatha Roberts. She had been born and bred in Ed Gein's hometown and had changed her name after moving to Milwaukee, shortly after the Plainfield Horrors became known to the world.

Stimpson explained that, over the past few weeks, he had begun to fear that Gein's bastard son might be the monster who had been terrorizing Milwaukee for months. As a result, he was deeply relieved when the killer turned out to be some psycho named Frewer who had just met his richly deserved end at the hands of the police.

Paul, meanwhile, had felt his heart start to gallop as Stimpson spoke. Ed Gein's son?! Living right there in Milwaukee?! What a remarkable discovery!

Studying the duplicate prints of the photos Stimpson had mailed him, Paul could only shake his head in amazement. The resemblance was uncanny! He just *had* to see this marvel for himself.

Suddenly, a realization had hit him with such force that it made his head jerk. *Of course! That was it! The secret Hobart was concealing! The reverend had known about Agatha and Leon Cobb all along—maybe even suspected, like Stimpson, that Ed, Jr. was Jack the Zipper.*

Paul had hung around for another hour or so, conversing with Stimpson, until it was clear that the old man was beginning to fade. As he got ready to leave, Paul announced his intention to pay a brief visit to the Cobbs before heading home.

Stimpson had looked resigned. "I figured you might react that way. Well, you're a big boy, Paul. I won't try to talk you out of it, but I want you to make sure you call me before you head home. I want to hear what happened."

Clasping Stimpson's hand with both his own, Paul shook it warmly and promised that he would.

Now, finishing his little circuit of the living room, Paul returned to the sofa and reseated himself. He had been half aware of the sounds from the kitchen—the shuffling of feet, the clinking of glasses, the opening and closing of the refrigerator door. Now, there was absolute silence. He was just leaning forward to pluck a *National Geographic* from the stack on the glass-topped coffee table when the old lady's voice called out.

"Hey, mister—c'mon in here and give me a hand."

Hand? Paul wondered. *Why does she need a hand?* He shrugged to himself. Maybe she had a trayful of treats—Oreos, Twinkies, whatever—she wanted him to carry.

"Sure," he called.

Rising from the sofa, he walked across the living room and stepped toward his death.

46

Thinking about it later, Paul would come to believe that it was *Psycho* that saved him.

Over the years, he had seen Hitchcock's classic more times than he could count. He had watched it again on videotape just two weeks earlier while preparing his lecture on Ed Gein's impact on American popular culture. Every scene from the film was engraved in his mind, including that harrowing moment when Norman Bates, disguised as his long-dead mother, bursts from a doorway and attacks the private detective, Arbogast, with a butcher knife.

Not that Paul was consciously thinking of the movie when he responded to Agatha Cobb's call for assistance. But something about the situation—being alone in the house with the mother of Ed Gein's son—must have set off associations with *Psycho* deep in his brain. At least that was the only explanation he could come up with for what happened next. The instant he stepped into the kitchen and saw that the old lady wasn't there, he felt a crackle of anxiety, like a warning signal shrieking in his chest.

When Agatha suddenly came up behind him and reached around with her knife, his right hand was already shooting upward in a reflexive motion of defense, so that the blade, instead of severing his throat, slashed across his wrist.

If she had managed to cut a vein, he would have died

anyway, bleeding to death on the kitchen floor. But his arm was angled sideways, so that the knife hit the bony outside of his wrist instead of the shallow-veined underside. Even so, the wound was nasty, slicing straight down to the bone. Paul let out a cry and staggered back against the sink, grabbing onto the counter for support.

The hulking woman glared at him savagely. "You damn runt," she shouted, gesturing at the blood that streamed from his wound. "I just finished cleanin' up the mess from that other pipsqueak!" Raising the knife high above her head, she came charging at Paul with a roar.

Paul wasn't conscious of picking up the frying pan. His left hand must have grazed the handle as he clutched at the Formica countertop. He acted instinctively, grabbing the pan and swinging it wildly as Agatha bore down on him.

It was like swatting at a stampeding water buffalo. The cast-iron skillet seemed to glance off her bulky right shoulder. Frantically, Paul smashed her again, this time on the side of the head. She sank to her knees with a grunt.

He dropped the pan and scrambled past her, feeling a tearing sensation on the back of his left thigh as Agatha, though stunned, struck out with the knife and caught him in the leg. He staggered out of the kitchen toward what he thought was the front door, but the shock of his wounds had disoriented him. Stumbling, collapsing to the floor, he found himself lying across the threshold of the living room. He heard a bellow from the kitchen and felt the floor shake as the lumbering woman came after him.

Frantically, he dragged himself backward into the living room, striking the rear of his head on the glass-topped coffee table just as Agatha appeared in the doorway. Her eyes were wild, her mouth flecked with spittle. "My rug!" she screeched. "You're bleedin' all over my rug!" Her face was lobster red and beaded with sweat, and her triple chin trembled.

Howling, she came at Paul, knife raised high. Desperately, he reached up behind him, groping around the coffee table for something—anything—to throw. There was nothing but the stack of *National Geographics*. With a frantic, sweeping motion, he flung them off the table, just to put something between himself and the rampaging madwoman. The magazines scattered all over the floor. Agatha's right foot slipped on a cover, and she toppled forward with a cry.

Hurling himself backward, half under the table, Paul shielded his face with his hands as she crashed through the tabletop. Glass exploded above him. The world went momentarily black as a crushing weight came down on him.

The next thing he knew, he was shoving and kicking, trying to free himself from the suffocating mountain of flesh. There were slivers of glass everywhere—in his hair, on his face, under his shoulders. A liquid gurgle filled his ears, mixed with the high-pitched rasp of his own frantic breathing. He could feel blood, sticky and wet, on his forearms, neck, and face.

Mustering what remained of his strength, he managed to squirm clear of the massive body and drag himself a few feet away. He lay on his back, gulping air, then elbowed himself up and saw the bloody shard of glass protruding like a dagger from Agatha Cobb's throat. The gurgle he had heard, the blood he had felt—both had been issuing from that ghastly wound. As Paul watched with gaping eyes, her enormous bosom heaved convulsively, then stopped. A big bubble of blood bulged from her open mouth like an apple in a roasted pig.

Paul put his swimming head back on the carpet, closed his eyes, and blacked out.

He didn't remember dialing 911 after regaining consciousness, but he must have dragged himself to the phone and placed the call, because the next thing he knew, the apartment was full of people.

He was slumping on the living-room sofa while a female paramedic bandaged his wrist. Another paramedic—a young black man—knelt in front of him, attending to his wounded leg. There were cops everywhere, crouching over Agatha's body, examining the shattered glass table, drifting into and out of the living room. One officer was stationed by the front door, keeping gawkers at bay. A detective in a camel-hair overcoat was hovering by the sofa, asking Paul questions and jotting the answers in a notepad.

A blinding flash made Paul squint as a cameraman photographed the ponderous corpse that sprawled a few feet away like a stranded pilot whale. Suddenly, from the direction of Leon's bedroom, Paul heard a muffled shout: "Holy shit!"

Seconds later, a cop wearing latex gloves appeared at the doorway of the living room. He was carrying a human skull that seemed to be decked out in a gray fright wig. It took Paul a moment to realize that the long wiry hair wasn't a wig. It was real hair, clearly that of an old woman. Though the rest of the flesh had been peeled from the skull, the scalp was still attached. Paul could see its ragged edge above the pale bone of the forehead.

The detective in the camel-hair overcoat hurried over to examine the skull and confer with the cop. A half-minute later, the detective stepped back to the sofa. "You say this Cobb guy is Ed Gein's son?"

Paul nodded.

'Looks like he inherited his daddy's hobbies," said the detective, nodding toward the skull. His mouth was puckered in distaste.

"His cleaning habits, too," said the cop with the skull. "You oughta see that fuckin' bedroom."

Just then, another cop strode into the living room.

Harold Schechter

"You get hold of Cobb's boss?" the detective asked him.

"Yeah," said the cop. "Hasn't seen him in a couple of days. Said that when we find the asshole, tell him he's fired."

The detective cast a querying look at Paul. Paul gave a weary shrug. There wasn't any need for words. They were both wondering the same thing.

Where the hell was Leon Cobb?

47

"What was *that?*" Wylie said. Seated on the edge of her daughter's bed, she looked up from the book and frowned.

"Mmmm?" mumbled Diana, her eyelids fluttering open.

"Sorry, baby," Wylie said, glancing down at her daughter. "Mommy didn't mean to wake you." She had been so absorbed in the bedtime story—*Ozma of Oz*—that she hadn't realized Diana had dozed off. Wylie had been reading the book to Diana, a chapter at a time, every evening since Paul's departure.

Tilting an ear toward the curtained window, Wylie listened hard. She had heard a strange noise—a sharp cry or whine from outside, instantly cut off. Had it been Melville? She had let the dog out before she came upstairs to put Diana to bed.

Leaning a little closer to the window, Wylie strained to hear. Faintly, she could make out the receding drone of a passing plane.

Otherwise, there was only silence.

Reaching out a hand, Wylie smoothed a wisp of golden hair from Diana's soft, untroubled forehead. "Want me to turn off the light, baby?"

"Uh-uh," said Diana, snuggling closer to Harvey, the beloved—if seriously bedraggled—stuffed rabbit who shared her pillow. "I want to hear more about the Hungry Tiger."

"Okay." Laying the open book upside down on the bed, Wylie patted her daughter's leg, swaddled in the flowered comforter. "Be back in a minute."

A crack of yellow light glowed beneath the closed door of Matt's room. Crossing the hallway, Wylie rapped on the door and paused, listening. No answer. Turning the knob, she pushed open the door, and poked her head inside.

Dressed in his Power Ranger pj's, Matt was sitting up in bed, a comic book in his hands and earphones clipped to his head. Up until very recently, he had been completely indifferent to pop music. A few weeks before, however, after hearing "Crocodile Rock" on the car radio, he had developed a sudden, intense interest in Elton John. Wylie took a dim view of kids who passed half their waking hours plugged into Walkmans. Still, she couldn't work up too much righteous indignation, having spent a significant chunk of her own adolescence listening obsessively to Billy Joel and David Bowie albums.

Quietly, she closed the door again. Whatever had made the peculiar noise outside, it was certain that Matt hadn't heard it.

Flipping on the stairwell light, she descended to the main floor and entered the living room. Normally, Matt and Diana retreated upstairs after dinner. But during Paul's absence, the three of them had congregated in the living room every evening, as though to seek comfort in each other's proximity. As a result, the room was something of a mess, strewn with assorted playthings—a coloring book and crayons, a half-completed wooden dinosaur skeleton, a few X-men figurines, and a buck-naked Barbie with a half-dozen fashion accessories scattered nearby. A Battleship game had been set up on the sofa; its little plastic pegs were sprinkled all over the cushions.

Well, she'd have the children tidy up first thing in the morning. Paul was even more of a neat freak than Wylie, and he'd probably flip out if he arrived home to find the living room in such a state.

Passing the fireplace, where a couple of logs hissed and crackled companionably behind the screen, she walked out of the living room and headed down the hallway toward the kitchen.

A small pottery lamp glowed warmly on the little wooden table. The cast-iron stove—a genuine antique that dated back to the Civil War—gave off a little light, too, through the circular damper she had left open earlier. Otherwise, the kitchen was steeped in shadows.

She checked the stove and closed the damper. By this point every evening, the wood had burned down to charcoals that would continue to warm the kitchen throughout much of the night for Melville.

She glanced at her watch: 8:40. Time for the mutt to come inside. Once he was settled in for the night, Wylie could finish putting the kids to sleep, then relax with a cup of tea and that new Amanda Cross mystery she was immersed in.

She stepped to the back door and flipped on the outside light. Lately, Melville had returned instantly at the signal. It was awfully cold outside. The weather reports were forecasting an overnight low of minus twenty. On nights such as this, Wylie believed that the big Lab secretly yearned to be inside.

But tonight he did not appear at the door, tail wagging, icicles hanging off his chin.

She brought her face close to the glass panes of the upper door and peered outside. Her eyes swept the snowy landscape, then returned to the small grove of spruces about twenty-five feet from the house.

There, at the base of the trees, clearly visible in the light spilling from the back door, a black shape lay motionless in the snow.

"Melville!" Wylie gasped. "Oh God, oh God." Was he hurt? What had happened? Hand trembling, she reached down for the key in the inside door lock.

On the opposite side of the door, a ghastly face sprang up behind the glass like a lifesize jack-in-the-box.

Wylie screamed and leaped backward.

Pressed against the panes, the grotesque face seemed to leer at her. In her shock and terror, Wylie couldn't make sense of its features. It looked like a Halloween mask made of some bizarre material—wrinkled and leathery, with black sockets for eyes and a smeared, bloodred mouth.

Wylie screamed again.

Taking one step backward, the grotesque figure raised its arms high over its head and brought them down. A big rock crashed the window and landed in a shower of glass shards and wooden splinters at Wylie's feet. She shrieked as a gloved hand reached in through the shattered panes and groped for the key.

Spinning, Wylie fled from the kitchen toward the stairway leading to her children's bedrooms.

Damn, but she's good-lookin'! Leon thought as he twisted the key and retracted his arm from the shattered pane. *Kinda like that exercise slut, Debbie.* Shoving open the door, he stepped into the gloomy kitchen. Maybe things would turn out to be okay after all. Maybe he'd even get to have some fun. That would be a nice change of pace. So far, the whole trip had been shitty. Real shitty.

Things began to go bad almost from the start. Leon's plane hadn't been in the air more than twenty minutes before he began puking out his guts. He'd never flown before—how was he supposed to know it was going to make him so sick? No one had been too nice about it, either—not that young bitch sitting next to him, who had leapt up and scurried to another seat, not the snooty-faced stewardess who'd looked at him like he was lower than a dog.

He'd spent the whole trip feeling greener than cow shit. When he'd finally staggered off the plane, he had to sit with his head between his knees for a full five minutes before he could go off in search of a car rental place. His mama had given him real clear instructions. Even so, Leon had a hell of a time before he managed to figure out which rental place was the cheapest, which car to choose, whether he needed insurance or not, and a million other damn questions he wasn't prepared for.

Though the pencil-neck behind the counter had provided him with a map, Leon still managed to get lost about half a dozen times as he navigated the strange roads in the gathering darkness. By the time he spotted the sign for Stoddard Bridge, he was almost weeping with frustration. Then he couldn't find the address. He'd finally had to stop and get directions from some old coot in a filling station. Even so, it had taken him another fifteen whole minutes to find the mailbox he was looking for.

Parking the car off the dirt road beside a stand of barren trees, he had tied on his mask, then stepped out into the cold and made his way carefully uphill through the snowy woods. He was almost to the crest of the hill when his foot caught a tree root and he went crashing onto his face, scraping his hands and tearing a hole in the knee of his pants. He lay there whimpering for a moment. That's when he'd heard the low growl. At least the dog hadn't barked before Leon leapt up and brained it. He could feel the bone crunch under the big rock as he brought it down hard on the mongrel's skull.

He'd been so fed up by then that he was damn near tempted just to turn right around and forget the whole thing, head straight back home and tell the fat old bitch that she could just go ahead and do the job herself for all he cared. The only thing that stopped him was thinking about how she'd react. He could just picture the look on her fat ugly face, hear that mean, yammering voice: *Can't do nothin' right, can you, boy? I shoulda known it all along. You're just a no-good, shit-brained sissy, like that dirty dog that spawned you . . . blah, blah, blah!*

Well, he'd show her—show her the kind of man he was.

He'd show that blond-haired bitch who just tore ass out of here, too. *Damn, she's a hot-looking slut!*

Glancing quickly around the countertops, he spotted a big, slanty wooden block with a bunch of handles poking out of it. Just what he was looking for! He grabbed the biggest handle and out slid a heavy-bladed butcher knife. He ran his forefinger over the edge, felt the sharpness and the sting, then stuck his finger through the mouth hole of the mask and sucked off the blood.

That'll do.

Though the skin mask chafed against his pimply skin, he liked the way it made him feel. Powerful. Like Batman or something. Only sexier.

There was a wall phone hanging right beside him—one of those portable kinds without a cord. Snatching it from its cradle, he hurled it to the tile floor, smashing the phone to bits.

He strode out of the kitchen, through a little hallway, and followed the lights into the living room. There was a fire going in the fireplace. Lots of toys and other shit scattered all over. He knew there were kids in the house—he'd read all about the Novaks in a *People* magazine article his mama had found in that Heckley shit's attaché case. Leon was planning on having some fun with the kids. Oh yeah. He was planning on having some fun with the whole damn family, though he intended to save the best for last—that long-legged blonde with the high tits and juicy ass.

There was another phone in the living room, this one a regular kind. It was sitting on a side table by the sofa. He grabbed it by the base and tore it from the wall with a savage yank.

Funny that he'd detected no sign of Novak. Maybe he wasn't home yet—the way Hobart hadn't been when Leon first arrived.

Well, he'd just amuse himself with the wife and kids

until the asshole got home and found a little surprise waiting.

A low sniggering escaped from the mouthhole of the skin mask as Leon strode from the living room and made for the carpeted stairs.

Diana was standing at the top of the stairs, clutching the scruffy rabbit to her chest. "Mommy?" she said in a thin, quavering voice. Her eyes were big circles of fear.

"Come!" Wylie screamed, bounding up the stairs. Snatching her daughter's hand, she yanked her toward Matt's bedroom, threw open the door, and burst inside.

Startled from his reading, Matt bolted upright in bed, tearing off his headphones. "What's wrong?" he cried.

"There's a man!" Wylie yelled, darting to his bedside. Reaching down, Wylie grabbed him by the wrist and half dragged him from his bed. Pulling both children behind her, she ran back to the doorway and paused, listening.

"Shit!" she cried. She could hear the intruder thudding across the living room. No time to make it back to her bedroom and call the police.

She slammed the door and leaned her back against it, panting. There was no way to lock it. Looking wildly around the room, she leapt to the big oak dresser, grabbed it, tried to wrestle it away from the wall. If she could just shove it in front of the door . . .

"Shit!" she cried again. The damn thing wouldn't budge.

"Lemme help, Mommy!" Matt cried, springing to her side.

"No! It's too heavy!" She struggled to quash her rising panic. Beside her, Diana hugged her stuffed animal tight to her body and made whimpering noises.

What to do? What to do?

Her darting gaze was caught by Matt's closet. *The attic!*

There was only one means of access to the unfinished attic: a little door—more of a hatchway really—in the very back of Matt's closet. The very first time the family had been shown the house, the kids had been thrilled by the hidden half door, which seemed like the secret entrance to another world. For the first few months after moving in, Matt and Diana had loved to crawl inside the closet, clamber through the little door, and pretend that they had entered an enchanted realm of make-believe. Paul, of course, had been a good deal less taken with the setup, since it was a serious pain in the ass to drag anything into or out of the storage space. But for the children, the little hidden portal was pure magic—like the marvelous wardrobe in the Narnia books.

"Quick, quick," Wylie cried, shoving the children toward the closet. "The attic!"

Matt went first, then Diana. Before ducking into the closet, Wylie stepped to the bedroom window and flung it wide open. Then hurrying after her children, she stepped into the closet, pulling the door shut behind her.

Hunched low, she made her way through the double row of hanging clothes, shoving aside the shirts and pants and jackets like a jungle explorer fighting her way through the undergrowth. The floor of the closet was a junk heap—Wylie had long given up trying to impose any kind of order on it. In the blackness of the closet, she couldn't see a thing, but she knew what was there— cartons of old toys, stacks of board games, dirt-caked athletic shoes, tennis rackets, baseball bats, the usual ac- coutrements of middle-class American boyhood. Getting to her hands and knees, she scrambled over the littered floor to the rear of the closet.

Matt had already slid back the metal bolt on the little door and was clambering through, his little sister close behind. Wylie followed, then yanked the door shut. Un- fortunately, there was no way to latch it from the inside. Squatting on her haunches in the dark, she listened to her children breathing hard beside her while her mind raced.

She was sure the intruder wouldn't see the small door,

even if he peered inside the closet. The floor of the closet was heaped too high with junk. For the first time, Wylie felt profoundly grateful for her son's slovenliness.

But what would the maniac do once he searched all the rooms and found them empty? She hoped that once he spotted the open window in Matt's bedroom, he would assume that she and the kids had managed to descend from the second story and escape through the woods. With his victims gone, there would be no reason for him to stay.

He wasn't a robber—of that she was certain. A robber wouldn't have smashed his way inside so brazenly. No. He was planning to kill them. She had no idea why. But somehow, she felt sure, this horror had descended on their lives because of Paul's book.

A sudden sickening thought made her throat clench. What if she was wrong? What if he *did* find the little door in the back of Matt's closet? She needed to find a place for them to hide.

There was only one light source in the attic—a sixty-watt bulb in a socket attached to an overhead beam. She reached up and groped blindly for the pull-string. On the third try, she felt it drag across the back of her hand. She clutched the string and pulled. Diana and Matt were still on hands and knees two feet ahead of her, blinking rapidly, their faces sickly and strained in the murky yellow light.

In a flash, she took in the contents of the attic. Several steamer trunks stuffed with baby clothes. Diana's dismantled cradle. A pair of old stereo speakers. A guitar case. A rolled-up Oriental carpet. A cracked mirror in an elaborate gilded frame. Some murky landscape paintings inherited from Paul's grandfather. A folded card table. A small wooden chest. Wylie's old camping equipment from her Girl Scout days. Two discarded end tables, one with a shadeless cast-iron lamp standing on it.

But mostly boxes and boxes of books. Neither Paul

nor Wylie could bear to throw away old books. There must have been fifty cartons of them piled up in the attic.

A muffled sound drove a spike of terror through her chest. The intruder was upstairs. She could hear him in the master bedroom, his footsteps clumping heavily on the floor. Suddenly he paused. An instant later, there was a loud, jingly crash. *The telephone.* She heard a muted grunt, then a door being jerked open. It was the door of her walk-in closet—it always stuck.

Wylie crawled past the children to where she could stand semiupright, her back hunched against the sloping roof. She held a finger to her lips. "Shhh," she whispered. "Like mice."

Squeezing between two tall stacks of cartons, she made her way to the very rear of the attic, sliding over and around the piled obstacles. Her children came after, Diana clinging to her sorry-looking stuffed rabbit, Matt at his little sister's heels.

Leaning up against the back wall of attic was a disassembled metal bed frame and a single mattress. The bed had served as a guest cot in their old apartment. Now, the mattress formed a kind of lean-to against the insulated wall. Kneeling, Wylie grabbed the bottom of the mattress and tugged it a little further from the wall.

"Here," she whispered to the children. "Inside."

Diana looked up at her mother. It was very dark back there at the far end of the attic. Even so, Wylie could see that her daughter's face was beginning to crumple.

Wylie stroked Diana's cheek with her fingertips. "Everything will be fine, sweetie," she whispered. "But you mustn't cry." She turned to Matt, who was squatting on his heels beside his sister. He was doing his best to look brave, but Wylie could see the fear in his eyes. "Matt, you go in first."

Getting onto his belly, Matt squirmed into the black cave between the attic wall and the propped-up mattress. Wylie reached down and touched his back as he disappeared into the hiding place.

"Now you, sweetie," she said to Diana. "Here. Let me hold Harvey until you're inside." She took the stuffed rabbit from Diana, who wiggled in after her brother. Crouching by the opening, Wylie shoved the stuffed rabbit behind the mattress, holding on to it until Diana tugged it from her grasp.

"Don't make a sound, no matter what," Wylie whispered. "I'll be right here."

" 'Kay, Mommy," answered Diana's tiny quavering voice.

Kneeling beside the mattress, Wylie quickly glanced around. A bunch of overstuffed book cartons were stacked a few feet away. Piled four high and arranged in a rough semicircle, they formed a kind of parapet.

In a flash, Wylie was hunkered down behind the boxes. At her back stood one of the cheap wooden end tables, holding the heavy, shadeless lamp—sentimental relics of her early years of marriage.

She listened hard, keeping one hand over her mouth as though to mute the sound of her own rapid breathing.

The madman had entered Matt's room.

She could hear the creak of the floorboards. Then a pause. Then his heavy footsteps crossing the room. Another pause.

Wylie strained to hear, her face muscles contracted with the effort. The footsteps seemed to move in the direction of the closet, then stop again. She held her breath as she heard him turn the door knob of the closet. After that, silence. Agonizing seconds passed. Hidden though they were, she felt frightening vulnerable—she and the children were not more than fifteen feet away from the maniac.

A dizzying realization hit her. *The attic light!* It was still on! What if he saw it seeping through the crack under the little door?

She squeezed her eyes tight and mouthed a silent prayer. *Oh God. Please make him go away. Don't let him see the door.*

And then, miraculously, as though in immediate response to her frantic supplication, she heard his footsteps heading away from the closet. Her relief was so overwhelming that she had to brace herself against the boxes to keep from sinking down. She could hear the heavy clump of his shoes as he moved down the hallway in the direction of Diana's bedroom.

A shiver ran through her, and for the fist time, she realized how cold the attic was.

Well, at least the children would be warmer, huddled together in the tight space behind the mattress. The three of them couldn't stay here indefinitely. But they'd be okay for a while. Until she was sure that the intruder had given up and gone away. Then—

An odd sound made her forehead pucker. *What in the world is he do—?*

She clamped both hands over her mouth to stifle an involuntary cry.

Oh Christ! He's coming back! Back toward Matt's room!

She could hear him in the hallway, feet pounding, as though he were returning at a jog.

Paralyzed with fear and confusion, she shrank down behind the boxes. She could hear him inside her son's bedroom now, quickly crossing the floor. He was coming toward the closet!

An instant later, the closet door was flung open. She heard a thud, like someone dropping to his knees, then a scrambling sound, growing louder.

He was crawling toward the back of the closet, toward the little attic door. . . .

She sank back on her heels, trying frantically to think. *Oh God, Oh God, Oh God.*

From the other side of the attic door came a muted sound that turned her bones to ice—a high, demented giggle.

Then the door hinges creaked.

48

Just climbing the stairs had left him panting. He had to admit his mama was right about one thing—he was in piss-poor shape. Maybe he'd actually start aerobicizing with Debbie once he got back home, instead of just whacking off to the show.

The mask wasn't making it any easier to breathe, that was for damn sure. He probably should've made the mouth- and noseholes bigger. But then it wouldn't have looked as much like the old cow he'd peeled it from.

He paused on the landing, gasping for air, and took a slow look around. All those doors! Leon had never been inside such a big house. This Novak fucker must've made a shitload of money. Imagine getting rich off a book about Leon's own daddy! Hell, it didn't seem fair. Maybe Leon'd write his own book one day and buy a house as big as this one. His very own place, just for himself alone—no fat old smelly bitches allowed.

Well, all that was in the future. Right now, he had more urgent matters to attend to. Like finding the blond-haired slut and her little bastards and having some fun with them until Mr. Paul Asshole Novak got home. *Oh, yeah. Mr. Paul Asshole Novak is gonna have some nice little surprises waiting for him.* Leon already had one idea in mind, involving the little girl's head and a broomstick.

A light was glowing from an open door across the hallway. Leon crossed the wooden floor and entered.

It was the largest bedroom he'd ever been in. It contained the largest bed, too, with a big wooden headboard and a mattress wide enough for a whole damn family to sleep on.

Must be where the bitch does her fucking, thought Leon, his lips curling beneath the desiccated circle of flesh that used to be Hannah Hobart's mouth. Well, he planned to have his own fun with the slut on that nice king-size bed before her hubby came home. Then he'd do something creative with the corpse, just as he'd done when he took care of the Hobarts. He could still picture the look on Hobart's face right before the old Bible-thumper croaked. *Haw!*

Now where the hell were they hiding? He walked to the closet, stopping first to snatch the phone from the bed table and smash it to the floor, and yanked open the door.

A light went on inside the closet when he opened it. *Pretty goddamn fancy,* thought Leon. They *needed* a light in there, too. The closet looked almost as big as his whole damn bedroom. He stepped inside, shoving aside the hanging clothes, peering up at the shelves and down behind the rows of shoes. *Nothing.* On his way out, he paused to slash a few of Wylie's outfits with his big butcher knife.

The cunt wasn't going to be needing any clothes after *he* got done with her, that was for shit sure.

He left the room and crossed the hallway to another, smaller bedroom. One glance told him that it belonged to the little boy. Dozens of little plastic figures—robots and soldiers and spacemen and shit—were scattered all over the floor. Stooping, Leon snatched up one of the toys—a helmeted figure in a skin-tight red suit, clutching a bizarre, long-barreled gun. Examining it in the lamplight, he imagined the little plastic warrior raping cheerleader Krystal with the gun. The idea made him chortle.

A sudden gust of icy air made him glance up at the window. It was thrown wide open. Leon shrugged. *Guess the little shit likes fresh air.* Leon hadn't decided exactly what to do with the boy yet. His fantasies never involved little boys. Maybe he wouldn't do anything *fancy*—just tie the kid up, let him watch while Leon took care of the mother and sister, then kill him.

We'll see. Gotta find the little bastard first. Gotta find all of them first!

Tossing the plastic figure back onto the floor, he went to check out the closet.

This one didn't have an automatic light, but there was a skinny white string hanging down just inside the door. Leon gave it a tug and a bulb clicked on. Taking a step inside the closet, he shoved aside some clothes and looked around.

The closet wasn't nearly as big as the one in the other room. In fact, it was just about the size of his own bedroom closet back home—deep but very narrow. It was a real mess, too, its floor covered with all kinds of junk. Not quite as chaotic as his own closet floor, but close.

Squatting on his heels, he peered beneath the hanging clothes. He couldn't see all the way to the very rear of the closet, but he could tell that there weren't any people hiding back there.

Standing upright, he backed out of the closet. The skin mask was making his face feel all hot and itchy. He shoved his right hand under the mask and scratched.

They're somewheres *around here,* he thought. *That's for shit sure.* He'd find them. And when he did, he'd make them pay *double* for all the bother they were giving him.

He was starting to feel a little impatient. He could hear his mama's voice inside his head: *You just do the damn job and get your fat ass out of there!* More and more, no matter where he was or what he was doing, he could hear his mama yammering at him, just as clear as if she were standing right there at his side.

Right now, for instance, her voice was so loud inside his head that he couldn't hear himself think. He had already crossed the hallway and was standing at the threshold of the third bedroom before the idea broke into his consciousness. He stopped dead in his tracks, then turned and hurried back.

In its size and general sloppiness, the little boy's closet had reminded him of his own. Maybe it was similar in another way, too. Leon had a secret place in the very back of his closet where he stored all his treasures. Could there be such a place in the back of the little boy's closet? A bigger one, where the blond bitch and her two little bastards could hide?

In a flash, he was on his knees in the cramped, messy closet, scrambling over the cluttered floor to the very rear. When he saw the little partly open door, its metal bolt slid open, a dull light glowing behind, he let out a delighted little giggle.

With his butcher knife clutched in his left hand, he reached out his right, pulled open the door, and crawled inside.

Crouching just inside the doorway, Leon took a slow look around. The attic was crammed with all kinds of shit, but mostly dozens and dozens of brown cardboard boxes, piled three and four high and extending to the very back. The bitch and her bastards could be hiding anywhere.

"Come out, come out, wherever you are," he sing-songed, like a kid playing hide-and-seek.

He listened hard but heard nothing. He stood as high as he could and peered around. Part of the attic was illuminated by the single bare bulb, but the back end was hidden in shadow. If Leon were looking for a place to hide, that's where *he'd* go.

"Here I come!" he called out in the same playful tone. Shoulders hunched, he began working his way toward the rear.

There was no need for stealth. He bulled his way through the gaps between the carton stacks, knocking boxes to the floor as he went. Suddenly, he froze, one ear cocked toward the rear of the attic. He thought he'd heard a noise—a muffled whimper, like the terrified sound that might escape the throat of a sleeping child in the midst of a particularly harrowing nightmare.

He shouldered his way past another pile of cartons . . . and stopped.

Directly ahead, leaning up against the back wall of the attic, was a mattress. Its bottom edge was shoved forward a couple of feet. *Just the place for the little bastards to hide their scrawny asses. And lookee there!* Poking out from one end was something that looked like a white stockinged foot. A little girls' foot!

Beneath the wrinkled mask he had made from Hannah Hobart's face, Leon Cobb smiled.

Then he sprang.

Leaping toward the mattress, he grabbed one edge and began to tug it away from the wall. Behind the mattress, little voices began to shout and scream. "Mommy! Mommy!"

Leon dropped to his knees, still yanking at the mattress. Under the hot, itchy mask, sweat trickled down and stung his eyes, obscuring his vision.

There was something soft and white there, all right. Between the darkness and his stinging eyes, he couldn't see it very well, but it was moving frantically, like the quaking leg of a child.

Raising his knife, he slammed the blade down on the soft, white thing, impaling it. A piercing screech rang out. He tried to raise the knife again, but the point was buried in the floorboard. Grabbing the handle in both fists, he struggled to work the knife free.

A maddened voice roared out behind him. It was her! The bitch! Leon ducked his head and raised his shoulders protectively.

Too late. Something exploded inside his skull—a blinding white light, accompanied by a crushing pain.

He let out a shuddering groan, fell forward onto the mattress, and slid to the floor.

* * *

Bellowing with rage, Wylie brought the heavy lamp down on the monster's head again. On the third blow, the cast-iron base caught him behind the left ear, half shearing it from his scalp.

Dropping the lamp, she fell to her knees beside the motionless body and frantically shoved at the mattress. Her children were shrieking at the top of their lungs. Reaching behind the mattress, she grabbed Diana by the wrists, dragged her out, and pulled her into a rocking embrace. Matt scrambled out after his sister and threw himself at Wylie, hugging her with the fierce, desperate need of a frightened toddler.

She clutched her children to her shaking body, running her hands up and down their heaving backs. Diana, her face buried against Wylie's chest, was saying something unintelligible.

"What, what, what?" Wylie cried.

"He killed him, he killed him, he killed him," Diana wailed, turning her face up to her mother's.

Wylie glanced down at the floor. Harvey, the stuffed rabbit, lay impaled beside the mattress, the butcher knife driven through its soft, scruffy middle.

"Matt," Wylie said breathlessly. Loosening his grip from her neck, the boy stared at his mother. Tears slicked his face and snot bubbled from his nostrils. He smeared his nose dry with the back of one hand and struggled to collect himself. "What, Mommy?" he said. His voice sounded so shaky and fragile that her heart gave a pang.

"Go," she gasped. "Take your sister. Quick—downstairs."

Nodding, Matt grabbed Diana's hand and pulled her away from Wylie. The two of them scrambled away, instantly disappearing over the spilled piles of cartons.

Still on her knees, Wylie looked down at the prostrate body inches away. Dark blood welled from the gash behind his dangling ear. He seemed not to be breathing.

She reached out a hand to feel his chest but withdrew it immediately. She could not bring herself to touch him.

Rising to a crouch, she made her way toward the lighted part of the attic. In her haste to get out, she slammed her forehead against a roof beam. For a moment, she could not see. She fell to her hands and knees and crawled forward, blinking.

Then she was out of the closet, moving across Matt's bedroom and into the hallway, toward the stairwell. She grabbed onto the banister and half slid, half stumbled downstairs.

"Matt! Diana!" she shouted, staggering into the living room. "Where are you?"

She could not hear them, and her mouth went dry with fear.

Then she heard her son's voice calling, "In here!"

Wylie followed the sound to the icy kitchen, where her shivering children stood by the sink, Matt with arms around his sobbing baby sister. The big rock that had smashed through the door pane sat on the tiled floor, broken glass and splintered wood scattered around it. A few feet away lay the shattered telephone.

Kneeling, Wylie took her children into her arms, stroking their hair, kissing their heads, pressing their damp faces to her chest. She wanted to embrace them forever; but she knew that they had to get out, into the car, drive to the police stati—

The realization struck her with stunning force. She squeezed her eyes tight and hissed, "Shit!"

"What?" asked Matt.

"My keys," Wylie said with a groan. They were upstairs in her bedroom, in her purse, on top of her bureau.

"Matt," she said, after gathering her resolve, "Take Diana into the mud room. Get into your snowsuits and boots."

As Wylie started to rise, Diana reached up and grabbed the hem of her sweater. "No, Mommy, no," the little girl cried fearfully.

Wylie took her child's face in her hands and managed a smile. "Don't worry, sweetie. The bad man can't hurt us anymore." Gently, she loosened Diana's grip from the sweater, kissed her fingers, and said, "I'll be back in a sec."

Without glancing back at her children, she hurried out of the kitchen, across the living room, and up the stairs.

She paused at the top of the landing, listening hard. The only sound was the sweep of the wind outside Matt's wide-flung window.

The middle of her forehead, where she had slammed herself on the roof beam, was beginning to throb. She reached up, touched a goose egg, and winced at the pain.

Drawing a deep breath, she quickly crossed the landing and entered her bedroom.

The big purse was exactly where she remembered leaving it. Grabbing it from the bureau, she stuck a trembling hand inside and groped for the key ring. *Where is it, where is it, where—?*

Suddenly, she froze. *What was* that? She thought she'd heard a noise. She strained to hear.

Silence.

Must have imagined it.

Her groping fingers closed on the keys. "Yes," she crowed aloud.

It would take them less than five minutes to drive to the police station. Another five minutes and the cops would be back at the house. The maniac would probably still be out cold. Hard as she had clobbered him, Wylie didn't seriously think he was dead. But he was down for the count—or so she hoped. She didn't want the bastard to escape before the police arrived. She wanted him locked away forever. Of course, even if he *did* regain consciousness, he was trapped in the att—

She clenched her fists so hard that the keys dug into her palm. *Damn! Damn, damn, damn, damn, damn!*

She couldn't remember if she had locked the little door! But given her haste and confusion as she fled the attic—particularly after she'd hit her head—she didn't think she had.

Her mouth was still very dry. She worked her tongue around the bottom of her mouth to generate some saliva, then dampened her parched lips.

Then, shoving the key ring into her jeans pocket, she darted out of the bedroom and across the hallway to Matt's room.

She paused at the doorway, peering inside. Her chest felt painfully tight.

The closet door was open, just as she'd left it, the single bulb still burning inside.

Quickly, she crossed to the closet, almost tripping as she stepped on one of the plastic superheroes littering the carpet. Taking a deep breath, she edged into the closet and crouched, pushing aside the curtain of clothes.

Swallowing hard, she scrambled over the clutter. Seconds later, she was kneeling by the little attic door. She was *right!* It *wasn't* locked! Reaching out her shaking hands, she shoved the door closed. Her heart was churning. In the closeness of the narrow closet, the only sound she could hear was her own ragged breathing.

There! she thought, sliding the bolt into place *That'll hold him.* She was beginning to feel physically ill. She closed her eyes tightly and shook her head.

Something brushed the back of her neck.

She let out a cry and froze, expecting to feel the blade plunge into her back, the hands wrap around her throat. Nothing happened. With a trembling hand, she reached up and touched the nape of her neck.

"Christ," she whispered, feeling the denim sleeve of Matt's jeans jacket.

Quickly, on hands and knees, she scuttled backward out of the closet. Emerging into the room, she leapt to her feet, dashed out into the hallway, and crossed to the head of the stairs. Grabbing the banister, she started to descend.

She was halfway down the staircase when she heard the shrieks—terrified shrieks—coming from the kitchen.

"*No!*" she bellowed, almost throwing herself down the final half-dozen steps.

She bolted into the living room just as her children came tearing in from the opposite side, Diana first, then Matt, both of them screaming as they ran. At their heels came the lurching madman, brandishing his butcher knife. His face was still masked, and his bloody left ear flapped as he ran. Spotting Wylie, he raised his knife high and came at her with a roar.

Without even thinking, Wylie sprang to the fireplace, snatched the wrought-iron poker from its stand and, holding it like a baseball bat, brought it down on his knife arm.

He let out an animal howl as the knife flew from his hand. Lowering his head, he butted her against the fireplace. Dropping the poker, she went over backward, her flailing arms sweeping the display objects from the mantel. She hit the floor hard. Before she knew it, he was on top of her, straddling her chest, his hands gripping her throat. Powerful thumbs dug into her windpipe.

Raking his face, she tore off the mask and stared up in horror. She had seen those features before, as if in a nightmare. At that instant of panic and terror, she did not remember the photographs in the envelope from Lewis Stimpson.

Blood rushed in her ears. Dimly, she could hear the frantic shrieks of her children.

The maniac tightened his chokehold. Clawing at his face, she shoved her thumb into his mouth and beneath his upper lip, her thumbnail digging a furrow of tissue from his gum. Clamping the knuckle of her index finger on the outside of his lip, she gave a vicious, twisting pinch, as if she were trying to rip his upper lip from his face.

He let out a gurgling cry and loosened his hold—just as two small arms wrapped themselves around his throat and began choking him. It was Matt. Screaming wildly, the boy had hurled himself onto the monster's back.

"No!" Wylie shrieked, as the madman broke her son's stranglehold and flung him halfway across the living room. Matt hit the front of the sofa and slid to the floor with a groan.

Nearby her on the floor lay the scattered objects from the mantel. Her groping hands closed on one of them— the New Guinea statuette that she and Paul had purchased with some of the royalties from *Slaughterhouse*. She scrabbled to her knees as the madman searched wildly for his fallen weapon. Then, with the carved wooden body clutched in her hand like a knife handle, she leaned toward him and brought the pointed end down on his leg, driving the four-inch spiked headdress deep into his inner thigh.

He leapt to his feet, shrieking, and grabbed the statuette with both hands, struggling to yank it free. Frantically, Wylie looked around the floor for another weapon. The madman gave another savage tug and the wooden spike came free in a spray of blood. Raising the statuette like a dagger, he charged at Wylie just as her hands found the wrought-iron poker.

He was almost upon her when she slammed the poker up between his legs and raked it forward, iron hook upward. She could feel the pointed hook catch on his genitals. With a wild screech, she ripped the point forward as hard as she could.

Roaring with pain, Leon dropped the statuette. He clutched his groin, and crashed forward onto the floor as Wylie scrambled out of the way.

"The knife!" someone cried. It was Matt. He had risen to his knees and was jabbing a finger toward the wing chair a few feet from where Wylie lay.

She flung herself at it, stretched out her hand, felt the smooth, shapely handle.

"Mommy!" Matt shrieked. As her fingers tightened

on the knife handle, she glanced over her shoulder. The monster was struggling to his knees.

"Bastard!" she screamed. Hurling herself at him, knife raised high above her head in both hands, she brought the blade down on him. Then again. And again.

He collapsed with a wheeze, the big knife protruding from his upper back.

Sobbing, Wylie staggered to her feet, stumbled toward her children, grabbed them by the hands, and fled the wreckage of her home.

Blood pumping from his thigh and back, the monster lay on his side. Dimly, he could hear a car engine turn over, then recede into the distance. Tears welled in his eyes, and his lips opened and closed like the mouth of a suffocating fish. He had no strength to produce anything more than a nearly inaudible whisper. A listener would have had to place an ear almost directly against Leon Cobb's mouth to hear his dying word:

"Mama."

Epilogue

Sales of *Slaughterhouse* had leveled off in the weeks before Paul's trip to Milwaukee, but thanks to the nationwide coverage of the Cobb affair, the book started flying off the shelves again. The sensational story was catnip to the media: best-selling author and beautiful wife, threatened by "Norman Bates, Jr." and the "Bride of *Psycho*," as *Hard Copy* immediately tagged Leon and Agatha. For several weeks following Paul's return to Connecticut, he and Wylie became the unwitting darlings of the tabloid press, their faces adorning the covers of the *Enquirer* and *Star,* along with the latest before-and-after shots of Oprah on her current diet.

Through his agent, Paul was besieged with requests for interviews. Everyone from Lionel Lemmick to Diane Sawyer was itching to have him on the air. Paul instructed Keith to turn down all the offers. He'd had enough of the limelight, enough of the endless, exhausting debate about horror and violence and the media.

Much to his agent's chagrin, Paul also demurred when his publisher offered him a huge advance for a book about the Cobbs—a kind of sequel to *Slaughterhouse.* He was renouncing horror writing, Paul said. His next book, he declared, was going to be a love story—as sweet and soothing as a "bowl of milk."

But even that project was put on hold for the moment. Right now, all he intended to do was take some time to treat the wounds—the wounds that had been inflicted on his body, his psyche, and most important—his family.

The last took the longest to heal. Three months after he got back to Connecticut—weeks after the stitches were removed from his gashed wrist and leg—his children were still having nightmares. And Wylie, though she struggled to resist her anger and resentment, couldn't help but blame him for the horror that had descended on their home.

Ultimately, however, their lives returned to normal. With the help of some professional counseling, Matt and Diana put the trauma behind them. And though their marriage suffered for a time, the tensions between Paul and Wylie eventually eased. In the end, only one thing really mattered: that the people they loved most in the world—their children, each other—were alive and well.

That the kids had escaped physical injury—or worse—was, of course, entirely the result of Wylie's heroism. After a while, this became something of a family joke—that Wylie had proven herself infinitely more "manly" than Paul. After all, she was the one who had defended their home against a knife-wielding psychopath. All he had done was scramble under a coffee table.

With a sharp eye for its commercial possibilities ("brilliant and beautiful supermom saves family from Son of Psycho!") various TV and movie producers contacted Wylie about buying the rights to her story. Several magazines, including *People* and *Us,* were also eager to run features about her. Wylie, amused, responded to each of these overtures with a polite "No thanks."

The only offer she accepted was an invitation to deliver a talk at a conference on violence and misogyny at Long Island University, where, by coincidence, she appeared on a panel with the feminist performance artist Christine Crowell, the same woman who had lobbed paper balls at Paul on *The Lionel Lemmick Show* a year earlier. At the end of the day, she was approached by a publisher's representative who had admired her speech and asked if she was working on a book.

The result of this encounter was a contract for Wylie's study of Emily Dickinson, which was published to glowing reviews in the academic press, securing her tenure and promotion at Connecticut State.

Wylie wasn't the only one who ended up with a prize. Detective Sergeant R. B. Streator, hailed as the hero who had rid the city of a monster, received a special commendation from the mayor at a formal ceremony at City Hall. The humility Streator displayed on this occasion was no act. A modest man by nature, he cringed at the attention, particularly since he believed that it was Sheila Atkins, not he, who deserved the credit for tracking down Jack the Zipper. Still, as Ellen pointed out, Sheila Atkins herself would have ended up a victim if it hadn't been for Arby's heroic dedication to the case.

Always admired by his colleagues, Streator became a revered figure around the city in the months that followed—the last, as it happened, of his life. The headaches he had begun to suffer in the final grueling weeks of the manhunt were not, as he had believed, a product of stress, but the first signs of the brain tumor that would kill him less than six months after he had put a .357 slug through Chuckie Frewer's poisoned heart.

Two weeks after Streator's funeral—which she attended along with the mayor, the D.A., the police commissioner, and a large contingent of Arby's colleagues (including, of course, Frank Turner, who delivered a moving reminiscence at the chapel)—Sheila Atkins, having experienced a profound sense of rebirth, called her own press conference. There, in the big ballroom of the Marriott hotel, she announced the formation of an organization named CEASE (Citizens Enraged At Sick Entertainment) dedicated to "promoting the ideals of the late Reverend Victor Hobart, who sacrificed his life in the struggle against the degrading and corrupting influences of today's media."

At the end of her announcement, a reporter for Milwaukee's alternative paper, *The New Times,* raised his hand. Referring to Chuckie Frewer's religious obsession, the bearded reporter asked if Sheila's crusade against violent books would include the Bible, which, he pointed out, was rife with killing, from Cain's original murder to the torture-crucifixion of Christ. Before Sheila could reply, this blasphemous query was answered with an outburst of catcalls and boos from the rest of the crowd.

Only a few weeks later, Sheila's position seemed confirmed when, searching the apartment of a suspect in a particularly brutal multiple murder, police discovered a copy of Paul Novak's *Slaughterhouse.* That the suspect's bookshelves also contained copies of *The Hobbit, The Catcher in the Rye,* and *The Celestine Prophecy* went unmentioned in the press.

In spite of Sheila's efforts, the media continued to revel in everything most abhorrent to civilized morality—violence and horror, deviance and crime, scandal, sleaze, and sensationalism.

Five months after he got back from Wisconsin, when life in the Novak household was just starting to feel normal again, Paul received one of the bundles of mail that his publisher forwarded every few weeks. Among the fan letters and hate letters and letters requesting everything from autographed pictures to writing advice was a clipping from a publication called *Nightsweats*—one of those amateur magazines produced by horror enthusiasts and dedicated to the weird and grotesque and outrageous.

Paul was very familiar with this offbeat brand of writing, since most of its practitioners tended to be fans of Ed Gein. While researching *Slaughterhouse,* he had combed through dozens of stapled, self-printed " 'zines" with names like *Splat!* and *Gutz* and *I Drink Your*

Blood. He had never come across *Nighsweats* before, but that was no surprise. Created on home computers and distributed to readerships that numbered in the hundreds (at most), the vast majority of these fringe publications tended to have exceedingly short half-lives, disappearing after only a few issues.

Oddly enough, however, Paul found a good deal to admire about these flagrantly cheap magazines. In spite of their crude production values (not to mention their unabashedly adolescent sensibility), most of them were genuinely lively and literate—no surprise, really, since the horror devotees who produced them tended to be voracious readers, not just of Dean Koontz and Stephen King, but of writers like Lovecraft and Poe. *Nightsweats* turned out to be no exception.

The clipping he received—headlined EDDIE'S BOY DOES PAPA PROUD!—was a high-spirited recounting of the Cobb affair. The story occupied an entire page and concluded with a quote from a "famous poet." Paul didn't recognize the quote, but when he showed it to Wylie, she identified it at once as an excerpt from a poem called "Nobody" by the English author Robert Graves.

"How apt," said Paul.

"The poem?" asked Wylie.

"That, too. But also the name."

"Paul. Please. Enough with the graves and ghouls and Geins."

"Right," said Paul, and kissed her on the brow.

Still, the article stuck in his head. Especially the ending. It went like this:

> . . . The untimely demise of Leon Cobb (aka Eddie, Jr.) has deprived the world of a unique opportunity to study the operations of a truly original mind. What shrink worth his exorbitant hourly wouldn't trade his best leather couch to get inside *that* head? Still, there may be hope. After all, if the "granddaddy of gore"

spawned one li'l bastard, perhaps there are more! Who knows? Maybe one of the Geiner's love children lives right next door to *you*. Think about it! That soft-spoken dork down the block may be stepping out on a Saturday night to dig up a date in the local boneyard. *What?* I hear you say. *That pasty-faced nobody with the shuffling walk and the shit-eating grin? No way!* But better watch out for ol' Mr. Nobody! In today's wacky world, ya never know! As a famous poet so wisely put it:

Nobody coming up the road, nobody,
Like a tall man in a dark coat, nobody.

Nobody about the house, nobody,
Like children creeping up the stairs, nobody.

Until this nobody shall consent to die
Under his curse must everyone lie—

The curse of his envy, of his grief and fright.
Of sudden rape and murder in the night.

HAROLD SCHECHTER

"One of the few names that guarantee quality."
—John Marr, *San Francisco Bay Guardian*

DERANGED
He bore the name of a great family...
and soaked that name in blood!
○ 67875-2/$5.50

DEVIANT
The gruesome true story of the original "Psycho."
○ 73915-8/$5.99

DEPRAVED
The shocking story of America's first serial killer.
○ 69030-2/$6.50

THE A TO Z ENCYCLOPEDIA OF SERIAL KILLERS
The minds. The methods. The madness.
(Harold Schechter & David Everitt)
○ 53791-1/$12.00 (trade paperback)

OUTCRY
A NOVEL
○ 73217-X/$6.50

Simon & Schuster Mail Order
200 Old Tappan Rd., Old Tappan, N.J. 07675
Please send me the books I have checked above. I am enclosing $_____ (please add $0.75 to cover the postage and handling for each order. Please add appropriate sales tax). Send check or money order--no cash or C.O.D.'s please. Allow up to six weeks for delivery. For purchase over $10.00 you may use VISA: card number, expiration date and customer signature must be included.

POCKET
B O O K S

Name _____

Address _____

City _____ State/Zip _____

VISA Card # _____ Exp.Date _____

Signature _____

1005-03

Read about the
SHOCKING and
BIZARRE
Crimes of our Times from Pocket Books

☐ **TED BUNDY:THE DELIBERATE STRANGER**
  Richard Larson ....72866-0/$5.50

☐ **DEAD BY SUNSET** Ann Rule.............................00113-2/$6.99

☐ **A FEVER IN THE HEART** Ann Rule.................79355-1/$6.99

☐ **CARELESS WHISPERS** Carlton Stowers ....73352-4/$5.99

☐ **THE DIARY OF JACK THE RIPPER**
  Shirley Harrison ....52099-7/$5.99

☐ **DEVIANT:THE SHOCKING TRUE STORY OF THE**
  ORIGINAL "PSYCHO" Harold Schechter ....73915-8/$5.99

☐ **DERANGED** Harold Schechter ....67875-2/$5.50

☐ **COP TALK** E. W. Count ....78341-6/$5.99

☐ **MISSISSIPPI MUD: A TRUE STORY FROM A CORNER OF**
  THE DEEP SOUTH
  Edward Humes ....53505-6/$6.99

☐ **UNABOMBER**
  John Douglas and Mark Olshaker ....00411-5/$6.50

☐ **IF YOU REALLY LOVED ME** Ann Rule ....76920-0/$6.99

☐ **A ROSE FOR HER GRAVE** Ann Rule....................79353-5/$6.99

☐ **EVERYTHING SHE EVER WANTED**
  Ann Rule ....69071-X/$6.99

☐ **YOU BELONG TO ME** Ann Rule.........................79354-3/$6.99

☐ **TEXAS JUSTICE** Gary Cartwright.....................88330-5/$5.99

☐ **STALKING JUSTIC** Paul Mones........................00201-5/$6.99

☐ **JOE DOGS** Joe Iannuzzi...............................79753-0/$6.50

☐ **THE RIVERMAN: TED BUNDY AND I HUNT FOR THE GREEN**

☐ **RIVER KILLER** Robert B. Keppel, Ph.D, with William J. Birnes
  ....86763-6/$6.99

☐ **UNFINISHED MURDER: THE CAPTURE OF A SERIAL RAPIST**
  James Neff..73186-6/$5.99

Simon & Schuster Mail Order
200 Old Tappan Rd., Old Tappan, N.J. 07675

POCKET BOOKS

Please send me the books I have checked above. I am enclosing $_____ (please add $0.75 to cover the postage and handling for each order. Please add appropriate sales tax). Send check or money order--no cash or C.O.D.'s please. Allow up to six weeks for delivery. For purchase over $10.00 you may use VISA: card number, expiration date and customer signature must be included.

Name _____

Address _____

City _____ State/Zip _____

VISA Card # _____ Exp.Date _____

Signature _____ 944-13